The White Satin Miter

The White Satin Miter

Second Edition

A Tale of Piety and Atonement

Linton Morrell

THE WHITE SATIN MITER
A TALE OF PIETY AND ATONEMENT

This is a work of historical fiction. The principal characters are fictional. Some characters are real. What they do and say reflect the political crises involved. There is no intent to defame them or impugn their integrity. The plot is fictional. Resemblance to actual circumstances is coincidental.

iUniverse books may be ordered through booksellers or by contacting:

iUniverse LLC
1663 Liberty Drive
Bloomington, IN 47403
www.iuniverse.com
1-800-Authors (1-800-288-4677)

ISBN: 978-1-4917-4496-3 (sc)
ISBN: 978-1-4917-4497-0 (e)

Printed in the United States of America.

iUniverse rev. date: 09/03/2014

Contents

PROLOGUE

FROM THE YELLOW PERIL

Hollywood, August 20.
Wanda Wannamaker reporting:
O.K. Kids! Get ready for the sleeper of 1974. One hundred minutes of music and dancing with a little bit of that old time religion thrown in to uplift spirits as well as hearts. The name of this cinematic gem is *The Signal Red Cadillac.* It is showing at a theater near you. How many of you fans would recognize *signal red* if you saw it? Ask your favorite cosmetician. Better still, if you are into lipstick, try some! The characters? Ten to one you never heard of any of them but you soon will. All are destined for celluloid immortality. My pick of the pack is Cherry Cokeland. She's a cute little brunette country-girl canary whose quirky voice reminds me of Ella Mae Morse. When Cherry-baby wails out the *Bordello Blues*, you'll wish you had listened to what your mother told you when you were a little girl wearing pigtails and pink panties under your mini jumper. And dig Aztec Sam, the big, bad, Mexican used-car dealer. Would you buy a red Cadillac from him? Susan Shams would. She's a redheaded sweetheart who works in a dentist's office and is always coming in late because her old clunker of a Studebaker is forever going on the fritz. In all fairness to the girl's intellect, she only bought a car after quite some long tire-kicking. In

these lengthy negotiations, boyfriend Lynn Landury, the stony-faced ex-football coach who never learned to smile, helped her. But he knows about second hand automobiles, especially what they are worth and he guides Susan to a cream puff of a Cadillac that matches her hair, sort of. Last but not least member of this kooky cast is a golfing chick named Meg Muffin-Driver. In her stylish short-shorts and a sun visor she comes in a few strokes under par every time. Get a gander of her on the links with a number one wood in her shapely hands. And get a second take of her kissing Aztec Sam. You'd think she could attract a higher class of beau but it takes all kinds and in this movie, we have all kinds. Washington's General Alexander M. Haig has a cameo as an EPA man. He wears his green and blue uniform with a purple and gold cap and carries his fume detector around in his hands as he checks out the smog capabilities of all those dogs on the lot including a real but toothless canine by the name of "Growler" who tries to chase him off the lot. He gets an eyeful of Susan Shams but Landury keeps a close watch on her and poor General Haig never gets a fair chance to make his play. Too bad, General Haig baby. Want to know who produced this flick of the year? Well kids, it was none other than our own Helen O'Reith. The director was Sir George P. McDonough. Remember him? Well, if you don't, he hangs out with Helen O'Reith's husband usually in some faraway place that nobody ever heard of. But when he is in town, sometime you can catch a glimpse of him entering the garage of the Casinghead Tower in the tonneau of a Nile green Chrysler Imperial limousine with tinted windows. His traveling companion is that sweet little geologist Genevieve Ste Jacqueline the famous religious curiosity whose discoveries are frequently reported right here! One other point before we sign off fans. Except for General Haig, all of the players are Pentecostals. When not on the set at the Hal Roach 18-acre comedy farm, they hang out at Estes Park near Aimee Semple McPherson's Angelus Temple. On Sunday morning they can harmonize a spiritual without overwhelming the organ. So hurry on out and get a sack of popcorn and sit back for *The Signal Red Cadillac*. Next Sunday, go to church. Pray a prayer. Sing a hymn. You'll feel better and it will be good for you!

Chapter I

Bid Boland

It was bumpy coming down into the top of the dust. O'Reith glanced at the altimeter. The sky above was lead gray. Below was a vast sand-colored haze. They were 10,000 feet above the Mars-like landscape of southeastern Persia. McDonough, in the copilot's seat, the brim of his Montecristo Superfino fluttering, had a worried expression on his lined face. He asked, "Clive, what does it look like?"

"We're OK, George," O'Reith answered calmly. "That flashing green light next to the fuel gauge is the Bid Boland splasher. It guides us in. The faster it blinks the closer we are. Only thing now is visibility right above the strip. It should be OK. Not to worry." O'Reith, in khakis, tall and angular, his once handsome face ruined by age, was cramped into the bucket seat of the airplane. On his head a pale-green golf cap with the Limejuicer Club logo was pulled low. His Ray-Ban sunglasses, of the darkest shade guarded his faded blue eyes. His left leg was half-asleep. His visage, lined and furrowed, resembled that of the aging matinee idol, Adolphe Menjou. Before leaving Los Angeles, his cosmetician, Sharon Mills, had dyed his hair jet black. But now the roots were gray for a half-inch or so above his skull as were his temples showing beneath the golf cap. Unless he could find a good hairdresser in Teheran, things would have to stay that way until he got to Paris.

"What if it's not, I mean the visibility?" McDonough's pink face was taut except for his sagging jowls. The tone of his voice was edgy.

"Pump station guy has a Very Pistol, George," O'Reith explained. "When he hears us, he'll put a green flare up over the end of the runway. I can't get the station-master on VHF because of the static. But he'll be listening for our engines. I'm bringing her down fast, George. Swap seats with the copilot? I'll need his help to keep her on the runway in this crosswind."

They were coming from the Poghdar Oil Field in the Naomid Plain near the village of Peshanjan. Through a fresh cut near a tiny salt lake, visible from their 15,000 feet cruising altitude, O'Reith had followed the pipeline running southeast. They had crossed the frontier between the Persian hamlet of Avas and the Afghan town of Ghurian where the pipeline threaded through the lower elevations of the Kuh-e-Baran hills. Over the Great Salt Desert he cut the oxygen as they dropped down to 12,500 feet. Near Ambar, coming up over the lower Zagros Mountains, he began the final, let down. Turbulence from a late summer front rocked the aircraft. The strong headwind worried him. Even as he scanned the fuel gauges, he got a red light for the right main tank.

The vast dust storm covered the entire oil field region of Khuzestan from the Persian Gulf all the way to the high massif of Zard Kuh. Wiping sweat from his pink face with a huge silk handkerchief, huffing and puffing, the big Englishman in the white linen suit, unsnapped his seat belt, labored out of the bucket seat and unsteadily groped his way toward the cockpit door. The brim of his Panama hat brushed against the upper bulkhead revealing what appeared to be a faint halo. Teetering slightly, he weaved his way into the passenger compartment. Tall and heavy with an egg-shaped head, wisps of white cottony hair showed beneath his hat even as his aura shone through the air holes. The copilot, a thirty year old ex-RAF man with a regulation mustache, sandy hair and a nonchalant attitude, seeing McDonough in the doorway, immediately jumped up, went forward, nodded to O'Reith as he snapped his seat belt and put on his headset.

"Tommy," O'Reith said, "My leg is half asleep. I can hardly work the rudder pedals. Besides that, take a gander at No.2 oil pressure gauge."

"Yes sir," the copilot answered. "Needle's down a bit."

"It began flickering a few minutes ago," O'Reith said. "I wanted you up here." He glanced over, met the copilot's eyes, and added. "Didn't want to upset Sir George. He's pretty nervous about the dust. Check out the oil cooler on your side. What does it look like?"

"Oil film running back over the wing catching dust. Feather her out, sir?"

"Roger, Tommy. Loose connection somewhere. If it pops open, pressure'll drop to zero. She'll freeze up before we can shut her down."

"Roger." The Englishman hit the feathering button, pulled off the rpms and chopped the throttle.

"I say Clive," McDonough rumbled, standing in the cabin door bulkhead behind the two pilots. "Everything still OK?" His sonorous bass was uneven.

"Tickety boo, Sir George," the copilot said over his shoulder. Not to worry."

"I can see that the right propeller is wind milling," McDonough said nervously. "Isn't that rather unusual?"

"It's OK, George," O'Reith said. "Precautionary measure. We're losing oil pressure."

"Well, I certainly hope the other engine continues on," McDonough added, still not satisfied that all was well. "I see a red lights on the panel, Clive. Does it signify that something is wrong?"

"Right main went dry, George. Left was already dry. We're taking out of a tear drop now. Not to worry."

McDonough returned to his seat, sighing audibly and wringing his hands.

The pilots grinned at each other. But not for long. The copilot said, "No. 2's not completely feathered. Prop's dragging."

"Restart her and try it again."

The copilot nodded. The engine sputtered to life, turned over a few times and seized. At least we didn't throw a prop blade," the copilot said. "That's something." Visibility continued to deteriorate as they descended. "Eight angels," the copilot announced. "I can't see diddly squat."

"We're pretty close," O'Reith said. "Should pick up the flare from the separation equipment pretty soon. Station-master said it was adjacent to the strip."

"Five angels," the copilot reported. "Splasher blinking like the devil."

"We're getting close. Something on the horizon on your side, O'Reith said. "Can you make it out?"

"It is a hell of a big fire all right," the copilot said.

"That's it then. You better drive, Tommy. My leg is asleep."

"Roger," the copilot said, taking control of the aircraft. He was slipstreaming towards the production station. "Three angels, sir. Red light on the right teardrop. Switching to the left one. We've got about five minutes of fuel left."

"Look for a green flare from the station attendant. He'll be standing at the end of the runway."

"Roger," the copilot said. "Wheels down sir, he ordered."

O'Reith lowered the landing gear and a red light came on. He said, "Down but not locked."

"We could try it again sir," the copilot suggested. It was an order.

O'Reith retracted the gear. A red light came on. "Uh-oh," he muttered. "Hydraulics, Tommy. We'll be lucky to get 'em down again."

"Better try, sir."

"Roger." O'Reith lowered the wheels again. The red light stayed on. "Not good, Tommy," he muttered.

"Level at one angel, sir. There's the green flare. Red light on the left teardrop," the copilot said.

McDonough was again at the bulkhead. "Clive, I have the impression that things are not all right. I see those red lights glowing on the instrument panel."

"George, we're going to be on the ground in a minute. Get back to your seat and strap in. The moment the aircraft comes to a stop, get out quick. If that hatch doesn't open, kick hell out of it. Understand?"

"Yes Clive. I think I'll say a little prayer."

"Good idea George," O'Reith said abruptly. "Now scram."

They were over the runway. Although the visibility had improved, with a 40-knot crosswind, the rudder was all the way around. Through the shimmering heat, a mirage-like image of the production station loomed up. The wheels touched. They were rolling. "We may make it OK," O'Reith said.

"Something blowing across the runway, sir," the copilot said. "It's painted orange. There's another."

"Empty Shell lube oil drums," O'Reith said.

"Ninety knots, General," the copilot said. "Eighty. There's another drum, sir. Coming right at us."

They were using up runway. The copilot said, "I'm scared of the brakes, General. Seventy knots."

"Tommy. We don't have a hell of a lot to lose."

"We're down to 50 knots,General, I'll hit 'em again".

"Roger."

When the copilot hit the brakes, the right wheel collapsed and the aircraft slewed around. The empty oil drum caught the right teardrop auxiliary tank and sheared it off. The aircraft stopped abruptly, right wing ripped open. McDonough kicked open the main exit hatch behind the cockpit bulkhead. The odor of high-octane gasoline came into the cabin. He hopped to the ground, the copilot right behind him, helping O'Reith. As the lame man's feet touched the ground, a flicker of lambent flame rose from the damaged wing and quickly enveloped the entire right side of the fuselage. The copilot raced to the nose compartment and rescued their three small bags.

In the sweltering 120° F. air, dust blowing into their faces, the three men trudged into the wind as fast as O'Reith's bad leg would permit. He said, "Couple of gallons of fuel left. It'll blow, sure as hell."

They were almost to the station when the wrecked, twin-engine Aero Commander vanished in a roaring blast of red, yellow and white flame. The pump station attendant, a black-bearded, axe-faced man of the QashQai tribe, had been coming to meet them. He stopped abruptly when the plane blew up and covered his face with his red and white burnoose.

"Egad!" McDonough exclaimed. "What a furnace!"

The Arab motioned the three men toward a Land Rover parked near the station. His hob-nailed boots digging into the red gravel of the strip, O'Reith, supported by his companions, caned his way towards the vehicle. He said, "I'm OK now, lads. Circulation improved greatly." They unhanded him and the threesome, all sweating profusely in the torrid air, followed the Arab.

"Hotter than the Coromandel Coast," McDonough muttered. "I suppose I shouldn't complain. We're lucky to be alive. Gadzooks!"

"You're over-dramatizing George," O'Reith chided. "We were never in any danger."

"*C'est a rire*!" McDonough blurted out. "Coo Bob!"

The pump station attendant held open the rear door of the Land Rover until the American and the two Englishmen were inside. The copilot took one of the jump seats. As the Arab started the motor, he hoisted a Gott can of ice water up from the floor to the cushion of the other jump seat. The Arab began the two-mile drive to Pump Station No. 5 on the Oil Company pipeline that ran from Bid Boland down to deep water at Bandar Shahpour. As they rode along the dusty blacktop, the travelers began to quench their thirst, McDonough first. After four tin cupfuls, his soiled white linen speckled with wet spots, he handed the cup to O'Reith, who passed it to the copilot. "Your turn, Tommy," the oil baron said.

When the copilot had his fill, O'Reith drank. He returned the cup to McDonough, closed his eyes and reclined against the cushions. He was already thinking about getting out of this place; worrying about Helen; thinking about Maxine; thinking about pussy; wondering if he could get his peter up. At sixty-eight, he had about as much business in Khuzestan as the Emperor of Japan. But George was determined to see his pet project come to a successful end. Since he had never seen a million barrels a day go on the line all in one fell swoop, O'Reith had gone along for the ride.

The Land Rover stopped at the entrance to the station house. The noise from the diesel-electric light plant was deafening. But once inside the insulated Portacamp building, the only sound was the purring of the wall air conditioners. It was a cool and comfortable 75°F. The newcomers shook hands with Production Superintendent Wally Durham. The beefy, gray-haired Yorkshire man greeted them by saying, "Welcome to Bid Boland even if you had to make it the hard way!" He laughed heartily. In khaki coveralls and a white plastic safety helmet that carried the Shell scallop, he continued, "Not often we get an American five star general and a peer of the realm in one visit. You gentlemen have a good flight from Poghdar?" He laughed again.

"Great except for the last five minutes," O'Reith said.

"That Arab said you came in on one engine and then lost her on the runway."

"Oil drum snagged us," O'Reith said.

"High wind took us by surprise and the dust knocked out the VHF." Durham said. "We should have had them empties secured." He showed them to the chairs that faced his desk. McDonough sighed audibly as he lowered himself into a swivel chair. O'Reith sat beside him. The copilot stood, lit a cigarette, and looked out of the window at the churning transfer pumps. Durham returned to his place behind his metal desk, eyed McDonough curiously and continued, "What's new from outside? Is it true a bloke has to line up for a tank of petrol in New York? And what's going on in Tripoli? I hear that crazy Qaddhafi has expropriated the oil fields down south in the Sahara. Anything to that?"

"Gasoline shortages here and there in the states," O'Reith explained. "Mostly in the cities. Plenty of fuel out in the countryside. Government has interfered with the distribution system. Too much in one place and too little in another."

Durham snorted.

"As for Qaddhafi," O'Reith continued, "he is threatening to confiscate the assets of some of the companies. He hasn't touched us yet, at least if he has, it has not come to my attention. I fully expect him to however. I don't have the latest details. Any messages?"

"Yes sir. Several from Teheran. I'll ask the tea boy to fetch them from the radio room. Well, good sirs, the world is sure running rough. And what about that new regime in Afghanistan? Daud Khan? Is he for real? Is he going to stay on seat? What happened to the king?" Durham concluded.

"Zahir Shah skipped," O'Reith said. "I don't know where he went. How about it George? Where did he go?"

"Paris, I hear," McDonough said.

"You gents have a valve opening ceremony?" Durham asked, grinning.

O'Reith said, "Wally, we had Poghdar on the line with all wells hooked up and running wide open at noon yesterday. No champagne. Not even warm beer. No ceremony. Not even a cheer. We were all whipped down. Line full yet?"

"Yes sir, one of them Arabs, woke me up about three o'clock this morning. He could hear the line a pinging and a hammering. The gauge began to flicker at sun up and by noon today, we were up to 1,000 pounds of pressure. I talked to the production foreman at No.6 Pump Station down south of Gach Saran a couple of hours ago. He was beginning to get some pressure too." He looked at his wristwatch. "Four o'clock now. We'll have another gauge reading in a few minutes. They know at Bandar Shahpour that it's coming. Standard Oil tanker tied up at the pier waiting to load. And Scotty Trevelyen called from Teheran about an hour ago. He wants one of you gentlemen to call him back."

O'Reith said, "Why don't you talk to him George?" To Durham he continued, "How long of a hitch do you fellows pull?"

"Two weeks on, one week off," the Yorkshire man replied. Not too bad."

"Family?"

"In Teheran. Kids go to the British School. Mum plays bridge. Not a bad life. Pay is good. This is temporary duty for me. I'm the General Production superintendent for Agha Jari. Soon as your man comes around, I'll be on my way", Durham concluded.

"Our man should be along shortly." O'Reith said. "Name of Hunter Holland."

Looking over at McDonough and pointing to the telephone on the desk Durham continued, "Just lift the receiver and wait for the Gach Saran dispatcher to come on the line. Tell him you want Teheran."

McDonough nodded, picked up the telephone and moments later, was listening to Scotty Trevelyen, an Oil Company director, as he gave him the information for the flight to Teheran and points west. While McDonough was on the telephone, O'Reith read his messages. Helen had an appointment with Dr. Max. She was asking how he was doing. Maxine complaining that she was hard up. Carolyn Cook saying she looked forward to seeing him in Rome. No business news of note.

When McDonough hung up the receiver he said to O'Reith, "The Very Large Crude Carrier, MV *R.G. Follis* is standing by at Bandar Shahpour. Remember Follis?"

"Oh yes! He and Blake are great pals. He's retired. Still lives in San Francisco. Standard Oil names tankers after retired executives. We have a beautiful contract with them, by the way; escalation clause and protection against political risk, at least up to a point." O'Reith added.

"Fokker Friendship on the way to fetch us," McDonough continued, "Be here within the hour. Scotty would like a word with us tomorrow. Shah wants to say hello in the afternoon. We can be on the night flight to Rome."

"Rome?" O'Reith echoed. "I want to go to Paris."

"Well I thought you wouldn't mind Rome," McDonough replied defensively. "I would like to show you a villa I've recently acquired there. It's a civilized city, Clive. As you know, I often have Church business with the Pope, God bless him. Clive, actually I want to talk to you about an idea that's in my mind. Since Carolyn is heavily involved with our interests, I thought it was only proper to invite her to meet us there."

"You gents care for some tea?" Durham interjected. "Hot or cold?"

"Hot is fine for me," O'Reith answered.

"Yes," McDonough agreed. "Any chance of crumpets?"

"I'll second the motion on that," the copilot said.

Durham nodded, reached across to a different telephone, a green one. He spoke Farsi into the mouthpiece.

"Say fifteen minutes," he announced, looking at his Rigid Wrench wall calendar featuring a scantily clad blonde-of-the-month with a pout on her face." Whatever you blokes want to do in August, you'll have to do it today. It's Friday and payday."

"You've been out here for a while?" O'Reith asked.

Durham's eyes had a Middle Eastern squint. He smiled. "I came out in 1952. Petroleum engineer at Masjid-i-Suleiman. Worked my way up over the years. I plan to stay as long as they'll keep me on. Your first time in this part of the world?"

"Quick trip in late 1945," O'Reith said. "I was treated to a ride down the Golden Staircase from Gach Saran to Baba Kalu. Some cliffhanger that was!"

"A trip down the staircase is a thrill. No doubt of that." Durham said. "First time in Afghanistan?"

O'Reith laughed. "First time in the west. I was on the Frontier in 1923."

"Looking for oil?"

"No. Indian Army. I was in Probyn's Horse. My brother was a battalion officer. I was a green ensign."

"Sandhurst?"

"1922," O'Reith said. "Long time passing."

"Your brother wouldn't happen to be General Warren Hastings O'Reith?" Durham asked.

"The same. Lives in Cornwall now. Raises African violets."

"He was at Gold Beach with Monty, artillery officer. So was I," Durham said.

"Long time passing," O'Reith repeated. My brother went to Woolwich RMA.

"I went there too. Royal Corps of Artillery. But you were with the Yanks, eh what?"

"Air Corps. My mother was an American," O'Reith explained. "Movie Actress. Upset about two sons on the Frontier. As Daddy's widow, she had some influence in those days. He was an Indian Army man too. Mother turned the heat on the India Office. Got me sprung, as they say."

"Well, the war was a long time ago. I can't forget those days," Durham mused.

"Nor I," O'Reith agreed.

"While you fellows refresh yourselves," Durham announced, "I'll line up a bulldozer and clear the airstrip. We don't want that Fokker to bump its bottom on the mess you made."

"Better tie down those empties too," O'Reith suggested.

They finished high tea, took turns showering in Durham's wash room, changed into fresh clothing and waited patiently until they could hear propellers over the hum of the air conditioners. Durham returned. "You gents ready to go?" he asked. "We'll take a tray out to the pilots. They don't like to stay on the ground very long in this heat."

"We're ready," O'Reith said.

Even though the wind had died down, there was still dust in the air and a yellow sky above them with the sun low in the west. Durham rode out to the strip with them. Behind them a pair of Land Rovers brought other passengers. "When do you get a break from the heat?" O'Reith asked. They were sitting on doubled up damp bath towels smoothed out over the scorching leather seats.

"A month from now," Durham replied. "End of September we get a breeze off the gulf. October is not too bad. Then we get a few good rains in December. Low clouds and fog near the coast. The Zohreh river valley turns green. I have garden fresh tomatoes with my lunch. Makes all the difference."

O'Reith checked to make sure his suitcase was in the luggage compartment. He said goodbye to Durham. Then he enplaned with McDonough and the copilot right behind him. The other passengers came on board and soon the aircraft was taxiing down to the end of the runway. A fine dust hung in the air. When the plane u-turned for takeoff, O'Reith could see the separator flare in the distance. He was in a window seat near the rear of the airplane, McDonough across the aisle from him. When they were in the air, O'Reith opened his briefcase and removed a sheaf of yellow paper, the pages stapled together. He began reading.

"I say Clive, is that a scenario?" McDonough asked.

"Yeah. Helen pushed it at me as I was walking out the door. Her latest. It's about Boris Godunov. He was some kind of a tsar in the latter part of the 16th Century. The title of it is *The White Satin Miter*. Helen calls it the last remake of *The Shoes of the Fisherman*. I've been reading it off an on at night in bed. I'm halfway through it. Helen's take on it is a kind of tragicomedy. Not the kind of movie I'd pay to see. But it's a mistake to knock her films in advance. She has a way of making them box office draws. Alice Ridley has given it the green light."

"The astrologer?"

"Yeah. If Alice says it's a winner, Helen will go for it. And I don't discourage her. She's been through holy hell with her titties. So anything to get her mind off her troubles has my full support."

"How is she holding up?"

"OK now. It was touch and go for a while. But Max found the right treatment and she's checked out with a clean bill of health. Been OK for about five years. Of course you can never tell about those things. Could come back tomorrow."

"I'm glad to hear she's well," McDonough responded. "Reminds me I wanted to mention to you that I know a faith healer in London who's a cut above your regular snake pit swami. If Helen gets in trouble again, I'll give you his phone number."

O'Reith laughed. "Max would blow a fuse if I pulled a fakir out of the hat. He hovers over Helen like a guardian angel. Any mention of a quack type would get him frothing at the mouth. Alice wouldn't like it either. Competition."

"Let's hope she stays well. As regards the *Miter*, Boris Godunov is an interesting bloke. There's a portrait of him in the Hermitage. He's togged out in his coronation finery, prancing around the Kremlin with a jeweled baton in his hand and an idyllic smirk on his face. I was fascinated because it was like looking in the mirror. Even Anastas Mikoyan, who gave me a guided tour some years back, noticed the resemblance. He and I are both theologians at heart. Godunov was an intensely religious person even if he was a bit of a rat. So I know something about the usurper. The rogue had no legitimate claim whatsoever to the throne. Legend has it he arranged the murder of the proper heir, Dimitri Rurik, a tot of three. Had the boy's throat cut and then packed his mother off to a nunnery. After that, things went down hill for him. He lost the good will of the people. Weather turned bad and crops failed. A young, unfrocked priest came to Moscow out of Poland and claimed to be the Dimitri that he had liquidated. The Polish bloke got on his nerves so bad he had a heart attack and died. That ushered in the fabled *Time of Troubles*."

"Helen says in this script, that old Boris has religious aspirations. He goes south to beat up on the Turks and make Christians out of them but they're too tough for him so he veers off into Italy. He sacks the Vatican and takes over as Pope himself. That's how the fisherman becomes involved. The movie came out some ten years ago. Anthony Quinn was a Russian bishop who got to be Pope. Kind of a screwy film. Forgettable unless you like heavy, medieval drama. I don't. I'm strictly a *film noir* man. Give me a Raymond Chandler flick. Like *Farewell My Lovely*. Christ George! That's a movie!"

"I don't suppose she's begun casting it? I'm referring to the Boris Godunov scenario." McDonough asked.

"She asked Jackie Gleason to read it. She was impressed with his performance in *Requiem for a Heavyweight*. I don't know if he's gotten back to her on it. He's pretty well hooked up in that television show, The "Honeymooners"."

"If he turns it down, you suppose she would consider me for the role?"

"She looked favorably upon your portrayal of Father Antonio in *The Golden Lane*. When I get back to LA, I'll tell her of your interest."

"Would she object if we copied the scenario in Teheran? I'd like to read it."

"She won't mind, George," O'Reith said. "Scotty will have a Xerox machine, surely."

"Where are we staying, by the way?" O'Reith asked.

"Hotel Caspien. Never been there. Scotty said it was your favorite inn."

"Indeed. Even though it fronts on Takte-Jamshid it is a quiet little place that doesn't attract the rich and famous. Bar on the roof. Good view of the dry side of the Elburz Mountains. Contemplate the meaning of life while you sip your vodka."

"Clive, have you been paying attention to this Watergate affair? Is Nixon truly in the soup?"

"Well he is taking some heavy flak from a congressional investigating committee. That is for sure. He has had to axe off his chief of staff H.R.

Haldeman and the other guy, John Ehrlichman, the second lieutenant. Bad omens."

"Possibly fatal? I mean the investigation," McDonough queried.

"Hard to say. Helen thinks it is movie material. She likes to see the politicians eating each other. She was fascinated with that 1936 movie that Jimmy Stewart made called *Mr. Smith Goes to Washington*. You know when it showed in DC, the pols hissed at it. Many of them walked out. None of them had any inkling that it would sweep through America like a hurricane and national politicians would never again have the respect of the people. Of course Helen is still bitter about the way Congress treated her during the Hollywood 10 hearings. I don't blame her. It is a luxury for us poor working stiffs to be left alone for a change. My concern is that the administration will use the oil price crisis to manipulate people away from the scandal. We get painted black again."

They were in the landing pattern for Mehrabad. The copilot came back to O'Reith's seat with a clipboard in his hand. He said, "Appreciate your signatures, sir. Lease ticket. The insurance report. The accident report. They're for the Air Taxi Company."

O'Reith signed them. He said, "Tommy, if you get in trouble with Teheran Air Taxi, you can come to work for me out of LA."

"Well sir that is a generous gesture," the copilot said.

"Tommy, good pilots are rare birds. That was superb flying back there."

The lights of Teheran were everywhere beneath them and suddenly the wheels touched the runway and they were rolling to the terminal.

"Scotty said he'd meet us," McDonough said.

Sure enough as they disembarked, standing at the bottom of the ladder was Viscount Charles Wheatley Mervyn Trevelyen, KCB, DSO, MC, OBE, retired brigadier of the Scots Greys and present Oil Company executive in Teheran. Sir Charles was also a Knight of Justice and Grace in the Most Venerable Order of the Hospital of St. John of Jerusalem. Although in civvies, he wore his MC and beside it, the eight pointed cross, embellished with lion and unicorn denoting his membership in the British Realm of the Knights of Malta. His face was no-nonsense with thin lips and dangerous-looking eyes. His cheeks puffed out like a squirrel carrying acorns and his plum of a nose was tomato-red. His long gnarled ears had been boxed around and one of them had a bullet-hole in it. His voice was gruff. He shook hands with O'Reith with a tentative smile, saying, "It has been quite some long time Clive. I trust you're keeping well?"

"Good to see you looking so dapper, Scotty," O'Reith replied. "I'm OK. Pleased as punch to have Poghdar on the line without complications."

"Aren't we all," Trevelyen replied, turning to McDonough. He shook the huge man's hand, slapped him on the back, saying, "George, you've sweated off a few stone in that blasted Afghan plain. How is your delightful companion, Sister Genevieve Ste Jacqueline."

"She's fine Scotty." Coming out for a meeting on our Bir Hakeim field in Libya. As a Dame of Honor and Devotion, she was wearing her habit as a matter of convenience when Scotty dropped by on the way to Teheran."

Trevelyen ushered them into the tonneau of his *Zim* limousine and got in beside them. A somber-faced Persian wearing black trousers sat inside on a jump seat. He had a square-cut black beard, an oriental slant to his eyes and a razor-sharp nose. His green jacket had gold buttons on the epaulets and there was a wide, white stripe running down the outside length of his pants. He seemed to be some kind of policeman. Trevelyen said, "Chaps, like you to meet Colonel Mansour Haghani of the Imperial Constabulary. If you gentlemen will present your passports, we'll settle the immigration affairs straight away."

The Persian policeman removed a portable hand stamp from his briefcase and leafed through the two passports looking for a suitable spot for a visa stamp. He asked, "You gentlemen flew directly into Poghdar from Bahrain Island, is that correct?"

"Just so," McDonough replied.

"Technically speaking," Haghani began, "You entered Afghanistan illegally. You really should have a valid Afghan visa in your passport. I take a liberty in overlooking it. While the Shah has taken possession of it, the Majlis has yet to ratify that action and make it part of Iran proper." He shrugged. Mustering a faint smile, the policeman returned their passports. The limousine rolled slowly away from the Fokker Friendship and stopped momentarily at the guard post to allow Colonel Haghani to exit.

"The ultimate Asiatic bureaucrat, Haghani." Trevelyen smiled. "He wants everything to be shipshape and Bristol fashion. But he's a stouthearted fellow. Does whatever needs to be done in that line of work. Shah looks to him for many things. I expect you chaps want to dine and get a night of sleep. I'll drop you off at the hotel. . You'll have a starlit dinner on the roof. I took a chance on the menu; Wiener schnitzel with French Fries and something green. Specialty of the house. Goes down nicely with chilled rosé. Hope you find it to your taste. What say we plan on meeting at noon tomorrow? I'll send the car around. We can chat, have a drink and drive out to Shah's villa in Shemiran, say two thirty."

"Sounds great to me. Hotel Caspien has the best Wiener schnitzel in town." O'Reith said. "By the way, what happened to your Rolls Royce? I never thought the Oil Company would use a Russky Limo."

"Shah doesn't like British automobiles approaching the flight line," Trevelyen explained; "Smacks of imperialism. He's not so sensitive to the Red Menace."

"Makes sense," O'Reith agreed. "Russkys won't stir things up with the Raj looking over their shoulder."

"Quite right," Trevelyen agreed. "And the *Zim* is a soft ride even if it rattles a bit going uphill."

O'Reith asked, "Scotty, any chance of seeing a hairdresser before we call upon his Imperial Majesty? I look like Hamlet's ghost."

"Say ten o'clock in your room?" Trevelyen suggested.

"Perfect," O'Reith replied.

No lights over the marquee of the Hotel Caspien. Dim lobby. A morose doorman with black eyes scrutinized them with a flashlight, took their bags and ushered them in. He held the flashlight over the guest book while they signed it. A slant eyed bellhop took them to the elevators.

"Dinner when you gentlemen wish it," he advised.

"Half an hour," McDonough suggested.

O'Reith nodded agreement.

"Ring the desk and I'll show you to the garden on the roof," the Mongol said.

It was well after midnight and they were the only diners. The night was clear and the Milky Way was a fantastic display of stars, nebulae and white mist. Brilliant, bright stars flashed and twinkled. O'Reith sipped a dry martini on the rocks. McDonough was drinking Johnny Walker Black and soda. O'Reith asked, "George, how is Carolyn holding up?"

McDonough squirmed uncomfortably. "She's OK, I've been seeing a lot of her lately. As a matter of fact we've been together for quite some little while, a completely chaste relationship. We're intellectually involved with one another. No hanky-pansy."

"More fun with hanky panky, George."

With mock indignity, McDonough put on a formal face. "General O'Reith, I beg your pardon," he said in his heavy bass voice. Then smiling smugly he added, "If there were any, it would be a matter for the confessional. Not something to discuss with a callow gentleman of the world."

"I'll bet my pocket change you're dipping into that, George."

"Well I'm not."

O'Reith laughed. The surly-faced waiter was serving their meal. Another appeared at his side, a bit friendlier with a sparkling rosé from Isphahan. "George, Carolyn shoots scratch golf and she plays a fair country-girl gin game too."

"You know that sort of amusement is beneath my dignity. The only golf course I've trod was that battlefield some years back at Aurora Airport in Guatemala City."

"Well if you're not making love to her, you need some activity in common." Maybe a jigsaw puzzle."

"We're doing just fine, Clive. No suggestions required. We attend mass together and other religious functions."

O'Reith said, "George I was a bit taken aback when that police colonel said that Poghdar was not officially part of Iran. I thought all of that was taken care of."

"That's what Scotty wants to talk about tomorrow. Bureaucratic delay, no more, no less. Don't be upset."

"George with $200 million invested in that field. I can't enjoy this meal for worrying about the payout."

"Nothing we haven't been through before, Clive. You know that. Remember all the fuss about Kavir Dome? That came off absolutely fabulously. Poghdar will too. No point in getting into it tonight anyway. Just be ground we have to cover again tomorrow. I say Clive; I overheard your chat with Durham back there while we were waiting to get out of

Khuzestan. I have heard about the Golden Staircase? But don't know anything about it. I didn't want to display my ignorance."

"Mountain road, George. Runs from Gach Saran down to Bibi Hakimeh. Crosses the Zohreh River near Baba Kalu. Indian Army built it back in the 1930s. Picture a broken saucer standing on end with a two lane rocky road cut from top to bottom, crisscrossing its face. Every switchback has a road sign in black Arabic with red skull and crossbones in case you can't read what it says. Get the idea?"

"How long to get to the bottom?"

"Well it is a drop of about a mile. But the road is much longer than that. Ideally, it takes about 45 minutes. That is, in a sedan with a careful driver if everything goes OK. It can be much shorter for the impetuous. I think the record is 25 seconds from the first hairpin to the bottom of the gorge. Leyland oil field tandem on a rain-slick road with a load of seven-inch casing. Rear wheels of the trailer skidded off..."

"Zounds!" McDonough exclaimed. His fork stopped halfway to his mouth and his eyes widened. Even in the dim light, the gleam of his yellow eyes paled.

The telephone awakened O'Reith at nine thirty the next morning. The hairdresser was in the lobby. He quickly showered, shaved and dressed. On the stroke of ten the bellboy appeared with his breakfast, the hairdresser and a sheaf of telexes that had arrived during the night.

A slip of a Farsi girl, twentyish with black eyes in a pretty oriental face followed the bellhop, opened her kit on the table and slipped on a white smock. As she got ready, O'Reith choked down a biscuit smeared with goat cheese and chased it with black coffee.

At the cocktail table, O'Reith read his messages as she dyed the roots of his thinning hair, trimmed the rest of it and carefully coiffed it to make the most of what he had. Then she gave him a facial, trimmed his fingernails and bowed to him when she was finished. He gave her two hundred rial notes. She bowed again, put her kit together and was quickly gone.

Most of the telexes were routine from the Tower in Los Angeles. One from Helen asked if he had read the scenario for *The White Satin Miter*. Since he hadn't and because McDonough had expressed an interest in playing the lead, he got it out of his briefcase and settled into it. Written years ago by Edward Dmytryk, Helen's friend from the days of the notorious Hollywood Ten hearings, in it Godunov falls in love with an Italian beauty ordered into the nunnery by a lecherous Pope for betraying Vatican secrets. The usual intrigue; a stabbing; a poisoned prelate, all rounded out by a secondary love affair between one of Godunov's infantry officers and an Englishwoman attending a cardinal in the Holy Office. In a second telex, Helen reported that their oldest, Rae Regan was now a grandmother. The baby was named Elaine. Helen's third message told him that their youngest child, Helen Simpson, was hanging around with a scroungy-looking beach bum in Santa Monica. Helen wanted him to come home immediately and put a stop to that affair. Message number four said that their son Clive Colin and his live-in, Ellen Mae wanted to remodel the bungalow on Summit Drive and asked O'Reith to clear out his desk from his den. O'Reith drafted a telex to Helen saying that Sir George P. McDonough would like to play the lead in her proposed movie. He ignored all the rest. Just as he finished, the hall porter announced the arrival of an Oil Company limousine.

McDonough, in the lobby, wiped sweat from his brow with a huge white handkerchief. He fell in beside O'Reith. The doorman closed them in to the tonneau of the Rolls Royce. O'Reith gave him a few coins.

Then they were off down Takte Jamshid in a sea of smoking, horn honking, Paykan taxis. Heavy, black smog blanketed downtown Teheran. "Christ, George, this is worse than LA," O'Reith commented. "I can't see to the end of the block!" Inching up to the Oil Company offices, not far from the British Embassy, the big car crawled along the last few yards and at noon sharp, Scotty Trevelyen, stern-looking and sober, with a handkerchief covering his nose, met them at the curb. He led them inside to the elevator bank and on the third floor, guided them to a conference room. An oriental tea boy with a vacant face stood by waiting for orders.

"Scotty, I told George last night I was disturbed by Poghdar not yet being officially part of Iran. Where do we stand there?"

"Well, as you can imagine, chaps, there has been a bit of a squawk out of the Russians. The new guy, Daud Khan, the war lord that booted King Zahir Shah, is in their camp. His government is new and shaky but the Afghans are officially crying foul play. The United Nations are addressing the matter and so the Majlis, understandably, sit on their hands. We have to sort it out with Shah this afternoon, get him to put the pressure on to ratify his Edict of Annexation."

"Scotty," O'Reith said in his musical tenor, if the Standard Oil Company becomes concerned about who has proper title to that crude oil stream, we're in the soup. We have an evergreen contract with them that calls for a million barrels a day for the next two years. They're paying us $2.35 a barrel, a slight premium to posted prices. That's on account of the shortages in the Far East. I have to be in position to reassure them they have a good solid flow of crude oil with a decent pedigree."

"I know."

"Clive, how long to payout?" McDonough asked.

"Eighteen months if we produce without interruption. That's another thing, Scotty. Are those Gurkhas going to stay as long as we need them? Without 'em, those Pathans will swarm that pipeline. We won't be able to run a barrel."

"Ah Clive," McDonough interrupted. "I've already had a word with Black Rod. We can keep the Gurkhas as long as we pay for them."

"The Shah is going to pay for them, not us," O'Reith said.

"Better be careful about that one, Clive" Trevelyen suggested softly. "Shah is testy these days. He wants to raise the price of oil too. Just like all the others. Will Standard Oil go along with a big price hike?"

"They'll go along up to a point."

"Shah is laying on lunch by the way," Trevelyen continued. "at his villa. Half hour drive. We can talk in the car." The Rolls Royce was waiting for them on the street; engine running and air conditioner wide open in the 100° F. September heat. The chauffeur, nodding behind the wheel, came awake as Trevelyen opened the door to the tonneau and let O'Reith and McDonough precede him. "Shah's moods change rapidly," Trevelyen remarked. "I never know what is going to set him off. What comes first?"

"Edict," O'Reith began. "We're running Afghan crude through a Persian pipeline to an American tanker. What will the bill of lading look like?"

"For the first cargo, we can label it as Oil Company crude, Agha Jari light 34 ° API. When Standard pays us, we pay you."

"With time running out, it'll have to be that way," O'Reith agreed.

"Then?" Trevelyen continued.

"The pay of the Gurkhas," O'Reith continued. "We've been reimbursing the Raj since we first began drilling, almost two years ago. Why can't that come out of the Shah's royalty?"

"Cover it up?" Trevelyen suggested. "Add it in to the cost of the pipeline. Labor and materials. He's unlikely to audit the books. Even if he does, arithmetic is not one of his long suites."

"I was hoping to get it back up front," O'Reith sighed.

"Bring that up at your own peril," Trevelyen said.

"We cover it up. It is peanuts anyway," O'Reith said.

"George, anything you want to bring up?" Trevelyen asked, turning to MacDonough.

"A personal matter," McDonough said. I only mention it because of your remark about his moodiness. I'll save it for the end of the interview. Sometime back, I telephoned Shah from Rome. I asked him to meet with the Metropolitan of Teheran. A bit sticky because Metropolitan is a Christian and Shah, of course, is a devout Moslem. I asked Shah to approach Metropolitan about a possible démarche in relations with the Roman Church. Specifically I want to know if the several metropolitans of the East would accept an invitation to become members of the College of Cardinals."

"George," O'Reith said in his military tone of voice, "if you're cooking up some new conspiracy that is likely to get the company into the limelight, I want to know every single detail of it in advance."

"Not to fret, Clive. These are small potatoes. Does not involve our company one way or the other."

They were at the gate of the Shah's retreat in Shemiran. A guard recognized Trevelyen and opened the gate for the black car. Another guard with a snub-nosed submachinegun opened the front door of the villa and pointed them to a flight of steps leading to the second floor. The Shah, smiling broadly, met them at the head of the stairs and ushered them in to his study. He beckoned them to the sofa and easy chairs that faced his huge desk.

O'Reith, caning his way to one of the easy chairs, looked him over top to toe, trying to recall how he looked a decade ago when he first met him in Babolsar. The Shah was a trim, athletic man in his middle fifties, darkish skin, slender, dark brown, curious eyes beneath bushy gray-black eyebrows, and black hair. O'Reith noticed immediately that his widow's peak had advanced considerably from its previous frontier.

His features were finely drawn. His immense nose was curved half way down from his forehead. His features, heavily made up, seemed drawn, as if he had had a face lift and the rouge and the talcum were there to conceal the surgeon's scars. He was wearing a white summer suit of silk, with a satin shirt open at the collar. On its left pocket was the royal Red Lion crest. His feet were shod in white Asiatic-looking slippers with paper-thin leather soles. Trevelyen took the other easy chair. McDonough had the sofa to himself. As the three of them sat, the Shah's frock-coated tea boy offered a tray of caviar canapes, icy vodka in tiny frosted glasses and chocolates. To be polite, the three men took vodka. A second tea boy, brought a tray of smokes which O'Reith and McDonough declined. Trevelyen accepted an Indian cheroot with an ivory mouthpiece. The Shah put a fat Turkish cigarette with gold markings into a short ebony holder and held it to his mouth. The tea boy lit it with a gold Ronson lighter.

"Shah it is a great pleasure to see you again after all these years," McDonough began. "All of us follow your career, of course. Your expeditionary campaign into Afghanistan was brilliantly conducted. Taking Poghdar will go down as one of the great conquests of the 20th Century. Yes indeed, Shah, your father and the entire Reza Pahlavi line can be proud of you. An emperor's coup! You truly earned that nice decoration from Her Majesty. It looks good upon your vest. You're in the company of Marlborough and Wellington and Montgomery!"

"Kind and gallant words, Sir George," the Shah retorted abruptly. "I do have a good opinion of myself and after all, I am a graduate of the General Staff College in Ft. Leavenworth. Why should I not excel in martial arts? I assume from the flattery that you want something important from me."

"Not at all Shah, don't be that way," McDonough soothed him. "The oil field at Poghdar is on the line and crude oil is flowing. Shah, you'll be getting a tidy little royalty payment ere long."

"When, exactly?" Without waiting for an answer, he turned to face O'Reith. "I'm pleased to see you again sir after such a long absence. I congratulate you for being promoted to the five star list. An elite group indeed. So you've been to that blasted pile of rocks called Poghdar? Not a good time of year for such a trip."

"Not every day one gets to see a million barrels a day go on the line, your highness," O'Reith said, smiling broadly. "Standard Oil will be glad to have it. That's a good contract, sir. In these times of shortages, quite welcome. I was a bit taken aback to learn that your Edict of Annexation has yet to be ratified by the Majlis. I thought we were running Persian crude. But it seems we're in fact, running Afghan crude. How long will it be until that problem is cured? Our customer, the Standard Oil Company may well be concerned about that."

"The price that our customer is paying is not good, even for Afghan oil," the Shah said testily. Two dollars and thirty-five cents is not enough. We should be getting six dollars and fifteen cents."

"Shah these are parlous times," McDonough interjected. "Standard Oil will be indignant if we up the price to more than double what they've agreed."

"Why would I care? They have a representative on the Oil Company board here in Teheran. Brigadier Trevelyen, I ask you to advise him of this matter."

"Your highness," O'Reith broke in. "I'll be in San Francisco next week. "It would be better to try a bit of diplomacy. We can likely get an increase. Perhaps not to six dollars. But we might get the fifteen cents. Then let the clock run. You know as well as I that Qaddhafi has taken a tough stand in Libya. We can let him be the goat. Let him raise prices. Standard Oil will be forced to go along. They'll be mad at him, not us. What do you say?"

The Shah's eyes narrowed to slits. He said, "Well, you can try that, General O'Reith. But don't think I'm giving in. If we don't get six dollars a barrel, I'll go over your head." He snapped his finger for emphasis.

"Highness, to return to the matter of sovereignty as regards Poghdar; can you give me an idea as to when the Majlis will address this matter?" O'Reith asked.

The Shah's expression softened. He suddenly seemed more sympathetic. He answered, "General O'Reith, our affairs with Afghanistan are not going as swimmingly as I could wish. The Majlis, perhaps rightly so, insist that I negotiate a Treaty of Annexation with the new Afghan Government. This is complicated by a contretemps regarding the boundary of the Helmand River. Finally they resent the Gurkhas. We may have to relent on that one, pull them out. Let the Afghan police patrol that part of the pipeline within Poghdar Province. Furthermore I don't know if the new ruler, Daud Khan will stick. He's a bit of a flake, if you follow me. By the time we get a pact worked out with him, some other chap may chop him off. Afghanistan is not long on civilized behavior, as you well know."

"I need to have a good story before I see Standard Oil. And pulling out the Gurkhas is not a great idea," O'Reith continued, trying to sound upbeat. "They keep the oil flowing."

"Shah we have always treated you properly," McDonough took up the conversation in his purring bass. "Remember you've always got the Raj behind you. Recall that bit of unpleasantness with General Edwin A. Walker a decade ago, the dust up that got you into the General Staff school at Leavenworth..."

"They treated me like a naughty boy!" the Shah interrupted icily.

"But it all turned out splendidly", McDonough continued. "Don't forget the Kavir Dome. What a wonderful windfall that turned out to be. Paid for a few of your Swiss chalets, I'll wager. That one at St. Moritz is as majestic as Saadabad Palace. Must have set you back the odd quid, eh what? And your successes in Poghdar were certainly improved by the presence of a brigade of Gurkhas."

The Shah cut him off. "Sir George, there is no call to discuss my skiing accommodations. Kavir Dome was a bonanza but that was a decade back. Production has been declining for some time now. Revenues are slipping..."

"All the more reason to safeguard the Poghdar," O'Reith interposed. "Your Excellency, your powerful army is equipped with the latest designs of American tanks, artillery and aircraft? Rattle the sabers at those heathens."

"And I'll be in trouble at the United Nations *tout de suite*. They are already after me for supposed human rights violations. If you crack a head and the Press picks up on it, you find yourself smeared immediately."

"Maybe not," O'Reith continued. "Nowadays they have fatter fish to fry."

The Shah ignored him. He went on, "Now we've got a world oil crisis and we must take advantage of it. Gentlemen, I insist that we get a better price for our crude. I'll do my best to resolve the impasse with Afghanistan. You may be assured of that. Now, sirs, may I offer you lunch?"

"I have a great appetite," O'Reith admitted. The four men enjoyed roast lamb with mint, carrots garnished with parsley and Caspian rice.

White sparkling Bordeaux served in chilled crystal flutes. Vanilla ice cream topped with maple syrup from Canada finished the meal. Over strong black coffee in tiny cups, McDonough asked, "Shah if you don't mind a meal time question, would it be an imposition if I asked you about the Metropolitan?"

The Shah smiled. "Well, sir, I did speak to that prelate, as you requested. He was sympathetic but quite skeptical. He thinks it extremely unlikely that the College of Cardinals, certainly as long as it is dominated by the Italians, would ever admit hierarchy of the Eastern Church. He found it preposterous to consider the possibility that Metropolitans might vote in papal conclave. He didn't laugh. But he thought it odd that I would bring such a matter up. Nevertheless, if miraculously, that should occur, then he would be pleased to meet with you to discuss those grand plans of reunification and spiritual rapprochement. Also, he expressed his congratulations, as do I, on your appointment as a Prince of the Roman Church. I have been in the presence of much royalty and nobility over the years but this is my first occasion to host two lay cardinals and a five star general all at the same time. It is a signal honor, gentlemen."

"We are pleased to be in your imperial company, Shah," McDonough said. "If you would set up an appointment for me, I would be much obliged."

"This afternoon sir," the Shah answered.

As the Shah was walking with them down the curved stairs to the front door, McDonough asked, "Shah, as a final point before we take leave of your splendid munificence, could I ask you about your brief sojourn in Guatemala? There was talk that you and the Colonel didn't get on. I hope that is untrue."

The Shah laughed and the first genuine smile of the day appeared. He bantered, "Have no worries on that score. He and I parted friends. I get a note from him now and again inquiring about my health. Asia is not Central America. Guatemala is what you westerners call a *Banana* Republic. I found it difficult to acclimate myself to Latin ways. Persia is the land of the puppet masters. I am more comfortable here. The Colonel may have thought that I was a bit arrogant but I was not. It became quickly clear that he needed no lieutenant. Then there was the urgency of Poghdar. All is well between us. Why do you ask?"

"In this matter of possible reunification of the Roman with the Eastern Church," McDonough replied, I may ask the Colonel for assistance. I wanted to be sure that the two of you would cooperate should that be desirable."

The Shah laughed again. "On matters of Christian faith we can cooperate."

On the way back to the Caspien, O'Reith asked, "Scotty, Where do we stand?"

The stone-faced British oilman was grimly silent for several long minutes. McDonough was breathing heavily and except for the whir of the air conditioner, that was the only sound in the automobile.

Finally, Trevelyen spoke. "Gentlemen, we have several serious problems. I may be able to solve one or two of them. First of all, Shah thinks that all of the production from Poghdar is his, that is to say, he thinks he can levy a royalty on every barrel. I have tried to explain to him that Poghdar is not in the same category as Agreement Area oil. The concept of equity oil escapes him..."

"It didn't escape him at Kavir Dome," O'Reith interrupted.

"Kavir Dome was out in the Gulf," Trevelyen explained. "Poghdar is on land which Shah claims to now belong to Iran but which in fact doesn't really belong to anybody. Let me continue. I can jolly Shah along if he gets his regular royalty payment. He has not named a figure but he will. Clive, when you talk to Standard Oil about the price, you can mention that Shah has to be placated or there will be no oil." The limousine had arrived at the Hotel Caspien and the three oilmen got out into the searing heat.

"Let's go up to the roof," O'Reith suggested. "Cooler up there and deserted at this hour. At the lobby desk, he asked for a several bottles of mineral water. The three men entered the elevator. At a table with a view of the Elburz they took off their coats and ties. After the waiter brought the water, Trevelyan continued, "Gentlemen, this affair is complicated by other factors whose significance I cannot completely evaluate. Surely you are aware that King Feisal visited the United States and gave interviews to the papers, especially The *Washington Post.* On American television, his message was that Saudi Arabia was prepared to shut off the crude oil supply unless Nixon changed his attitude toward Israel. Should that happen, what do you suppose would happen to the price of crude oil?"

"It would go up," McDonough said. "No doubt about that."

Trevelyen's face became clouded. "A Queen's Messenger from Riyadh came through day before yesterday. He said that Anwar Sadat had been in a hush-hush meeting in the Saudi royal compound. Trouble is brewing. Clive, when we were talking to Standard Oil about Poghdar, George Parkhurst said that they intended to refine it and sell it in Japan to cure chronic power brownouts in Tokyo. No mention of a clean bill of lading then. After all, it was going East of Suez so what difference did it make? But in the cable exchanges regarding the load out of that VLCC, we saw language about a bill of lading that would allow them to bring that cargo to their Richmond, California refinery. Something is going on that we don't understand."

"Scotty, it is Qaddhafi. In Rome, I'll lay all this out for Carolyn. She will surely be aware of the pressure being exerted by King Faisal. I'll go to San Francisco and put it to Standard Oil. We're on good terms with Parkhurst, Miller, Haynes and Hamilton. We have to lay some of the cards on the table. Is there any expectation that Shah will sign a treaty with Afghanistan?"

"Practically none. Too much hostility. Too many issues."

"Can we get him to open negotiations?" O'Reith probed. "Standard Oil has its hands full around the world. They won't understand the Shah's difficulties. If I can assure them that talks are in progress and we have every reason to think that Poghdar will soon be another province of Iran, they will be more amenable to a price rise. If Aramco goes down, they will have a good steady alternate throughput that they can bring into the U.S. without legal complications."

"When I see the Shah again in the morning, I'll make that point," Trevelyen said, rubbing his chin.

O'Reith asked McDonough, "George what time is our flight tonight?"

"Midnight. An Iran Air 747 non-stop to Rome. Arrives in the early hours."

Trevelyen rose, tied his tie and started putting his coat on. He said briskly, "I'll have the car to fetch you at eight o'clock. That's plenty of time to get through the formalities."

Riding down to the lobby together, "O'Reith said, "Scotty, soon as Carolyn and George and I kick all of this around, one of us will telephone San Francisco and set up a meeting. I'll call you from George's place and let you know where we are and you can bring the Shah current. Probably be the middle of September."

"I'll tell Shah that tomorrow."

"O.K," O'Reith said.

They arrived at Fiumicino Airport as dawn was breaking. Weary from the long flight, after clearing customs and immigration, they got their bags and made their way out to the arrival gate where McDonough's black Mercedes-Benz limousine was idling. The chauffeur closed them into the soft seats and turned onto the coast road. O'Reith laid his head back and dozed. He stirred at Lido di Ostia when the driver slowed and again at Tor Valancia where they turned inland to Pomezia and on to Lago Albano.

"We're getting close, Clive," McDonough said softly. O'Reith opened his eyes and sat up straight. McDonough pointed to a magnificent edifice beside which rose the dome of an observatory, all behind a high stone fence. "Castel Gandolfo, Clive. The Vatican Observatory next to it."

"Some swell layout, George," O'Reith replied yawning. "Is His Holiness in residence?"

"Should be," McDonough said. "Be a couple of weeks before he heads back to the city. See that yellow brick villa with the red tile roof and the conical topped turrets just beyond the castle, the one with the flower garden in front?"

"Yeah. Fancy joint. Looks like some kind of oriental girlie joint."

"Well it is not. It is my house!"

"Carolyn will be up at this hour?"

"To be sure. She will greet us."

"George, I need a hot bath and a big breakfast and then a long walk around the grounds."

"We'll take proper care of you including the grand tour."

Carolyn Cook met them at the side entrance wearing the habit of a nun of the Dominican Order. She was fifty-three, slender, with a weathered, freckled face, and thin, determined lips around small, pearly teeth. Her deep-set brown eyes and falcon-like nose gave her a predatory appearance, like Clare Trevor. Her features were easy on the eyes. Over the years she had discovered several billion barrels of oil in Venezuela, North Africa, Sumatra and California. Her greatest claim to fame was her discovery of gold on the Malheur River in the early days of WWII. An outstanding exploration geologist dedicated to O'Reith, she first worked for him in Maracaibo when he was just out of the army and Manager of Foreign Operations for Calitropical Oil, a subsidiary of the Calitroleum Corporation. After Standard Oil bought Calitroleum, she helped him organize the Casinghead Company and was now its president. From Enid, Oklahoma, a graduate of UCLA and a lesbian, for years she had lived with a cheroot smoking, bull-fighting red-hot from Caracas. But they had drifted apart. She had had a string of short-term affairs with several of the girls in the tower. But she had finally given up on all of them. McDonough saw that she was lonely and became personally interested in her. During the development of the Kavir Dome in the Persian Gulf in the middle 1960s, they became close. Later, they made the pilgrimage to Santiago de Compostela together. In the cathedral in Santiago, she took the name of Genevieve Ste Jacqueline and now they were inseparable.

"You look neat in that get up Carolyn," O'Reith said.

"Blends in with the local scenery, General O'Reith," she answered, her head up and at an angle to let the smoke from her cigarette miss her eyes. "Lots of religious types in this part of Italy. Probably the only place on the peninsula where nuns outnumber prostitutes. I'll show you your digs. Breakfast on the table when you're ready."

After a bath and a shave O'Reith joined McDonough and Cook for bacon and eggs. Then the three of them walked all the way down to Castel Gandolfo, a mile or so and then a stroll through McDonough's garden. It was set between the silo-like turrets. Large and square, brick-lined up to the austere turret walls, symmetric clusters of yellow marigolds, orange marigolds and red and pink carnations filled the many parterres. The grass around the circles was soft and mossy and smelled of freshly turned earth. Narrow brick paths ran between each line of flower clusters. In the center of the garden was a tulip-like fountain that loomed up head high with bubbling water tumbling down to the catch basin and into drains that irrigated the entire plot. In a corner was a plot of herbs. Dill. Thyme. Rosemary. Mint. Basil.

O'Reith found it an elevating experience.

Back inside the villa, the three of them settled into the vast morning room. Windowed to the front garden with a chocolate tiled floor and stuccoed walls, the ceiling was canary yellow. Above the fireplace an oil painting showed three smiling girls on their knees looking at their reflections in a pond. Above them three tiny, nude cherubs of indeterminate sex with stubby wings and golden halos hovered approvingly. McDonough wore a scarlet zucchetto covering the bald spot of his domed head. Through an open window, the perfume of marigolds permeated the room. Shards of sunlight illuminated patches of the dark tiles. A cool breeze blew in from the lake. On the table and the mantel above the fireplace were more carnations in bright pottery vases. The tick-tock of the clock echoed from the walls.

O'Reith recounted for Cook their trip to Poghdar, the start up of production and the visit with the Shah. After that, his yellow eyes dancing, McDonough began, "Clive, Pope Paul is receptive to an expansion of the College of Cardinals. Last time I counted there were about ninety. Pope has disqualified those over eighty and plans to appoint some new ones quite soon. He would like to see 120 voting cardinals. I suggested to him that he bring in we lay cardinals, Scotty, myself, the two dozen or so scattered around in Europe and the Americas. France alone has six or seven including Marcel Riboud. And of course the Metropolitans of the Eastern Rites. Paul is not against it. Just wants more time to think about it. You know that we are good friends."

O'Reith, looking non-judicial, nodded. "I remember that you lobbied for him at the conclave. Can you pop in on him George, like a next door neighbor, or do you have to ring up his secretary for an appointment?"

McDonough raised his right hand and snapped his fingers. "I can call him directly on his red line. Usually I can see him on five minutes notice. Clive, Paul's papacy has been clouded from early days. That weird 1967 encyclical, *Humanae vitae* has caused him much pain and anxiety."

"Yeah I recall a ruckus over that," O'Reith answered, laughing. My youngest, Helen Simpson was sixteen at the time and going to a Catholic college. Boy crazy in spades. She just giggled at it. She called it 'goofy'. I knew it had something to do with birth control but I never read it. What the hell was it all about?"

"*Humanae vitae* condemned contraception pretty stringently. Latex producers. Rubber fabricators. Birth control pill makers. School kids. Young marrieds starting families. All up in arms. *Humanae vitae*, as you Yanks say, came a cropper. Today, it is a dead letter. The tragedy of it all is that it has been so completely misunderstood. Paul pays attention to demographics. In fact, he's somewhat of a fanatic on the subject of exploding populations. He likes to point out that only one person in five is white and that by the end of the century that ratio will be one in eight. All the rest of the people are black or brown or yellow or red or some shade in between. Worse, people of color for the most part, are not Roman Catholic. They are Hindus and Moslems and Buddhists and Confucians. And that's merely Asia. You get down into Africa and the situation is even more complicated."

"Those masses have never heard of contraception," O'Reith replied. "They breed and breed and breed. The Colonel was vocal on that subject. He claimed he had to get rid of about a million people in Guatemala to make a go of it. He even imported some man-eating tigers from India to help him out. He got a grant from the 'Save the Tiger' oil company. I doubt if he played it straight with them."

"Rightly so," McDonough agreed. "How did that work out, by the way?"

"Do you recall that the Colonel got religion on the road to Santiago de Compostela?"

"Those wild dogs," Cook interjected, tittering. "They shredded the pant legs of his Oleg Cassini pilgrim's outfit."

"Yeah, they changed his mind all right," O'Reith said. "The man-eaters got to be a hell of a problem. While I was there, we fed them U.S. Army beef. But when I left and the troops went to Vietnam, the Colonel had to scramble to keep them going. He tried to get them to eat beef-flavored bananas but they wouldn't go for them. Eventually he returned to his original plan. He turned them loose in the countryside. Hell of a stir in the newspapers. In DC, the Society for the Prevention of Cruelty to Animals got into the act. The ACLU got after him because the tigers were roaming the country, eating villagers. He still has a problem with them."

McDonough said, "Frankly Clive, I am a bit surprised that you've managed to keep him in Guatemala City. As I recall he had strong hankerings for Caracas."

"I still have the Bull of Excommunication against him. He's afraid of that."

"Ah yes, I should have remembered that. To return to the subject of discussion," McDonough resumed, "what Paul would like to do is to get the white folk, the European and American Catholics, that is, to step up their breeding. Try at least to stay even with the sub-human hordes in Asia and Africa. If that doesn't happen, Christianity will be finito in a few decades. So I am hoping that an expansion of the College of Cardinals will lead us in that direction. If Paul will bring in the lay cardinals plus the Metropolitans of the Eastern Churches, then we'll have a forum in which this delicate subject can be discussed universally."

"George," O'Reith suggested slyly, "Why don't you put the Pope up to issuing another encyclical, one that gives the nod to plain old fornication? Omit all talk about contraception. Just get the glands going. You know..."

McDonough jumped. "Completely unrealistic, Clive. You know that!"

"I'm not so sure," Carolyn interjected, holding back a giggle. "Properly titled, and with obscure language that has to be interpreted, he might go for it. By the way George, you've a message from the Shah. He's set you up to see the metropolitan."

"Splendid!" McDonough exclaimed. He became thoughtful, rubbed his chin, said nothing more.

"O'Reith said. "Let the Pope come to grips with some biological realities. Men are attracted to women, for the most part. We do have homosexual relationships but, from a theological point of view, they are in a minor key."

"But they should be addressed in any encyclical of a general biological nature," Cook insisted.

"I don't disagree with that," McDonough demurred. "Paul might. You two know as well as I that those issues are quite sensitive."

"We'll get to that later," O'Reith retorted, his expression hopeful looking. "If there is one facet of human behavior where we are world-class experts, it is putting the pressure on high religious and political authorities. So let's get down to it. Remember that song, *Sin and that's what I'm agin*? It's a Johnny Mercer lyric. George for example, if Maxine gives me a blow job, has either of us committed a sin? I'm Anglican and she's Roman Catholic. Where do we stand on that?"

"I'm sure I haven't the foggiest notion, Clive," McDonough replied, nose in the air. "You seem to have forgotten we have a lady in our presence."

"She looks like a nun to me," O'Reith said laughing. "And she's not blushing."

"You two guys are so funny," Cook said, removing her wimple. "But it is an interesting question. What if she were a Buddhist, George? Would that make any difference?"

"How is all of this related to the general encyclical on human biological behavior?" McDonough asked. "I'm speaking *Urbi et Orbi*."

O'Reith had noticed the last, faint glow of a halo when Carolyn dropped her wimple but he pretended he hadn't seen it, He smiled, looked directly into McDonough's yellowish eyes. "Just as I thought. George somewhere in all of this grand planning, you've got your eye on a white miter to replace that red skull cap. Am I correct?"

Cook's eyes widened. Hand over her mouth, she gasped, "George no!"

McDonough simpered, shrugged. "It is a possibility, of course. But for the nonce it is just a thought, Clive."

"So in this papal phantasy, " O'Reith continued derisively, "we are going to set out what is sinful and what is not in the biological relationship between human beings. How can we determine these matters?"

McDonough fell circumspect. He replied unctuously, "Monsignor Gerard Josepin is the Vatican resident theologian dealing with carnal matters. I could take this up with him."

"George, you and Carolyn can make a list of all biological acts between humans that could under certain circumstances be interpreted as sins. To carry matters a bit further, in a loving relationship between a man and a woman, why wouldn't a blow job be in the same category as a French kiss?" O'Reith enjoyed himself immensely with McDonough squirming defensively in his chair.

"I'll have to ask Josepin?" McDonough responded laconically. "Clive why are you pressing this issue?"

"Because the Middle East is on the verge of blowing apart," O'Reith said prophetically. "A significant fraction of our combined fortunes is located there. The basic issue between the Israelis and the Palestinians is control of the land around the Dead Sea and Jerusalem. The Palestinians are breeding faster than the Jews. To counter that, the Israelis encourage emigration of Jews from Russia and other parts of the world. The Jews are settling on Palestinian lands. The U.S. Government supports Israel. It is going to explode. If the Pope puts out a double-gaited encyclical that clarifies the natural biological relationships of human beings, while at the same time condemns what the Jews and Arabs are doing in Palestine, it can be debated by all concerned. We could put some language in it that applies directly to the tensions we now witness. Perhaps even defuse some of them."

"I suppose it is worth a try," McDonough sighed.

O'Reith, relentless, said, "I'm serious, George. When I get back to LA, I'll ask Stan Ethering to help us with the language. As a practicing Roman Catholic, he'll bring a legal, scholarly approach to it."

"I was unaware that Stan was a Catholic," McDonough said, startled. "Would it be too much to ask him to lobby for me; to expand the College of Cardinals?"

O'Reith laughed. "Carolyn, you can tell him his stock option depends on it."

The three of them laughed together. Cook clapped her hands mirthfully. Smoke from the cigarette in her mouth went everywhere as she moved her head around vigorously.

O'Reith said, "George, how long since you've talked to Maurice LeBel?"

"Quite some long time, why?"

"Don't forget he's a Foreign Legion guy. He's wired in to high political and ecclesiastical authority in Paris. He could lobby those frog cardinals. Maybe you'd like to have them on the team."

"I would indeed," McDonough replied. "How do I get in touch with him?"

"He's on the red line down in Port Grimeux. I'll give you his number. I'm going to Paris when we're finished to visit my daughter Monique and her new husband, a geophysicist that works for *CFP*. While I'm there I'll call down to Maurice and give him some background."

"I would be grateful for that."

O'Reith turned to look at Cook. "Carolyn, how much crude oil are we running out of the Bir Hakeim Field?"

"Couple hundred thousand a day to Shell's Rotterdam refinery. Gas goes back in the ground."

"Any official communication from the Libyan Government?"

Cook made a wry face and said, "They've told us to send a representative to Tripoli for a meeting on September 17. That is usually bad news. I plan to go."

They were silent for a minute, looking at one another. Then O'Reith, rubbing his chin thoughtfully said, "In that case, I'll go to the Kremlin in San Francisco and work out the price problem for Poghdar Field. I promised Scotty we'd get right on it. The Shah is pretty well torqued up. Carolyn, Can you get me on a plane to Paris this afternoon?"

"I'll ask Betsy Everdeen to book it. She's next door in my office."

O'Reith asked, "Was she not once your projectionist in the map room?"

Cook smiled. "You remember that?"

"You were going to take her on a trip to Babolsar for being a good girl. Did that ever happen?" O'Reith probed.

"She preferred Capri." Cook said rising abruptly, pulling up her wimple, and going to her office.

"OK, George, I guess we're set. I'll call you after I've talked to Stan."

"Clive, there is one more small favor you could do for me."

"Anything, George."

"The Colonel. Would you have a word with him? He'll know, or Flor will know, all of the high church officials in Central and South America. "Would he lobby in my behalf?"

"I'll call him."

"How will he like the idea of a biological encyclical?"

"He won't like it. He doesn't like any kind of papal announcement. He claims the Pope interferes in his affairs. He twisted off with the Vatican way back in 1957. He was threatened with excommunication then. That is why he is sensitive on the subject. I'm not going to give him the details. I'll put it to him that you're trying to wedge your way into the College of Cardinals and we need his help. That is all he needs to know."

"Clive I am not trying to 'wedge' my way in. I am a churchman trying to move ahead in the papal chain of command." He sighed, "I leave those matters in your good hands."

"George, what name do we give this grand encyclical? Stan will ask me that question. You know..."

"How about *Casti connubii redivivus*," McDonough suggested. "It goes back to 1930. Pius XI put out *Casti connubii*. In English, that's Of Pure Marriage. So this new shot at it will be called Of Pure Marriage Revisited."

"Fabulous. I'll just make a note of that in my little book. Let's call it *Casti Connubii II*. In fact my Latin is just fair. You write it in. George, why don't you ask the Pope to bring a few ladies on board? Maybe those designated as Dames of Honor and Devotion. I'm sure Carolyn would like to be a member of the College of Cardinals. Some distaff input might fetch a better Pope."

McDonough's face brightened momentarily. He nodded, said, "That's a thought, Clive. I'll ponder it."

A businesslike Cook returned with a slip of paper. She said, "General O'Reith, you're booked on an Air France Mercure to Charles de Gaulle. It leaves in about three hours. It's an hour's drive to the airport. What do you say?"

"Ready in ten minutes. Ride to Fiumicino with me? We can talk on the way."

In the tonneau of McDonough's Mercedes-Benz, sitting beside Cook, O'Reith began, "Carolyn, I can't remember a time since I've been in this business when international affairs were so unsettled."

Driving along the lake on the way to Fiumicino, the road was lined with pink, purple and yellow blossoms, poppies and violets and daffodils. The afternoon breeze carried their perfume. The fields were green. Here and there, a creek cut across the meadows. Small houses and grand villas were spaced out along the road.

"The truth of the matter is that we're running out of oil," Cook said.

"In the states," O'Reith agreed. "On a world-wide basis, there is plenty of oil. But it is in the wrong places and controlled by the wrong people. Worse, those OPEC cats realize that we can be blackmailed in the face of continuing shortages."

Cook put on her fretful look. She said, "Well, general, our world-wide situation is not very good."

"Mexico?"

"Salt dome fields in the Yucatan are making water. Production is plummeting. To make matters worse, the president of Mexico is ranting at the United Nations. He wants those provinces back. The Colonel is worried."

"Venezuela?"

"Pressure problems in the lake. Water encroachment in Tachira. Government is pissed off at us about the Colonel. No new concessions. In fact they plan to nationalize what we've got now. Taxes are already confiscatory."

"Sumatra?"

"Production steady but only because we're steam-flooding those heavy oil sands. No new concessions there either."

"Carolyn," O'Reith replied, "We're not the only oil company with problems. Gulf Oil Corporation, while it has a good reserve position, also has a financial problem. Their stock is trading too low. Smart money is telling us they are vulnerable. Their top people have made some powerful political enemies. But I think they are undervalued. If the management were straight, Gulf would have a future. An investment banker at JP Morgan called me looking for business. He used to work for Mellon Bank in Pittsburgh and he's got the skinny on Gulf's reserves and finances. I'll call him. He'll give you what he's got."

Somewhat puzzled, Cook turned her chin up and asked, "Are you thinking of making a run at Gulf?"

"Yeah but we need to know what they're worth. After the Morgan guy calls, we can line up extra credit from the Linen Bank in London. Could be a good play."

"Yes sir."

O'Reith became sharp-eyed. Looking intently at Cook, he added, "Carolyn I don't want George to know about this just yet."

"Yes sir."

The Mercedes-Benz pulled up under the marquee of the departure lounge at Fiumicino. The chauffeur opened the door of the tonneau and O'Reith caned himself out. He said, "Carolyn, I forgot to call my daughter. When you get back to the office would you ask her to send the car for me?"

"I'll do it," Cook answered. "That's Monique isn't it? And the number is the same, where you and Maxine used to live."

"That's it."

The Chauffeur handed O'Reith his suitcase. He waved back at Cook and he was on his way. Now that he was back into civilized surroundings, far from the fiery Khuzestan rocks, he was beginning to fall into one of his occasional blue moods, mainly because Maxine was far away. Depression had dogged him all of his life. But he had learned to live with it. He could be down all day but at the cocktail hour, he always perked up. Gin was his magic potion. Now in the middle of this afternoon, having left McDonough and Cook, feeling friendless, he wondered how he would find Monique. He had always been crazy about her and often thought fondly of her as a giggling tot and later a little girl that he would joyfully toss in his arms after a long absence.

Her laugh and pattering patois uplifted him. But now, twenty-five and newly married, perhaps even pregnant, although he looked forward to seeing her, even with a frog of a husband, who actually was really a nice boy, he was down. Once the jet was in the air and leveled out at cruising altitude, he closed his eyes and dozed until the captain announced their imminent landing at Charles de Gaulle. Waking, he looked down at the green French countryside. He recalled his day's as a squadron commander flying deep penetration missions into the Third Reich. Yes, he knew these skies. He had over flown Paris many times, more than once with three or fewer engines. Then, he thought the world was complicated. Looking back, it was pretty simple. He only had one woman and his insurance was paid up. Now....

For twenty years he had been caught between Helen and Maxine. He knew he had to give one of them up. But he was forever undecided. Now with Helen recovering from a bout with cancer, he could hardly put her out of his life and yet at the same time he would be content to run out his remaining days with Maxine. At 68, he was far from controlling his destiny. The plane approached the runway. Having landed so many aircraft over the years, even when he was a passenger, he was attuned to what the pilots must be thinking. In his mind, he helped them land, sighing with relief when it slowed, u-turned and taxied back to the terminal gangway.

Monique, in the arrival lounge, jumped into his arms. They embraced fondly. Full of banter, just like in the old days, she asked about his travels and told him of her recent adventures. Then they were in the tonneau of the 1947 Cadillac limousine. The graying family chauffeur, somewhat stooped, hunched forward and now wearing thick-lenses, tooled the big car out to the roadway.

"Daddy, I have news," Monique said. She was a willowy young lady with jet-black hair tied back with a red ribbon and crystal blue eyes like her father had had when he was a young man. But her oval face was that of her mother, who resembled the French film actress Mylene DeMongeot. Monique was wearing blue jeans and one of O'Reith's old white satin shirts open at the throat. Like her mother, she was endowed.

"Yeah?" O'Reith answered. Although he smiled fondly, fear gripped him. Full of angst, he awaited the dreaded revelation that she was with child.

Jolly looking, Monique continued, "Jean-Louis is in Hassi Messaoud. He's finding a place for us at the *Maison Verte*."

Jean-Louis Picot, Monique's husband, was an exploration geologist with the *Compagnie Francaise des Petroles.* The two had met at a dinner party thrown by Gabrielle and Maurice LeBel in Port Grimeaux.

LeBel and O'Reith went all the way back to World War II. Some weeks after the invasion of Normandy, at an Eisenhower-hosted gala, LeBel, one of Charles de Gaulle's staff officers in London casually mentioned that he too, like O'Reith, was in the oil business. The two hit it off and in 1950; Lebel's influence gained for Calitroleum an oil concession in Algeria that led to the discovery of the Tidikelt Oilfield, one of Cook's triumphs. After Calitroleum was sold to Standard Oil and O'Reith formed the Casinghead Company, LeBel became a shareholder and director. Now he no longer lived in Paris. He and Gabrielle often invited their friends down to their villa on the Mediterranean. It was there, in 1970, that Monique met Jean-Louis. They were married in the Madeleine in the summer of 1971 and O'Reith still had not gotten over it. "Headed south, eh." O'Reith said, relieved that she was not yet pregnant.

"Yes Daddy. When we're settled in, you and Mommy can come to see us. Jean-Louis said we would have a large flat with plenty of space."

O'Reith had visited the *Maison Verte* often during the exploratory campaign that led to the discovery of Tidikelt. The French had moved a slice of France down to the Sahara. He had been in some fancy oil field camps in Venezuela but nothing that compared with that. There were several dozen villas. An apartment block for couples without children and single employees, a movie theater, supermarket, school and clubhouse complete with a billiards room, tennis courts, swimming pools and petanque grounds. *CFP* had brought in ton after ton of rich black loam from the detritus alongside the northern slopes of the Atlas Saharien to make a garden around the magnificent camp. Double rows of plain trees ringed this mini-oasis. An immense irrigation system kept it all green. A high, paled fence encircled the camp, keeping out the dust.

As they drove into Paris, O'Reith, digging into his memories, described it for her. She listened with the rapt attention of someone who expects to see it with her own eyes. Soon they were pulling into rue de Surene where O'Reith and Maxine had lived for so many years, where Monique first saw the light of day and a place he truly loved. They rode up to the fifth floor in the 1945 model Otis elevator O'Reith had installed when he bought the building for Maxine.

Settled in, Monique, with an elfin grin asked, "Daddy, ready for a drink?"

He laughed and asked, "Is the Pope a Catholic?"

Martini in hand, he rattled the ice cubes contemplating that first restorative sip. He asked, "Sweets, how long since you've spoken with your mother?"

"When Miss Cook called to say you were on your way I rang her."

"She OK?"

"Yes Daddy."

"Let's call her back."

Maxine squealed when she heard his voice. He let her talk until she ran dry. He said, "Sweet face, I'm booked out of Charles de Gaulle tomorrow on TWA 801 for JFK. I've requested space on their afternoon flight out to the coast. It's a 747 so I should be OK. I'll see you tomorrow night."

"You'll call me from JFK?"

"Soon as I'm on the ground."

"I'll meet you at LAX."

As he hung up the telephone and took a second sip of his martini, Monique said, "Daddy, the teleprinter downstairs has been clacking like crazy all day."

Concerned, O'Reith said, "I better go down and see what is so important. Dinner in or out tonight?"

"I don't mind cooking," Monique said.

O'Reith nodded, said, "That suits me. OK Sweets. I'll finish my drink downstairs, read the messages and rejoin you in an hour."

A steel stairway in the bedroom where O'Reith and Maxine kept their things spiraled down to his den. Taking care not to splash his drink, he cautiously worked his way down. Telex paper had cascaded from the printer into a stack on the floor. He ripped it all off at the top of the machine and rolled it into a scroll. In his chair, he pulled on his drink and telephoned Helen. He listened for ten minutes to a repeat of all the problems enumerated in her telexes. Then he gave her his travel plans, agreed that when he arrived, they would resolve matters with their son, visit their granddaughter and counsel their younger daughter. Helen had doubts about McDonough for the role of Boris Godunov in *The White Satin Miter.* O'Reith listened but was noncommittal. After saying goodbye he turned to the scroll of messages. Most of them were from executives of the international oil companies who had learned of his recent audience with the Shah. They were curious about how the Persian winds were blowing. He telephoned each one in turn and lined up meetings during the weeks to come. Work done he climbed up again to catch up on the news from The *International Herald Tribune, Le Monde* and *Financial Times.*

Monique fixed a chicken and shrimp East Indian curry, as tasty as if Maxine herself had prepared it. With dill flavored white rice, a succulent mango and fresh ripe tomatoes, it was a meal for a magnate. He washed it down with "33" Export, a Parisian beer, not his favorite, but tonight he was not complaining. Then it was off to a hot shower and bed. He had been on the road for over three weeks, one of them under the burning desert sun. In bed he turned and tossed, occasionally sitting up as a burst from the teleprinter below floated up the stairs. More messages coming in.

How happy he was just a few short days ago to see the master valve opened in Poghdar. But he knew it was the riskiest investment he had ever made in his life. The session with the Shah had unnerved him. Then there was McDonough and his aspirations. O'Reith really didn't object to his ecclesiastical ambitions but he fretted it would interfere with company business. Finally, as dawn was breaking, he fell asleep thinking about the encyclical that could emerge from all of this, a pastoral letter that would reduce the tension in Palestine and Israel and by extension, throughout the Middle East. He tried writing it in his mind's eye but his powers of concentration were dwindling and soon he was asleep.

In his dream he was horny as hell, bringing a burning B-17 down through low mist and fog over the English Channel with two coughing engines. He was trying to level out at two angels, the prescribed altitude for returning allied aircraft to avoid being shot at by the British. But he could not stabilize the bullet-riddled bomber and he was falling, falling, falling...

Chapter II

Yom Kippur

In the summer of 1945, O'Reith was released from active duty because of a shrapnel wound. Calitroleum sent him straight away to Maracaibo to put out a bad fire on the lake. The fire extinguished, Hunter Holland his lieutenant, threw a celebration party at which he met Maxine deMoustier, a fluffy blonde with slate blue eyes, a cute nose, a neat figure and 'plenty of titty'. It was a flirtation that just kept going on. Then it became a romance, burst into flames that he could not extinguish. She was then 30 and he was 38. He tried to break off the affair but he was in too deep. He loved her. Now she was his trusted companion. Born in Buenos Aires to a second-rate movie actress and a failed French priest, she was fluent in Spanish, French and English. She rarely read books but she adored the movies; liked the bright lights and fancy restaurants. If she dined in a place that served good food and had a Hungarian violinist, she was in ecstasy. She dressed stylishly and was fond of Chinese red silk. She often spoke of Paris, wanting to see the land of her father. When O'Reith suggested they set up housekeeping there, encouraged by the Orinoco Witch Amanda Macabra, she jumped at it. It was then that he bought the building in rue de Surene. She furnished her new flat with exquisite taste. When they were together in

Paris, despite his bad leg, they often went dancing. No one could give Maxine tango lessons.

When O'Reith was away, she tended the flowering plants she kept in pots on her window ledge. Behind the building was a large garden with cherry, peach, pear and fig trees. Between the rows of trees were alternating plots of hyacinth and African violets. A Portuguese girl named Dina Maria helped her. The two of them would pass the entire day pulling weeds, watering the flowerbeds, planting seeds and picking fruit.

While not particularly religious, she enjoyed organ music and attended early mass regularly at the Madeleine just down the street. She lived for O'Reith's caresses. Of course, after the birth of Monique, things changed. Monique filled an empty spot in her heart. So, for many years now she lived for O'Reith, for Monique, for the organ at early mass and for her garden.

Now, thirty years after falling in love, much of the ardor was gone, but she could still excite him. When together, they would strip down to the buff and hold each other tight until with some effort, he could get a decent erection. He delighted in 'wobbling it in' as he described it to his diary. In her arms, he could dismiss everything, particularly business worries like the ones that had haunted him so recently. As they had traveled the yellow brick road to Emerald City, he held her tight. When they met the wizard, he was in Nirvana. When it was over, he slipped loose, turned her backside to him, and encircled her with his arms, one hand over each titty. His hands full, nipples between his fingers, he would drop off into a state of torpor for quite some long time.

Years ago, when they were still living in Maracaibo, Maxine advanced the theory that when two lovers were close together, certain health-giving endocrines flowed from one body to the other so that each person was renewed. The flow was of maximum intensity when they were joined together but it continued at a lesser rate for as long as they were touching. O'Reith, in the beginning, did not take that seriously, although he was careful not to scoff at her. Now, all these years later he had come to the conclusion that there was something to it after all. There was never any question about her ability to rejuvenate him in mind, body and spirit. So if it was endocrinal, so be it. He thought of these things as he woke up the next morning and packed for his trip across the Atlantic.

He would need a full week of Maxine's ministrations to completely recover from the trip to Poghdar. Unhappily, events had overtaken him. His calendar was full to overflowing. He would only get three days of her therapy. There was Helen to attend in Long Beach, of course. But that was a daylight affair. Nights he'd be with Maxine. Then, too soon he would be off to the Kremlin. Standard Oil could not wait.

Alan Prescott, his Vice President for Production could take care of the myriad tasks covered in the file of telexes in his briefcase. O'Reith set up a meeting with him for September 10 in the Casinghead Tower on Sepulveda Boulevard. When Standard Oil bought Calitroleum, O'Reith ran his new company from a suite of rented offices in the Fullerton Building on Wilshire Boulevard. Then some years later, Standard Oil sold him the Calitroleum Tower, now rechristened as the Casinghead Tower. Unexpectedly, the Fullerton Building came up for sale too. O'Reith liked it and bought it; converted it into flats and installed Maxine in a penthouse on the 25th floor.

He flew TWA to Los Angeles. After a night with Maxine, he visited Helen in their Long Beach penthouse. The problem with the Santa Monica beach bum had evaporated. Their daughter had abruptly 'kissed him off'. They drove to Holmby Hills to see their great grandchild, Elaine. O'Reith advised his son that he had no plans to move his den. If they remodeled, they would have to leave his place untouched. His son was miffed.

On the fourth day of his return, Wednesday, September 9, his chauffeur drove him to LAX where he took a Pacific Airlines 727 to San Francisco and a Green Top Cab to 225 Bush Street. Soon he was in the office of W.R. (Bill) Hamilton, an up and coming Standard Oil Company executive in the Production Department. Hamilton, of medium height, sturdy-looking with a blond crew cut in a square, forthright face, was a petroleum engineering graduate of Texas A&M.

A copy of their contract lay on Hamilton's desk. With a sympathetic expression, he began, "Clive what in the hell was an old duffer like you with a game leg doing in that blasted desert?"

O'Reith laughed. "I went along to keep George company. He wanted to see a big oil field go on production. Poghdar qualifies. I get peter fatigue hanging around LA anyway. I thought if I got out of town for a few days, my dick might develop some strength if not strength of character. At the Bid Boland pump station Scotty Trevelyen called, asking us to pay a courtesy call on the Shah. It never occurred to me that he would be up in arms. He demanded more money. He said he was going to read the riot act to the local Standard Oil representative. Scotty and George and I were all three of us sitting there. I suggested to the Shah that it would be more diplomatic if I came to talk to you in person, not to demand a change in the contract but just to see if Standard Oil would review the Shah's demands."

Hamilton asked, "Clive just exactly where is Poghdar? Is it in Afghanistan like it appears to be on the map or is it in Persia as the Shah seems to think it is?"

"It's about a hundred miles south of Herat, if that helps."

Hamilton smiled. He said, "Clive, our problem, like every one else in the business is the looming threat of OPEC going berserk. If the Israelis and the Palestinians tangle, oil prices can go crazy. This has been discussed with the Executive Committee ad nauseam. In the fine print of our contract with you, we can find no language that gives the Shah any authority to raise the price on oil that originates outside Persia. On the other hand, we have got to have the oil. If things blow up in the Middle East and ARAMCO shuts in, we're in deep you know what. A Saudi embargo hurts us. We have to play this one cagey."

"What if the Shah can get the Majlis to approve his Edict of Annexation?" O'Reith asked.

"He'd need for the government of Afghanistan to OK that; some kind of a treaty. Sure, if the Shah gets his act together, we'll consider his needs."

"What if we merely get the negotiation going? "O'Reith asked.

"If it were a bona fide negotiation, we could probably get EXCOM to agree on the grounds that the outcome was predictable."

O'Reith's face brightened. He said smoothly, "I'll report that to Scotty. It buys time. I worry about Libya. If that crazy Qaddhafi leapfrogs the system and imposes higher prices, the Shah will be back after us. We have to do something. With the pipeline running through Khuzestan, he can shut us in. We don't want that and neither do you."

"Clive, I'll present that important point to EXCOM," Hamilton said. "With Qaddhafi acting up in Libya, we want to be prudent. Give me a couple of days?"

"Sure."

"Another thing, Clive. If things go well, Poghdar crude goes to the main intake manifold at Sodeguara that refines crude oil for Tokyo Electric Power. If there is an embargo, we'll have to bring it to California. It will need a pedigree. The government will be after us for violation of God knows what kind of import regulation. So the Shah has got to clean up his act with Afghanistan."

"We're working on it, Bill," O'Reith said.

"All that aside, I'll stand you a drink and lunch. Parkhurst and Haynes are in town. They're expecting to see you and hear some war stories. What do you say?"

"Have you ever known me to turn down a dry martini?"

The two oilmen laughed together and took the elevator to the Executive Dining Room. After a joke-telling lunch with the top brass, O'Reith thanked them; nodded agreement on all points discussed and headed back to Candlestick Airport. That night he telephoned McDonough in Rome. He and Maxine fooled around that night and slept late.

That afternoon, his chauffeur helped him into the Cadillac and in an hour, he was in the elevator going up to his penthouse in Long Beach. His youngest, Helen Simpson, now 26, wearing a white silk blouse and a green velvet mini-dress met him at the door. She shouted, "Mommy, Daddy Cool is home!"

The terrace of the penthouse overlooked Ocean Boulevard and the broad Pacific beyond. O'Reith and Helen often had cocktails there in the evening where they would discuss the affairs of the day. Helen had looked good when he left to go see Hamilton but now she seemed poorly. He greeted her warmly and embraced her. She was in a basic black party dress trimmed with rhinestones that fell to her knees. She wore black velvet slippers and smelled of Chanel No. 5 as she had for as long as O'Reith had known her. She was wearing it the afternoon they became engaged. A first lieutenant at the time, she insisted that he marry in uniform. An enlargement of the wedding photograph now hung from the wall of his office in the tower and when he looked at it, as he often did, he wondered how they could have appeared to be so idiotic. She was then a sassy-eyed blonde who strikingly resembled Joan Bennett. Now she was still a blonde but it was a wig. She had lost most of her hair during the radiation treatment some years ago. It had never grown back properly so her cosmetician kept what little was left cropped. Even with two face-lifts, her visage was ruined by age. Without plastic surgery, O'Reith managed to look marginally better than she did and it convinced her even more strongly that throughout life, men got a better deal than women.

She would not be in a mood for romance this evening. She had returned home earlier in the afternoon from tests at Hollywood Central Hospital. Max Parkinson, now retired as the company Health Director, had warned her to expect more bad news. Helen O'Reith was 58. She had discovered a malignant lump in her right breast in the fall of 1964. Parkinson prescribed a therapy that had saved her from radical mastectomy but resulted in a series of small operations that she described as 'cutting off the boobies, nipple by nipple'. Three years later, Parkinson declared her 'as cured as anybody ever gets' and indeed although only half of her right breast was still part of her body, she had compensated for it with a specially designed version of the Howard Hughes High Altitude Brassiere which the noted aviator and cocksman had created for Jane Russell of *The Outlaw* fame. More importantly than the nice appearance that the brassiere provided, she no longer worried about her condition and more or less happily returned to making motion pictures, most of them, oaters. From time to time she got the yen to make a serious movie, one with substance and a message for posterity. Thus she was looking forward to directing *Miter*.

Helen took repose on a chaise longue with crimson cushions and yellow wooden legs. O'Reith sat beside her in a swivel chair. Helen Simpson sat briefly in his lap then hopped up to help the butler mix the drinks. Her curls were tied back with a green ribbon that matched her miniskirt and she had on green ballet slippers.

Over martinis, O'Reith reminded Helen she had been through tough times before and reassured her more than once that Max would see her through whatever complications lay ahead. She was not to worry. Their daughter took it all in but said nothing. Relations between mother and daughter were still strained over the beach bum incident. But Helen said nothing about it and he was certainly not going to dredge it up. The gin brought a happier and more relaxed expression to her face and soon she was ready to talk about McDonough's desire to play the part she described as Big Bad Boris. "Ace," she began. "George is too heavy. He is old and he has a speech impediment. I'll cede you that he is a great dramatic actor in the Shakespearean tradition."

O'Reith laughed. "He's not quite as heavy as he was. Those two weeks in the plains of Afghanistan cost him a few pounds. He's my age. I guess that's old all right. I've got arthritis so bad I can't swing a golf club anymore. George is not one to complain but I can tell that he is feeling his years. The speech impediment has vanished by the way. I didn't ask him about it. He may have had surgery. Maybe he went to a voice therapist. Whatever, you can't rule him out on that point. Don't forget that his cameo appearance in *The Golden Lane* attracted the attention of the critics."

Helen sighed. "Yes, I agree that when the role has a messianic aspect to it, George makes the most of it. He can get lost in the part if it fits his mysticism."

O'Reith asked, "Did he get any notice for playing the role of the Archbishop of Bogotá in the last remake of *Four Feathers*?"

"Don't mention that celluloid catastrophe to me Ace," Helen snorted. "Nobody got any credit for that bomb. But to get back to reality, George is just too bulky. He would have to lose five or ten stones, and we would have to suppress that silly halo", Helen added. "Would it be beneath his dignity to test for it?"

O'Reith became animated. His eyes lit up. " He'll switch his halo off and test in the nude if that is what it takes. You know how he is."

"Well, Jackie Gleason has turned it down. He's committed to his TV show."

At that moment, the butler ushered in Alice Ridley, Helen's astrologer pal. Like a shot, Helen Simpson, ignoring Ridley, was up and gone.

O'Reith rose, embraced her and asked, "Martini, Alice?"

"Make it a double. With lots of rocks. I really need to rattle the ice cubes after all I went through at lunch!" Ridley, a fine-boned peroxide blonde of 61 going desperately on 39 was five feet five in heels. Her round face, lifted at least twice that O'Reith could remember, was perfectly made up by Sharon Mills. Ridley invariably smiled the inane Hollywood smile. Fashionably thin, she always wore black. Her jewelry was heliocentric with at least one Virgo ring, sometimes two, in keeping with her star sign. On this late afternoon in early September, her face was drawn.

"Who's giving you a hard time, sweetie?" Helen asked, trying to look interested.

"That dolt, Jock Rumsford."

Helen giggled. Rumsford, one of her leading men a decade ago was in his prime, a muscular matinee idol. Now he was fading. He was also, as O'Reith put it, 'as queer as a three dollar bill'.

Helen said, "Well, I'm not interested in that hulk of a has-been. I asked you over to help me decide about George McDonough playing the role of Big Bad Boris."

"Jock doesn't think he's a has-been," Ridley said. He asked me out to lunch because he had heard you were looking for a leading man. He knew it was some kind of religious flick but he didn't know it was Boris Godunov. He wouldn't know a tsar from a tout. Jock is unaware we once had the Middle Ages."

Helen giggled again, asked, "What about George, Alice? He won an Oscar nomination as best supporting actor in *The Golden Lane*. He has a Shakespearean background. That's a plus."

"Jesus Christ, Helen, George must be seventy if he's a day," Ridley barked.

"He's sixty-eight," O'Reith said, "Helen that script was a Dmytryk scenario from his salad days. Why not produce it? Hire Eddie to direct it. He'd go for that. Let him cast it. George can talk to Eddie. That way, you're out of it."

Helen was glum. "Ace, Eddie is making a TV series called "Bluebeard"."

Ridley pulled her martini down, faced Helen and asked, "How long since you've laid eyes on George, honey?"

"Long time but Clive saw him in Rome last week."

Ridley gave O'Reith the hard stare. "What does he look like now, Clive?"

"Big, bulbous Englishman, "O'Reith said "Like Sydney Greenstreet. You saw him last time he was out here. He looks about the same. Wispy-haired. Jowls sagging."

"Halo?"

"Once in a while, It slips out, I guess he can't always control it."

Ridley shrugged. "Why not test him?"

"That's what I've been thinking about," Helen said, looking cheerful. "On the strength of George's great dramatic presence, if he can get through the screen test, I'm inclined to take him on."

Ridley rattled her empty at O'Reith. "Could I have a refill, Sweetie? A single this time? I won't break up the crystal."

In a fresh glass, O'Reith fixed her a solid single with new ice cubes. Handing her the new martini, he said to both of them, "Why don't you film it in Italy?" Up north, part of the country looks like the Ural Mountains."

Helen, exasperated railed, "Ace my one experiment with Italian film making convinced me never to try that again. Remember Ventimiglia?"

"This would be different," O'Reith answered reassuringly. "You're running the show. It eventually comes when Big Bad Boris sacks the Vatican. What better place to shoot those scenes than in Rome? George could help you."

"You have a point there, Ace," Helen admitted, "I'll ponder that one.

"Middle of the afternoon in Rome." O'Reith observed, looking at his Rolex Oyster. What say we give him a ring?"

"Good idea."

Ridley polished off her gin with a gulp, said, "I've got to run kids. I'm having dinner with Clint Eastwood. After what I've been through today, I need a facial and a hot soak. Ta-ta."

As Helen saw Ridley out, O'Reith dialed Rome. Moments later; Cook was on the line.

"Carolyn," O'Reith began. "You got my message on Bill Hamilton?"

"Yes, George has relayed it to Scotty."

"You're still set up to go to Tripoli on the 17th?"

"Yes sir, leaving on Sunday."

"George around?"

"Sitting beside me."

"Helen wants a word with him."

"I'll put him on."

"Hey, Big George, baby," Helen began cheerily.

"Ah fair maiden of Camelot," McDonough replied, "Helen, how have you been keeping?"

"I'm having my ups and down, George. Clive tells me you want to play Boris Godunov."

"I do."

"Willing to test for it?"

"If it comes to that?"

"It does. Willing to lose a few pounds? Boris is a good sized boy but you'll have to slim down a bit to wear his kingly robes."

"I begin my fast immediately," McDonough rumbled emphatically." I'll not have dinner tonight?"

"George, I'll set you up for a test around the middle of October. OK?"

"Yes. Two days notice. I'll be on the coast ready for it. Slim, trim and in voice."

"All Right, George. Not too trim. Good to talk to you. Here's Clive again."

"George, I'm to meet with Alan Prescott in the morning. With Carolyn tied up in Libya, Holland in Khuzestan and you and I with political problems, I'm going to put Alan out to run our day to day business. Pass that on to Carolyn. After that, Stan Ethering is coming in to talk about that encyclical. With luck, we should have some language in a few days. I'm going to New York later in the week to see Jersey, Mobil and Texaco. Then on to London. Shell and BP. Then to Rome. I'll advise you my flight plan. British Airways has a 747 going in to Fiumicino every day. You can send a car for me."

"Right you are Clive. See you in Rome soon."

A young Alan Prescott resembled Audie Murphy; baby-faced war hero turned movie actor. Now 55, he was burly, brown hair turning gray, and his tight-lipped face had lost its cherubic set. He had put on weight was now was pear-shaped. Today, waiting in O'Reith's office, in a dark business suit and black cowboy boots with Cuban heels, he rose.

In a brief meeting, O'Reith asked about Prescott's wife, Sally now the mother of three. O'Reith hadn't seen her since a Christmas party a couple of years back. He said, "Alan, if Sally wants to come back to work in the tower, I can sure use her?"

"I'll pass that along, General O'Reith," Prescott said in his east Texas drawl. Like most of the company executives, Prescott idolized O'Reith. So did Sally.

"Alan," O'Reith began, "We're stretched so thin I'm putting you in charge until Holland returns from Poghdar. Whatever you need, call Carolyn in Rome. She's fully up to date. OK?"

"Yes sir. Is she living with George?"

"More or less," O'Reith said, smiling.

As Prescott departed, Ethering entered. Now General Counsel, he began his career with the company as Chief Lobbyist. His pie-shaped face was tomato-nosed and he wore a perpetual grin. In his late fifties, liver spots marred his cheeks, temples and neck. His white hair was crew cut. In a dark blue pin-stripe suit with a white stiff cotton shirt, his navy blue tie had on it a picture of the Spirit of St. Louis. His black brogues were highly polished. He had the expectant look of a con man in hot water certain that all would end well.

Eyes heavenward, O'Reith asked in his musical tenor, "Stan are you not a practicing Roman Catholic in good standing?"

"I am that, sir. Early Mass every Sunday with Kathleen. Attend all Church devotions. I follow the Christian path, teach catechism and try not to stray off the reservation. I belong to the Confraternity of the Sacred Heart. Kathleen belongs to the Rosary Society." He smiled and added; "I go on the wagon each Good Friday, bribe no pols during Lent and stay dried out until Easter."

"That is commendable, Stan. George would approve. Do you know very much about papal encyclicals?"

"The pastoral letters? Yes. I have a compendium of them. I'm not a student of papal literature but if a question of faith and moral behavior arises in my class, I can always come up with the right answer. Why do you ask?"

O'Reith began, "Stan, over the years, you've made more state and federal law than just about any politician I could name. How would you like to have a crack at some canon law?" O'Reith paused, carefully appraising the expression on the bewildered attorney's face.

"Bribe the Pope?"

O'Reith said, "Of course not, Stan. We want to help Paul VI undo some of the damage caused by *Humanae vitae.* Are you familiar with that one?"

"Hot potato, Clive. It never got off the ground. Yes, I would do what I could for the Pope. Is George involved in this? His face took on the appearance of an intelligent bagman trying to bribe a politician on the cheap.

O'Reith continued, "Stan, I represent George on this one. He and Pope Paul are pals. George is a lay cardinal, you know."

"Yeah. And a Knight of St. John too."

O'Reith continued. "More than that, the Pope holds him in his heart of hearts as a full cardinal. George bought a red hat that he carries in his briefcase. For political reasons, he can't wear it in public. George wants to get an invite to join the Curia. The Pope was deeply wounded that *Humanae vitae* went down in flames. He considered it at the time, to be his best shot for getting good Catholics off dead center. He fretted that those Asians were breeding fast while Christians were birth controlling themselves into extinction. But when he put the encyclical out, the negative reaction knocked him to his knees. George wants him to come out with a new encyclical that will fly. George thinks a rework of a 1930 encyclical called *Casti connubii*, will be a winner. He wants to call this one *Casti connubii redividus*, 'Pure Marriage Revisited'. The message is that Christians should procreate. It would be nice if this could be done within the framework of a chaste marriage. But given social conditions as they exist today in the world in general and the USA in particular, the emphasis is on breeding, in or out of wedlock. In this work, we can touch upon certain mating rituals such as French kissing, connubial blow jobs, *soixante neuf* and the like. But the language has to be vague and circuitous or the Pope won't go for it. Think we can put something like that together?"

Ethering wheezed out a long, low whistle. He said, "Jesus H. Christ! Clive that's a tough one. That's like trying to get a monogamy law through the Utah Legislature. Yeah, I suppose I can do it but I may have to make a good Holy Confession afterward. We'll be bordering on immorality if not apostasy. Yikes! Could even be heresy for Christ's sakes!"

Leaning over close, O'Reith touched Ethering on the knee with his right index finger. He muttered "Only if the Pope nixes it, Stan. If he puts it out, it's canon law. Instead of immorality, we'll be bordering on sacred immortality."

"When you put it like that, I guess you're right. You really think he'll go for it?" A perplexed grin returned to his mottled features.

"George thinks he will," O'Reith said. He was silent for a few moments, looking at Ethering's face. "Stan, you know how federal legislation works in this country. A bill that gets signed into law, has something in it that the POTUS wants pretty badly. It also has something in it that Congress wants and that the POTUS would veto because it is pure pork. But to get what he wants, he has to give the Congress what they want."

"Standard stuff," Ethering agreed. "That's the name of the game. No other way to get it done."

"Stan, I want to put some language in that encyclical for our company. Doesn't have much to do with procreation. I want to scare hell out of OPEC, particularly those cats in the Middle East. I want the Pope to press the Jews and the Arabs to quit fighting in the Near East. Some strong language that will get the attention of the U.S. State Department. I want the Pope to condemn both sides, to cite their behavior as uncivilized and barbaric. I want him to indite the United States for abetting both sides through armaments sales. American money goes out there making mischief."

"You'll have DuPont pissed off at us. To say nothing of Lockheed and Boeing and the rest of the defense dogs." Ethering said. "Even if we could make that happen. Even if the Pope would put it out, do you honestly think those cats would quit whacking each other?"

"George will get him to put it out," O'Reith said emphatically. "Maybe we can't expect much of an effect in Israel. But in the Middle East, Iraq and Iran and Saudi Arabia and Pakistan, it wound resonate. Let them know the Church is on their case. Our job is to get the language right. Can you do it?"

"I'll consult with Archbishop Harley here in town?" Ethering said. "He spent a year in Rome at the Holy Office. I wouldn't tell him what we're up to. Merely sound him out on how he feels about the Pope condemning both sides in the Near East. As a new bishop when *Humanae vitae* came out, he took some heat. He'll remember that business."

"As long as he doesn't know what we're doing, sure."

"When do we need it?"

"I'm going to New York in the morning," O'Reith said. "Meetings with Jersey, Socony and Texas Company. Then I backtrack to Pittsburgh to see Gulf Oil. He looked at his desk calendar. Today is the tenth. I'll call you from the Waldorf Astoria around the 16th or 17th. When you have something, send me a wire. Nothing in writing before we talk. If it looks OK, you can DHL it to George.

"OK."

"Stan, if we make this happen, there could be something in it for you."

"Like what?" Ethering asked warily, puffing out his cheeks and arching his eyebrows. He knew that O'Reith was a pretty big thinker.

"Would you like to become a Prince of the Church?"

Ethering broke into a broad grin, said, "Would the Pope like to be canonized?"

They laughed and got up. Ethering continued, "Clive I never heard of a man becoming a lay cardinal without putting out some heavy lettuce. The only one I know much about is Peter Grace, the WR Grace Corporation heir. The word is that he kicked in a couple of hundred grand to get his knighthood."

"Stan, the company will do that. You've more than earned it"

O'Reith returned to the Fullerton Building where Maxine awaited him. He was feeling horny so they had a quick French dip before the cocktail hour. Now, O'Reith was mixing the drinks. He said, "Maxine, let's call Monique. We can ask her how long before she joins Jean-Louis in Hassi Messaoud. If it is going to be a week or so, we can travel together tomorrow and when we get to London, you can continue on to Paris. When I'm finished at Shell and BP, I'll hop across, we can spend a day together and I'll go on to Rome to see George. What do you say?"

"Good idea," Maxine replied, picking up the telephone and dialing their Paris number. She spoke to Monique in French, listened to her response and then turned to O'Reith. She said, "She'll be there at least two more weeks."

O'Reith handed Maxine her martini and they clinked glasses.

On September 12, a non-stop TWA 747 brought them to JFK. Next morning Maxine shopped 5th Avenue while O'Reith took a cab from the Waldorf Astoria to Rockefeller Center. At ten o'clock he was in the spacious 20th floor office of Peter Knowles, a trim Jersey production executive whom he knew from an American Petroleum Institute Convention in Chicago. Knowles, saturnine and eagle-eyed wore a dark blue suit and black shoes.

Taking in the extraordinary view of the East River, O'Reith listened as the Jersey man began, "Clive, it looks like the entire house of cards is coming down. Qaddhafi is acting up. He forced Oxy to curtail. We're next. OPEC meets in a couple of days. We have a wire from them; get that Clive, summoning us, to a meeting with their executive in Vienna set for October 8. So they have already made up their mind about something. We just don't know what it is. Socony and Standard Oil and BP and Shell are all invited. I assume Qaddhafi will be represented. Do you have an invitation to that meeting as well?"

"Carolyn Cook was called to Tripoli for a meeting with Qaddhafi. They're no doubt fixing to put the squeeze on us. If we're invited to the Vienna meeting, she will know about it."

Arching an eyebrow, Knowles continued, "We expect a game of leapfrog to commence. "Qaddhafi goes first. Yamani ups the ante and then the Shah jacks it up another five dollars or so. One thing is certain. The 1971 Teheran Agreement is a dead letter. I have no idea where this will all end."

"It will end when the price of gasoline gets too high for Joe Six-pack to fill his tank. That could be $15-20 a barrel."

"We have asked John J. McCloy to help us out at Justice Department," Knowles continued. All of us, Standard Oil, Socony, Gulf, the others; we're asking for antitrust immunity so we can present a solid front at the October 8 meeting. If we get the clearance, are you with us?"

"Certainly, Peter. I'll visit Texas Company in the Chrysler Building this afternoon, and then Socony. Tomorrow I'm going to Pittsburgh. After that to London. I can't imagine any circumstance in which we would go counter to the Seven Sisters. We do have the unique problem that we're running a million barrels a day out of the Poghdar Field and we don't know whether we're in Afghanistan or south Persia. Standard Oil is taking that stream East of Suez for the Japanese market. But if we all get into trouble in Libya, they may want to ship it around the horn to their Richmond, California refinery. I'm walking on eggs."

"Aren't we all," Nobles concluded gloomily.

They flew to London over the weekend. On Monday, September 17, he met with Shell in the morning and British Petroleum in the afternoon. Neither Shell nor BP had any clear idea of the direction the confrontation with OPEC would take. They all agreed to sit tight. O'Reith and Maxine were watching TV in a corner suite of the Cumberland Hotel in Marble Arch when Ethering called. He had a draft text of the encyclical ready. O'Reith asked, "Stan, how does it look?"

"Not bad, Clive if I say so myself. Poetic in places. Shall I read it to you?"

"Please do." O'Reith listened as the attorney read. When he was finished, O'Reith said, "Just the ticket, Stan. Make three copies and send them by courier to George. Maxine and I are leaving tomorrow for Paris. I'll see George on the 21st and let you know how things look."

"OK, Clive. Good luck and good traveling."

When Ethering was off the line, O'Reith telephoned Knowles to confirm that the Casinghead Company stood with the sisters. They dined in the hotel, went to bed early and next morning took an Air France Mercure to Paris. That evening they joyously dined with Monique at Lasserre in rue Franklin D. Roosevelt. Next morning it was a threesome on the golf course. But then O'Reith had to go.

On Friday, September 21, in Rome, McDonough met him at the airport. By noon they were in his villa. At a lunch of baked sole with lemon butter and steamed rice with dill, O'Reith recounted the substance of his many talks. He was relating the details of the London meetings when the courier arrived with the draft encyclical. McDonough's insisted that they put aside oil talk. He wanted to read the Ethering text. Scanning it quickly, on the second page his lemon eyes lit up. He smiled and said, listen to this: "The Church recognizes the amazing diversity of the connubial caress in all of its many variations as well as its erotic intensity. The Church declares that this is completely acceptable human behavior within the general context of *Casti Connubii*. Further, after a search of the Holy Soul, the Pope has come to see that the persona of a woman may be imprisoned in a man's body and vice verse. This may lead to a form of union previously considered illicit. The Pope has concluded that any issue resulting from such union will be a Christian birth.

"O'Reith asked,"Will Pope Paul go for the word *erotic*?"

McDonough blinked. "Hard to say. Even expunging that, the rest looks quite acceptable. Let me scan the part about the Near East. He read carefully but rapidly. Soon he paused and said, "Egad, Clive, that language about the Jews and the Arabs is strong as a whore's breath. Listen to this: "Islam is a 7th Century religion which has never evolved. It is completely lacking in regard for human rights, enslaves women and is without grace. As for the Jews, they cause nothing but trouble wherever they are found in the world. They are mercenary and unscrupulous in their pursuit of material wealth." He sighed. "I am not sure that Paul will agree with that."

"Shall we edit it before he takes a look at it?" O'Reith asked.

"My inclination is to present it as drafted," McDonough said, rubbing his chin. "Give us a chance to read his mind."

"When are you going to drop it on him?" Cook asked.

"Tonight!" That is, I'm going to run it by Monsignor Josepin tonight. If he gives me the green light, I'll call Paul tomorrow. He's still at Gandolfo. So it could be in his hands over the weekend."

"George," O'Reith replied, "With Helen's contacts in the entertainment world she could get up some PR for this pastoral letter. Maybe get Peter Paul and Mary to write an encyclical song. What rhymes with encyclical?"

"I have no idea," McDonough muttered, his face becoming slack-jawed. "Clive that may not be a great idea. After all, this is a religious matter."

"George, it was the young people who torpedoed *Humane vitae*," O'Reith countered. "They can put the skids under *Casti Connubii II* if we're not careful. Paul could be standing double nought zero as they say out in western Oklahoma."

"I have never heard that expression, Clive," McDonough said. His face had turned pensive. "You know, you may be right. The exuberance and effervescence of youth is something Paul overlooked in his early years. I'll review that with Josepin. He has a long head when it comes to such matters. I'll ask him if he knows of any word that rhymes with encyclical. When will you be talking to Helen again?"

"I'll call her tonight from Paris. She wants to get out some PR for the *Miter*. If we tie the movie to the encyclical, we kill two birds with one stone."

"Get your kicks on the Pope's encyc!" Cook exclaimed, snapping her fingers and doing an impromptu dance around the floor. "How does that sound?"

"That's neat," O'Reith replied. "And I just thought of one too. If the Pope's encyclical bombs he will be in a picklacal. How about that one?"

"Heh heh heh," McDonough muttered. But he didn't sound convinced.

"George," O'Reith continued, "We'll get the best songsters and lyricists in LA working on this. The music will jump and so will the encyclical. A song that goes something along the lines of 'Doing it for the Pope'. How does that sound?"

“You’re making me nervous with your constant flippancy. But I’ll run up a trial balloon tonight anyway,” McDonough said.

O’Reith asked, “Carolyn, how did you make out in Tripoli?”

“Our company has been seized, production stopped. We’re invited to negotiate for compensation. I’ve asked the Production Department to put a value on the property. Should have something in a few days. Then it is back to Tripoli.”

O’Reith said. “Send Betsy, Give her instructions”.

O’Reith returned to Paris. After dinner that night while Maxine and Monique were cleaning up in the kitchen, he took the spiral staircase down to his study and called Helen.

“What’s up, Ace?” she asked.

“Helen, George and Carolyn and I kicked around the Pope’s idea for an encyclical on procreation this afternoon. We thought it could be a good idea to hire some pop musicians to write some snappy songs in support of it. Good idea?”

“Ace, there are several so-called Christian groups that specialize in what they call ‘popular’ religious music. Some of it is terrible. But once in a while they come up with a tune that swings. The current rage is a Country and Western ditty called ‘I’ve got a Chancre on my Soul’. Melancholy but it has a hopeful lilt. Like maybe the guy is taking medication for it.”

“Jesus!” O’Reith winced.

“Want me to look into that? Try to get a license to use it in the PR?”

“Yeah, I guess so. It doesn’t catch me just right. A chancre song is at odds with our love angle. I’ll ask George if he wants it in. Helen, we discussed tying this PR into the “Miter”. It could be a boost for the film.”

“I like it.”

“OK. I’ll call you Monday. Anything new with Max?”

“He says if I don’t go for radiation or chemotherapy, he has no other answers.”

“George knows a faith healer in London. That’s how he cured that odd hesitation in his voice. George thinks the guy hung the moon. Of course curing a speech defect is not in the same league with tackling cancer. You want to hear more?”

“Max would explode if he knew about it but I need help, Ace. I’m at wits end. None of these Hollywood quacks could cure the clap. Find out more about him. By the way Ace, did you get the news on Henry Kissinger?"

"What has he done now, Helen?"

"He's Nixon's new Secretary of State."

O'Reith laughed. "If there is nothing going on, he'll do OK."

"Don't forget the faith healer, Ace."

"You got it baby, Good night."

O'Reith called Dr. Parkinson. After the pleasantries he asked, "Max, how about giving me the straight goods on Helen. How sick is she?"

"I don't know how sick she is, Clive. Clinically, the cancer cells have moved into the lymph glands of her armpits. Radiation might kill them off. But she won't go for it. Can't say as I blame her."

"How would you feel about bringing a faith healer into the act?"

"They are a dime a dozen in Hollywood. All that I know are Mexicans pretending to be from Tibet and solidly in the quack column. I mean 100%."

"George was telling me about a guy in London that has a track record," O'Reith said. "Helen needs emotional support more than anything else. Things are so screwed up in the Middle East that I really can't give her the attention she deserves."

"Find out who the guy is and how he operates," Parkinson agreed. "George has a long head and we have to respect that. I'll call Helen right now and give her some assurance that it is not the end of the world."

"OK, Max. After I talk to George, I'll call you back."

It was after ten. Even though it was late, he called McDonough. To his surprise, the Englishman picked up on the first ring. "George, it is late but I wanted to talk to you."

"I'm reading my lines, trying to get into Godunov's mind. No dinner tonight. Just a saucer of caviar with champagne. I'm starving. Can't go to bed. I'd never fall asleep. Tomorrow will be worse. Coffee and toast. What will a man do for fame?"

O'Reith laughed. "Anything."

"What's on your mind, Clive?"

"George, remember that swami you were telling me about?"

"Helen ailing again?" His voice was filled with genuine alarm. McDonough idolized Helen O'Reith.

"Yeah, I just got off the phone with Max in LA. Cancer cells migrated to the lymph glands. She won't go for any more radiation or chemotherapy. I told her about the healer in London. She wants to know more."

"Russian bloke, at least he travels on a Russian passport. Looks like he's from Mongolia if you ask me. His name is Sergei Kondratieff. He's a hypnotist. His specialty is lowering the heart rate down to just about nothing. Pulse practically disappears. Patient becomes comatose. He does it in stages. He recites metaphysical poetry to get the patient's mind off the source of illness. Then it is music. First treatment is fifteen minutes. Second is a half-hour. Third is an hour and he keeps it at that level until results appear."

"On the level guy? Los Angeles is full of quacks that prey on the rich and ill."

"He seems upright. I have talked with him on a number of occasions. He says that we don't know much about the internal chemistry of the body. Emotions trigger the release of opiates when we need them. And famously, fear induces the production of adrenaline. Clive, not to seem pontifical but those of us in religious service, those of us who labor in the spirit of the Lord, those of us who communicate regularly with the Divinity, often see remarkable transformations of the human psyche and sometimes of the corpus too. I could tell you many tales of young German soldiers, fanatic Nazis on the outside, quivering sinners in the confessional. So we have to take faith healers seriously because we cannot know the extent of the power they can exert if they are in communication with the Holy Powers. You may scoff at men of Kondratieff's ilk but I take him seriously. He's treated some ministers and some prelates and other intelligent people; the kind who would know better. They go to him because he's the last resort. He has received many favorable recommendations."

"I'm not knocking him George. However I am definitely circumspect. I depend upon Max to keep things logical. Will Kondratieff come take a look at her?"

"Have to ask."

"Would he talk to a regular physician about his methods?"

"He is a regular physician, Clive. I don't know his pedigree but he's licensed to practice. He's from a good family, a relative of the noted economist who died in a Stalinist salt mine in Siberia. Friend of the

Mikoyans. I can't think of a reason why he would not talk to Max. You want Max to give him a green light to treat Helen?"

"That's the idea, George. I'm leery of springing him on Helen without getting Max to say it is OK."

"Monday morning soon enough?"

"Yeah."

"I'll let you know something then. You're staying in Paris?"

"Until the end of next week."

"We'll talk again on Monday then."

Monday, the 24th of September was the end of the OPEC meeting. Nothing had happened. No price increase. Quotas remained the same.

"A lull before the storm," O'Reith muttered. He called McDonough in the middle of the morning. "George, did you have a pleasant weekend?"

"Indeed. Lovely weather this time of year. I had to get up early. Clive, we have some encouraging news. Monsignor Josepin signed off on the text of the encyclical. Couple of minor revisions. Nothing of substance. At first reading, he wanted to drop the word 'erotic'. We knew that, of course. But on a second reading he decided to let it stand. He didn't change a word about the Arabs and the Jews. So the text of it is in Paul's hands. I had a word with him just minutes ago. He's inclined to go with it *in toto* without alteration of tint or tone. At lunch he said that he was inclined to publish it on October 6, which is Yom Kippur."

"Good idea. Emphasize the nature of the message. What about my swami, the faith guy?"

"Just got off the line. He's from the south, near Kiev. He's about fifty; medical training at an academy in Yalta. After that, he took an advanced degree in tropical medicine from the University of London. Then at Ecole Polytechnique he studied psychiatry. He practiced tropical medicine in Baku for several years before coming to London. He is a gifted musician and he uses musical instruments in the practice of his craft. With a fife-like whistle he induces hypnotism with a certain form of Russian lullaby. Now well established, he is given credit for some remarkable recoveries. He said he would travel to Los Angeles for a preliminary look and an interview. He will gladly discuss Helen's case with Max. If need be, he could treat her once every couple of weeks on a test basis. If she improved, a routine could be worked out. What say I telex you the details with his address and telephone number?"

"I appreciate the effort, George. Looking forward to your telex. I'll call Helen tonight."

"I say Clive; I meant to ask you this last Friday. Did you discuss my idea of enlargement of the College of Cardinals with Ethering? You said you would."

"I didn't because I wanted him to focus on the encyclical. I'll call him tonight."

"And the Colonel?"

"George, I don't know if I can talk to Guatemala City or not. If I don't get him, I'll ask Stan to. That OK?"

"Splendid. Anything else?"

"A telex from Hamilton at Standard Oil in San Francisco confirms our thinking on Poghdar. We have some work to do there. He says that to keep peace in the family in these extremely uncertain times, EXCOM is willing to go along with a price increase to be effective the day the Shah enters into formal negotiations with Afghanistan to settle the boundary dispute. They would like to keep the increase under $5.00/bbl. We have to look the Shah in the eye and make the best deal we can. What say we travel next Saturday, September 29? That gives me the rest of the week with Maxine."

"Let's discuss it again tomorrow. I think it is all right."

"OK George, ta-ta."

O'Reith was having his after breakfast coffee when the telephone rang. It was Cook. "General, we are out of business in Libya."

"Carolyn, we have a lot to talk about. I can get out of here around noon. Ask George to send a car for me to Fiumicino. Alitalia. Gets in around two PM."

"Yes sir."

In the afternoon room of the villa with walls of yellow stucco and adorned with 18th Century portraits of noted religious personalities, none smiling, McDonough and Cook were sitting on the sofa. She was wearing blue jeans with her wimple rolled back on her head. O'Reith, in a chair of burnished oak cushioned in leather with brightly polished brass brads was silent, pensive. The open window beckoned an occasional bumblebee to bang into the screen. The sun was still too high to shine directly upon them but altogether it was fresh and pleasant and the fragrances of the flower garden wafted through the chamber. O'Reith began, "Give me the details," he said, looking at Cook.

"Betsy Everdeen called. The Libyan National Oil Company has officially seized the Bir Hakeim field. They suggested we stay on to operate it for them for a fee."

"You agree to that?" The tone of O'Reith's voice was stern.

"No sir. Betsy called our production superintendent and told him to finish loading the Shell tanker at Tobruk Terminal. After that he was to close the master valve at the main production unit, pay off the locals and lay down the contract rigs."

"How many do we have in there?" O'Reith interrupted.

"Two Bell and Burden rigs out of Santa Fe Springs. Two Green & Heiser rigs out of Bakersfield. And we have six Poole truck-mounted rigs out of Texas setting gas lift valves. We'll have to pay demobilization freight back to the states."

"Let's send them to Poghdar. Force majeure in effect?"

"As of midnight, September 24."

"Nothing will prevent Libyan National from opening the master valve and selling our crude oil to all offtakers that will accept it," O'Reith said. "Who might that be?"

"The Chinese. Maybe North Korea. India and Pakistan," Cook said.

"Have you filed suit against Libyan National?" O'Reith asked.

"They offered us $75 million as compensation. I called Stan last night. He said he would have something in The Hague by the end of the day. He's going to demand $250 million."

O'Reith turned to McDonough. He said, "George that 200,000 barrels a day of *Es Sidar* light was good money for the company. We've got to replace that. We can develop those two structures adjacent to Poghdar, Mishan and Ilam pretty quick. Soon as the rigs from Libya arrive at Bandar Shahpour, we'll need permits to move them. Money may be a problem. Without clear title, financing is tricky. Can we talk to Scotty from here?"

"Sometimes we can get a call through. Sometimes not."

Cook rose, started for her office."

They were in luck. Within the hour Trevelyen was on the line. O'Reith took the receiver, said, "Scotty, can you line us up to talk to the Shah?"

"It may take a few days."

"We'll travel over the weekend. Line him up with good news from Standard Oil. We'll fill you in when we get there. Are you up to date on Libya?"

"Just got the news. BP is out. We've been expropriated."

"Our representative rode back from Tripoli on the BP plane and had a drink with Sir Eric Drake. It made her day. We'll telex you our travel plans," O'Reith said. Turning to McDonough, he asked, "George, what kind of pressure can we put on the Shah from Ten Downing Street? Will Ted Heath fire a shot across his bow?"

"He's a timid fellow, Clive. And he would want to be careful not to stir up the United Nations. What did you have in mind?"

"I would like for him to notify the Shah that the Raj was displeased about the unsettled state of affairs in Poghdar Province of Persia. He could suggest putting in a second brigade of Gurkhas."

"Let me ponder that, I'm inclined to call Black Rod." McDonough answered.

"Do you know him?"

"Yes, Admiral Frank Twiss. He became skipper of H.M.S. *Exeter*, one of the cruisers that tangled with the *Graf Spee* off Montevideo. *Exeter* banged up and had to have major repair. Then it went out to the South Pacific. Twiss was the skipper. He retired and and was appointed Black Rod about three years ago."

"Point out that both Shell and BP are going down in Libya. Say that if we can get the Shah off dead center on that Edict, we can lay down 200,000 barrels a day of Asmari light into steel storage at Grangemouth terminal by the end of December. We can even call it Urals Export."

"Twiss"ll go for that," McDonough said.

Inasmuch as Cook was central to the operation of the company, the three of them would travel from Rome to Teheran over the coming weekend. O'Reith returned to Paris, ran out the week enjoying Maxine's charms, and talked again to Parkinson and Helen about the faith healer.

It was ten o'clock in the morning of October 1. Cook, McDonough, O'Reith and Trevelyen were in the foyer of the Ivory Hall at Golestan Palace, awaiting the pleasure of the Shah. In the quiet interior of the small waiting room, far removed from the din of the street, the odor of roses was cloying. The wait signaled that the Shah was not in good humor, at least as far as they were concerned. Then a small bell tinkled. They were summoned. The Shah greeted them at the entrance to his second floor office and showed them to sofas that were facing his immense glass-topped, teak desk. His indignant-looking face with severe black eyes drilled into McDonough. He barely acknowledged Cook, looked suspiciously at O'Reith. Only for Trevelyen did a trace of a smile and a nod of civility appear. He was wearing his white silk uniform with a high collar trimmed in lamé. Gold piping ran down both trouser legs on the outside. His shoes were of red leather, oriental in design with medium heels. When the wizened tea boy had served everyone, the Shah fixed McDonough with his hard eyes and asked, "What have you done now?"

"Shah, we bring glad tidings. General O'Reith will explain."

"Indeed your Imperial Majesty," O'Reith began. "The Standard Oil executive in San Francisco told me that they desired to keep their relations with you cordial and correct. In view of the uncertainty surrounding crude avails, if your Imperial Highness felt that a moderate price increase would resolve the matter, then we can negotiate something."

The Shah sat up straight. His dark glaring eyes went from one executive to the other until he had made contact all around. His visage was impassive, stony. He opened his taut, rattrap lips and announced, "No negotiation required. The price is to be $6.15 per barrel."

"Ah, Shah," McDonough intervened. "Standard Oil wants us to resolve the ownership of the oil. If the Edict of Annexation were ratified and the treaty with Afghanistan were in place, we'll get a tidy little increase."

The Shah appeared exasperated. He proclaimed, "You gentlemen, and Mademoiselle Cook, know well that complications attend ratification of the Edict."

McDonough air-washed his hands before the Shah's eyes. With a supplicating-look, he smiled confidentially and asked, "Shah have you given thought to prorogation of the Majlis? If they were on a sabbatical, say, then you could proclaim the Edict ratified and so it would be."

The Shah was now more than exasperated. He was exercised. He slapped his hand vigorously on his desk. "So I hear that song twice. His Excellency your ambassador to the Peacock Throne was here yesterday with that same message. You seemed to have forgotten that the thrust of the White Revolution is that of the Shah and his people acting as one. What would my subjects think of me if I sent my Majlis packing?"

"Some of them would not care one way or the other, if you don't mind my saying so," McDonough said carelessly.

The Shah put on his dealing-with-a-child face. After a ponderous sigh, he said, "Sir George, you English are getting to be just like the Americans. Sending the British Ambassador to see me with such a message reminds me of the time that President Kennedy sent that arrogant General Edwin A. Walker to tell me that I was to be pulled, like an abscessed tooth. And now that foolish Richard M. Nixon has appointed a Jew to be his Secretary of State. Is he going to come around demanding tribute?"

"The business with General Walker was an unfortunate occasion, Shah," McDonough agreed. He was in high gear now, his voice purring and melodious. He sensed the Shah was amenable to reason; the moment he was waiting for. He began, "As for Mr. Kissinger, Shah, we shall have to wait and see how he turns out. But remember that the Raj is acting in your best interest. Shah, you have to ask yourself. Which would I rather have? A non-cooperative, indeed even rebellious Majlis or a nice little price increase. Ponder this too, Shah. The British Government would like to see those two other oil fields in Poghdar brought on the line. Instead of running a million barrels, by year end we could be running a million two hundred thousand by next summer, a million and a half."

"You wouldn't have to prorogue the Majlis indefinitely," Trevelyen broke in, looking optimistic. "Give them a long autumn vacation. Bring them back next spring."

"And the treaty?" the Shah asked.

"The Raj is prepared to put pressure on Daud Khan," McDonough said. "Another brigade of Gurkhas waits in the wings." He raised his chin slightly and gave a quick glance to the side as if those soldiers were at the Shah's door even as they spoke.

The Shah followed his glance, smiled faintly at the bit of implied deception. He sighed and capitulated. "Very well, I will dismiss the Majlis tonight. We may have a reaction. The army may have to go to the streets."

"Just so, Shah," McDonough agreed.

"And am I expected to go to Kabul to negotiate this treaty?"

"Of course not, Shah. You can send a fugleman. Going yourself would abrogate your dignity. Nominate a plenipotentiary and we will provide him a proper military escort."

O'Reith said, "Your majesty, the most important thing is to begin the negotiation and inform the press of that. It would be desirable if the Afghans took similar action but your telex to them would satisfy Standard Oil. And of course, something needs to appear in the leading European newspapers."

The Shah smiled. "I'll put out a press release immediately."

"That will take the pressure off of us," O'Reith said sincerely. "Also Shah, we'll have a number of drilling rigs arriving in Bandar Shahpour soon. They'll need permits for Poghdar."

"I'll arrange that today, General O'Reith."

"Shah, I am always amazed at your ability to come to grips with reality and to take the appropriate action," McDonough said.

In the limousine on the way back to the Caspien Hotel, a self-satisfied McDonough said, "Let's check out and go straight to the airport and book a flight out of Teheran to somewhere in Europe. When Shah dismisses the Majlis, there will be a bit of a flap. Riots, Strikes. Civil disorder. He'll have to put the army in the streets to calm those bearded Muslims down."

"Unfortunately, I must stay," Trevelyen said. "I work here."

"Not to worry Scotty," McDonough said. "Three or four days and the furor will die down. When it does, you can call on Shah anew. Ask him to summon a rump Majlis, of only those faithful to him and ready to do his bidding. They will ratify the Edict and later, the treaty."

O'Reith asked, "If the rump Majlis ratifies the Edict and it is published, won't that stir up the Afghans?"

"Good point," Trevelyen said.

"We have to chance it," McDonough said. "Insist that Shah put out the press release. Get our price increase from Standard Oil and then let the clock run."

"That's the ticket all right," Trevelyen agreed. "I'll wait in the lobby while you fellows pack. Then I'll take you to the airport. I'll call my office from the desk here and ask someone to start work on your reservations. Is Rome OK? Alitalia has a late night flight."

"That's fine McDonough said."

O'Reith and Cook nodded agreement.

It was Tuesday, October 2. Again in the afternoon room of McDonough's villa on Lake Albano a doleful-looking Cook said, "We're all flanged up in Libya. Top expatriates on the way to Poghdar."

O'Reith nodded. He said, "Well, Carolyn, it's the rub of the green. I suppose I'll go back to LA. Nothing I can do here."

"I'll be going with you, Clive," McDonough said. "A telex from Helen. I am to be screen-tested next week."

"So I stay in Rome and travel each time one of those rag heads summon me? Is that it?" Cook asked acidly.

"Why not put Holland in Teheran for the time being," O'Reith suggested. "Let him do the traveling. You and George proceed to LA. I'll return to Paris, fetch Maxine and we'll all meet in the tower on, say October 8. That's a Monday. We can see where we stand then."

"All right," McDonough said. "Tomorrow we close up the villa and send the help to our flat in Vatican City. I'll speak to Paul tonight, perhaps even pop over for a word with him. Just to make sure the encyclical is going OK. He'll be returning to the city before October 6, the official publication date of the encyclical. Clive, while I'm in LA, Ethering could bring us up on the enlargement..."

"Sure."

"Clive, have you spoken to the Colonel?"

"Not yet. The Roman Catholic Church is a sticky subject with him. After you complete your test, we can drop in on him in Guatemala City."

Although disappointed, McDonough nodded his agreement.

"Clive do you remember ten years ago when we were first looking at Poghdar, we thought of bringing that crude stream out through Vladivostok?"

"I do," O'Reith said smiling. "Had we known what we were up against now, we might have gone ahead. But it was a long pipeline, 4,000 miles as I recall."

"When do we spring it on Shah that he's going to get $6.15 a barrel?" McDonough asked.

"I'm going to ask Hamilton for $8.15, George. That's $6.15 for the Shah and $2.00 for us."

"Clive, going beyond those other two structures, Mishan and Ilam, what does it look like?" McDonough asked.

O'Reith looked over at Cook. She said, "There are at least three more structures to the north visible from an airplane. But the further north we go, the wilder those tribesmen become. They may be Pathans for all I know."

"You suppose those structures contain oil?" McDonough asked.

"More than likely they do. Oil or gas. The Asmari is usually good. The closer to the surface the better, but the only way to find out is by drilling."

"Could they be as big as Poghdar?"

"No. They are smaller," Cook explained. "The Bangestan could be productive too. Sour no doubt. But it is far deeper and more expensive to test."

"Where will those northern structures be once Shah gets his treaty signed, Poghdar Province, Persia or Herat Province, Afghanistan?" O'Reith asked.

"I don't know exactly, probably in Afghanistan," Cook said.

"Clive, say you and I went in to Kabul to see Duad Khan," McDonough suggested. "Say he gives us a concession covering those structures beyond Ilam. We could test them and if they are any good, we could run that oil out through Vladivostok."

"It's a thought," O'Reith agreed. "It's a question of money. But that Duad Khan guy is a Johnny-come-lately. He may fade." He turned to Cook, said, "Carolyn let's remap that region including those structures to the north. Scotty can pop it on the Shah and get the Edict amended accordingly."

Cook nodded, jotted it down in her little black notebook.

"Clive, I know you make light of my desire to expand the College of Cardinals. You think I'm being selfish and egotistical, trying to manipulate the odds in my favor so that if Paul were to die, I might be elected in his place. Is that not correct?"

"I don't make light of it," O'Reith said. "George, you are a world class manipulator, whether it is Ted Heath, Harold Macmillan, Paul VI or Colonel Marcos Pérez Jiménez. None of that bothers me at all. If you can become the Pope, that's fine, at least it's fine if you don't go to the length of getting rid of the one we've got."

McDonough said huffily, "Clive, you know I would never do that."

"No, I don't think you would."

"Clive, I do not wish to become Pope to fulfill some egotistical dream. I wish to make fundamental changes in the way Christianity is practiced. Today the Roman Catholic Church exists as a plaything of the clergy. There is not much there for the laity. Great change is impossible so long as the papacy is passed from one Italian aristocrat to another. Mark you, these men can practice a medieval form of statecraft but rarely are they men of God. Even Paul, and he is my friend, can only make superficial changes."

"George, I've never heard you speak that way before," Cook said. "How would you reform the Church?"

"That encyclical, we're working on," McDonough continued. "That is a tiny start. The problem of the Church is that it only reluctantly recognizes the enormous physical attraction that exists between men and women. Whatever they are, those priests are not biologists. The bishops grudgingly admit that making babies can be fun. But they wish it were not and more or less, they devise ways to deny it. From that arise many of our woes."

"You're beginning to sound like the Colonel," O'Reith said. "He's all in favor of artificial insemination. He would have made it the law of the land in the Co-prosperity sphere but Flor nixed it."

"He was on solid ground as far as the Church is concerned," McDonough said. "And that is the difficulty. Until the Church comes to grips with the reality of the human condition, there is little hope for the poor, miserable Christians. Would you like to explore the underpinnings of Holy Confession? As a former counter intelligence officer I know a lot about that rite."

"Some other time," O'Reith said. "But I would like to know more about how you work that halo trick. Right now my interests are crude oil avails. George, Pope Paul is not going to let the language of that encyclical leak out before he signs it, is he? If Kissinger had any idea the Pope was getting ready to stick it in the Jews; he would try to get the thing toned down. I don't want that to happen."

"Not to worry, Clive," McDonough reassured him. "Paul has a long head. What kind of a bloke is Kissinger, anyhow?"

"Phony as a three dollar bill as far as I'm concerned," O'Reith said. "His German accent fools people into thinking he knows statecraft.

George, he couldn't shine shoes for the Colonel or Franco. Tito would eat him alive."

"He brought peace to Vietnam. Or claims so anyhow."

"Le Duc Tho in Hanoi had him by the balls. He knew Nixon wanted out. He tossed Kissinger a few crumbs. South Vietnam is a goner. Not that anybody cares."

Cook's eyes narrowed to slits. She yawned, looked at O'Reith, asked, "When do we travel?"

O'Reith pursed his lips; looked to McDonough, asked, "Tomorrow?"

"I'll have a word with Paul. If everything is tickety boo, off we go."

Maxine flew to Rome to join them for the trip to the U.S. They took an Alitalia 747 to New York. Late getting into JFK, they spent the night at the Hilton Hotel in the airport. Next morning, the foursome caught a TWA 747 for the coast. So it was in the afternoon of October 5 that they deplaned at LAX. A company Cadillac awaited them. The chauffeur dropped O'Reith and Maxine off at the Fullerton Building. Then he drove McDonough and Cook to her penthouse in Hollywood Hills.

O'Reith fooled around with Maxine for the rest of the day. They went to bed early and he was up by seven. After breakfast, he shaved in the shower and washed off with lots of soap. He was generous with the aftershave lotion because he was going to see Helen. He didn't want her to smell Maxine's scent. At ten o'clock he entered his limousine for the ride to Long Beach.

Helen, her wig on the deal table, was sitting in their morning room wearing a gray pantsuit and penny loafers. Sharon Mills, in a white smock, her kit open on the table next to the wig, was making up Helen's face. Mills, a nice-looking, pigeon-cheeked woman in her mid-fifties with short hair rinsed to an ash color had worked for the family O'Reith for 20 years. Her hazel eyes were beginning to have lines around them. Many years ago, an MGM talent scout spotted her in the Beverly Hills Hotel barbershop and hired her as a make-up artist. She quickly gained respect for her neat work. When O'Reith turned fifty and his features began to harden, Helen hired her. Mills had an office in the tower next door to O'Reith and when he was to appear in public, make a speech or testify before Congress, she always touched him up so he would look his best. She still had her tower office but nowadays, most of her time was dedicated to Helen and Alice Ridley in Long Beach.

"How's it going, baby?" he asked Helen, bussing her cheek.

"Not too bad, Ace. Max is coming out later today bringing Dr. Kondratieff. George called a few minutes ago. His test is lined up for next Wednesday. Sharon is going to size him up at Cook's place after she's finished with me. Listen to the news this morning?"

"No, are the vultures after Nixon again?"

"Egypt attacked Israel, Ace. Big war going on."

"Jesus, I'll have to go to the office this afternoon. What's with Kondratieff? Get acquainted or is he going to treat you?"

"Depends upon how he looks. Alice is coming too. If he smells of garlic and has a long shaggy beard, it's a no go."

"Surely Max told you what he looked like?" O'Reith asked.

"He said he looked like a Chinaman."

Mills was finished with Helen's face. She carefully installed the wig, handed Helen a mirror and packed her kit. "Look OK, babe?" she asked.

"Yeah, Sharon, good job," Helen replied.

Mills gave O'Reith a quick embrace and a kiss on the cheek, saying, "OK kids, I'm off to attend Sir Sydney Greenstreet."

"Call me after you've checked him out, Sharon. Let me know what you think?" Helen requested.

"Take my car, Sharon," O'Reith said. "Send it back for me."

With a wave of her hand she was gone. Minutes later the butler announced Dr. Max Parkinson and the Russian faith healer. It was almost noon and his chauffeur would not be back for at least two hours. With a war on in the Near East, his teleprinter would be running non-stop. On a Saturday, no one would be there to attend the machine and it would soon run out of paper. He telephoned Cook; asked her to send someone to take care of it.

He didn't care much who would win the war. In the short run, for the company, it simply did not matter. But an Arab victory combined with an unstable American executive could prove problematic, mainly in his dealings with the Shah, his principal concern. An Israeli victory could trigger an oil embargo. That suited O'Reith fine. Instead of $8.15 a barrel, he could get $18.15.

Parkinson introduced the Russian physician. He was nicely dressed in a blue pinstripe suit, was clean-shaven and smelled of some English after-shave lotion that O'Reith couldn't put a name to. He carried a regulation doctor's black bag and a stethoscope hung around his neck. His professional-looking face was thin with a yellow cast. His eyes, dark and penetrating, flashed fire when O'Reith shook his hand. His grip was firm.

O'Reith, Helen and the two physicians sat on sofas in the morning room. Parkinson began, "Helen, Dr. Kondratieff proposes a hypnotic treatment. By reducing physical activity to a minimum, that is, by bringing your blood pressure down to a low level, the white corpuscles in your blood stream can stay in longer contact with the cancer cells, thus destroying them at a faster rate. It is a theory, untested until now, and we can't predict the results. If you agree to try it, I will be at your side. The initial treatment will last fifteen minutes. Dr. Kondratieff will monitor how easily you revive. If all goes well, tomorrow the second treatment will last thirty minutes. Then we will evaluate the results. Following each treatment, bed rest is required. My nurse will be here during the treatment."

"Helen, I'm going to be here too," O'Reith said.

"Well, let's get on with it," Helen replied.

The nurse arrived, helped Helen into her pajamas, turned the bed down in the extra bedroom and when she was installed comfortably, the faith healer began his incantation. With the shades drawn, in the dim light, O'Reith counted the minutes from the luminous dial of his Rolex. The monotonous rhythm of the Russian poetry began to do its work. In two minutes she was semi-conscious. With a small, silvery flute from his black bag, Kondratieff created a mesmerizing tinkle of oriental music. In five minutes, Helen was out. Kondratieff asked in a whisper, "Dr. Parkinson would you like to measure her blood pressure?"

"Parkinson nodded, lifting her wrist.

O'Reith tiptoed out of the bedroom, walked to their den and turned the TV on to KTLA. Israel had been attacked simultaneously by Syrian armor in the north and Egyptian infantry from the west, a coordinated attack making solid gains. It began in the early hours as Israelis were preparing for Yom Kippur observances across the nation. Kissinger was quoted as saying that the State Department was trying to organize a cease-fire. Golda Meir, Prime Minister of Israel was demanding military assistance from the U.S. After a half-hour of news, he turned the TV off and returned to the bedroom where Helen had been wakened from her hypnotic nap. She was resting quietly, the nurse seated beside her and the two physicians standing at the foot of the bed. Parkinson said, "Clive we're going to sedate her and let sleep through the night. She should be in much better condition in the morning. Nurse will be at her side all night."

O'Reith nodded, turned to Kondratieff, asked, "Next treatment?"

"Tomorrow. And again early Monday before I return to London. Dr. Parkinson and I will set up a schedule for continued treatment over the weeks and months to come. We can expect results in six weeks or so."

"Can she continue with plans for her movie?" O'Reith asked.

"But of course," Kondratieff replied with assurance. "After Monday's treatment, she can rest up on Tuesday and proceed with her project on Wednesday."

"That's the day for McDonough's screen test," O'Reith noted.

As the conversation continued, the three men walked into the hall. Parkinson asked, "What kind of a screen test for George?"

"He wants to play the role of Boris Godunov in Helen's remake of *The Shoes of the Fisherman*."

"I saw that movie," Parkinson said. "There was no Boris Godunov in it. It was about a Russian spy who had been in prison for twenty years. He was elected Pope in Rome."

"Well, in this version, Boris Godunov becomes Pope in Rome."

"Incredible!" Parkinson said.

Kondratieff said, "I rarely go the movies. I prefer ballet."

"You are probably better off," O'Reith said. "This one that Helen is making will appeal to a narrow audience."

The telephone was ringing in the den and O'Reith excused himself to take the call. It was McDonough. He said, "Clive, I've just had a word with my secretary in Vatican City. *Casti connubii II* was published this morning in *L'Osservatore romano*. The text is almost identical to what Stan Ethering proposed. When do you plan to see him?"

"Later today, George. Helen is just waking up from her treatment. Max is going to sedate her. When that's done and everything is OK, I'm going to the tower to read the telexes. Ethering will be there."

"I'm coming too," McDonough said. "Carolyn said we had a stack of messages. I'm just finished with Sharon. She want's a word with you."

When she came on the line, O'Reith said, "All's well Sharon. Helen is resting."

"Wonderful. Will she need me again today?"

"No, but come around in the morning. Say ten o'clock."

"OK. Sir George looks pretty good, by the way. Properly made up, he'll be a swell Boris."

"That is good news indeed," O'Reith said, hanging up the telephone. Parkinson and Kondratieff were still talking in the hall. O'Reith asked, "OK if I go read my mail?"

"Sure, Helen won't be in the mood for conversation until in the morning."

The Cadillac was parked out front, his chauffeur napping behind the wheel. He woke up when O'Reith entered the tonneau. "The Tower, Waters," O'Reith said, looking at his watch. It was after four. With all the news, it was shaping up as a long Saturday afternoon. The big Cadillac tooled north finally turning into Sepulveda Boulevard. Then they eased into the underground garage and O'Reith caned himself out in front of the executive elevator that ran non-stop all the way to the 39th floor. Soon behind his desk, he called Maxine for dinner plans. The cook was off duty so they opted for the Formosa Club. He told her he would be home by seven o'clock. Then he summoned Cook, McDonough and Ethering.

"Where do we start?" he asked, looking at the sheaf of messages that Cook had in her right hand.

She said, "We start with a telephone call to Bill Hamilton in San Francisco. I have his home phone number in Nob Hill. Urgent request for you to return his several calls."

O'Reith smiled. "That's good news." He put on his reading glasses and dialed.

The answer came before the end of the first ring, "Hello?"

O'Reith purred into the mouthpiece, "Bill how's a boy?"

"I'm OK Clive. Torqued up but OK. Christ Clive am I ever glad to hear from you! I guess you know that all hell has broken loose in the Near East."

O'Reith laughed. "You jerked that phone off the hook like it was a fire axe in a Roman Candle factory. Carolyn, Sir George and Stan are here with me. Teleprinter went berserk. Carolyn has a stack of messages that looks like the Sears Roebuck catalog. We definitely have all that we can say grace over."

"Clive, I'll get right down to it," Hamilton began in an even, unhurried voice, "With Libya down we're standing short across the board. Suddenly that put-through coming out of Poghdar is our lifeline. We gotta have it, babe! Gotta have it! Price no object."

"We got into it with the Shah last week. You fellows think you could stand still for $8.15/bbl. That's $6.15 for the Shah and $2.00 for us. We still have the pedigree problem. The Shah put out a press release on the negotiation with Afghanistan the day we left. We'll have copies to you in a day or so. With Scotty's help and some imaginative forgery, we can guarantee you a clean bill of lading. While the negotiation is ongoing we'll call the crude stream Agha Jari light. That OK?"

"Clive, it looks like Feisal will force Aramco to shut in to support Syria and Egypt," Hamilton said. "If they do, then we'll run Poghdar crude into California. Agha Jari on the bill of lading would be perfect."

"You got it, babe."

"That's a load off my mind. I'll advise EXCOM right away." Hamilton said, relief in his voice. "If Aramco stays up, we'll continue selling it East of Suez. If Aramco shuts in, California here we come."

"Bill, you know that several additional structures exist in that area," O'Reith replied. We're thinking of putting four strings in there to develop another 200,000 bopd. Would Standard Oil like a first right of refusal?"

"Refusal my rear end! We'll take every barrel of it. Contract in the mail, babe."

"OK, Bill, we'll get a wire off to Scotty. You can tell your EXCOM that the million barrels out of Poghdar is firm with more coming. We'll have to get confirmation from the Shah but he's sure to go for it. We're thinking of running the extra 200,000 bopd into the Grangemouth Terminal. I'll be back in touch." O'Reith hung up the telephone and wheeled around to face the others. "Anything interesting in that stack of telexes, Carolyn?"

"Alarm bells ringing across the board. Every refiner in North America is looking for crude oil. We could sell five million barrels a day if we had it. Oil company executives want your opinion about the war."

"George?"

"A wire from Eric Drake at BP. Shah is nervous. Worried the war may spread into Lebanon and Iraq. Too close to home for him."

"I suppose we could print up the encyclical and drop it on the battlefields," O'Reith said. "With them at each others throats, fat chance either Jew or Arab will have heard about it."

"It would go for bum wad," McDonough sighed.

"George, it's back to Teheran and explain all this to the Shah. We don't want him to get any delusions of grandeur." O'Reith continued. "I don't want him to get the idea he can jack the price up again."

"We could go after my test. Say next Thursday. That would be the 11th."

"OK. Wire Scotty today. Wait for him to see the Shah and confirm everything OK. George I don't want to fly anywhere in the Middle East on a commercial jet. Too many heat-seeking missiles crossing the air lanes We have one of our B-17s hangared up in Paris. It is slow but with our own pilots we can leave in a hurry, fly a circuitous route, and if if things get out of control head for Baku. Any news from Scotty by the way?"

"Telex last night said the war has sparked bad rioting in Teheran and Ahwaz. Police couldn't handle it. Shah had to set the army on them. Several hundred dead. Prisons overflowing. Gasoline shortages. Food shortages. The usual commotion. Fairly quiet now."

O'Reith turned to Ethering. He asked, "Stan what do you know about Kissinger? Is he any good?"

"World class sycophant," Ethering answered. "But all of those cats are. Diplomats!"

"Can he stop that war?"

"Not by himself. Maybe with help from the Russkys. The only way to stop the war is to quit giving them arms and ammunition. We supply Israel. The Soviet Union supplies Syria and Egypt. They can keep it going until everyone is a casualty or they run out gun cotton."

McDonough spoke up. "Clive is it all right if I ask Stan about helping us expand the College of Cardinals?"

"Sure George, shoot," O'Reith answered easily. He reclined in his chair.

Ethering wore a blank expression on his round face and he seemed dazed. A faint smile began to flicker around his nose and lips as he looked at McDonough and echoed, "Expand the College of Cardinals?"

"Yes, Stan. Pope Paul VI has come to the conclusion that little can be done to reform the Church so long as it is dominated by a corps of aristocratic Italians. He's thinking of an immediate expansion to somewhere around 150 members. That's an increase of 70. He's thinking of the inclusion of lay cardinals, Eastern Rites metropolitans and Dames of Honor and Devotion of the Order of St. John. Inasmuch as you are a Roman Catholic of some visibility and with good connections throughout the country, we were wondering if you could help us lobby. You could contact the elite laity here in North America. Sound them out on the idea of becoming princes and princesses of the Church. If reactions were favorable, I could report that back to the Pope and we could advance the scheme."

"Well, I can kick it around with Archbishop Harley here in LA. Get his opinion. He helped us with the encyclical. If he gives the nod, we can take a systematic approach. Put out a circular letter to all of the American and Canadian Cardinals and the one down in Mexico City. Then, once they have the message, I could telephone around and try to pump up some enthusiasm. Maybe a few discreet contributions to their favorite charities. Would that strain the budget?"

"Of course not, Stan," O'Reith said. "Do the necessary."

Ethering consulted his calendar. He said, "You fellows are getting out of here on the 11th. How long will you be in the Middle East?"

"Get to Teheran on Sunday the 14th. See the Shah on Monday. We may see him again on Tuesday for a follow up. We're going to shoot for one day in Kabul to see Duad Khan. We should be back in Rome on the 16th and back here on the 18th."

"I'll give you a preliminary report on the 19th." Ethering concluded.

"That's wonderful Stan," McDonough said, beaming and washing his hands in the air. "We're going to ask the Colonel to do the same for us in Central and South America. With your report, I'll be able to give him some background."

Ethering nodded. He turned to O'Reith and asked, "Can we do anything to shut down the war in Palestine?"

"Nothing, Stan." O'Reith said. "But we may be able to take advantage of it. Carolyn, get together with our treasurer on Monday and line up financing. I'll advise my contact with JP Morgan that you'll be in touch."

"What about a trip down to see the Colonel, Clive?" McDonough asked."Remember you promised."

"One of those messages is from the Colonel sir," Cook said. He asks that you call."

O'Reith was thoughtful. He drummed his desktop with his fingers. He picked up the telephone and dialed the *Palacio Nacional* in Guatemala City. When there was an answer he asked to speak to Colonel Marcos Pérez Jiménez, President of the *Greater Central American Co-prosperity Sphere*. When he was on the line, O'Reith began, " Colonel Jiménez how's a boy?"

"General O'Reith!" the Colonel squealed in seeming ecstasy. "How splendid it is to hear from you! And how is my sweet *Pecos Lil*?"

"She's ailing Colonel. But not to worry. She'll be OK in a bit. How's your family?"

"Flor is well. She's here. Margot is in New York. Shopping as usual."

O'Reith said, "What's on your mind? How are your affairs in Venezuela?"

"Not good. Government raised the taxes. They're threatening expropriation."

"We could talk about that. But not on the telephone," the Colonel said, laughing.

"George would like some help from you. A religious matter."

"He should talk to Flor. That is her department. But why don't the two of you pop down for a quick visit? I have to address the *Co-prosperity sphere* on national TV tomorrow. How about Wednesday, the 10th?"

"Sir George is slated for a screen test on Wednesday and we're off to Persia on Thursday," O'Reith said. How about one week later, Thursday the 18th?"

"A screen test?"

"Yeah. Helen is making a new movie."

"I'd like to hear more about that. What about Saturday?" the Colonel suggested.

"The 20th? Yes that would be OK. Pan American has a DC 8 flight non-stop from Los Angeles on that day. Arrives in the early afternoon. We could chat for a while," O'Reith responded.

"You gentlemen could stay for dinner." the Colonel suggested.

"Are there any night flights back to Los Angeles on that day?"

"You can make book that there will be at least one," the Colonel replied, laughing. "That's a new American idiomatic expression I just picked up."

O'Reith laughed too. "Quite apt, Colonel. OK. We'll see you on Saturday, the 20th and I'll call you before we take off."

Chapter III

The Screen Test

Next morning he called his penthouse in Long Beach. The nurse answered and he asked, "How is she?"

"Dr. Parkinson sedated her after the second treatment. She is in bed asleep."

"Parkinson still there?"

"No but I have his telephone number."

"OK," O'Reith signed off. "I'll be around later when she wakens."

Then he called Parkinson. "Max, how does it look?"

"Too early to say, Clive. First treatment was a snap. Today was a bit different. Kondratieff normally uses a musical instrument known as a Theremin to bring his patients out of their trances. But it is rather large and delicate so he used an LP of Theremin music. He put it on the turntable at low volume and gradually brought it up until she wakened. When she came out of her trance she was disoriented. Kondratieff said that was somewhat unusual. Still, her vital signs were all OK. She should be conscious in a bit. The nurse will call me."

"OK, Max," O'Reith said. "I'll look in as early as I can get away. She still on for a third treatment on Monday?"

"If she's in good shape tomorrow, yes."

"You're coming out?"

"I'll be there by nine at the latest, Clive."

"See you then," O'Reith said.

O'Reith rose at six the next morning and was at Helen's bedside before she awoke. "How's a girl?" he asked.

"Ace, What time is it?" she asked, sleepily. "How long have I been out?"

"It is Monday baby. Almost 8 am."

"Surely not."

"Yeah, you had two treatments and lots of sleep. Feel any different?"

"Ace, I don't remember a goddamned thing. I feel pretty good. Hungry as a horse."

O'Reith said, "I'll wait for you in the morning room. When you're up and about, we can breakfast together."

Downing her orange juice in a gulp, Helen said, "Ace I remember meeting Dr. Kondratieff and after that it's a blank. What happened?"

"He hypnotized you and kept you down for fifteen minutes. Max was beside you all the time to measure your blood pressure. Kondratieff brought you around with some kind of weird music. You were a bit confused about it all so Max sedated you. Yesterday you got a second treatment and today you get a third if you're up to it. Kondratieff is on his way."

"Well, I'm up to it. George is in town, right? Screen test on Wednesday?"

"That's it. He would like to come around later to say hello," O'Reith said. I told him I'd call him to let him know how you are doing."

"I really don't want to see him. I don't want to see anybody. But he arranged for Dr. Kondratieff. I suppose it is the least I can do. Maybe this afternoon, say four o'clock?"

"Will you be in the mood for a cocktail tonight?"

Helen laughed, said, "Ace I'm in the mood for one right now. That is a good idea. Instead of four, let's ask him to have a drink with us. Say six."

"I'll call him while you're getting dressed."

"Ace, he's going to have his hands full with that test. It is thirty minutes long. He'll be wearing heavy robes encrusted with jewelry and he'll have to sing part of his lines. He'll be wearing a crown made of gold-plated aluminum. I don't know how much it weighs. Those Klieg lights will wilt him down too."

"Maybe not. Who does he sing to?"

"Olga. She's a girl that is trying to win his favor. She wants to be his tsarina, or at least, one of them."

"Who's playing that part?"

"In the test it will be Eve Arden. She wants the part. I told her we'd have to see how it turned out."

"She's no slip of a girl, Helen. Eve is 60 if she's a day."

"Ace, I'm directing this movie for laughs," Helen explained. "You recall that *The Shoes of the Fisherman* was somber. I don't want that. This is going to be a tragi-comedy. Besides, Sharon is no slouch at taking years off. She'll have Eve down to a winsome thirty-nine in a wink of an eye. It'll be a good flick."

"With George and Eve, it is well on its way," O'Reith agreed.

The nurse came to help Helen up. O'Reith kissed her and departed.

"When McDonough answered the telephone at Cook's place, he was elated and it was in his voice. "Clive, the Sunday papers have noticed that the encyclical was published yesterday. The *New York Times.* The *Los Angeles Times.* The *San Francisco Chronicle.* Isn't that something?"

"I suppose it is, George. Are the notices favorable?"

"I haven't read them. Stan called. He's bringing them over now. Clive what is the *Yellow Peril*? They noticed it too."

"It's a newspaper that prides itself on printing what it considers to be the unvarnished truth. Often with a cynical take on the events of the day, especially in matters political and religious. Stan bringing that one over too?"

"Indeed."

"Well read that one first. We'll know where we stand pdq. George the reason I called is that Helen is up. She gets her third Theremin serenade in a few minutes. If all goes well, she'll be ready for cocktails at six. Does that suit you?"

"Indeed, may I bring Carolyn?"

"Of course. Do you have your scenario handy?"

McDonough chuckled with satisfaction. "I've been sleeping with it."

"Flip it over to where Olga enters for the first time. Boris sings an aria to her. Then she sings one back to him. That's what the test is going to cover. Study that before the camera rolls. Good luck."

"I'll be properly prepared," McDonough said. "I say Clive, if I should propose a cameo appearance for Carolyn, would Helen go for it?"

"No idea," O'Reith answered.

"Carolyn gets along OK with Alice?"

"That's the key to it. George, Alice will be coming tonight. You and Carolyn can think about how you want to cue it up."

"We'll be ready."

"George, what about the Shah? Did he put out a press release? Copies for us?"

"We have something coming from the *Financial Times* and another from *Le Figaro*. Should be here in a day or so."

"That's great. See you tonight."

Helen's third treatment left her tired but by six o'clock she was eager for a drink. Sitting around the cocktail table in the parlor were McDonough, Cook, Ridley, O'Reith and Helen. Mills had just finished making up Helen's face and was taking off her white apron and packing her kit. O'Reith said, "Sharon, you're welcome to join us."

"Thanks but I've got a date with a gentleman. At my age, that's a rarity." She shook hands with McDonough and Cook, bussed Ridley, Helen and O'Reith and flew through the door with a wave of the hand.

The butler rolled in the drink tray. Pitcher of dry martinis for the O'Reiths and Ridley. Johnny Walker Black for McDonough and Ron Pampero for Cook.

"George, how did it go?" Helen asked.

"Helen, it went well. Alice coached me. Helen. I must have the role. It is so me!"

"That test covered the very core of the movie," Helen began. "It goes downhill from there. The film ends seven minutes later. This one is for laughs. Of course Godunov has his solemn moments but he is elated at having attained the pinnacle of success. Enjoys every minute of it. He comes to a bad end but not just yet. The audience will be glad to see him get what he deserves. But this is a moment of jubilation. Did the bejeweled robe and the aluminum crown drag you down?"

"No. It was a snap." McDonough said proudly. "I held my head high and sang the aria with brio in my operatic basso".

"How did you get on with Eve?" Helen asked. She is one of the silver screen's truly gifted actresses."

"She tried to steal the scene. What else?" McDonough replied cagily. "But I did enjoy performing with that remarkable actress?"

"I'll take a look at the test tomorrow," Helen said. "We'll go from there."

"Understood."

Cook took the big man's hand and caressed it. She said, "George, my hero!"

"How did you like our Grand Hall of the Tsars of Russia in St. Petersburg?" Helen asked.

"For a sound stage at Culver City, it was a faithful replica," McDonough said. "Helen," he continued, "Is there a possibility of a cameo for Carolyn?"

Helen looked across the cocktail table to Ridley who gave her an approving nod. "Of course there is. Carolyn could appear as Genevieve Ste Jacqueline, come to bless Boris. She says her prayer and then lifts the crown off of the red satin pillow and places it gently on George's head."

Turning to Cook, Helen added. "You just stand there smiling until a royal attendant removes the pillow. Then you bow and depart the set."

"May I flash George a quick halo?"

"That may be overdoing it," Ridley said.

"OK. No halo," Cook agreed.

"I'll call Edith and ask her to design a costume for Carolyn," Ridley said.

"Good idea," O'Reith said.

They were having refills. O'Reith asked, "George, did you check out those reviews of *Casti Connubii II*?"

"*Los Angeles Times* was noncommittal. They reported on it like it was a soccer match. *San Francisco Chronicle* about the same. The *Yellow Peril* was unkind. At least I thought so. I brought it along. Would you like to read it?"

"Yeah I would."

From the *Yellow Peril*, only honest newspaper on the West Coast

> "Los Angeles. Sunday, October 7, 1973. At the same time the Arabs were attacking the Jews from Syria and Egypt, the Pope in Rome, His Holiness Paul VI was putting out another encyclical, which was duly published in the Saturday issue of *L'Osservatore*

romano. The name of this one is *Casti connubii II.* In English it would be called 'Of Pure marriage again' and it is a remake of an encyclical originally put out in 1930 by Pope Pius IX. We don't exactly know what to make of it. Readers of this regular Sunday column will recall Pope Paul VI's previous literary endeavor, published in 1967 called *Humanae vitae,* which bombed. Everybody, from condom manufacturers to teenagers doing it in the back seat of the family sedan, was upset. The negative reception staggered the Pope so he swore off encyclicals. At least until yesterday. The remake is a bizarre document, to put it in its best light. Our religious editor has checked back through every encyclical put out over the last ten centuries and this is by far the most explicit in terms of definition of sexual idiosyncrasies. Even the notorious practice of *soixante neuf* finds a place in this pastoral letter. What the Vatican is saying, reduced to cold statistics, is that the Christian World needs more Christians to keep up with the wild, unfettered breeding of non-Christians, mostly in the Middle East and Asia. His Holiness follows world population trends and it does not look good for Christians. Since birth control in general was coldly rejected by the Roman Catholics who bothered to note the Pope was against it, this approach is a little different. Now the Pope wants to get Christians to start making more Christians and he does not much care exactly what biological process is followed. If a so-called French kiss results in pregnancy, the Pope will bless it. Even more curious than the language on procreation is his violent condemnation of Jews and Arabs for upsetting the peace of the world, what little there is of it. In times past, a pastoral letter was confined to one subject. This one has two and they are only tangentially related. Reminds us of federal legislation. Well, we'll give it a chance. See how it plays out on the hustings. Will it become a permanent part of Roman Catholic legacy? Or will it, like *Humanae vitae,* go down the tube? Dear thoughtful readers, *Casti connubii II* looks to our staff like it might come another cropper. Check us again next Sunday. We should have plenty of reaction by then."

"Not a great endorsement," O'Reith said, handing the news clip back to McDonough. "I hope the Shah's press release is more to our liking."

"Don't worry. It will be. Perhaps by next Sunday, world opinion will be more favorable," McDonough said, miffed.

"Don't count on it," Ridley interjected. "When the *Yellow Peril* nixes something, it usually stays nixed."

"Clive, you were telling me we might get some religious group, a Christian pop band, to write a song or two on the encyclical. Have we done anything?"

"George, there is a group called The New Hope Pomona College Pentecostal Minstrels." Helen said. "You'll get to meet them. They are putting together a portfolio of ditties that could be used to support the encyclical."

"I can hardly wait," McDonough sighed, smarting from the *Yellow Peril's* pan.

After two martinis, Helen was feeling OK. She suggested that they drive to the Limejuicer Club for dinner. It was agreed instantly. O'Reith, Ridley and Helen rode in the Cadillac. McDonough and Cook followed along in her Lincoln Continental.

The Limejuicer Club, organized around the time of World War I by British expatriates in the motion picture industry included O'Reith's mother, Rae Regan who was a silent star of the silver screen, and widow of a British officer of the Indian Army. When she became inactive, O'Reith took over the membership. Located in the hills north of Hollywood, it had once been the estate of a matinee idol and was surrounded by orange groves on three sides and steep, sagebrush-covered hills, on the fourth. The wrought iron entrance was carefully guarded. Members, chauffeurs and guests were closely scrutinized. Past the gate, the narrow asphalt road wound along for a half mile with lemon trees lining the route on both sides and ended under the marquee. A uniformed attendant helped them from the limousine.

They dined on barbecued beef, cole slaw and baked beans washed down by Olympia Beer on tap. They gossiped long into the night, giggling and tittering. The evening was all enjoyed by all. Helen, exhausted by the long day, fell asleep in the car.

O'Reith was up early and at his desk before nine. Departing for Rome on Thursday, he had much to do. Parkinson called. He said, "Clive I know you're traveling but I need to review a few things with you."

"Can you come around this afternoon?"

"How about three o'clock?"

"See you then."

When the two men were together, Parkinson began. "Clive, Helen's second treatment, like the first was without complications. But this last one was a bit irregular. It took longer for Helen to awaken. Kondratieff seemed concerned. I wanted to prepare you in case he spots something we didn't expect."

"Did you schedule a 4th treatment?"

"Yes, a month from now. Kondratieff will call me after he reviews the EEGs. We'll confirm it then."

"OK, Max. I look to you to keep her in good spirits."

Next morning, KTLA reported intense fighting continued between the Israelis and the Syrian-Egyptian combination. McDonough called to inquire if Helen had seen his test. Cook called to tell him that Ethering had departed on Sunday for Vienna to attend the meeting with OPEC ministers. She sent the Shah's press release by courier to Standard Oil. O'Reith spent the afternoon with Helen. In good spirits, she claimed that she could feel herself recovering. McDonough's screen test was a borderline case. Eve Arden's aria, written for a mezzo-soprano, turned out flat. For the movie itself, Helen was torn between hiring a professional and letting Arden sing her own song. Although not famous as a singer, she could carry a tune and had indeed, more than once, performed in motion pictures as a singing actress. So in the end, Helen had decided to let Arden have a crack at it. Her logic was that after all, it was only a test and she was under no pressure to make a decision.

At cocktails, O'Reith asked, "Helen what's with Helen Simpson and Alice? The other day when Alice came in, she ignored her and ran out of the room."

"Something to do with that beach bum she kissed off. In the heat of their affair she asked Alice to prepare a chart on him. She didn't like the chart."

O'Reith laughed. "Maybe that's why she told him goodbye."

"Who knows?" Helen asked philosophically. "At least he is out of our hair. Ace, I'm having a bowl of soup with Alice and then early to bed. I've had it for today."

O'Reith returned to town and upon arrival, greeted Maxine and immediately switched on the TV. The Russians were airlifting supplies to the Syrians and the Egyptians. The administration was dithering.

White House Chief of Staff Alexander Haig announced the formation of the Washington Special Action Group to address the crisis in the Near East. There was speculation that Vice President Spiro Agnew would resign later in the day. President Nixon remained on high alert in Key Biscayne, Florida. The newscast gave the impression of tension in Washington. A Congressional Committee was demanding more Watergate papers and tapes from the administration. He telephoned the corporate treasurer, Roland Gresham, to explain that he was considering various plans to expand the company. All required financing over and above their cash generation. He reviewed his discussions with Cook. He concluded by telling Gresham that around the end of the month the three of them would decide how much to borrow, under what conditions and from whom. Late in the afternoon, McDonough called. "Clive, I'm totally exhausted."

"Where are you George?"

"At Carolyn's in a vast tub of steaming water. I'm worn down from the pressure and the heat and all the rest of it."

"Carolyn in the tub with you?"

"Clive I must say you are a bit impertinent!

"Yes or no, George."

"W-e-l-l, yes."

"George, we're on TWA tomorrow for JFK. It's a 747. Leaves around eleven in the morning."

"We'll meet you at the airport."

"OK, George," O'Reith said.

O'Reith dined with Maxine and it was early to bed.

The flight to JFK was routine. Traffic flowed easily on the Van Wyck and the Long Island Expressways. Congestion at the Queen's Tunnel slowed them down. It was dark before they arrived at the Waldorf Towers. O'Reith said, "I'm going to dine in the room. See you two in the morning."

After ordering dinner, he turned on the TV to WNBC. The big news was the resignation of Spiro Agnew. There was speculation about who would replace him. The war continued to rage in Israel. Cook called to say she had spoken with Ethering in Vienna. Still no decision on oil prices from OPEC.

They were on the daylight Pan Am 707 to Paris. Cook and McDonough had a connecting flight to Fiumicino on Air France. O'Reith said, "George, I'm spending the night at my place in Paris. One of those old B-17s is hangared up at Le Bourget. Company pilots and navigators will get it ready for a trip to the Middle East. Tomorrow I'll fly to Rome. Get a message off to Scotty that we're coming."

"I must say I prefer to fly jets but I'll admit to being uneasy about flying anywhere around Israel. Will you be talking to Helen tonight?"

"Top of my list, George. Helen. Then Max. Then Hamilton with Standard Oil. Carolyn should have news from Stan by tomorrow. So when I arrive, we can huddle and put the pieces together."

"Clive, I'm anxious about the outcome of the screen test. You'll ask her about that, won't you?"

"I will, George. Not to worry."

"Clive, it would be better for Carolyn to remain in Rome unless you feel that we need her."

"I agree. She has plenty to do and communication can be difficult from Teheran."

O'Reith bade his traveling companions goodbye at Charles de Gaulle. His limousine was waiting and by midnight he was in his place in rue de Surene. Because of the time lag, he decided to skip dinner. As soon as he was out of the shower, he called Helen in Long Beach where it was three o'clock in the afternoon. She picked up on the first ring and he asked, "How's a girl, baby?"

"Ace, I'm not feeling too bad but I've looked at the screen test again and while it is not a disaster, I'm disappointed."

"George?"

"Yeah. Ace, he is really too old for that part. He was struggling."

"How about Eve?"

"The same. On the good news side, I got a call from Rod Steiger. He's interested in playing the Godunov role. What do you think?"

O'Reith laughed. "What does Alice think?"

Helen laughed. "I knew you would ask that."

"Seriously, what did Alice say?"

"She doesn't like him. She says there is something wrong with him. She thinks he's a psycho."

"Baby," O'Reith came back, "there is something wrong with all of them, George included. But I guess it is difficult for you to go against Alice."

"In these trying times, it is Ace. She looks after me, stays near at hand and well, I can't do without her."

"Ask her what she thinks about a test for Steiger. She'll then realize you're taking him seriously. Baby, what do I tell George? I'll be in Rome tomorrow night and that will be the first question out of the box."

"Say the test is inconclusive. Technical problem with the film or something. Tell him we may have to do another. Perhaps that will discourage him."

"Not a chance. I'll stall him along until you make up your mind about Steiger. If you go with him, we'll have to figure out some way to keep George in the movie. We can't just tell him it's a no go. He would spit a snake."

"Let me think about it, Ace. Will he go for a supporting actor role?"

"I'll sound him out but it will be like walking on eggs. If he suspects you're going to dump him, that will be very bad news indeed. You know baby, you could just scrap the whole idea. After all, the original film didn't make any money. Your scenario is even direr. Remember that Ed Dmytryk is basically a *film noir* guy. His scripts are heavier than .45 caliber slugs. Why not make a musical; a remake of the *Ziegfield Follies of 1933* for example? Plenty of young kids in Hollywood that can sing and dance. They'll work for a song. When it comes out, the bobby-soxers will flock to it swooning, screaming and pulling off their panties."

"Ace, must you always have your mind on your well, you know what?"

O'Reith laughed. "Anything from Max?"

"He was in this morning, Ace. Took my pulse, looked down my throat, measured my blood pressure. Putting on an act. Nothing has changed. Said I was doing OK. We're waiting on Dr. Kondratieff."

"Max say anything about that?"

"Said he'd let me know. He mentioned that an EEG report from Kondratieff was routine."

"Are you going to look at it?"

She laughed. "What for?"

"Did they confirm your next treatment?"

"November 6th. He told Max that it was too early for any predictions."

"What about the kids, baby? Are they in the loop on all of this?"

"Helen Simpson knows. I have said nothing to Rae Regan nor little Clive Colin and I don't intend to. I want to make my movie and go about my affairs without answering questions."

"Fair enough, I'll stay silent. If they ask, I'll refer them to you."

"Is there anything else we need to discuss, baby? I'll be in Rome tomorrow with George and Carolyn. Then out to Teheran. Telephones don't work as well out there as they do in Europe."

"I'm interested in knowing how big of a shock it will be to George's nervous system when he gets the bad news," Helen said.

"I'll sound him out. Take care." As he hung up on his call to Helen, he dialed Parkinson. "Max," he began, "just talking to Helen. She said Kondratieff reported on the EEG. Must be normal since he confirmed the next treatment? Everything going OK there?"

"Clive, Kondratieff was a bit upset because it took him a few minutes longer to bring Helen around than it did the second time. He said that was unusual. He does not understand the significance of it. He's not finished yet."

"Is he going to report back to you?"

"He's going to call me when he has a theory. He wants to go ahead with the next treatment but he might cut it short. Depends on what he can dope out from the EEG. When can I talk to you again?"

"We'll be in Teheran most of next week. One day in Kabul. Be back in Rome on the 21st."

"I'll leave a message for you," Parkinson concluded.

Then O'Reith called Maxine to say he had arrived in Paris and was sleeping in their bed.

The flight plan took them from Paris to Rome, from Rome to Athens, Athens to Ankara and Ankara to Baku. Then, it was an easy flight down to Teheran. He called McDonough, asked, "George, can you raise Mikoyan in Moscow and get us a landing permit?"

"I expect so. When will you be here?"

"In the morning. We can get out of Rome in the evening. Fly all night. Refuel in Athens and Ankara. With the delays, we should get into Baku around dawn. We can spend the night. Rest up. You suppose we can find a hotel with running water?"

"Mikoyan can help us there, Clive. He'll put us up at a government guesthouse. Might as well be comfortable."

"OK, see you tomorrow."

For a change, O'Reith let the pilots fly the *La Cruz de la Cañada*. After a late lunch with Cook, the two oilmen motored to Fiumicino and by five pm were in the air headed for Athens. In the mid-section of the airplane were two half beds and behind them, four swivel chairs bolted to the main fuselage spar. After refueling in Athens, "they looked at the Grecian Isles in the moonlight from the swivel seats. The windows had once been gun ports for .50 caliber machine guns. But now, with Plexiglas installed, they had a fine view of the tranquil Aegean. McDonough, swirling a snifter of Martell Five Star cognac asked, "Clive, did you call Helen from Paris?"

"I did, George. I asked about the test. She said the test was technically flawed. May have to do it over."

"Well of course, I will be glad to do that. But I hoped that all was well, that she had good news for me."

"George, these things take time. Patience is the watchword. *Gone With the Wind* had more screen tests than it had actors in the cast. In due course, all will be resolved."

"Of course Clive. Of course you're right."

As they circled to land at Baku the early sun reflected light from the cockpits of dozens of obsolete Tupelov and Ilushyin aircraft stacked out along the fringes of the runways. A Mikoyan man in civvies met them at the main exit hatch and escorted them through an array of brown-uniformed customs and immigration officials, many of them beefy-faced women who had not smiled since May 9, 1945. Wearing a huge Red Army cap a stout, gray-haired crone with black eyes and a hawk nose sat at the immigration desk, the last hurdle before leaving the lounge. She shouted at the government man, "This is highly irregular! These men have no visas for the Soviet Union. You ask me to break the law!" Mikoyan's man presented a telegram to the furious woman. She read it slowly and carefully; finally handed it back to him and angrily stamped the passports. As the men departed she raised a closed fist, shook it at them and shouted after them, "This is not Moscow, you Bolsheviks!"

The government man shrugged, said "Soviet life in the provinces You will get used to it."

Mikoyan's man turned them over to an agricultural functionary who escorted them to a Zim limousine under the marquee of the arrivals building. He explained that they would be quartered at an experimental Soviet agricultural project south of the city. The drive took them in a southwest direction for some minutes until they turned into Khatai Street on the outskirts of town. At the Square of 28 May, downtown, which commemorated the execution of the Commissars in 1919, they turned into Chingiz Mustafayeh Street, which ran all the way to the western suburbs. There they picked up a two-lane black top that ran along the coast. Pump jacks of the Baku oil field bobbed up and down in the low swale near the shore. On the right were high sandy bluffs. Vegetation was sparse and swirls of dust eddied up from time to time. Ancient grave markers rose up here and there along the way. After an hour's drive, they arrived at the agricultural station on the seashore. It had its own water well, electric power plant and sewage disposal system. In luxurious rooms, clearly built for important visitors from Moscow, McDonough gazed lovingly at the giant-sized tub in his bathroom. The agent showed them row after row of hydroponically grown green vegetables and a surfeit of hothouse fruit. He explained that the Caspian was a sulphate rather than a salt sea. Chemicals precipitated the sulphates making the water suitable for drinking as well as irrigation of the garden grown produce. Once settled in, McDonough telephoned Mikoyan in the Kremlin to thank him for the munificence. As he talked, a second limousine rolled up with the pilots, the navigators and the crew chief. O'Reith treated himself to a marvelous hot shower. McDonough opted for a soak. After ice cold Moskovskaya vodka, they dined on baked sturgeon, Caspian rice with dill, sliced cucumbers and tomatoes with hot peppers and mixed fruit compote for dessert. All of that washed down with a chilled white wine from Bulgaria. O'Reith couldn't remember dining any better, not even at Lasserre's. After dinner, on a late evening stroll, limicoline birds along the Caspian verges serenaded them with night songs. A vibrating string of vertical lights indicated an offshore drilling rig turning to the right. McDonough said, "Clive, Mikoyan relayed a bit of sweet news."

"Yeah, what's that, George?"

"Clive after all these years of wandering in the wilderness, I'm to be brought into the green garden."

"Yeah, how's that?"

"Clive, I'm on the Queen's List for 1974. I'm to become The McDonough of Grangemouth."

"Lord of the Oil Company refinery," O'Reith chuckled. "How would Mikoyan know that?"

"Ten Downing Street routinely notifies the Russian Ambassador." And it is not the refinery that I'm to be lord of. It's the river, the Grange River."

"Congratulations. Am I to be invited to the investiture?"

"*Bien sur*! And Helen and Carolyn."

"Looking forward to it, George."

"At what hour do we take off in the morning, Clive?"

"Chief pilot is requesting a take off clearance from Moscow. Try to be in the air by nine o'clock. Put us into Teheran around noon."

McDonough picked up the telephone and began speaking slowly in elegant Russian. He hung on as first one and then another, long distance operator came on the line. With each new voice, he repeated his request for a direct line to Trevelyen's flat in Takte-Jamshid Boulevard in Teheran. After a half-hour, he hung up in disgust. "Eight hour delay," he muttered.

"That's the Middle East for you," O'Reith said.

"In any event, he's expecting us."

The Zim came around for them next morning at seven. By ten o'clock, after a half-hour dealing with the functionaries, they were back on board the B-17. The flight to Teheran took two hours, complicated by a 20,000-foot climb to clear the Elburz Mountains. As they crossed the top of the range, Teheran was almost directly below. During the rapid descent, McDonough complained about his aching ears. No one met them at the airport but Trevelyen was notified when they arrived. By the time they cleared customs and immigration an Oil Company driver arrived. Twenty minutes later they were in Trevelyen's office.

"How did you chaps find Baku?" Trevelyen asked McDonough. "Russkys take good care of you?"

"Yes. We were put up in a well-appointed set of digs on a model farm. Moskovskava Vodka, that's a gold medal drink. Wonderful food. Hot water. Nothing like good Russian hospitality when you're on the Kremlin's guest list."

"I'll call Shah," Trevelyen continued. "Tomorrow OK?"

"No chance to see him this afternoon?" O'Reith asked.

"Probably not but I'll ask." Trevelyen picked up his telephone and requested a connection to Golestan Palace. "When was the last time you fellows listened to the news?"

"Several days," O'Reith said. "What's up?"

"War in Israel going wide open. The U.S. Air Force sending supplies. Arabs upset. Negotiations with OPEC broke down. They've upped the price of oil to $5.11/bbl. That includes the Shah as well. He's going to read us the riot act by the way," Trevelyen added.

"Serious or mere theatrics?" O'Reith asked.

"Mostly theatrical."

"Standard Oil has agreed to $8.15," O'Reith said. Nothing to worry about there. I'll advise the Shah that we need $2.00 out of that to speed up the payout of Poghdar. From those two adjacent structures, in six months we can be running a million and a half bopd. Shah's getting what he wants so he shouldn't have any kick?"

"He'll go for the million and a half," Trevelyen said. "Nothing would please him more. He won't like the $2.00/bbl for us." His telephone rang. He answered and listened, then said, "Very well." Turning to McDonough and O'Reith he said, "We're in luck. He'll see us at five o'clock. You can freshen up at the hotel. I'll be around with the car at four thirty.

"That's fine," O'Reith agreed. "I need a shave and a shower."

"And I," McDonough echoed.

The traffic to the Golestan Palace was heavy as usual. Even on a clear October day with a breeze from the mountains, the smog was overwhelming. The Rolls Royce inched along in the bumper-to-bumper, horn-honking flow of taxis, minivans, power tricycles, fruit-laden go-carts and other imaginative forms of transportation. At the Ivory Hall, the guards, seeing that it was an Oil Company limousine, opened the massive wrought iron gate just wide enough to let the big car through, but not wide enough to let the peddlers, gawkers, accordion players, rug merchants and other riff-raff in. The limousine moved silently through the vast rose garden along the black top to the parking lot at the edge of the palatial compound.

A bearded guard opened the door of the tonneau and helped them descend. Some minutes later the Shah met them at the door of his den. He was in a blue pinstriped banker's suit with black oxford shoes and a dark blue tie hanging down over his starched white cotton shirt. The expression on his face tended toward hostility. After the usual greetings and hand shaking, the Shah beckoned them to the leather seats that faced his desk. He then placed himself in his high-backed, throne-like swivel chair. He leaned over the desk expectantly as one of his slippered tea boys shuffled across the room to light his gold-tipped Turkish cigarette.

McDonough began, "Ah Shah, it is nice to see you again. I trust all is well with you?"

"I'm fine, thank you Sir George," the Shah replied. "A pity the entire region is not in a state of tranquillity. I don't know exactly whom we can fault for that. I suppose the new, untested American Secretary of State can take some of the blame. It is a tragedy. I can't imagine why the Americans or the British or anybody else could really care what happens to the Jews or for that matter, the Palestinians. Who needs them? I ask you. Who needs them?"

"They are all children of God," McDonough uttered piously.

"You traveled all the way from London to tell me that?"

"Actually we came from Rome, Shah," McDonough continued unctuously. "You may make light of it but in fact our Holy Father, His Holiness Pope Paul VI is quite upset about the state of relations between the Palestinians and the Jews. He has gone to extreme lengths to put out an encyclical on that subject."

"Well he could have saved both his ink and his parchment. They are at each others throats and likely to remain that way. Since you mention it, my minister for religion advised me of some bit of idiocy recently put out by the Pope. Was it a letter that encouraged Christian immorality? Now that's a *tulipe noir*!"

"It is somewhat unusual at that," McDonough agreed.

"As long as we Moslems are kept out of it, I am not overly concerned," the Shah stated, spreading his arms to dramatize the situation. "But if in the final analysis, as seems more and more likely, the effect of the encyclical is to pit Islam against a Jewish-Christian coalition, then such a tragedy would be of great concern. As you know I am not an Arab. But I am a Moslem and that is a fundamental part of the White Revolution, the bond between the Shah and his people."

"We all understand that, Shah, of course," McDonough said.

What news do you bring?" the Shah asked, impatiently.

"Considering the parlous state of the OPEC group, the Standard Oil is prepared to be flexible as regards pricing for Poghdar crude oil, your highness," O'Reith began. "I spoke often with their representative in San Francisco. He now has copies of your press release that appeared in the European newspapers. I refer to the negotiation with Afghanistan regarding the boundary dispute."

"Actually nothing is going on," the Shah said. "But if they want to talk, I'm ready."

"Negotiations between OPEC and the several international oil companies have broken down," O'Reith continued. "We can expect general price increases in Libya, Saudi Arabia, Iraq, Iran and Venezuela."

"Yes my dear General O'Reith, that is substantially correct," the Shah said.

"Perhaps the first point," O'Reith continued, "is that we three, Your Highness, Sir George and I, agree that Poghdar crude oil is outside the OPEC cartel."

"Well, of course but what is the point?"

"The flow would not be subject to an OPEC embargo," O'Reith explained.

"Ah! Good point," the Shah agreed. A faint smile came across his face. "But as Lord Trevelyen can verify, I have no intention of joining in any embargo against my friends in the west."

"How do things stand between you and the Majlis?" O'Reith asked

"Well sir, that body of mullahs and bazaar keepers is quite upset with me. As Sir George suggested, I sent most of them packing. But on Brigadier Trevelyen's advice, I stopped short of having the Edict ratified. Ratification now, in the light of my press release would inflame whatever government exists in Afghanistan. But those sacked parliamentarians are all pouting and moping, clamoring to be brought back. They have tried to raise a street with that in mind. My faithful army and air force has sequestered them and I expect they will remain so indefinitely. But I grant you the situation is tense. Maybe tedious is the better word."

"And the negotiation with Afghanistan?" O'Reith asked. "Is there a chance that it could become a reality?"

"There is no forward motion," the Shah lamented. "Alas."

Trevelyen said, "Clive, we gave the Shah's minister an armed escort from Herat. We tried to reach Kabul. Bandits and brigands at every turn of the road."

"How about flying in?"

"Impossible," Trevelyen continued. Total anarchy in Kabul. An aircraft would be shot down by small arms fire as soon as it entered the landing pattern."

O'Reith looked over at McDonough and smiled. Remembering the airstrip at Bid Boland, McDonough seemed relieved that the trip to see Duad Khan would never take place. O'Reith said to the Shah, "Your Highness, Standard Oil has indicated that if we develop the two structures in echelon with Poghdar, Ilam and Sarvak, they would agree to take the extra oil."

"Let's do it," the Shah agreed.

"There is a question about funding the additional development, your Highness," O'Reith continued. Of the present million bopd run from Poghdar, as your Highness is well aware, the Casinghead Company earns sixty cents a barrel. That is not enough to fund the new drilling. To carry forward and arrange bank financing, our company would have to earn something like $3.00/bbl. We could set the price to Standard Oil at $8.15/bbl. We know they will pay that. So $4.15/bbl for you and $4.00/bbl for us. And we pay Scotty's company ten cents/bbl for use of the Gach Saran pipeline to tide water at Bandar Shahpour.

The Shah's nose went up in the air. "Gentlemen," he chided them. "Such an arrangement flies in the face of my contract with the people to get the maximum value for the oil so that improvements in the way of life can continue. As things presently stand, much of our revenue goes to buy armaments to protect ourselves against external threats."

"And internal as well," McDonough added.

"Do you suggest, Sir George that the bond between the Shah and his people is fraying?"

"Shah, you can answer that better than I. Clive's suggestion as regards Poghdar crude oil is worth examining. Standard Oil desires that the oil have a good pedigree. That is to say each cargo should carry a bill of lading that is not controversial. Clive thought that we might label it 'Agja Jari light'. That effectively takes Afghanistan out of the picture. Internally, we will call it Poghdar, which takes your government, coffers out of the picture. Your share of the profit would go straight to Switzerland. What do you think of that?"

"You suggest I betray the confidence the people have in me?" the Shah asked.

"Not at all Shah," McDonough said suavely. "You would be merely the custodian of the funds and after a bit, after things have cooled down and the people are not involved in streets raised by the mullahs, then you could quietly transfer the funds back into the national treasury. And do remember Shah, there are dynastic concerns to be addressed. One day you will want to see your treasured little son on the Peacock Throne, one day when you want to spend more time in St. Moritz. Running crude oil according to that scheme would please the Raj, your friend, perhaps your only really true friend."

"The Raj today is a ghost," the Shah said.

"Those Gurkhas guarding the Poghdar pipeline are not ghosts. Without the Raj, they would not be there," McDonough insisted.

"I grant you that much," the Shah agreed.

"So, where does that leave us Shah? Do we call it Agha Jari light?" McDonough asked. His facial expression was hopeful.

"Such an arrangement clearly has a certain appeal." The Shah turned to Trevelyen. "Sir Charles, inasmuch as that would be somewhat irregular, would the Oil Company think ill of me if I were to do it?"

"Who would tell? Not I, Your Highness."

The Shah sat straight in his chair with his hands behind his neck and said, "In principle then gentlemen, we are agreed. General O'Reith, you are confident that Standard Oil will accept these arrangements?"

"I'm sure of it," O'Reith said. "They have pressing requirements. If we can accelerate the development, they may even pay us a bonus. Do we agree on the profit split?"

"I suppose so. At the least I'll get a new villa out of it."

O'Reith smiled. "I'll push hard."

The Shah was buoyant as he showed them down the stairs.

In the tonneau of the Rolls Royce, as they edged their way back to the Caspien Hotel, O'Reith said, "Scotty, I'd like to get out of here tonight. Can you get us a clearance for a ten pm take-off?"

"I'll call from the hotel. I have the Shah's direct line. He'll still be there."

Turning to McDonough, O'Reith continued, "George, I give you credit for wire-working the Shah. He was half way pissed when we when in to see him. When we left, he was beaming. Your diplomatic skills are invaluable."

McDonough said, "I try to make the most of the few talents given me by the Lord."

Trevelyen said. "And such a modest bloke too. Clive you did well. He agreed to the split."

So it was back to Baku for an early morning refueling and then on to Ankara, Athens and Rome.

Late in the afternoon of October 16, a Tuesday, they found themselves back in McDonough's villa on the shores of Lake Albano. The odor of marigolds and carnations wafted through the screened windows. Flies buzzed against the screen. McDonough in white linen, breathing heavily, with his eyes closed, reclined on the satin-covered chaise longue. Cook in a white, frilly lace blouse and black bolero pants sat in one corner of the red leather sofa with her legs hanging over the raised end smoking an English Oval in a foot-long, silver FDR holder. O'Reith opposite her, looked at the stack of paper on the cocktail table.

Cook nodded, said, "Messages."

O'Reith said, "I'm too beat to look at them. Separate the ones I need to see. I'll read them after dinner tonight and make a few phone calls back to the states. And I want to fly to Paris in the morning."

"Sure," Carolyn answered. "Like for us to book a flight?"

"Say ten o'clock."

"All right. Too tired to talk business?"

"No. Shoot."

"When will you return to LA?"

O'Reith said, "George and I are going to Guatemala City on the 19th. So I rest up in Paris tomorrow and meet George on Friday." We travel that same day. Come back on Sunday."

"We could meet in the tower Monday the 22nd, to discuss finances? The J.P. Morgan and the Linen Bank representatives could join us," Cook suggested.

"Suits me," O'Reith agreed. "OK with you, George?"

"Indeed."

"I'm going to stretch my legs," O'Reith said. "Anybody want to go?"

"Not me," McDonough replied. "I don't have it in me."

"I'll read some Holy Scripture to George," Cook said, giggling.

"Cocktails at six?" O'Reith asked.

"On the terrace upstairs," McDonough said.

O'Reith took up his cane, put on his homburg hat and limped out through the front garden for a long restorative walk around Lake Albano. He knew that the *Le Ville Pontificie di Castel Gandolfo* had ancient origins but he was surprised to find a plaque dating it back to 1623 during the time of Urban VIII. His leg was threatening to go to sleep but after a quarter mile, circulation restored, he was feeling snappier. He took in the gardens of Belvedere and would have done more sightseeing but he was weary. He headed back to McDonough's villa. With plenty of worries, he soon forgot his small infirmities. Declining oil production in Venezuela, the loss of the Libyan concession, Helen's health and finally, McDonough's screen test. Helen would resist any pressure to give him the role. Still, if he didn't get it... Well, he refused to consider that possibility. The sun was sinking behind clouds drifting in from the Mediterranean. A cool breeze rippled the surface of the lake. O'Reith could smell rain above the odor of the flowers. Although his leg was quite stiff, he stepped up the pace a bit and as he came through the front garden of the villa, the huge grandfather clock in the hall was tolling the hour. The bells in Castelo Gandalfo were also ringing. He could already taste the gin.

They dined on Osso Buco, pasta with a fruity red wine from the Turino region and caramel flan prepared by the matronly gray-haired cook, a veteran of Rome's finest restaurants. Retiring to his bedroom, O'Reith addressed his messages. A telex from Helen advised that Rod Steiger was making a movie called *Lolly Madonna*. When that one was in the cans, he was committed to another called *Innocents with Dirty Hands*. Helen was about ready to give the part to McDonough but not just yet. A telex from Kondratieff suggested that he come by his office in London to review Helen's EEG. The Colonel asked if the meeting for the 20th was still on. Hamilton's telex confirmed Standard Oil's readiness to purchase the extra throughput from Poghdar. In a hurry to establish the timing of the increased production; asked if drilling could be stepped up. Ethering, back in Los Angeles from Vienna, reported a lobbying program to expand the College of Cardinals.

He would fly to London tomorrow night to see Kondratieff and then proceed to New York. He sighed. In his declining years when he should be sitting near the fireplace reading *Variety*, he was traveling as much as when he was in his prime. More than anything, he was lonesome for Maxine. She was truly an oasis in the desert. He was thankful that his good judgment had prevailed. His heart had kept her close to him when his head told him to kiss her goodbye. On impulse he picked up the telephone and called her for a happy twenty minutes. They laughed and joked and murmured sweet nothings. Although he still had messages to read, he said to hell with it, took his shower and drifted off to sleep with Maxine on his mind.

That afternoon in his Paris flat, he read the accumulated papers, The *International Herald Tribune, Le Monde* and *Financial Times.* War still raged in the Holy Land. Nixon had nominated Gerald R. Ford to become Vice President replacing Spiro T. Agnew who was facing charges of fraud and tax evasion. Ford's confirmation was considered to be a shoo-in. Lots of oratory from political leaders about shutting down the Arab-Israeli War but not much indication that anyone was doing anything about it. He telephoned Kondratieff to confirm the meeting. After dinner at Lasserre's, nine am in Los Angeles, he telephoned Helen. "How are you doing?" he asked.

"Ace, I'm certainly glad to hear your voice again," she began. "Everything in the Middle East OK?"

"Peachy keen, baby. I got your telex about Steiger."

"OK. Ace, I'm strong for George. You can tell him that much. Those hypnotic treatments have done me some good. I'm looking forward to the next one."

"Helen, I'm calling on Kondratieff in London tomorrow. He volunteered to explain those EEGs. It will be an education for me."

"Great, then you can explain them to me?"

"So you still want to make the *Miter*, eh?"

"Oh yes. I'd go nuts without something to keep my mind occupied."

"OK. I'll call George tomorrow. He'll be flying out anyway. We're going down to talk to the Colonel."

"Well, with Steiger out of the running, I don't have any good alternative."

"What do I tell him?"

"Tell him that I want him to take another test. I'm going to set it up differently."

"With Eve Arden?"

"Yeah."

"OK, I'll tell him. Like to go with us to Guatemala? No doubt the Colonel would like to see his sweet little *Pecos Lil*."

"I'd like to see him too, Ace. I'll think about that. When are you going?"

"Fly down on the afternoon of Friday, the 19th. Back to LA on Saturday."

"When will you leave London?"

"Pan American has an evening flight. Gets into JFK early afternoon. I'll see you day after tomorrow if the planes are on schedule."

"That's great Ace. Our daughter is getting into politics."

"Is she a Democrat or a Republican?"

"How about a streaker? We need to discuss it"

"Yes. We definitely need to talk about *that*. See you baby."

Next day in Harley Street at eleven, the mandarin-like Russian physician welcomed him into his study and said, "General O'Reith I'll come right to the point. In a case of this nature, we use hypnotism to overcome the resistance of the conscious mind. The trance leads us to the subconscious, which in turn, works to overcome the illness. The theory is that the immune system is subject to suggestion. We stimulate it so that it will attack the tumor. The EEG tells us if we are getting through. The wave pattern of a normal person in a hypnotic trance is symmetrical. In the case of your wife, the pattern suggests an incomplete trance, as if she were dreaming. For the treatment to be successful, that is, to contact the immune system, I will have to put her into a much deeper trance, which takes longer and is attended with greater risk."

"Risk of what?"

It took several minutes longer to bring her round after the last treatment. Alarmed, Dr. Parkinson was emphatic that you be brought into the picture."

"He called me. Said the next treatment was scheduled."

"Yes. November 6, a Tuesday."

"I do not want my wife subjected to a life-threatening procedure. I am fully aware that your treatments are speculative. I don't mind that. I just want to be sure that she will come out of the trance. I don't want her to slip into a coma that we couldn't get her out of."

"Understood. After the first three treatments, I aroused your wife with a recording of my special music. A record has its limitations. This time, although it is rather bulky, I propose to bring my Theremin with me." He led O'Reith into his treatment room and showed him the musical box with two metallic rods protruding from the top. He plugged it in and moving his hands across the box some inches above the antennas, played an eerie oriental melody, vaguely reminiscent of Rimsky-Korsakov. He said, "With the instrument I can vary the tone and pitch of the music and if she is reluctant to awaken, I can increase the volume. I feel more comfortable doing it this way."

"Will your Theremin work on American current?" O'Reith asked.

"Oh yes. I have a converter."

"Great, bring it along."

"Well, sir I will consult again with Dr. Parkinson about the length of the treatment. Whatever we agree upon will have his blessing."

"Fair enough Dr. Kondratieff. I appreciate your taking the time to fill me in."

He flew from Heathrow to New York and caught a TWA flight west. At seven pm PST, he arrived at LAX, rum dum and totally exhausted. Maxine met him and rode with him to the Fullerton Building. With his head back on the cushions, his eyes closed, he told her of his visit with Kondratieff and that in the morning, he would call on Helen. At home, stripped, Maxine lathered him up in the shower and washed him down. She dried him off and put him to bed and he was out before she had the covers up. He slept well, awoke around five am with a nude, scented Maxine curled around him. She stirred and began to caress him. Soon he had a partial erection, which her perfume reinforced. When it was stiff enough to 'wobble in', they skipped off down the yellow brick road to the Emerald City and arrived with the angels singing hymns. When Maxine drifted off for a post-pronging nap, O'Reith got up, showered and shaved and then breakfasted on fruit with a bowl of oatmeal. As he drank his coffee, McDonough called. "Clive I got in late last night and wanted you to know I arrived OK."

"Carolyn with you?"

"Of course."

"Well, George, I'm on my way to spend the morning with Helen. Shall we get together around two?"

"Just the two of us?"

"Yes. We'll call the Colonel."

"Ah, Clive, I know you have many things on your mind but..."

"George I spoke with Helen from London. She said that she wanted a second test. The set up will be altered but you'll still be playing against Eve Arden. Carolyn gets her chance too. OK?"

"Kind of you, Clive," McDonough said. "I look forward to this afternoon."

O'Reith in a white Polo shirt and navy blue slacks with matching black oxfords donned his golf cap and entered his limousine at eight. By nine, he was in Helen's bedroom. Ridley, in a canary yellow pantsuit ornamented with star signs, was preparing Helen's horoscope for the day. Mills, with a green surgical gown over her clothing, had just finished making Helen up. She was adjusting her wig.

O'Reith kissed his wife, greeted Mills and asked Ridley, "Alice, what's the prognostication for today?"

"Clive, things are looking pretty favorable. No planetary interference to speak of. I predict a neat day."

As Mills departed, Parkinson arrived. O'Reith said, "Max, I saw Kondratieff in London. He's going to bring his music box. Says it is far superior to the LP."

"He called me after you left and we decided to go ahead as planned."

"I wish it could be sooner," Helen said.

"Helen, George called at breakfast. Wanted to know about his new test."

"I haven't scheduled it but I will. You two still go to Guatemala tomorrow?"

"In the afternoon."

"Tell George we'll do it next Monday, the 22nd."

"That means you're not going with us?"

"Ace, I don't want the Colonel to see how far I've fallen. The last time was ten years ago in Spain. I was looking OK then. Now I look like a...well, you know."

"I'll tell him you are busily working on the Boris Godunov film."

"And don't suggest him for a cameo. Tell him the movie is fully cast."

"Very well dear."

Ridley said, "Clive, tomorrow is not auspicious for people in the political arena. The Colonel may be off his feed."

"Not the first time, Alice. What do you predict for him?"

"I see turmoil in Central America."

O'Reith laughed. "You don't have to be a seer to predict that! What else?"

"There's trouble blowing in the wind for our native son of the Golden West. Tomorrow could bring a reverse for him."

"Nixon?"

"Yeah. He's in trouble over those tapes," Ridley declared.

"Ace, that's what our daughter is going to streak against," Helen interjected.

"Against Nixon?"

"She thinks he should release the tapes."

"That's fine with me if she doesn't make any headlines," O'Reith said.

"She's joining some kind of an oddball group. *Yellow Peril* may pick up on it," Ridley said. "I stand by my prediction for some kind of a flap tomorrow."

"You're too pessimistic," O'Reith objected. "Besides it is a Saturday. Washington takes a powder on Friday afternoon. Alice on the subject of forecasts, what was in the cards that put Helen Simpson into a snit?"

"That goofy Lamar de la Torre, the beachcomber. She wanted me to predict that they were compatible and they weren't. She's a Leo and he's a Taurus. That's asking for trouble in spades."

"But she dumped him. That's something," O'Reith said.

"She dumped him because she discovered he was double-gaited," Ridley added.

O'Reith laughed.

"Not funny Ace," Helen snorted. "What if she had married him? What then?"

"She is a sensible girl when you dig deep enough," O'Reith said.

"I feel in my bones that something will happen back east," Ridley said.

Helen said, "Ace I'm running late. I'm to be in Culver City even as we speak."

"Before you go my dear," Parkinson interjected, "let the good family doctor check your pulse and measure your blood pressure."

Helen said, "Max you've been watching too many of those Kildare reruns. You're even beginning to look like Lionel Barrymore."

"I'm a better doctor than he is, Helen. He guesses a lot. I'm going to measure your blood pressure and if it is not up to par, no Dr. Kondratieff."

"Tyrant," she said. But she took her place on the chaise longue and let him get on with it. Then, going downstairs she asked, "Ace, cocktails at six?"

O'Reith smiled. "I'll be ready. Fighting off the shakes."

"Max, want to join us?" Helen asked.

"I'm on the wagon."

She laughed and with Ridley behind, took the elevator down to the foyer. As Helen and Ridley left for Culver City, O'Reith said, "Max are you playing this straight? Do I know everything you know?"

"Clive all of the tests, all of the indications, all of the history we have on cancer, tells me that Helen is getting on down the trail. She's 58 and looks 78. It has been six months since I've seen her without any make up and she looked terrible then. Sharon is keeping her painted up but I can see her appearance declining. I assume you can too."

"Yeah."

"Clive, if she would consider further treatment, radiation or chemotherapy, it might do some good. Might not. I'm far from sold on these modern theories. I'm concerned about the next hypnotic treatment. Kondratieff is too. She might take even longer to come around this time. She could fall into a coma. We couldn't bring her around and she'd vegetate. Kondratieff wants the treatment in hospital so that if we experience difficulty, resources would be available to..."

"I doubt if she'll go for it," O'Reith said.

"I have to bring it up, Clive. Professional ethics. If she says 'no', what then?"

"You could change your mind about the cocktails. You could ask her with me sitting across the table and we could figure out how to deal with it."

"Good idea."

"In the tower with Cook and McDonough, he telephoned Guatemala City and confirmed the meeting with Colonel Jiménez. While they were talking, O'Reith's secretary brought a flimsy on a silver tray to Cook. She read it aloud. "Bad news. Nixon announced a big arms package for Israel. Saudi Arabia retaliated with an oil embargo. Looks like Libya and Iraq will join the party. We could see oil going to $15.00/bbl."

O'Reith smiled. "That's good news. A solid price hike can put us ahead of the game for a change."

Cook asked, "What exactly is your agenda with the Colonel?"

"We're going to ask him to help us extend the College of Cardinals?" McDonough replied.

"Nothing else?" Cook asked

"What did you have in mind?" O'Reith asked.

Cook continued. "Maybe now would be a good time for the Colonel to knock Honduras over. You recall we have discussed it with him before. He was never to keen to go for it. He was afraid of General Arellano. But he seems to be standing strong now. Our Central American exploration specialist has picked an area there that looks interesting. Soon as the Colonel puts the troops in and gets things stabilized, we could run a few seismic lines and drill a well."

"Would you like to come along, Carolyn?" O'Reith asked. "How long since you've seen him?"

"Ten years. When George was elevated in the Church, he was at the party that Scotty threw in Rome. I'd like to see that little imp again."

"OK," O'Reith said. "You can spring Honduras on him. I'll watch to see if he flinches. He said he wanted to talk about Venezuela. He may have some skinny."

The three of them laughed. McDonough said, "He wants to go back."

In the limousine on the long ride out to Long Beach, O'Reith told Parkinson he had tried to get Helen to forget about Boris Godunov and switch over to musical comedy and that she wouldn't go for it. Parkinson said, "She's so strong-willed. Maybe better if she stays with Boris. She's enthusiastic about it. What difference does it make if it is a good movie or not? It is keeping her alive."

"You've got a point there, Max," O'Reith agreed.

A tired-looking Helen greeted them in the living room. Draped, in a straight-back chair, Mills was preparing to remove her make up. Ridley was seated close by. Helen said, "I thought I would be cleaned up by now but we ran late. You don't mind Sharon, do you?"

"Of course not," O'Reith said. He rang for the drink trolley.

As it rattled its way across the parquet floor, O'Reith asked, "martinis for everyone?"

"Not for me," Mills said. She was working quickly to remove the foundation, the rouge and the powder from Helen's face. "I've got to run back to town."

"On the wagon, Max?" O'Reith asked.

"I think I'll have one tonight," Parkinson said.

Helen turned her head to look at the physician. She said, "More bad news for me?"

"No, not at all," Parkinson said. "But I do need to get your opinion on something."

Mills finished up. The make-up gone, she washed Helen's face and toweled her off. "I'm on my way, kids," she said. "See you in the morning, hon."

The butler served martinis around and bowed out.

Helen said, "Out with it Max?"

"Helen, Dr. Kondratieff brought up the possibility of a complication in the therapy. He suggested we set up the third treatment at Central City."

"Never!" Helen objected violently. "If I ever am forced to go to a hospital again, I'm going to die en-route."

"Well it was just a thought," Parkinson continued. "Helen, on occasions, patients falls into coma. In the hospital, they're set up with emergency equipment..."

"Forget it, Max. If that happens, give me a double shot of morphine. Finish me off."

"Against the law, baby," O'Reith said. "Besides, others are involved. Little Clive Colin. Rae Regan. Helen Simpson. Me. All of us want you to come around properly. If you went into a coma, then you'd *have* to go to a hospital."

"I'm not going into a coma. I have strong powers of recuperation. I can't enjoy my drink with that kind of talk. So there."

"We talked to the Colonel," O'Reith said. "We're going down as planned. George is looking forward to his test next week"

"I've had second thoughts, Ace. Tell George he's got the part."

O'Reith was secretly pleased but he tried to suppress his delight. He said. "He'll be overjoyed when I tell him. What made you change your mind?"

"Alice, you say," Helen responded.

Ridley said, "Well, for one thing, screen tests cost money. For another, after a close look at their star signs I saw that they are compatible and playing together should bring out each others best. Both have comedy talents that should outweigh the fact that they are both pretty creaky.

So on that basis, after kicking it around, we decided to go that way. Eve was happy to get that news. She felt comfortable playing against George even knowing what a scene stealer he is."

"She's no slouch," O'Reith said.

"Scene stealers make good movies," Helen said. She had drained her glass and was rattling ice cubes at O'Reith. He refilled her glass as he glanced at his Rolex. It was after six thirty. "Dinner at the club tonight?" he suggested.

Helen said, "I'm all in. We had a full afternoon in Culver City. Sharon would have to come back to put a new face on. It would be ten o'clock before we got there. It's a light dinner for me with Alice. We're going to discuss tomorrow's plans. And I will be in bed asleep by eight thirty."

"How about you Max?"

"I promised the better half I'd join her for home cooked."

Ridley showed the two men to the front door. O'Reith looked at her, smiled and said, "Alice, I owe you one. George will be tickled pink"

"It is better all the way around," Ridley said. "That flick is not a high priority item."

O'Reith kissed her forehead. "Thanks anyway."

In the limousine on the way back to town, O'Reith said, "Max, we didn't come completely clean with Helen about the odds of lapsing into coma."

"That's as clean as I'm coming. She has her mind made up. What really bothers me is that Kondratieff insists that the treatment is most effective when the trance lasts for an hour. These half hour shots are just warm ups for the real thing."

"No. 4 is to be what?"

"A half hour. Because of the long wake-up time before. This entire program is on go slow as far as I'm concerned. That Helen thinks she is being treated is as good as the treatment itself. Maybe next time we go for a full hour."

"You'll go along with that?"

"I'm thinking about it," Parkinson said. It was dark and the lights of oncoming cars cast his face in an eerie white from time to time. It was a long thoughtful face and O'Reith could see that he was deeply concerned."

"Max, I'm not much of a medico but at least we can be concerned together," O'Reith said.

"Thanks for that, Clive," Parkinson said, relieved that it was not completely his burden. If we worry together, maybe it will come out all right. Clive I'll have adrenaline lined up in case we need it and an ambulance..."

O'Reith slapped his knee. They caught each other in tight smiles as headlights momentarily illuminated their faces.

Chapter IV

The Greater Central American Co-prosperity Sphere

Following the Bay of Pigs disaster in April of 1961, Potus John F. Kennedy realized that to prevent the spread of communism throughout Central America, strong measures were needed. Particularly worrisome was Guatemala. The country was lawless and chaotic. The leader, one Miguel Fuentes, a left-leaning and vacillating friend of Fidel Castro, was taking the country into the bosom of the Soviet Union. Aggravated that the hapless troops set to invade Cuba staged in Guatemala, Castro could easily retaliate given his access to Soviet resources. Thus Kennedy requested the Central Intelligence Agency to recruit an able man who would lead the land out of its quagmire. One was Augusto Pinochet down in Chile, a robust, chesty, light colonel in the Chilean Army with military police experience. His right wing views were known internationally and the U.S. Department of State considered him completely reliable. The difficulty with Pinochet was that he spoke an inflected Spanish that was peculiar to Chile, a dialect not admired in the northern zones. Furthermore, Chilean customs might as well have been Chinese as far as Guatemala was concerned. Another candidate was Pedro Estrada, former chief of secret police in Venezuela. He came to the United States in January of 1958 along with Colonel Jiménez. The Venezuelan secret police was held in some odium by the more faggish State Department types and a campaign to oust Estrada began immediately, even during the Eisenhower Administration when Colonel Jiménez, living in Miami, was *persona muy grata*. Facing a wall of resistance with regard to Estrada by human rights purists, JFK deported him to Spain. Reluctantly, Franco took him but soon became suspicious. The CIA reasoned that since Eisenhower had awarded Colonel Jiménez the Legion of Honor citing his responsible leadership of an important South American ally, he would be an ideal candidate. Jiménez was a proven strong man, thought to be deeply religious and his wife Flor, was a member of the Caracas Altar Society. Now she played a prominent role in the affairs of the Roman Catholic Church in Miami. Jiménez had a nice family of three daughters. A man of the right and a friend of the Rockefellers, a scratch golfer and had many associates among the executives of the American Oil companies. He had, however, a strong enemy. During his term as Dictator of Venezuela, he had refused Edward Kennedy an oil concession. Kennedy, well connected to United Fruit, a premier banana producer located in Boston, lobbied against his appointment. It was the largest American concern in Guatemala and dominated its politics. They wanted to continue to do so. As political decisions at high levels often go, they went nowhere for quite some long months. Unhappily, neither Ted Kennedy nor the United Fruit Company were content to to allow Guatemala to continue its slide into the abyss of *fidelismo*. Thus by the middle of 1962 the tide in favor of the Colonel began to turn when the new Venezuelan democratic government of Venezuela, headed by President Romulo Betancourt, formally requested that Jiménez be extradited back to Caracas to stand trial for peculation and murder. To put it mildly, the Colonel did not wish to stand trial in Caracas for anything; certainly not high crimes, which included the liquidation of his enemies. Jiménez had become friendly with Great Britain's Harold Macmillan who personally lobbied JFK in his behalf. The administration wanted to do Macmillan a favor to make up for the shoddy way Eisenhower had treated him during the Suez Crisis. Also by allowing Jiménez to voluntarily leave Miami for Guatemala, the plea by Betancourt would become moot. So in the fall of the year, the Colonel was *transferred* to Guatemala City where, with CIA backing, he was immediately elected president. Some of the neighboring Central American republics, notably Honduras, squawked because they all knew the Colonel was a dangerous kind of guy and nobody wanted him around. But nothing could be done about it. Several South American republics, particularly Venezuela, complained too. The idea that a recently booted tyrant could be propped up in a nearby country was somewhat unsettling. But after all, banana republics had that feature built in to them. Soon the furor faded into the background.

O'Reith had risen through the ranks of Calitroleum to become its COO under CEO Vincent Barkett Blake. Some years later, Standard Oil bought Calitroleum. With his share of the profit, O'Reith formed his own company. In 1956, Colonel Jiménez, then President of Venezuela, allowed independent oil companies to compete with the likes of Shell, Jersey and Mene Grande. The Casinghead Company applied for and was given two blocks in Lake Maracaibo. Cook, O'Reith's friend, had grown up with Calitroleum. Over time she rose to become Exploration Vice President. When Standard Oil bought the company, she joined O'Reith. She personally picked the two Lake concessions. O'Reith and Amanda Macabra negotiated the contracts with the Colonel. Soon they were running crude oil to steel storage at Punto Fijo.

During the negotiations, O'Reith, discovered that the Colonel was a movie fan with private theaters both in the presidential palace at Miraflores and his hideaway on Orchid Island. He particularly liked western films and the beautiful Helen O'Reith was one of his favorite actresses. She had played the role of *Pecos Lil* in a western farce about the life of Judge Roy Bean, *The Law West of the Pecos* in turn-of-the-century Texas. Soon O'Reith and the Colonel were fast friends. When the Casinghead Company inaugurated the oil storage terminal at Punto Fijo, the Colonel and *Pecos Lil* jointly and gleefully opened the master valve allowing the first flow of crude oil from the Lake Maracaibo oil fields. The gala occasion made the Colonel's day. He had never forgotten it. So now in late 1973, the President of Guatemala was inclined to help his friend O'Reith in any way that he could. All the more so because his friend could get him excommunicated at the drop of a hat. And as the Colonel well knew, General O'Reith was fully capable of dropping the hat himself.

The *Greater Central America Co-prosperity Sphere* was more or less a by-product of JFK's desire to stabilize Guatemala under a rightist democratic regime. At the time the Colonel took over, Prime Minister Harold Macmillan indicated that he was willing to cede British Honduras, thus ending a long-running, often acrimonious exchange concerning the legitimacy of the British colony. Macmillan's largesse, if that was the word for it, pleased Kennedy because another Monroe Doctrine obstacle was going to disappear. He could hype that to the public as an example of a strong American foreign policy. The fact of the matter was that the colony was so poor it could not afford to pay for fuel to run the one light plant in the capital, Belize. With a shrug, the British Prime Minister unloaded its operating cost on the equally impoverished Guatemala. Still the country was enlarged and as he applied to JFK for a subsidy to operate Belize, Jiménez began calling his adopted nation Greater *Guatemala*.

Communism threatened Mexico as much as Guatemala. After all, Leon Trotsky had sought refuge in Mexico. The various socialistic governments of the PRI always leaned left, were quick to expropriate foreign property, shelter known revolutionaries, and foment trouble wherever capitalism flourished. Worse, insultingly worse, Lopez Contreras was a pal of Fidel Castro. JFK was, at a minimum, annoyed that while Contreras was smoking a *Grande Claro de Havana,* he had to settle for a White Owl. From one of the president's greatest supporters, Senator Quirk Q. Quigleyson, Democrat of Nevada, came the suggestion that it would be a relatively simple matter to hive off the five southern Mexican provinces that were collectively called the Yucatan. Specifically Chiapas, Tabasco, Campeche, Yucatan and Quintana Roo. It was a fact that Quigleyson knew very little about Mexico and cared less. But his handler, one Stanley Ethering, General Counsel of the Casinghead Company did and he put him up to it. Invariably, Quigleyson did what Ethering wanted him to do. He knew that Ethering would snap the head off of his dick if he balked.

Reading a study made by the National Security Adviser, JFK decided to act. Mexicans who lived in the Yucatan were unruly, often at odds with the central government in Mexico City and tended to banditry. Government offices in those regions were frequently plundered. Attempts by the National Guard to subdue the rebellious Chiapans had met with failure. Government men were shot at; sometimes killed.

JFK reasoned that it would take only a small effort to jar the Yucatan loose and not much more to connect it to Guatemala.

When the idea was broached to the Colonel, the color drained from his face and his small hands twitched uncontrollably. He balked, saying it was madness to stir up the powerful Mexico. But when it was clear that both the United States and Great Britain were willing to commit troops to the effort, he cautiously began to come around. An offer of an increase in his banana subsidy convinced him. JFK wanted to use northern Guatemala as a training ground for troops destined for Viet Nam. Macmillan, worried about Argentine designs on the Falkland Islands, agreed to station troops in the recently 'liberated' Belize. The Colonel was led to believe that these troops would be at his disposal. Since he was a military leader of note, with a bona fide Legion of Honor medal from Eisenhower, which he proudly and conspicuously wore on his tunic, the expectation was that he would quickly prevail over the sonorous tribes of the Yucatan. A Washington think tank came up with the name *Isthmia* to replace the somewhat pretentious *Greater Guatemala*. The American and British ambassadors to the United Nations then introduced the concept of *Isthmia* as a guarantor of liberty in a distressed region to the Security Council. It was controversial. Mexico and Russia took immediate exception. Honduras, Costa Rica and El Salvador all protested that such an agglomeration would prove to be provocative. Other countries, including Venezuela, scoffed.

Nevertheless, military operations began. As often happens in affairs of this nature, the original campaign miscarried. Perhaps the Colonel was over-confident. Perhaps the troops lacked training. Whatever, O'Reith and McDonough, willy-nilly, found themselves caught up in the enterprise. In an effort to bring things round, O'Reith did exercise some leadership, ultimately bringing success to the expedition. McDonough, not caring for the name *Isthmia*, suggested the more eloquent *Greater Central American Co-prosperity Sphere*. The Colonel liked this and it stuck. *Isthmia* was consigned to the dustbin of history. The United Nations was notified of the new political entity. Further military action that followed the original disappointments was more successful. In due course, the Yucatan was formally incorporated into the sphere. A new nation was created.

During that time often referred to as the darkness before dawn, when the light at the end of the tunnel was the will o' the wisp, the Colonel became disheartened and abandoned his military responsibility, leaving O'Reith and McDonough to hold things together. The Colonel decided on the spur of the moment to make the pilgrimage to Santiago de Compostela. Going a step further, he invited *Pecos Lil* to join him and she, recovering from cancer treatments, accepted. Helen had the foresight to bring Sharon Mills along on that trek so there could be no talk of hanky-panky. Not that O'Reith mistrusted her, but it would have been easy to misread the Colonel's intentions. O'Reith did mistrust the Colonel with regard to a widow woman from Tachira who had leased the company her oil lands. She was going on the pilgrimage to atone for knifing off her rat of a husband. The Colonel was plotting a return to Venezuela and the widow was his political enemy. O'Reith suspected that the Colonel would chase down and liquidate her in the mountains of Léon. He set out in hot pursuit, hoping to prevent the worst.

Before the pilgrimage was over, it came to include Cook and McDonough. The widow was not harmed. The Colonel returned to his job in Guatemala City where fortune began to favor his governance. Although never seen as a hero by the peasants of the highlands, the Colonel was reluctantly accepted as president of the country by the city folk.

Thus the bonds between the Colonel and his North American friends were strengthened. All was well. But that was almost a decade ago. O'Reith knew that the Colonel still had it in the back of his mind that he would one day return to Miraflores. A presidential election was in the cards for December of 1973 and one Carlos Andres Pérez of the *Accion Democratica* party was favored to win. *Accion Democratica* in general and Pérez in particular were anathema to the Colonel. O'Reith fretted that he could decide that now was the time to vie for control of his country.

So on this bright Saturday of October 20, 1973; O'Reith, Cook and McDonough were the only passengers in the first class cabin of a Pan American DC-8 headed for Aurora Airport in Guatemala City, a three and a half hour flight; old friends calling upon another old friend in the spirit of camaraderie. When they made the appointment, it was to discuss religious matters, notably the College of Cardinals. But now, with turmoil in the Middle East, the agenda was expanded to include the persuasion of the Colonel to invade Honduras. While this was something that the Colonel would like to do, he would like to do it with American and British troops. To get him to do it with his own resources was a delicate matter. Nevertheless, McDonough had remarkable powers of persuasion. On this bright morning at thirty-five thousand feet flying over the Chihuahua Desert, with the semitropical sun beaming in through the ovoid windows and bubbling flutes of Mumm's champagne in their hands, anything seemed possible.

As he watched the tiny bubbles from his champagne, McDonough said, "Clive, if it is OK with you, I would like to get into the College of Cardinals with him first. Let me induce him to help us, then we can get into the controversial business of Honduras. I don't want him to be in a cold sweat while we're talking religion."

"Good idea," O'Reith agreed. "Once that's done, Carolyn can discuss the signs of oil accumulations along the Honduran mountain chain. If he sees a few dollar signs, we can edge him into the invasion. See if he'll go for it." He smiled broadly and sipped his champagne.

"Do I bring up the possibility of invasion?" Cook asked.

"No, it will be better if I do that," O'Reith said. "The Colonel knows that I'm capable of hammering that Bull of Excommunication up on the door to the Guatemala City Cathedral. He'll think twice."

McDonough chuckled.

"Does it still have force?" Cook asked. "The bull?"

O'Reith laughed. "Ask George?"

Cook turned to George who was smiling conspiratorially. "What about it, George?"

"Carolyn, I doubt if Paul VI is even aware of it," McDonough began. "Cardinal Grannito Girolo has been moldering in his grave for five years now. He would never have mentioned it to the Pope. And in fact it is based on an error of translation. The bull charges the Colonel with castrating the male population. Actually, what he did was force them into circumcision in an effort to improve hygiene. I would be reluctant to bring it up. Paul has plenty of worries right now."

"The Colonel doesn't know that," O'Reith said. "Even if it is a paper tiger, I can tell him we'll have it published in *L'Osservatore romano*. Put the fear of God into him."

They were circling the city of corrugated-tin roofs. O'Reith spotted the miniature Eiffel Tour. "Just a few minutes now," he said.

"I say Clive," McDonough exclaimed. Look down there at the golf course adjacent to the main runway. It is much longer now."

O'Reith quickly appraised the course with the eye of a pro. "Look at that!" he said. "The Colonel said he was going to make an 18 holer out of it. Times like these I wish my legs would hold me up. I'd give anything to play 18 holes."

"Maybe you can," Cook suggested.

"Too old and broken down by decades of double martinis and amorous activity," O'Reith said glumly.

"You could ride a cart," Cook suggested, laughing.

"Well that's a thought," O'Reith agreed. "Maybe that's the place to bring up the invasion. Out on the fairways."

"We don't have time," McDonough said, "unless we stay overnight."

"That's a possibility," O'Reith agreed.

"Let's do it," Cook said. "Take a day off."

"Agreed," O'Reith said. The champagne had softened him.

"Aye," echoed McDonough. Though not a golfer, he had walked the course ten years ago when it was a shell-torn battlefield. Now he might enjoy the colorful birds, the water denizens and the serenity.

The jet lined up with the long runway and soon the wheels were screeching. Presently they were turned around and taxiing to the terminal. By the time the plane had pulled into its berth, they had their carry ons and were ready to deplane. The Colonel's driver, waving a Casinghead Company sign above the scurrying passengers, waited just inside the terminal. Minutes later they were in the tonneau of an aged Lincoln limousine on their way to the *Palacio Nacional*. From the terminal, they pulled out on 11 Avenida down to Diagonal 12, turning right at the city zoo, crossing the northern flight path of Aurora Airport to the traffic circle at *Parque Independencia* and then going north on *Avenida de la Reforma* past the hotel *El Camino Real*, past the *Torre del Reformador*. They were in *10a Avenida* now going through the Olympic City, crossing over the railroad all the way to *8a Calle.* Then turning right to the Central Plaza, they turned into the gate leading into the huge compound of *Palacio Nacional.* The big Lincoln was crunching gravel as they drove through the garden to the *Residencia Presidencial.* The compound included the palace itself, the annex, and the presidential guard annex. Inside the palace were the various government offices and the infamous Regional Telecommunication Center installed by the

CIA. At the residencia, a soldier in fatigues ushered the trio inside. A rickety steam-driven elevator vibrated them up to the third floor and the soldier led them down the parqueted hall to the Colonel's office.

Beaming broadly, Jiménez removed his heavy, tortoise-shell eyeglasses, rose from his vast desk and came around to greet them. In an elaborate white uniform with a high, silver-brocaded collar and a coat that fell to his knees and displayed six brass buttons the size of half-dollars, he shook hands. He was decorated with the seal of the republic and his Legion of Honor as well as several Venezuelan medals plus two *Co-prosperity Sphere* decorations for victories in the Yucatan. His white tubular pants were sharply creased and fell to the top of his thick-soled, highly polished elevator shoes. He stood a tall five feet and one inch. At fifty-nine, his round, cherubic but crafty-looking face was remarkably unwrinkled and his hair still jet black, possibly dyed. O'Reith had seen that same get up ten years ago at Babolsar on the Shah. The Colonel must have copied it.

He said, "General O'Reith, I am disappointed that you didn't bring *Pecos Lil*. How is that splendid actress keeping?"

"Colonel Jiménez, you remember that on the pilgrimage to Santiago de Compostela, she had just received word of a cancerous lesion in her breast."

"Yes I recall that. We prayed often for her health to return and we were rewarded for it. I must say, General O'Reith I treasure those days on the road in Spain with your remarkable wife. Her fine sense of humor brightened our days along that difficult trail to the splendid cathedral in Santiago."

"Well, she's ailing again. Same complaint. She's getting regular treatment. But she's older now and well..."

"I'm sure she will recover. Nevertheless I will begin praying for her immediately, as will Flor and our daughters. Never underestimate the power of prayer, my dear general."

"Oh I don't. When I tell her you and your family are with her in this trial, the tears will come to her eyes. Despite her travail, she continues to work. She has begun another motion picture."

"An oater?" the Colonel asked.

O'Reith laughed. He said, "No. Everyone has religion under the skin these days. She's making a film about a Russian who becomes Pope in the 15th Century."

After a sumptuous lunch of roast suckling pig, *platanos* and avocados, the Colonel guided them through the plants and flowers of his dripping tropical garden, which surrounded the palace on three sides. Much had changed over the years and proudly the Colonel pointed out his new irrigation system paid for by the U.S. Department of Agriculture. While they walked, O'Reith said, "Circling to land we saw that Aurora Golf Course is now 18 holes. Quite an improvement."

"Would you like to play a game?" the Colonel asked.

"We would," O'Reith responded.

"Why not stay over? On the tee at nine o'clock, play a round, have lunch and you can depart in the afternoon" the Colonel suggested,"

"Agreed," O'Reith said.

The thick carpet in the parlor, of Mayan design, had snakes, parrots and the national bird, the quetzal, in the center. A dozen Doric columns enclosed a huge sitting room. In the colonnade, portraits of past Guatemalan presidents, none of them smiling, were evenly spaced at head-high level along the walls. Their solemn features did not create a favorable impression of Guatemalan politics.

As the four of them sat on sofas that faced each other, the Colonel waved a hand in the direction of the portraits, saying "my long-faced predecessors." Then looking across at McDonough, he added, "We begin?"

"President Jiménez," McDonough began, you may be aware that Pope Paul was deeply disappointed with the outcry over his 1967 encyclical *Humanae vitae...*"

"Aware!" the Colonel snorted. "Never have I been bombarded with so many objections as from my three daughters. It was as if I had written that screed. Indeed! And now he has come out with another insane message. What is it called? Oh yes I remember now. *Casti connubii II.* What are we to make of that idiocy? Here I have dedicated ten years of my life to population reduction in the *Co-prosperity Sphere* and what does that fool of a Pope do? He puts out a pastoral letter telling people to procreate without limit. Incredible!"

"We should not judge him too harshly," McDonough suggested, washing his hands in the air. Pope Paul is concerned about the unrestricted breeding of the Arabs of the Middle East and other undesirable Asiatic and African populations. His worry is that Christianity will disappear under a massive wave of Islamic incursions into Europe."

"Well that may be," the Colonel retorted angrily. "Here in Central America, Christianity was about to disappear under a horde of marginal animists. I liquidated a cool million of them and could easily have chopped another half million. I may find it necessary to do so yet. Make no mistake about it, Sir George, these indigenous savages can do just as much damage in this part of the world as the Mullahs can in your part of the world. I humbly suggest that his Holiness is in error with *Casti connubii II.* Perhaps you can induce him to repeal it. I can't tolerate unrestricted breeding here. I don't allow the Parish priests to proclaim that encyclical from the pulpits. The bishops are under threat of deportation if they disobey me. Luckily the several man-eating tigers we imported a decade back have found our jungles to their liking. Hundreds of them on the prowl with population control on their minds. What would I do without them? But they are not universally admired. Every month or so, an agency of the United States Government sends a mission down here to protest that the tigers are interfering with human rights. How do I handle them?"

"That's easy," O'Reith said. "Apply for a grant-in-aid."

"What is that?" the Colonel asked, bewildered.

"Ask POTUS Nixon for federal funds to study the problem of the tigers."

"How much?"

"Couple of million. Maybe more."

"Really!"

"How do I apply?"

"I'll ask Stan Ethering to fill out the papers and mail them in."

"Will the government send the money to my bank account in Zurich? I'm getting quite a few subsidies of one kind or another now from the U.S. but they all go into the public treasury. Worse, they keep an auditor down here to see how the funds are spent. It is difficult for me to touch it personally."

O'Reith chuckled. "I'll have a word with Al Haig on that."

McDonough began "Colonel, when I am again in Rome, I will have a private chat with Paul. I will make your views tactfully known. Not to change the subject but you do remember that the primary reason for our visit is to ask you help in the enlargement of the College of Cardinals."

"You wish to pack it like President Franklin Delano Roosevelt tried to pack the Supreme Court in the United States in the 1930s."

"Not exactly," McDonough continued. "Let me explain. Paul wants about 175 cardinals in the college eligible to vote. My idea is that the lay princes be brought in as well as a few women, such as Carolyn here. She is a Dame of Honor and Devotion."

"I attended the ceremony where she was decorated. But ladies in the College of Cardinals, well sir, that is bizarre."

"Colonel Jiménez, besides lay princes and dames, Paul is thinking of bringing in a few of the Eastern Rites metropolitans."

"What is the point?"

"Paul would like to make the college more like the world. Now, in his view, it is too Italian."

"And in your view, Sir George?" Jiménez asked.

"I am a servant of His Holiness."

"I see. Well, let us not misunderstand one another. Although I am a good Catholic, I leave the practice of the religion to Flor. She does it for both of us and in my turn, I practice statecraft for both of us. I am no great fan of Pope Paul. I was even less of a fan of John XXII bless his dear departed saintly soul. I will help you as a personal favor but I doubt if I can do much. We don't have many lay princes in this part of the world; even fewer Dames of Devotion. Why couldn't Flor become one of the new cardinals?"

"She could, indeed!" McDonough said.

"There, we're making progress already. Maybe my daughter Margot too," the Colonel suggested. To O'Reith, he asked, "Why are you interested in this murky affair?"

"Like you, I want to help Sir George. If he thinks the college should be bigger, so be it."

"Well, there is more to this than meets the eye," the colonel said. He turned to Cook. "Putting aside the religious changes looming before us, "What is happening in the never-ending *Guerre de Petrole*?"

In a plaintive voice, Cook began with, "War in the Holy Land. Big price increases in crude oil. An oil embargo against the U.S. That's the bad news. On the credit side, we just put a big field on the line in eastern Persia. That's about it. Oh yes, we've been looking at Honduras. Some interesting structures run along the mountains."

The Colonel's reply was quick and discouraging, "Honduras is what you Americans call a hot potato. In Central America we don't have much interest in a war in Asia Minor. Of course, I'm always pleased with an increase in oil prices. Too bad those oil fields in the Yucatan are in decline. Honduras, is a delicate situation. Pity we don't have that little state under our control. You know that fellow down in Tegucigalpa, Oswaldo López Arellano, was an army general of some stripe, and as you might suspect, a despot to the core. He has been in charge a couple of years now and is far from popular. The United Fruit and the Standard Fruit own him body and soul. In my view, he is vulnerable. But I could never handle him alone. Maybe with American troops..."

It was getting on in the afternoon. Flor, and Margot appeared and suggested a tour of the palace. They agreed on dinner at eight-thirty. O'Reith, ready for a soak, made for his quarters, stripped and got into the long bathtub with gargoyle legs. In the steaming water, he drifted into a semi-sleep. And there he remained for quite some time until his telephone rang; McDonough summoning him for cocktails.

At dinner, the three Venezuelans, the two Americans and the one Englishman began with prawns from Belize in a horse radish sauce. Then Santa Barbara beef fillets in American barbecue sauce with fried plantains and garden fresh asparagus. As they finished dessert, a messenger brought the Colonel a slip of paper on a silver salver. He looked over at O'Reith and said, "Radio news. A shooting at the White House. Chap by the name of Archibald Cox killed. You know him?"

O'Reith said, "Not personally. He's the special prosecutor nominated by the American Congress to delve into President Nixon's Watergate affair. Who killed him?"

"We don't know yet," the colonel said. "No details. Apparently he and his entire entourage were executed. It is described as a massacre. We'll have a telephone report from our ambassador in Washington tomorrow morning."

"Scary!" O'Reith exclaimed. "I thought we were more civilized than that."

"Do you suppose Nixon had him shot by the secret service?" McDonough asked.

"Surely not," O'Reith answered.

"In this part of the world such assassinations are routine," the Colonel said. "They rarely make the newspapers."

"Well in the U.S.A. it would be taken seriously," O'Reith replied. "Nixon is in the doghouse. Shooting off the Special Prosecutor gets him deeper in the hole."

"Well, we'll know more tomorrow," the Colonel said yawning. There was a rap on the door and a spidery, long-jawed, tough-looking Latino entered. He spoke in rapid Spanish. The Colonel answered him equally fast.The Colonel said, "Captain Anthrax. Night man at the *Seguridad Nacional*. Getting ready for the eleven o'clock patrol."

"He looks capable enough, McDonough said."

On the No.1 tee at nine o'clock, tropical birds were singing. Here and there nutrias darted across the fairway. The trees were leafy and green. The temperature was about 70° on a day with fleecy white cumulus clouds blowing in. McDonough was along for the ride; to enjoy the fresh air; to watch the stately clouds cross the sky; to listen to the music of the endangered animals and of course to smell the lavender and hyacinth which grew alongside the fairways in great perfumed profusion.

The Colonel's ambassador reported that last night had not seen a real killing. Reporters and newscasters called it the 'Saturday Night Massacre'. Nixon had fired Cox. Attorney General Elliot Richardson and his assistant Richard Ruckelshaus had resigned. Henry Kissinger in Moscow met with Brezhnev trying to stop the Holy Land war. Nixon had flown off to Florida to play gin rummy with his pal Bebe Rebozo. With Haig running the government, nothing to worry about.

No.1 was a down hill par four of 385 meters with the fairway curved slightly to a postage stamp green adjacent to the fifty foot high concrete wall that ran parallel to the main runway. Military policemen were discreetly posted among the trees and shrubbery. The Colonel hit first, a long high drive that carried the curve and fell in the middle of the fairway. O'Reith hit next, a good drive but shorter than the Colonel's. He had his work cut out getting on in two. The carts chugged down to the ladies tee. Cook hit a No. 2 wood a long, low ball that came to rest alongside the Colonel's. O'Reith elected to walk, McDonough beside him. The Colonel, Cook beside him, chugged off down the fairway. McDonough asked, "When are you going to put it to him about Honduras?"

"Fourth hole, George," I should know by then on how his pulse is beating. I don't want to run his blood pressure up too high."

"He seems to be in a pretty decent humor," McDonough noted. "The events in Washington apparently amused him."

"Yeah, so far," O'Reith agreed. A caddy hovered over his ball; a Dunlop with two red dots. With a No. 2 wood, O'Reith hit a flat sizzler that fell in the fringes of the green. The mogul and the prelate walked down to where the Colonel was sizing up his shot. He put his ball on the green with a No. 2 iron, about ten feet from the pin. Cook's shot came in hot, bounced once and spun up to within inches of the pin. As the threesome putted out, a jet roared off over the high wall. The Colonel shouted, "The barrier is not high enough. How can anyone putt out with that din?"

"I agree," O'Reith said.

Cook birdied the hole. The Colonel parred it and O'Reith made a bogie.

At No.2 tee, McDonough asked, "What happened to the concrete bunkers that were here in 1962?"

"I had them knocked down. Things are quieter these days, Sir George," the Colonel said proudly. "The marginals are in check. Not so many loose firearms out there anymore. The snipers have been liquidated. As you see I've torn down all those slums that were once hotbeds of criminal activity. That's where the new nine holes are located. We'll come up on them before long."

From the ladies tee, Cook stood 167 meters from the center of the green. Her No. 3 wood whipped the ball down the fairway to drop a foot from the flag. The Colonel's seven iron shot fell near the pin; O'Reith's further out. Cook birdied again and the Colonel and O'Reith parred.

On the tee of the next hole, a 304 meter par four, the Colonel said, "See those flamingos jacking around among the lily pads, that's a new swamp, fully stocked with alligators and snakes. I intend to expand it so that it circumscribes the city. The only way in or out will be across trestles. They'll be heavily guarded. Marginals, degenerates and defectives will have to take their chances with the reptiles."

"That must be expensive," McDonough said.

"Costs us nothing," the Colonel said. Nearly every week some functionary of the U.S. Government comes. Note that line of pussy willows and fern trees near the fringe. Courtesy of the U.S. Department of Agriculture. Last month an official of *Alianza Para el Progreso* was here to determine if we had any endangered species. I told him that everything we had was endangered. Marginals were eating them. I didn't mention the man-eating tigers up north. He said we qualified for $20 million if we used the funds properly. When it showed up a couple days later by wire transfer, I ordered another three dozen tigers from India. Days later, a fellow from the Agency for International Development appeared. He wanted to know if I had any construction projects that required financing. I told him of my plan to extend the swamp and he put me down for $10 million. So I am in good shape as far as projects are concerned. What I need is some money to buy arms and ammunition. It has to be invisible to the United States."

"Why?" O'Reith asked.

"To support my return to Miraflores. Of course."

"That is a no-no Colonel. Have you forgotten?" O'Reith's voice was unmistakably as clear as it was cold.

"I imagined that after all these years you might have forgotten."

"Well I haven't."

"Things change, General O'Reith. Your oil wells are not as valuable now as they were a decade ago."

"Yes. That is true all right," O'Reith agreed.

"And you could use some new concessions in Venezuela," the Colonel continued.

"Yes, they would be welcome," O'Reith admitted. "I cannot deny that. But the tax regime is onerous now."

"That could be easily changed."

"Elections are scheduled for December," O'Reith said.

"Chaos could result from that. Well?" the Colonel finished.

"We may be able to get funds to beef up security right here," O'Reith suggested. "They could be pigeon-holed with Miraflores in mind."

From the ladies tee, Cook hit a beautiful drive that fell far down the fairway. The Colonel rifled a shot that cleared the creek, a nine iron shot from the green. He answered, "Well, sir, I get an annual allocation to keep the military police force in tip top shape. The Pentagon wired me last month that I was entitled to an upgrade. I don't know exactly what to reply."

"Send them a request for arms and ammunition," O'Reith said. "Get some new tanks and the latest in artillery. And new trucks too. Six by sixes with V-12 Cadillac engines in them and automatic transmissions."

O'Reith hit a straight shot that just cleared the creek. McDonough alongside, he walked to his ball. The Colonel and Cook chugged down the fairway, waited as he walked up. O'Reith hit an eight iron to the fringe of the green. The Colonel's wedge put him three feet from the flag. Carolyn Cook hit a wedge too and her ball rolled up close to the pin. For the third time, Cook birdied, the Colonel parred and O'Reith bogied.

"I'm glad we're not playing for money," the Colonel said grinning. "That woman would clean us out."

O'Reith chuckled. "She's good all right."

At the No. 4 tee box, O'Reith asked, "What about the CIA? Do they come around?"

"Oh yes. With regularity. Always asking if the situation is stable. Stable! Ha! What a laugh. At last count we had four active insurgencies, each one militant as all get out. First and most worrisome to the CIA is the Communist Workers Party, called (PGT). Then we have the Guerrilla Army of the Poor, called (EGP). A particular nuisance to me is the Rebel Armed Forces called (FAR). Finally we have a gang that is called Organization of the People in Arms or (ORPA).The CIA likes to think it monitors the activity of all of them. In reality they can't even tell them apart. For that matter, neither can I. There is a shabby, abandoned building not far from the palace that I tell them it is the Communist Party headquarters. The police erected a couple of sophisticated-looking antennas on the roof to give the appearance that somebody is in there talking to Moscow. They keep it under close surveillance. A workman goes inside from time to time to raise and lowers the shades. CIA perks up. So when they ask how things are, I tell them that I worry about the Communists. The last CIA chap mentioned some trouble with a bad actor named Allende in Santiago de Chile. This far north we don't pay much attention to that long land. It could be the Middle East for all we care."

No.4 was 445 meters from the men's tees to the flagpole. After the men drove, Cook walked down to the ladies tee. O'Reith hit his usual. The Colonel out drove him by twenty meters or so. Cook's ball fell near the Colonel's.

"What about the border with Honduras?" O'Reith asked. "All quiet?"

"Torpid," the Colonel responded. "We had a dust up in Chiapas some time back but the troops settled their hash quickly. Wild-eyed banditos that had too much to drink broke a few heads. Nothing we wished to report to the CIA."

"You should have anyway and asked for more money," McDonough suggested.

"I hadn't looked at it that way."

"Colonel Jiménez," O'Reith began, "what do you think about Honduras and El Salvador? Is it time to knock those two over? Expand the *Co-prosperity Sphere.* Run it all the way down to the Costa Rica line?"

The Colonel's nose went up into the air. "Asking for trouble," he snorted. "You recall our previous brush with those savages. It was a bad scene."

"Carolyn thinks we might find some big oil fields next to that mountain range that runs down south. You wouldn't have to rely so much on those U.S. agencies."

"Well I suppose if we had a large enough force, we could manage it. But things are not what they seem. I control Guatemala City. My troops patrol the pipelines and keep the Mexican peons away from the well heads. However with production declining rapidly, even that will soon be pointless. We guard the banana plantations for the Fruit Company. Beyond that I have little control over the countryside. *The Greater Central American Co-prosperity Sphere* is fundamentally a myth; it exists only on the map. It could collapse at any time. To subjugate Honduras, we require a foreign army, American or British. I need a corps?"

"You can't handle it on your own?"

"Heh heh heh," the Colonel tittered nervously. "You jest."

"George," O'Reith asked. "What are the chances of getting a Gurkha brigade?"

"Slim to none." McDonough snapped back tersely. "Harold Wilson will hardly speak to me. Clive, you know better than to ask. Problems enough hanging on to those troops in Poghdar."

"This is a bad time to stir Washington up," O'Reith continued. "What with war in the Holy Land and his personal problems haunting him, Nixon must be distracted. And surely he still remembers Vietnam and the bad publicity related to it. But I'll go this far. Ethering has useful contacts in the capital. Maybe a propaganda campaign can generate some support for an attack on Honduras. Colonel Jiménez, do we know of any communists there?"

"Arellano long ago liquidated what few were there. The fruit companies insisted on it. Something like that would be a long shot."

The players all hit satisfactory second shots and for a change, all three parred. As they chugged up to No. 5 tee, Cook observed a pair of long-tailed, scarlet birds with golden-green heads in a flowering Bougainvillea tree. "Are those quetzals?" she asked.

The Colonel looked up at them and said, "Could be. They are not parrots. We don't have anything like that in Tachira."

"George, what do you think they are?" Cook asked.

"No idea my dear. They seem to be fooling around. Looks as if they are going to create some additional specimens?"

"They are getting down to it all right," Cook giggled.

From the elevated No.5 tee, one could look down into the swamp. Alligator eyes protruded from the murky water. Frogs hopped from lily pad to lily pad. Agile, fast swimming, water snakes skimmed across the surface. Giant green and blue, gossamer-winged dragonflies hovered. Flamingos stood stilted up in the shallows. Bubbles gurgled up from decaying plant matter. Stinging gnats swirled around their heads. The Colonel said, "Next time the *Alianza Para el Progreso* agent comes down I will treat him to a round of golf. He can see for himself the endangered species. In there are newts and efts and mollusks and nutrias. Nutrias, by the way, are water rats of some description. In America, the newts and efts are called 'water dogs'. Then we have fish with teeth. Everything out there in that morass is either being eaten, is eating one of his fellow denizens or if they are not doing either of those things, they are breeding. You cannot imagine the chaos that exists in a swamp."

"I can imagine it," Cook said. "And as for eating, these gnats are eating us. Let's get away from this noxious bit of real estate?"

The threesome quickly teed up and drove down the fairway. McDonough, whose thin skin was quite delicate, was already wiping away tiny bloodstains left by the vicious gnats. No. 5 was a 480 meter par five located along the runway about where the jets became airborne.

As they went down the fairway, a Pan American Boeing 747 headed for Lima, roared above them. Their balls, far along the fairway, were away from the swamp. Gnats were no longer a nuisance. O'Reith hit a No.3 wood to the green. Cook's ball got hung up in the fringe and the Colonel hit a bouncer that stopped thirty meters short. O'Reith, his ball inches from the cup putted out for a birdie. Cook could only par and the Colonel, heaven forbid, bogied.

At No. 6, a par 3, O'Reith was tiring. Here, the swamp curved inward making the green a peninsula some 160 meters from where they stood. O'Reith got on with an 8 iron. The Colonel, did the same. Cook hit a nine-iron high and straight. She watched with delight as her ball plummeted neatly into the hole."

"Nice shot, Carolyn," O'Reith said.

"Excellent!" the Colonel said.

"You are entitled to a kiss for that, my dear," McDonough said.

"I'm not even going to the green," Cook said. Too many midges. George would you retrieve my ball?"

"With great pleasure, dear."

The Colonel and O'Reith parred and they were on their way to No.7, a par four 395 meters long. The rough between the fairway and the swamp narrowed as they played down course. Mosquitoes and gnats were acting up. By No. 8, the rough had narrowed to about thirty meters and by No. 9 it was less than ten.

No. 10 began the new holes, constructed where favelas once stood. Only five meters of rough separated fairway and swamp. The sun's warmth brought swarms of insects into the air, buzzing and humming as they descended upon the players. In addition to stinging midges, huge black mosquitoes hovered over the fairway swales wet with casual water. Halfway down the fairway, the rough tapered off to nothing. A mishit ball to the right would fall into the swamp. A bad shot to the left would strike the concrete barrier, carom off, roll across the tilted fairway and also into the swamp. Since No.5, O'Reith had either bogied or double bogied every hole. His leg had given out, and forced to bounce along in the cart with the caddies, was ready to say the hell with it. Although Cook was playing well, she too had had enough of the insects. McDonough's pristine white linen suit was speckled with tiny blood spots.

They packed it in. After a shower and a change of clothes, lunch in the Colonel's private dining room at Aurora, they boarded his private jet for the flight back to Los Angeles, arriving late in the afternoon.

O'Reith went to the Fullerton building to spend the night with Maxine. Next morning, at his huge desk in the corner office, O'Reith put a call through to General Alexander M. Haig, Chief of Staff to the POTUS. To O'Reith's annoyance, it took quite some while for the call to go through.

When it finally did and he picked up the phone he heard an enthusiastic "Clive!" from the affable General Haig. "What a long time since we've chatted. How are you getting on?"

"Not too bad, Al. Congratulations on achieving the apogee of power."

"I'm not there quite yet," Haig said laughing slyly. "I'm still working on it. Nixon and Kissinger still give me marching orders. How is that remarkable movie actress getting on?"

"She's ailing again but not to worry. Good Dr. Parkinson looking after her. Al, how about a favor?"

"Anything Clive. What do you need?"

"Troops."

"Like soldiers?"

"Yeah, maybe a light corps. Two armored divisions."

"Where?"

"Al, this is in strict confidence. Sir George P. McDonough and I just returned from a visit with Colonel Jiménez in Guatemala City. He's keeping quiet on it, but there has been a build-up of hostile forces in the south. Frankly, he fears an invasion from Honduras and El Salvador. He thinks that both countries are about to be taken over by communist insurgents and that in the end, they will unite in an effort to upset him. It worries him."

"Sounds like typical McDonough intrigue. You guys trying to get the Colonel to knock off Honduras?"

"Al! How could you ever suspect such a thing?" O'Reith objected. "No sir, you have it wrong. George was with me on a religious mission. The Pope wants to beatify some outstanding Christian martyr from that neck of the woods. George was down there to sound the Colonel out on a suitable candidate."

"Why not beatify first and ask questions later?" Haig suggested, laughing.

"Funny Al, how about my corps?"

"I could let you have the First United States Army Group, Clive," Haig suggested. "Patton's old unit. Much larger than a corps. Two armies in fact. Twenty divisions."

"Al, are you referring to FUSAG?"

"That's it pardner," Haig chuckled.

"Well I'm not interested in that old canard," O'Reith said. "It fooled Rommel but it doesn't fool me. Al, I'm serious. Throw us a bone. How can we make the world safe for democracy if we can't get some oil concessions in Honduras?"

"Negotiate with that guy down there, what's his name?"

"His name is Oswaldo Arellano. The Colonel says he's no good; a tool of the banana companies."

"That is not a capital sin. Clive, you've been out of circulation too long. Last Saturday afternoon, Nixon told Elliot Richardson to fire Archy Cox. Richardson refused. He and his deputy, Bill Ruckelshaus resigned. Nixon finally found a federal judge named Bork who agreed to axe off Cox. Since then things have really been in a mess. Telephones are ringing off the wall. The rag heads and the Jews are trying to liquidate each other. Kissinger is in Moscow to pry the Russkys loose from Anwar Sadat. I'm here all by myself running the government. Not easy with Congress stirred up. Clive, this Watergate break-in is totally out of control."

"Maybe it is Waterloo," O'Reith suggested. "Where is the POTUS, anyhow?"

"Florida. Playing gin rummy with Bebe Rebozo. Both of them sauced up."

"Al, we might be able to help the POTUS. A good, well-run, anti-Communist diversion in Central America could take the heat off of him."

"Clive, you and Sir George don't have a really good reputation in this town. You think all those odd shenanigans pass unnoticed but they don't. You two guys have been known to pull some weird-looking rabbits out of the hat. Frankly, Nixon is leery of you. Communist scares are a dime a dozen. Yawners. Can you come up with a better ploy than that?"

"We'll come up with a plan with more traction. He helps us. We help him."

The telephone line fell silent. Haig had just put his thinking cap on. Over the mouthpiece O'Reith raised an eyebrow and grinned at McDonough, breathing heavily.

Haig cleared his throat. "Clive, I could arrange a meeting down in Florida. The POTUS, you and Sir George, Henry and I. At the Winter White House in Key Biscayne. Strictly informal. Off the record. Just an exchange of ideas. I could do that without getting my tail caught in the dashboard. The POTUS respects Sir George even if he doesn't completely trust him. Actually he doesn't trust anybody, not even his mother. Maybe he trusts Pat but that would be it. He knows you by reputation. I've heard him mention your name. That's something. Would Sir George ask the Queen to say something nice about POTUS? He could use an endorsement from her. How does that sound?"

"George just walked in Al. He's catching his breath. He and I could kick this around and call you back."

"OK. I'll be here. At least I think I will."

"Try to answer the telephone a little faster next time."

"Funny, Clive, really funny. Ta-ta."

"George," O'Reith began eagerly in his musical tenor. "A glimmer of light at the end of the tunnel. Richard Nixon has got his dick caught in a light socket over that break-in at the Watergate. Those Democrats smell blood. They'll turn the switch on. Smoke him out, peter first. If those tapes have damaging testimony, he could get himself impeached. Let's come up with a strategy to save his skin. We can get an army corps for the Colonel and knock Honduras and El Salvador off easy."

"Don't forget Nicaragua," McDonough admonished.

"Yeah, you're right. I forgot about that. George, Haig said he would agree to set up a meeting with Nixon. He needs encouraging words from Buckingham Palace. Could you have a word with...?"

"Wilson won't talk to me but Black Rod will. That is a direct connection to the Queen, God bless her" McDonough said.

"That's better than monkeying around with Parliament. OK. George, if we get something for Nixon from the Queen, we'll be in a good position. We'll fly down to Florida. Have a meeting, the two of us, Kissinger, Haig and the POTUS."

McDonough pulled at his lip; stared off into space. After some thoughtful moments he said, "Any way we can avoid Kissinger? He often has ideas of his own. We don't need that."

"George, that's a tough one. Haig and Kissinger are allies. How can we save Nixon?"

"I truly don't know, Clive. If the Colonel knocks off Arellano and then returns to Caracas, it would create an opening in Guatemala City."

"An opening?" O'Reith repeated slowly.

"Nixon," McDonough replied. "If the committee runs him out of Washington, he could become president of the *sphere.* Where is Stan?"

"Down the hall. I'll call him. O'Reith picked up the telephone and summoned the General Counsel. When the affable, round-faced attorney took his seat, O'Reith began, "Stan, we're trying to build support for the Colonel so he can expand the *Co-prosperity Sphere* down to the Costa Rica line. We want Nixon to let us have some troops. It is a tough call for him because of all the flak over Watergate. Then there's the Holy Land. I told Haig that we could help Nixon get out of the clutches of that committee. Any ideas?"

"Not off the top of my head," Ethering said. "As things stand they've got him by the balls. If we could get them to thinking about something else, maybe they would loosen their grip."

"I asked Haig if we could pump up a grand communist conspiracy to threaten Central America and take the Panama Canal away from us," O'Reith proposed. "But he said that idea had been overused. With the Russkys tangled up in the Holy Land, it could be sensitive too."

"Let's try it out on him anyhow," McDonough began, "Suggest that Nixon makes a foreign policy speech linking the Soviet Union to the conspiracy. At the end of the speech, he declares a national emergency. With that in place, we find something the Democrats badly want and link it to legislation that trivializes Watergate. Stan, whatever happened to that senator from Nevada that used to help us frame legislation? He was a godsend when we were trying to get the *Co-prosperity Sphere* going."

"Quigleyson?"

"Yes, that's the bloke. A scandal some years back cost him his seat."

"He runs a strip joint in Vegas. And he's a Justice of the Peace on the side. Pretty much out of it, I mean national politics."

"Does he still have influence," McDonough asked.

"Not much," Ethering replied. "Ruptured duck."

McDonough said, "If Nixon were to appoint him as an ambassador, the Democrats might see it as a step toward reconciliation and call off the dogs. Who is the American ambassador in Guatemala now?"

"No idea," O'Reith said. "Whoever he is, the Colonel could get him declared *persona no grata* with a snap of his fingers. Create an opening for the Quig."

"Long shot," Ethering said tersely. "Of course we can explore it. But in all candor, we have to write the Quig off. Democrats consider him a disgrace. And Sir George, we don't have to look far afield to find something the Democrats badly want. They want Nixon axed off."

"Stan, George has the idea that if the Colonel went back to Caracas, Nixon could take his place if he gets impeached. Is that a good idea?"

"Yikes! Sounds wacky at first blush but I don't know. The U.S. needs a strong ally in Central America. The Colonel is an ethical embarrassment. The government in Venezuela is sitting on the fence. Elections are weeks away. The Colonel, back at Miraflores, would be another strong U.S. ally. We could hype that. As long as Castro is hanging out in Cuba with the Russkys propping him up, American foreign policy has to be flexible. I would say that properly sugar-coated, it is doable. The committee chops Nixon. He gets a new job in Guatemala. The Democrats win the next presidential election. American defenses are strengthened. It could work."

"George after you talk to Black Rod, I'll call Haig back. Line the meeting up," O'Reith said.

"Good idea," McDonough agreed. "But this will take more than a few hours. Let me cogitate overnight. I'll have a plan of action in the morning. Clive, try to keep Kissinger out of it."

This time O'Reith got through to Haig in five minutes. "Al, we're ready for a meeting with the POTUS. Can we leave Kissinger out of it? George says he is a man of ideas. The meeting would be brief. We'd make specific proposals. If Nixon went for them, we would be on our way."

"I can't keep Henry out, Clive. Nixon likes to have him around especially when it is some kind of a goofy deal like you guys are going to spring. I'll call the POTUS later on and get back to you," Haig said.

At ten o'clock in the morning Tuesday, October 23, O'Reith was standing in the door of McDonough's make-up cubicle at Helen's Culver City studio. The big Englishman looked set to burst the canvas-backed chair with his name on the back strap. Its legs were bowed and his bulk caused the bottom to sag ominously. Mills was fixing his face and adjusting his wig. In minutes they would begin shooting the opening scenes of *The White Satin Miter.*

McDonough said, "The Queen has agreed to make Nixon an honorary Knight of St. Swithin. She will invite him to Buckingham Palace. Short speech, drinks and a state dinner, the works. He returns to DC with his little bronze medal. How's that?"

"That's great, George. Who the hell is St. Swithin?"

"Said to be a rain maker. The Pope made him a saint."

"Haig called me at home late last night. He and Nixon do their talking after the moon sets. We're on for a chat at Rebozo's place in Miami on the evening of October 25. The two of them have to fly down from DC. Nixon has a press conference scheduled for the 26th. No dinner just coffee and White Owls. We have to be there at ten. Kissinger has been in Moscow and Tel Aviv. He will brief Nixon on the war in Israel. Haig can't predict how long that will take. So we leave tomorrow afternoon when you finish shooting. Take a chartered jet and then return after the meeting. You can sleep on the plane and won't miss any time on the set. That OK?"

"Yes indeed. Clive I'm excited about this chance of cinematic immortality. I certainly expect to live up to Helen's high expectations. I met some of the other actors and actresses on the set today. They all sing together in a Christian group called the New Hope Pomona College Pentecostal Minstrels. One of them is an actress named Cherry Cokeland. She seems a pretty little piece but rather vacant. Eve called her a 'bubble-head' which I think is rather cruel. Also of that group is an actor who calls himself 'Aztec Sam'. He doesn't look much like an Aztec but he may be. Then there is an ex-football player named Lynn Landury with a Texas drawl. His girl friend is named Susan Shams and she works in a dentist's office. Finally we have another actress called Meg Muffin-Driver. She is a bit odd but you would probably enjoy her company as she claims to be a scratch golfer. She is quite buxom."

"Well, I'm sure you will have a great time of it playing against all of those exciting types, George," O'Reith purred. "Given any further thought to what we're going to strap on the POTUS?"

"Clive, it came to me in a flash as I was showering this morning. Nixon must announce a history-making breakthrough with the Soviet Union. On national television, he will say that the two nations have decided to reduce their nuclear arsenals to zero. It will be a long, complicated negotiation that will completely consume the president's time for the next two years or so. He will ask the people to be patient with him as he sorts through all of the complexities inherent in this détente. So the Watergate affair suddenly becomes a detail of the game which must be set aside. What do you think?"

"That could be all right," O'Reith agreed. "If he went for it, we might get our green light on Honduras?"

"Then a couple of weeks later," McDonough continued. "Another TV address. This time the discovery of a Cuban conspiracy to overthrow the *Co-prosperity Sphere.* Of course, it cannot be a communist threat. That would queer the détente. But it could be a *fidelista* conspiracy. Nobody likes Castro. He's the goat. While Nixon is negotiating with Brezhnev, we can be liquidating Honduras."

"George, what if Brezhnev won't go for it? What if he wants to keep some of his nuclear weapons?"

"I'll telephone Mikoyan tonight," McDonough said. "If we can get the talks going, it really doesn't make any difference what they do with the weapons. So long as it looks like progress..."

"If the talks stall, George, the Democrats will get back on his case."

"I can work that out with Mikoyan," McDonough said. "From time to time we can announce a milestone. Keep people glued to their TV sets." Helped by O'Reith and Mills, he got to his feet. The chair creaked a sigh of relief. The red light came on; the bell was ringing and it was time for the cameras to roll. O'Reith gave Helen a hug and a smile and left the thespians to their cameras and megaphones.

On the plane to Florida, O'Reith said, "George, we cannot rule out the possibility that the committee will prevail in the end. Do we expose that thinking at this meeting?"

"We could expose it to Haig," McDonough allowed. "I'm afraid of letting Kissinger see that far into our crystal ball."

"Yeah, me too."

At midnight Haig finally appeared in Rebozo's magnificent parlor and summoned the man of oil and the man of God. At the door of his den, shadowy-jowled and worried-looking in a dark blue suit, white shirt and a red tie, Nixon stood anxiously. Behind him, the floor lamps with orange shades cast a warm glow on the red and brown carpet. Nixon smiled, speaking in his famously hollow-sounding voice. Beside him, like an evil gnome, a hunched over Kissinger in a rumpled dun-colored suit and mustard yellow tie, glowered. O'Reith got ready for a tough go. Haig said, "President Nixon, allow me to me present Sir George P. Cardinal McDonough."

Nixon, a super-friendly smile on his face offered his hand to McDonough saying, "A great honor indeed to meet you, your Holiness."

"I'm just a simple parish priest from the north of Ireland, Mr. President. You can call me Father George."

Nixon laughed, pumped his hand vigorously, said "Father George it is!"

He turned to O'Reith saying, "Well sir, you need no introduction! The nation owes you more than it can ever repay. Men of your fervent patriotism are rare indeed."

"Thanks for the kind words, Mr. President," O'Reith responded.

Haig then presented the two oilmen to Henry Kissinger. With cold civility, he greeted them as if they were lowly State Department supernumeraries.

Coffee was poured and cigars passed around. Haig began, "Gentlemen, the president, an intensely patriotic person, fully aware of the your influence in this world, looks forward to hearing your ideas as regards the national safety."

The glass-topped coffee table was covered with newspapers and back copies of *Time Magazine*. In both the *Washington Post* and The *New York Times,* the word 'Watergate' appeared as a headline. A picture of the entrance to the apartment complex was on the cover of *Time*.

O'Reith began. "Mr. President, to derail this Watergate investigation, we have to come up with something truly astonishing, an epic event, something that will eclipse all other topics of conversation. We must convince the man on the street that it is in his best interest to telephone his Congressman and tell him to cool it until you have completed your mission. We must postpone the investigation so far into the future that it becomes moot. This is not a stonewall, rather it is a statement that the new situation completely overwhelms the triviality of Watergate."

"I like the concept," Nixon said in his brisk, authoritative, echoing voice. Framing his ideas with his hands, he continued, "The problem is that some of our campaign activities can be narrowly construed as being illegal. The rest of it is just chaff, the stuff of misdemeanors. I am definitely interested to hear just what can it be of such dimension that the Congress will return to their normal business."

"George," O'Reith said, "your turn."

McDonough quickly explained his plan for nuclear détente, revealing that Mikoyan had already assured him of his support.

Kissinger gasped, stiffened and tried to speak. He sputtered, "An enormity, Mr. President. Gauche diplomacy. I cannot agree!" His mouth opened and closed rapidly but further words failed him. He shook his head, rolled his eyes. Totally nonplussed, he struggled to regain his poise; said in his heavy German accent, "Mr. President, I find this a very dangerous position for you to put yourself into."

Nixon laughed. "Worse than the position I'm already in?"

Everyone laughed except Kissinger. He said heavily, "I find nothing amusing here. Such diplomacy is foreign to me, Mr. President," he stammered. "As you well know, the negotiation of a nuclear limitation treaty is properly the business of the State Department. Actually your role would be quite small. It would be my job. There would be no reason to halt the Watergate investigation. Yes sir, I must insist that a matter of this gravity should be left in the hands of professional diplomats. I must say that I find discussions between the lay reader McDonough and Mikoyan rather unusual and hardly conducive to an effective foreign policy After all Mikoyan is subordinate to Leonid Brezhnev, my boar-hunting companion."

McDonough rose, pulled himself out of his chair up to his full six feet six inches and said, "I do beg your pardon, your Excellency but a Prince of the Church is at least one notch up on a lay reader." To emphasize the point, he opened his cavernous, battered leather briefcase; first laying out on the floor his Webley-Fosberry .44 revolver in its cumbersome army regulation holster. Then he found his breviary with gold letters showing it to be a gift from Pope John XXIII and laid that out beside the pistol. Finally he found what he sought, his scarlet zucchetto which he smoothed out and smiling at the POTUS, placed on his white-fringed, bald dome. It was the first time that he had worn it outside his villa on Lake Albano.

Nixon guffawed and pointed a forefinger at Kissinger. In his resonant voice he said, "Take a gander at that red skull cap Henry. Mind what you say to such high ecclesiastic authority." He slapped his knees and howled with laughter.

Turning to Kissinger, McDonough stared him down. When the Secretary of State shifted his eyes downward, McDonough laboriously restored the pistol and the breviary to the briefcase. O'Reith made a mental note to congratulate his comrade for a masterly coup. It was a pity that there were no cameras."

Nixon's agile mind was racing ahead of the theatricals. He said, "I can say in my press conference tomorrow, as I announce the beginning of the negotiation, that I cannot surrender the tapes because of conversations with Chairman Brezhnev."

"Mr. President," Kissinger said, "Brezhnev speaks no English."

"That doesn't make any difference, Henry. Who the hell will ever know?"

"You can say, Mr. President," McDonough suggested, "that the conversations are in Russian and that I was your interpreter."

"I like it," Nixon said. Then turning to O'Reith he continued, "I assume you gentlemen are not doing this as a public service. If détente is the quid, what is the quo?"

"O'Reith answered, "Colonel Jiménez, down in Guatemala City, has been getting flak from the *fidelistas* in Honduras and El Salvador. We went to see him a few days ago. He thinks now could be a good time to expand the *Co-prosperity Sphere.* Take it all the way down to the Costa Rica line. That would remove the threat. As you know, Mr. President, the Colonel has been a great supporter of democracy in that region and with Honduras and El Salvador incorporated into the *sphere*; the "Bulwark of Freedom" would loom that much larger."

"I like it," Nixon said. "Al, make a note of "Bulwark of Freedom". Bill Safire can work it into my next speech. Troops required?"

"Yes sir, we need an armored corps." O'Reith said. I've already discussed it with General Haig."

Haig grinned at Nixon. "We spoke in terms of FUSAG, sir."

Nixon laughed. "Old FUSAG. George Patton would turn in his grave. But I assume this time it would be the McCoy."

"May I ask, Mr. President, what is the "McCoy"?" Kissinger asked, puzzled."

Nixon chuckled. "The real thing, Henry. The original FUSAG was a ghost to throw the Germans off the track." Turning to O'Reith, Nixon continued, "We would have to hold off on the announcement until Henry here gets the war in the Holy Land shut down. Can't fight on two fronts at once." Turning back to Kissinger, he asked, "Henry, when will you have your cease fire in place?"

"I haven't the faintest idea. As things stand right now, Golda Meir still thinks she can cream out the Egyptian Third Army. If she does that, the Israelis will be in Cairo in a week. We can't allow that to happen. Now that the Soviets have backed away from military confrontation, I have to call Golda back and tell her she has to let the Egyptians escape. If she doesn't, the Soviets will balk. They really would put troops into the Sinai. So I can't say for sure."

"Surely by mid-November," Nixon insisted.

"Well, I hope so," Kissinger replied wearily.

Nixon turned to O'Reith. "Think in terms of November 15. Al, where is your calendar?"

Haig looked at his date book. He said, "The 15th is on a Thursday."

"Well let's set up a press conference for Friday the 16th then. You and McDonough can come up with some language that suits everybody."

Kissinger said in his heavy voice, "Mr. President, this combination of détente tied to a change in Central American thinking constitutes 'linkage'; always a dangerous proposition in foreign policy."

Nixon laughed. "Henry the only linkage that matters is that of 1973 to 1978. Once inaugural day of 1978 rolls around, they can investigate Watergate as much as they like. There will no longer be any tapes to subpoena."

"Mr. President," Haig said, "It is getting late. Remember you have a press conference scheduled for tomorrow afternoon in Washington. If we have no further business, perhaps we should adjourn."

"Good idea," Nixon agreed. He turned to McDonough and asked, "Father George, would you lead us is prayer?"

"Of course," McDonough said, reaching back into his briefcase for his breviary.

Nixon said, "Henry I want you to kneel right here beside me. And Al, you can kneel on the other side. General O'Reith you are excused inasmuch as you have a game leg."

O'Reith acknowledged his exemption, clasped his hands, put on a sober face and assumed a pious position.

As if by magic, McDonough's halo appeared. He began in his majestic bass, pitched low for the solemn occasion.

> "Holy Father in Heaven, we mere mortals now humbly gathered here in Key Biscayne at the Winter White House ask you to look favorably on our small enterprises which we undertake to bring peace to a troubled globe and prosperity to the little people who find themselves in reduced circumstances. We know so little of your divine intentions that we can only grasp for solutions that will please your eternal longings. We ask especially that you look with favor upon the presidency of our Friend and leader, Richard Milhous Nixon and that you allow him to keep this dedicated office for its complete term and that you further favor Friend Nixon with serenity and wisdom so that his leadership will be evident in the great statecraft that it is his lot to undertake. Lord we further ask you to look with kindness and charity upon your servant, his Excellency Heinz Alfred Kissinger, known with great friendship and amity to his friends as Henry. We ask you to bless his Secretaryship and favor him such that he is remembered as a great and powerful diplomat whose skills are only exceeded by his honesty. Lord we ask you to look after and take care of your devoted Catholic servant, General Alexander M. Haig, who in his capacity as Chief of Staff of the White House must daily make great decisions about the safety and security of the United States of America. We also ask that at some time in the future the government to which he has steadfastly been so loyal recognize the great genius of Alexander M. Haig and that he be inducted into the ranks of the five star generals of the Army of the United States. Also Lord, help Henry Kissinger here in shutting down his war in the Near East. Please Lord, give all of us gathered here tonight the fortitude to bear our travails with honor and dignity so that the world will be improved by our being here in it. Goodbye for now, Lord. We keep thee in our memory."

"Great prayer!" Nixon exclaimed jumping to his feet and helping Kissinger up.

"My congratulations, Father George!" Kissinger said sardonically acutely observing as he spoke that McDonough's halo began to fade. "But it is not my war. It belongs to Golda Meir and Anwar Sadat and that Syrian lunatic."

Nixon laughed.

Haig slapped McDonough on the back. "Wonderful oration, Sir George. You are a man of imagination."

From a deal table Nixon plucked two books. The jacket showed a picture of a thoughtful Nixon quite a bit younger than he now looked. He handed one to O'Reith and the other to McDonough saying, "Fellows, a token of my esteem. This is my autobiography. *Six Crises* that I have lived through. I hope you find it interesting."

O'Reith straightened up in his chair, unclasped his hands, took the book and said, "Well Mr. President, this is an unexpected pleasure. I look forward to sharing these difficult moments of your life."

McDonough graciously accepted his copy saying, "Mr. President I always like to read a book written by a man who likes to write. I will treasure it. He noted the inside autograph. "This will someday be worth a fortune, Mr. President."

Nixon laughed and slapped him on the back.

O'Reith said," When we get through this one, Mr. President you can write another book. Call it: *My Seventh Crisis*."

Nixon laughed and slapped him on the back.

In the limousine on the way to the airport, McDonough asked, "Clive, what did you think of it?"

"The meeting?"

"The prayer."

"It was OK. If you intended to lather those three guys up, you certainly did. Turning your halo on was a masterful touch. One of these days when we are not so busy, I would like for you to expand on how you learned that trick."

"I got it from J.C.Masterman. He gave it to me when he asked me to become the Bishop of La Roche Guyon. We had to work that through Pope Pius XII. He had been the Nuncio before that and met Hitler in 1933 during concordat negotiations. But we can explore that a better time. You were not offended that I excluded you from consideration in my prayer for Nixon?"

"Of course not, George. Including me would have diluted the overall effect. After all, we're trying to get those guys to dance to our tune. Kissinger seemed a bit put out by it."

"My thinking too," McDonough agreed.

"George I'm going to call Haig in the morning. I'll spring the idea of the Colonel going back to Caracas and Nixon taking his place."

"That's OK," McDonough said.

CHAPTER V

BORIS GODUNOV

It was late on a clear afternoon on November 5 (Gunpowder Day), a Monday. O'Reith, sitting in Helen's dressing room, scanned an article in an old copy of *Variety* about the possibility of a sequel to *The Godfather*. Aside from his concern about his wife's health, things were not too bad. The war in the Holy Land had been stopped for a week now. Crude oil, in the face of the embargo was selling for $16.20/bbl and Standard Oil was glad to get it at that price. The Shah had agreed to split the windfall. Nixon had announced the 'Nixon-Brezhnev Doctrine' which would result in total elimination of all nuclear weapons except for those aimed at China. As of today, the company had the four strings from Libya in Poghdar cutting long ditch. O'Reith was pleased at the prospect of running another 200,000 bopd at the new price within the next ninety days.

Helen leased cameras, lighting, production equipment and a sound set from the Hal Roach Studios, sometimes described as 18 acres of comedy. Shooting had started at seven o'clock in the morning and O'Reith expected that Helen as well as the cast would be utterly beat down. He wanted to offer moral support on the ride home. Tomorrow she would get her next treatment from Dr. Kondratieff. As soon as he saw her, he knew it had been a rough day. Even beneath the heavy make-up, her face looked terrible. He asked, "How did it go, Baby?"

"Ace, I'm whipped. Hardly anything went right. We had to re-shoot half of the scenes. I was hoping to make a big dent in the schedule. But it didn't happen. Ace, I have decided to use the screen test with George and Eve just as it was shot. It looks better each time I run it through the movieola. And I'm going to splice some archival material into it as well. Alice thinks that is a good idea."

Just then, Ridley and Mills appeared. Helen said, "Sharon, I want you to clean me up immediately. I can't stand this goo on my face a minute longer."

As Mills went to work," Ridley said, "Honey, you're pushing yourself too hard. This movie isn't that important."

"Ace I don't know what to do. I have the cast on hire and we can't work tomorrow on account of my treatment and it is going to cost me a bundle. What's more I'm disgusted with those new players. I thought they would bring some youth and good cheer to the film. But they're wackos. That Cherry Cokeland is one weird chick. And I can't stand Aztec Sam. What a fraud he is. Landury has such a stiff face. All they can talk about is football, hotsy-totsy girls in short-shorts, golf and used Cadillacs. Ace, my judgment is getting terrible these days. The only saving grace is that they can harmonize pretty well. They sing some neat songs. What am I to do?"

"Let George direct for you tomorrow," O'Reith suggested. "He knows what to do. If they don't do to suit him, well..."

"Alice, what do you think? Can George direct that movie?"

"Honey, he can. He has an interest in its success. He's got plenty of experience at a lot of different things. And after all, it is just one day of shooting. Even if you have to re-shoot some of it, you're still ahead of the game. Since those cats sing so well, why not plug some extra songs into it?"

"Ace, you think he'll do it?" Helen asked.

O'Reith laughed. "George? For sure. Alice has a good idea. More music and some jumpy songs will help out. Where did you find Aztec Sam and his entourage, Helen?"

"Aztec Sam came to see Hal Roach looking for work. Hal didn't have anything and sent him to me. I didn't know about the others. Aztec told me that he was a born again Christian down on his luck. He offered to work as a janitor. I felt sorry for him. So I hired him as an extra. Next morning he brought Cherry and Susan and Meg Muffin-Driver and Lynn with him. Grinning like possums in a persimmon tree, they belted out a couple of Gospel songs. They belong to Aimee Semple McPherson's Church of the Foursquare Gospel. They hang out in Estes Park at a cheap hotel near the Angelus Temple. I think they have lurid patches in their lives."

"All the more reason to let George do it. He can cope with those trey balls."

Mills had removed Helen's pancake and washed her face, using a Q-tip to clean some of the deeper furrows." She said, come over to the sink and I'll wash your hair."

O'Reith, Helen and Ridley were deep in the cushions of the tonneau of his Cadillac. Mills sat in the jump seat with her kit bag on the floor. Helen had a Limejuicer Club Golf cap on her head and a green mesh veil over her face. Cruising down San Diego Freeway on the way to Long Beach, a thirty-five minute drive in traffic, Helen said, "Christ Ace am I ever ready for a drink!"

"We'll be there in a few minutes, baby," O'Reith purred. "Close your eyes. Relax in the cushions. Max is going to join us. He wants to make sure we're agreed on tomorrow's treatment. Kondratieff arrived around noon. He's at the Beverly Hilton."

"It's at ten in the morning, isn't it?"

"Yeah," O'Reith affirmed. "Max wants to discuss the length of the treatment. Another half-hour or a full hour which is what Kondratieff considers the standard?"

"I want to go for the full hour," Helen said vigorously. "We're paying for him to fly back and forth from London. I want to get my money's worth."

"The concern," O'Reith began "is the period when Kondratieff brings you out of it. He has studied that EEG he made last time and there is some small risk that bringing you out may be complicated. You recall Max suggested a hospital..."

"No!" No hospital. I'll take my chances."

In their study they met Parkinson. The butler had rolled in the drink trolley. As Mills was giving Helen a facial, she said, "Ace, I'm dry as a bone. Mix me a double and don't spare the gin."

Parkinson said, "Helen, at your age it takes longer to metabolize alcohol. You don't want to go into treatment with a hangover."

"I don't give a damn about my metabolism and as far as a hangover; I seem to have one all the time. I'll take my chances."

"You're determined to have a full hour's treatment," Parkinson said.

"Yes," Helen said, taking a long restorative pull from her drink.

"OK then. We'll schedule it that way. Kondratieff thinks that with his theremin, he can avoid the delay we encountered bringing you around before. But if despite everything, something goes wrong, you'll have to depend on adrenaline to pull you out of it."

"That's fine. Line me up for double adrenaline on the rocks." She laughed feebly and then began to sob. O'Reith quickly reached over and put his arm around her. He soothed her until the weeping ceased. Helen took a gulp of her martini, wiped her eyes dry and turned to O'Reith. She said, "Ace, I'm having a light dinner in my room with Alice and then it is off to bed. Will you talk to George about taking over in the morning at Culver City?"

"I'll call him right now, baby." He got up, put his arm around her, caressed her and left the room.

O'Reith called from the telephone in the downstairs foyer. He asked, "George, are you up to standing in as director for Helen tomorrow?"

"Of course, I'm flattered."

"OK. She's having a light dinner with Alice. I'm on my way to the Fullerton Building. I'll come back in the morning when the medicos set up for the treatment. Hopefully, it will be routine I don't know why I'm so goddamned torqued up about it."

"Not to worry Clive," McDonough said in a gentle voice. We know that everything will be fine, Clive. I had a word with Sergei. He's tuning up his Theremin, sure everything will turn out tickety-boo."

"It has to be that way, George. If you run into difficulty on the sound stage, call me."

"Clive, do you think Helen would object if I added a bit to the film?"

"I have no idea, George. She can be mercilessly abrupt with fools, as you well know."

"Clive, my thought was that at the end of the picture when Godunov has just pronounced himself to be the Vicar of Rome and taken the name Boris I, as a final shot, he would sing out *Casti Connubii II.* I have adapted it to the music for *God Save the Queen*. It only adds about four minutes of running time."

"George, may I ask what motivates you in this regard?"

"Clive, the encyclical is not getting famous reviews. Paul is disappointed by the lack of enthusiasm. In retrospect it may have been a mistake to put that Holy Land language in it. It seems to have only made matters worse. Surely Helen wouldn't mind a little PR for the Pope."

"George, it is not in the script that I read in the Hotel Caspien. Better run it by Alice."

"Yes, of course. You'll let me know how things go tomorrow?"

"I'll call you in the afternoon. She should be around by then with her eyes focused."

"Clive, did you talk to Al Haig?"

"I did. The idea stunned him at first but he got used to it. I told him if Nixon could face up to his string running out, we had a place for him. Haig said he would look for a chance to get that to him. He knows we're nervous about Henry the K."

"OK. Take care, Clive."

O'Reith arrived in Long Beach a few minutes before nine. Helen was having breakfast with Ridley and Mills in her bedroom. Doctors Kondratieff and Parkinson were setting up the spare bedroom for treatment. O'Reith, still sleepy, closed his eyes and let his mind wander to McDonough's saying that the origins of his halo could be traced back to La Roche Guyon. O'Reith was no stranger to extra-natural events. He could vividly remember being attacked by *foo fighters* over Posen. He could recall Amanda Macabre's hyper-magic incantations and his near brush with disaster when she gave him the evil eye. He was certain she had bewitched Maxine so she would fall in love with him. Then the stories his brother told him about Morgan Le Fey and her ability to create mirages in the Western Desert of Tripolitania. Morgan Le Fey was the sister of Arthur, legendary creator of the British Army. What British Officer did not know of her power as the "Mistress of Mirages"? All of that was of a piece with McDonough's halo.

Parkinson shook him out of his day dream."Clive, Sergei and I have agreed that if today's treatment goes well, we'll repeat it again tomorrow. With two treatments, twenty-four hours apart, we should get some idea of how she is responding. So around ten o'clock, Helen will be hypnotized and left in a trance for one hour. Then she will be awakened. No sedation is planned but she will rest in the quiet of her darkened bedroom for the day. After a light dinner, she will go to bed and remain thus until seven o'clock in the morning. After breakfast, Sergei will give her another hypnotic treatment. If all goes well, we plan another series of treatments in two or three weeks. How does that sound?"

O'Reith said, "It sounds OK to me. But you guys are calling the shots. What do I know about it?"

"Just wanted to make sure you were in agreement," Parkinson said.

O'Reith nodded.

Helen took her place on the half bed. Parkinson explained what was to happen. Kondratieff plugged in the theremin and began to summon its eerie music. In minutes, Helen fell into deep slumber. O'Reith went up to the den and tuned in KTLA. Kissinger was on the road again to Morocco and Tunisia before going on to Cairo with Anwar Sadat. No big negotiations were under way. The Near East was quiet. Oil liftings from Saudi Arabia were curtailed and shipments to the USA were forbidden under the Arab embargo. Gasoline lines in the cities but not in the countryside. Chevron stock was up sharply. Nixon was preparing for a summit with Brezhnev in Keflavik, Iceland. After the news, O'Reith turned off the TV and returned to the treatment room. Kondratieff was working his hands over the antennae of the theremin. High-pitched, oriental music filled the room and reminded O'Reith of a dancing goblin in the Mirrored House of Horrors. Helen still slept. The Russian physician turned up the volume and increased the pitch. The whine of it got on O'Reith's nerves. As Kondratieff played, Parkinson eyed his wristwatch, monitored Helen's pulse. He said, "Three minutes Sergei and no change."

Kondratieff nodded and increased the volume. Parkinson spoke again, "Five minutes and no change."

Kondratieff moved away from the musical instrument and looked into Helen's eyes with a penlight. "Six minutes," Parkinson said.

Kondratieff began playing the theremin feverishly. Parkinson said, "Seven minutes, Sergei." How about a shot of adrenaline?"

"Three more minutes," Kondratieff replied.

O'Reith, edgy and upset, beginning to fret, said nothing. There was nothing he could do. He depended on Parkinson. After nine and a half minutes Parkinson said, "Pulse stronger."

Kondratieff nodded, turned down the volume of the theremin. He looked across the instrument to Helen, unconscious on the bed. He said, "Her eyelids are fluttering. She's coming around." Shortly she opened her eyes and rose up on her elbows.

"Almost eleven minutes," Parkinson said, noting the details in his book.

Kondratieff began, "Helen you have just awakened from your fourth treatment. All is well. For the rest of the day, meditate on things that make you happy, give you good feelings. Avoid thinking about problems."

"May I think about the movie I'm making?"

"Only in a positive sense," Kondratieff said. "Think of ways to make it better, more poignant, more effective but avoid thinking of the problems associated with it. Have a light lunch and then a nap in the afternoon. When you awake you may resume your meditation. After a bland dinner, it's early to bed for another treatment in the morning at ten o'clock"

"May Alice stay with me while I meditate and help me get through the day? May I have a martini tonight?"

"Of course."

Ridley assisted Helen to her bedroom. Parkinson asked, "Sergei, should we go ahead so soon?" I'm concerned about the time it took to bring her around."

"Ten minutes was what I expected," Kondratieff said. "Eleven is within the standard deviation. Tomorrow should be better. She will be stronger."

"She'll probably have a stiff slug of gin with Alice tonight," O'Reith said.

"Hardly a problem," Kondratieff said. "That's medication too."

O'Reith rose, went to Helen's bedroom and rapped on the door. Ridley opened it and let him enter. Helen was in an easy chair with her head back. "How are you doing, baby?" O'Reith asked.

"I'm weak but all right. How do you suppose George is making out?"

"Like for me to go see?"

"That would be nice of you."

"I'll be back at the cocktail hour with a report."

She nodded, closed her eyes and seemed to fall asleep. O'Reith stood at her side for quite some long while. Finally she stirred and said, "Alice, would you get me a glass of sparkling water?"

O'Reith tiptoed to the door. Ridley let him out. He rejoined the two medicos in the parlor. "Where do we stand, fellows?" he asked.

"We've agreed on another one hour treatment in the morning," Kondratieff said.

"OK. I'm off to Culver City to see George. I'll have a drink with Helen around six tonight. I'll see you both in the morning."

After checking the office mail, he went to the studio. The cast had just called it a day. Mills was removing McDonough's make-up. O'Reith asked, "How's it going George?"

"Quite well, old chap, quite well indeed!" Helen will be proud of me. We're making splendid progress. Tomorrow we're going to shoot a side-scene."

"A side-scene, George?" O'Reith asked. He was suspicious.

"It is a cousin to a flashback. In a side-scene, you touch on an interesting event that is outside the main thrust of the plot."

"Like what? Give me an example," O'Reith said.

"This particular side-scene was suggested by Aztec Sam," McDonough said. "He plays the part of a used Cadillac salesman. His girl friend, played by Cherry Cokeland is a stripper in an upscale cocktail lounge in the Fairmont Hotel in Dallas, Texas. Her friend, Susan Shams works for a dentist out near Love Field. She drives an old Studebaker that is always breaking down. The dentist complains that she is missing too much work. He wants her to get a newer, more reliable car. So in the side-scene, Cherry introduces Susan to Aztec Sam with the expectation that he will sell her a used Cadillac that is in good condition."

"George, Helen will blow a gasket. She regrets hiring Aztec Sam and his hangers on anyhow. She would never have done it if she were well. How does that unfold? Do you just interrupt Boris Godunov and cut to the side-scene?"

"Yes, there's nothing to it. We simply fade out and segue into it. Then when it is complete, we return to the *Miter*."

"George, I don't want to get into the soup with Helen about this."

"Not to worry. She'll be pleased. Are you going to tell her we discussed it?"

"Of course I am."

"Well that's being a bad sport about it all."

"George, you and I have a number of important irons in the fire. Remember that Helen is my wife. I can't afford to have her annoyed with me."

"What if I told you that I cleared it with Alice and she said it would be OK?" McDonough asked.

"That puts it in a different light. If Alice agrees, you're on solid ground. I'm having drinks with them tonight."

"Give me a call afterward, Clive. Let me know. How is Helen by the way?"

"She's OK. At least she is for now. It took longer than usual for her to come out of hypnosis. Parkinson is watching over her. He has confidence in Kondratieff. He also has a hypodermic needle loaded with adrenaline just in case. Another treatment tomorrow. What about the encyclical, George? Did you film it?"

"I did and it is beautiful. I've looked at it several times."

"Does Alice know about that?"

"She does."

O'Reith patted McDonough's shoulder as he walked to his limousine, muttering.

Under a heavy cloud cover, by six o'clock it was dark on the terrace. It was the 10th of November. A soft breeze blew in from the ocean. Helen sat in a lawn chair with no make-up, no wig and wearing a cloche with a veil. Ridley, in a tan pantsuit, sat beside her. O'Reith standing over the drink trolley poured the martinis and added ice cubes. As he gave Helen one, he looked over at Ridley and said, "Alice, when I saw George tonight, he mentioned a side-scene involving Aztec Sam and Cherry Cokeland. He said that you knew about it. What is that all about?"

Helen said, "Relax Ace. Alice thought it was not too bad of an idea. The *Miter* is a heavy drama. George thought a comedy interlude would lighten it up. Those Pentecost jokers are under contract. I may as well get some useful footage out of them."

"What about several side-scenes with a little plot development?" Ridley suggested. "A movie within a movie. And more singing too.

When they form a choir and put on their best smiles and sing those sweet little religious songs, I feel good all over. I said nothing about it to George but my idea is to continue with the used Cadillac dialogue over three or four episodes. In the end, Susan buys the Cadillac only to discover it is in worse condition than her Studebaker. As she drives it off the car lot, the radiator explodes or something like that. What do you think, Clive?"

"I don't know much about the movie business," O'Reith said, taking his chair and rattling the ice cubes in his martini. "You two are the experts. But there is nothing wrong with music. Maybe we should get some songs written specially for them. What's Johnny Mercer doing these days? George, by the way, is having the time of his life. He said you approved the encyclical scene."

"It can only have a positive effect," Ridley said. "George is not too bad of a chanter himself. I don't know about Johnny Mercer. Last I heard, he was ailing. I agree we should have some songs written for them. Burt Bacharach could do it. I'll go to work on that."

"That is wonderful," Helen said. "It is such a relief to have someone directing the movie that I can rely on. Ace, George has been a real friend over the years. How is his romance with Carolyn going?"

"They take tub baths together. She washes his back and gives him a massage. I think that is as far as it goes."

Helen said, "If George can find his, he can probably find Carolyn's."

The three of them laughed together. It was the first time Helen had smiled in several days and O'Reith was pleased that she was enjoying life. He said, "Baby I have said nothing to the kids about your treatment. Do they know of the recurrence?"

"Helen Simpson knows that something is wrong. I have said nothing to Colin Clive or Rae Regan. It is none of their business," she said emphatically.

"What if Helen Simpson tells them?"

"She's too wrapped up in her own odd-ball affairs," Helen said.

"Am I invited for dinner?" O'Reith asked, hoping he was not.

"Alice and I are having a salad and an omelet," Helen said. "Not enough for a man of your appetite. Dine at the club. Be here when Kondratieff knocks me out tomorrow."

"So be it," O'Reith said. His limousine was waiting outside. He finished his drink, kissed Helen, embraced Ridley and headed for the Fullerton Building and Maxine.

The treatment was now routine and went off exactly as planned but with one little glitch. After 11 minutes of wake-up music Helen was still out. After 14 minutes, a grim-faced Parkinson gave her a shot of adrenaline. After sixteen minutes Helen awoke with a blank expression on her face. She was speechless and could remember no one. O'Reith dumbfounded, looked at the two physicians and asked, "So where does that leave us?"

"I expect she will come around," Kondratieff said. "But it may take several hours. Often in cases like this, she will fall asleep naturally and when she awakens, she will have regained her memory."

O'Reith looked to Parkinson.

Parkinson said, "The first thing for me to do is line up a nurse to look after her. Then we have to consider what to do in case she does not come around."

"What would that be?" O'Reith asked.

"We have to suspect brain damage," Parkinson said. "We'll have to hospitalize her for tests. Could be that the malignancy has spread to the brain."

"What do you think, Sergei?" O'Reith asked.

"I don't think it is a tumor. I think she will come around shortly."

To a distraught Ridley, O'Reith said, "Alice until Helen comes around, you and George have to be responsible for the movie. Can you carry on? Do we complete it or abandon it?"

"Helen would not want us to abandon it," Ridley said. "I can hear the scorn in her voice now."

"OK. We leave Helen in the hands of the medicos. Let's go to Culver City."

In McDonough's dressing room with Ridley beside him, O'Reith said, "George, Helen is out of it for now. The best thing is to go ahead, complete the movie."

"Agreed," McDonough said.

Ridley said, "One of Hal's comic writers can do a series of side-scenes for Aztec Sam and his cats?"

"Sounds OK to me," O'Reith said.

"We don't want the side-scenes to detract from the main thrust of Boris Godunov," McDonough said.

Ridley smiled. O'Reith asked, "George how much of it is already filmed?"

"We have a total of 35 minutes," McDonough said. "A balanced approach is required here. We have the 15-minute coronation scene, my screen test. Helen bought 10 minutes of archival material from Films on File. Five minutes from *The Sands of Iwo Jima* and another five minutes from *A Farewell to Arms*. Mostly troops on the move seen from a distance to be spliced in as required. Then the side-scene is ten minutes. We need another hour to make a 95 minute feature"

"Hal Roach is a past master of comedy," O'Reith said. "He could even look at the script for the *Miter*. Maybe give it a lighter touch."

"We have to be careful about that," McDonough said. "Paul knows of my involvement in this motion picture and above all, we must preserve the dignity of the papacy. *Casti Connubi II* is off to a slow start. He's catching flak from some of those puritanical South American bishops."

"Just having Boris Godunov as a Pope is pretty much of a negative," O'Reith observed.

"Well we can overcome that by a proper choice of dialogue," McDonough said.

"Do we get help from Hal or not?" Ridley asked.

"I say yes," O'Reith said.

McDonough sighed. "Well, I suppose we should. We can always control whatever comes out. Medicos have an opinion as to how long Helen will be *hors de combat*?"

"Kondratieff thinks it will be a matter of hours. Parkinson is not so sure."

"Clive, have we an idea as to the financial picture? How much did Helen budget? Is it her money?" McDonough asked.

"We'll have to look into that," O'Reith said. "She usually has a couple of partners but I didn't ask her about this one. Who's looking after the expenditures?"

"Robert Walters is the office manager," McDonough interjected. "Down the hall."

"He's been working for her for years," O'Reith said. "I know him pretty well." He picked up the phone and dialed his number.

"Business manager," a cheery voice sang out.

"Robert, Clive O'Reith. How's a boy?"

"General O'Reith! Well sir, been a while. I'm OK. I hear that Helen is ailing."

"Yeah. She's having a sinking spell. George and Alice and I are trying to decide what to do. Are all of the contracts signed?"

"Yes sir. Cast. Crew. Props. Rent. Utilities. The works."

"Time and budget?"

"Thirty days. Nine hundred grand and 95 minutes long."

"Thanks, Robert. George will keep you filled in." O'Reith hung up the phone.

Clive do you have power of attorney over her affairs?" McDonough asked. "Without that, we can't do anything."

"Yes. I have that. So does Alice with regard to her motion pictures. We can proceed. George, what do you say we go to a 24 hour/day schedule? Work around the clock. You and Alice take turns directing the picture. We're a third of the way. Let's try to finish it before the end of November. If we can get five minutes of usable film per day we can make it easy. String what we've got together for the movieola. That will give us some perspective. We have so many irons in the fire that you can't afford to be tied up any longer than that."

"Aztec Sam and his pals may squawk about the hours," McDonough said.

"Read their contracts, George. Let's get as much as we can out of them in the shortest possible time. Do they appear in the main story?"

"Aztec Sam appears as Godunov's court jester," McDonough explained. "Cherry Cokeland is Eve's lady in waiting. Susan Shams is Godunov's secret girl friend. Lynn Landury is the royal stable keeper. Eve finds out about Susan near the time when Boris becomes Pope. In a raucous scene she tries to have her executed but it doesn't work. Susan ends up being exiled to a nunnery in Warsaw."

O'Reith said, "OK. George you and Alice direct the movie. Let's line up one of Hal's writers for the side-scenes. By December first, we want to turn the movie over to the distribution company. Are we all agreed?"

"Suits me," Ridley said.

"I agree," McDonough said. "Any word from the White House on FUSAG?"

"Haig has promised troops middle of December. But no general officer. He fears that puts too much emphasis on American involvement. We need a guy."

"Have we got anybody?" McDonough asked.

"I'm thinking of using David Penrose. Artilleryman. You met him in Poghdar. Production Superintendent out there. Haig stressed that our man needs experience, a seasoned officer that he could recommend. I'll work it out one way or another. When the *Miter* is in the cans we'll go see the Colonel and tell him the plan."

"Is Nixon's nuclear deal with Brezhnev taking the heat off the Watergate fiasco?" McDonough asked.

"Haig said that so far, that committee was still after him to cede the tapes. Nixon is nervous and ready to get things stirred up in Central America. He's hoping that will ease the pressure. Haig hasn't sprung the *sphere* on him yet."

"I agree that it is somewhat premature."

That evening, O'Reith returned to the penthouse in Long Beach. Ridley remained in Culver City to line up a comedy writer. Kondratieff was attending Helen in her bedroom. Parkinson was in their den. O'Reith asked, "Any change, Max?"

"No. She's awake, staring at the ceiling. Hasn't said a word. Doesn't seem to recognize anyone. Sergei and I take turns staying with her. Long night ahead."

"Count me in," O'Reith said. "With three of us, we can all get in a nap."

"Sergei canceled his travel plans," Parkinson said. "He wants to see Helen up and going before returning to London."

"Max, Alice and I discussed the movie with George. We decided to keep the cameras rolling. In fact George and Alice are going to shoot around the clock. Could you prescribe some pep pills for the cast? Something to keep them going when they're tired and worn down."

"Clive, I am definitely not in that line of business."

"Well, it was a thought."

Helen Simpson in a white shirt and tight blue silk go-go pants arrived. She had a date for the evening and wanted Mills to give her a facial and a make-up. O'Reith asked her if she wanted a drink.

"A light one, Daddy-Cool. I have a long, rugged disco evening ahead of me."

The butler rolled the tray in and began mixing martinis. Helen Simpson got up to help him. When she and her father had their drinks and the butler departed, O'Reith said, "Sweetie, how much of a problem would it be for you and Alice to kiss and make up?"

"Why?"

"Because your mother didn't come out of her treatment in good shape. She has amnesia. Alice will be spending a lot of time here. It would be nice if the two of you could get along."

"Is mother going to die?"

"I don't think so. But she is ill. We have tedious times ahead. When Alice comes, will you talk to her?"

"When you put it that way, what can I say?"

O'Reith took her hand and squeezed it. "Long night ahead, sweetie. Max and I and Kondratieff are going to keep a vigil over your mother."

"Daddy-Cool, I could break my date and help out."

"No. Keep your date. Make up with Alice."

"You got it Daddy-Cool."

Next morning, when O'Reith looked in on Helen, she appeared to be sleeping. The nurse shrugged when he inquired about her. With no reason to hang around, he went to the office. After lunch, he returned to Long Beach. Kondratieff was in the parlor. O'Reith asked, "Any change?"

She is awake and alert. She had a good breakfast and a good lunch. She took her shower and brushed her teeth. She is in control of her bodily functions. But her memory is still missing. She looks intently at the nurse, then Dr. Parkinson, then me, as if trying to figure out who we all are. She has spoken not a word."

"How long do we allow things to remain thus?"

"I suggested to Dr. Parkinson that we bring her to the edge of a trance using an incantation. It could be a soft prayer. He is pondering that. My idea is to keep her on the edge of a trance for a few minutes and then waken her again."

"Sounds kind of like restarting a balky airplane engine. Any reason to think that would work?"

"Her condition resembles a Pentecostal hysteria. There are cases in the literature where penitents suffer spells of amnesia but eventually come out of it. Often the revivalist 'prays such a person through' as they refer to it. I can't do that but I can bring her to a full mental recovery. Her amnesia tells me that she has had a shock of some kind quite recently that left an indelible scar on her mind. Something sudden. Something frightening."

"Maybe that idiotic movie she's making. Where is Dr. Parkinson?" O'Reith asked.

"At her side."

"We better put our heads together and decide on a course of action." O'Reith continued. "This is no time for a shot in the dark. I'll look in on Helen and bring Max down and we can talk about it."

"Very well."

Parkinson paced the floor with a pensive look on his face glancing from time to time at Helen, propped up in bed on two pillows. Her face was a blank. As O'Reith entered he said, "Clive, I'm glad you're here. Helen is doing just fine but her memory is gone. She won't talk. I don't know what to make of it."

"Let's go down to the parlor and kick it around with Kondratieff," O'Reith said brusquely. Then he approached Helen, took her hand and caressed it. She gave him a vague stare. He put his palm against her forehead. She was compliant; gave no sign of recognition. He took his hand away, nodded to Parkinson.

The three men stood in the center of the parlor looking at one another. O'Reith asked, "Max, what about Sergei's idea of partial hypnosis?"

"I don't know, Clive. This is out of my line. We can look after Helen. She is in no danger that I can determine. I doubt if there will be any deterioration in her condition. She may regain her memory spontaneously. Sergei can return to London. A couple of phone calls should turn up an expert on amnesia. There must be many similar cases considering the type of people who live here. Once we have a better background, we can consult with Sergei by telephone. Maybe partial hypnosis is the answer. Maybe not."

"I leave matters in your capable hands, Max," O'Reith said. I'm off to Culver City to see how the motion picture of the century is coming along. I'll call you tomorrow."

O'Reith found a haggard pair in McDonough's dressing room. "Such long faces," he said to McDonough and Ridley.

"Clive, it isn't going to work the way you wanted it," Ridley said.

"We have a rebellion of the cast on our hands," McDonough added. "We worked all night. I looked at the dailies. None of the takes meet Helen's high standards."

"Clive, my place is at Helen's side," Ridley said. "She needs me and I don't know anything about direction anyhow."

"What about the side-scenes, Alice?" O'Reith asked, ignoring their complaints.

"Hal assigned a comic writer to us for free. Complete scenario in a couple of days. It is a tribute to Helen."

"OK George, you're on your own. Make peace with those Pentecostals. How is Eve holding up?"

"She is doing superbly. A trouper."

"Great." O'Reith said. "Put Boris in the cans quickly and artistically. Alice, Helen needs you more than this film does. Max is still with her. If you hurry you can catch him before he goes home. He'll fill you in while I talk to George. See you at the cocktail hour. OK?"

Ridley's face brightened. She kissed McDonough on the cheek saying "Ta-ta big George." She hugged O'Reith, kissed his cheek, winked at him and was gone.

"George, here in the autumn of our lives, we find ourselves in the kind of trouble that we were in thirty years ago," O'Reith said.

"That's true but for me it is easier to bear," McDonough said. "Carolyn keeps me company. And I don't have to worry that some fanatic Nazi will throw a potato masher into the confessional."

O'Reith laughed. "George did you ever really think that would happen?"

"I thought there was a good chance that I would be found out, that I would find myself kaput in some dank prison cellar. But I had an ace in the hole that John Masterman gave me. I counted heavily on it.

"What was it?"

"It was after the krauts were cleaned out of North Africa. Rommel was commander of Army Group B at La Roche Guyon, several hundred thousand troops. The bishop was a frog and the krauts suspected he was tied in to the resistance. The Kraut High Command wanted him replaced with a more reliable confessor, one that would not share confessional revelations with the frogs. They put the problem to Pius XII. Masterman suggested we meet in Lisbon in the Tivoli Gardens the seats used by *Deuxiéme Bureau*. He advised me that he had been in contact with Pope Pius XII and that I was the logical choice to go to LaRoche Guyon, a shocker. Of course I had to go. Masterman presented me with a small prayer-book and asked me to keep it on my person and use it religiously before every confession that I heard. What he didn't tell me was that all of my priests would be British Agents, combat chaplains with experience. He wanted to know what kind of sins the Germans were confessing. Especially sins of officers."

O'Reith said,"I worried about being captured. I came within an ace of being shot down over Regensburg. Thought for a while I might have to ditch it in Lake Constance leaving Helen a widow with two small children. I had a couple of close calls after that. A bad day over Bremen and then Berlin. But after the invasion, I thought I might just make it back. I had some top-notch gunners but those were not really good cards."

"But you made it. That's all that counts now. By the way, does Helen have partners in this flick?"

"George, I had a word with Robert Walters her accountant. She's doing this one straight up. Her traditional partners thought it was too risky."

"I can finish it for about three hundred thousand," McDonough said. "We are OK on that part of it. The big question is getting all that lolly back."

"All I want is for Helen to come to. If she has forgotten about this movie, I won't remind her of it."

The two men nodded agreement.

"George I'm going to have a drink with Alice and see if there is any change in Helen's condition. If she's still out of it, I'll spend the night with Maxine. When you get a scenario from Hal's comedy guy, give me a ring and we can read through it together. See if it fits in with the general scheme of things."

"OK, Clive. See you tomorrow."

Over drinks, Ridley advised O'Reith that in the hour spent with Helen, nothing had changed. Parkinson planned to examine her in the morning as she awakened. He was looking for a clinical psychiatrist with experience in hysteria. She said, Clive I'm sleeping in the guest bedroom tonight."

O'Reith, badly in need of affection, returned to the Fullerton Building and Maxine. If he were to stay out of the frog pond, it would be because of her.

Next morning in the Tower, McDonough called to say that the comedy writer had delivered the side-scene scenario. O'Reith, on his way to Culver City, had no doubt at all about McDonough's ability to direct and produce a gripping motion picture, even with the idiotic side-scenes. His sense of drama was as sure as his knowledge of human foible. Nor did he doubt that he would work swiftly and economically. He was not a man to waste anything; not prayer, not time, not money not food. McDonough's commanding presence could get the best from his actors, as good or as bad as they might be. They would render unto him the best performance of which they were capable. But it was also a certainty that he would take this opportunity to craft a subtle propaganda message in support of the Pope and *Casti Connubii II*. What was not a certainty was Helen's recovery and beyond that, what if anything she would remember about *The White Satin Miter*. So it was likely that the days immediately preceding Helen's *event* would be erased forever. Parkinson called it the fugue stage. O'Reith hoped that was right. He did not want an enraged Helen discovering when it was too late to do anything about it that her film had been fatally monkeyed-around with.

As his limousine pulled up in front of the studio gate, the guard opened it and his chauffeur tooled the big Cadillac up to the front of McDonough's dressing room. O'Reith found him quietly reading the scenario. "Clive, how are you keeping today?" the Englishman asked.

"OK considering everything, George. Side-scenes?"

"Indeed. Not bad. The comedy is provided by Susan Shams. She is reluctant to put out the kind of money required for a really good car. The second side-scene depicts her futile negotiation with Aztec Sam. It ends with her agreement to return tomorrow to look at a cheaper vehicle. That's as far as I've got. The third and fourth are more of the same with Susan becoming increasingly desperate. Want to read them?"

"O'Reith laughed. He said, "No!" then he added, "George, driving out here today I pondered how much of recent events Helen will remember when she snaps out of this sinking spell. She may not remember anything about this movie."

"That's possible."

"Well, I suppose there is nothing to do but finish it. It worries me."

"It will be mid-December at the earliest," McDonough said.

"Carry on, George, I'm going to Long Beach."

He had no more than entered the parlor than the telephone was ringing. His older daughter Rae Regan, forty-three, long married to a Douglas Aircraft Company executive was on the line. She said, "Daddy! I'm furious with you. Helen Simpson called to tell me mother was in a coma. She said a Chinese quack had put her into it. How could you let something like that happen? Did that nutty Englishman you pal around with drag that oriental shrink out of the woodwork? It sounds exactly like something he would do. He's weird, Daddy. I mean weird, weird, weird! Where is Dr. Max?"

"Rae, sugar, I'm not going to get into this with you over the telephone," O'Reith answered her patiently. "Come out here, I'll tell you the entire story."

"I'll be there for cocktails," Rae Regan said angrily.

"Bring your brother too so I won't have to go through this twice," O'Reith said.

"I will if I can find him."

"See you at six, Rae. Don't drive too fast and don't jump to any further conclusions." The commander had spoken. She knew that voice.

That evening over cocktails, O'Reith explained to his three children by Helen that their mother was gravely ill with recurring cancer and that the faith healing of Dr. Kondratieff was a last ditch effort to cure her. He added, "Your mother didn't want you to know. She didn't want you to worry. She has always let you kids follow your stars. Your mother treasures her privacy so I didn't tell you."

Rae Regan turned to her younger sister, Helen Simpson and asked, "How did you find out?"

"I called from downtown and Alice answered. She said mother was resting. So I called Dr. Max. He was evasive. So I drove home and saw Dr. Kondratieff in the parlor. He was taking turns with Dr. Max looking after mother. Then Daddy-Cool told me what had happened to her. Needless to say I was in shock. I had no idea she had been ill with it some years back. To discover she was being treated for a relapse floored me."

"Daddy, this all your fault," Rae Regan repeated.

O'Reith said, "You kids can forget the recriminations. Your mother and I don't need any advice from you on anything. Anything! Have you got that? Now, it would be nice if you went in to see your mother for a few minutes. You can touch her and hold her hand and even if she does not respond, she will be aware of your presence. Max is fully confident that she will soon come around. He is in consultation with psychiatric experts. It is rarely a permanent condition. As for Dr. Kondratieff, his treatments seemed to have helped your mother. All of us, including your mother, were aware of the risks."

Chastened, the three offspring finished their drinks and filed up the stairs to their mother's bedroom. O'Reith caned his way, behind them. Helen Simpson in the rear looked back into her father's face as they climbed the stairs. He glared at her mercilessly. She shivered. O'Reith sensed her distress, smiled at her. She stopped. He caught up with her on the next step and she took his hand.

During this period of crisis, O'Reith slept with Maxine. Up early he would arrive at Long Beach about the time Helen awoke. After a chat with Parkinson, O'Reith went to Culver City to see McDonough about the motion picture. Then to his office. He lunched at the company dining room with Cook who brought him up to date. The afternoons he spent with Maxine, the cocktail hour at Long Beach. He liked to get Ridley's take on Helen's condition. Then it was back to the Fullerton Building for dinner with Maxine.

Nixon held his press conference on November 16 bringing out new wrinkles of the Nixon-Brezhnev Doctrine for nuclear restraint stressing how important it was for the nation that he remains at his post 24 hours a day. Next day, a Saturday, he gave a major Middle East speech from the White House. He castigated Saudi Arabia and the other Arab states for the oil embargo. He said that for all Americans now, the focus was on energy conservation in the face of rapidly increasing gasoline prices. He urged the people to begin car-pooling, turn down thermostats and wear heavier clothing when the weather turned cold. He suggested that many New Englanders consider moving to Florida, south Texas, Arizona or southern California. He announced the formation of a new bureaucracy; the Federal Energy Office and he appointed a functionary named John Sawhill to run it. He said that rationing was just around the corner and even as he spoke, the printing presses were grinding out gasoline coupons. Then he announced that trouble was brewing in Central America. The CIA had discovered Cuban plots against American interests in Honduras and El Salvador. He said that the Department of Defense was working closely with the friendly government of the *Greater Central American Co-prosperity Sphere* headed up by the Guatemalan patriot, Colonel Marcos Pérez Jiménez. The U.S. was preparing to send the First Army Group down to reinforce our great, steadfast ally. It was a stirring speech and O'Reith listened to it intently.

It was a rainy day in December and he was not in the mood for a drive to Long Beach. Helen's condition was unchanged. Having a cocktail with Maxine when the telephone rang, he picked up and it was Haig who asked, "Clive, how are you holding up? How's Helen?"

"I'm OK Al, for a broken down old driller. Helen is still under the weather a bit. How's a boy?"

"Not too good, Clive," Haig said in a raspy, worried voice. "That committee is banging war drums, still after the POTUS to cough up those tapes. The nuclear thing with Brezhnev isn't slowing them down much. Nobody is worried about Central America like they should be. I think it is keeno for RMN. I'm ready to spring the *sphere* on him."

"It is your call Al," O'Reith began, "If he goes for it, let me know immediately. As you know, Carlos Andres Pérez was just elected president of Venezuela. The Colonel hates his guts. I've told him many times that if he tried a *golpe de estado* in Caracas, I'd put out his excommunication order. We still have oil concessions on the lake and I didn't want any trouble over that. But Pérez is bad news. He wants to confiscate our property. If we give the Colonel a go signal, it is a reversal of our Company policy which, no doubt, the Colonel will accept. But at the same time, he will have to scamper to get his act together. Those cats in Caracas are sure as hell not going to invite him back. He'll have to go back loaded for bear. That means U.S. troops."

"OK. That we can do. Will a division do the trick?"

"That should be enough. I'll see George in the morning. He may be able to get a brigade of Limeys to stand in reserve just in case a fuse blows somewhere. He is a master arm-twister of Whitehall types. When he's thinking about oil, he has good, innovative ideas. His imagination is something to behold."

"Can you catch a plane to DC after you've talked to him?" Haig pressed. "This thing is kind of hot. I'm at my wit's end and the POTUS wants the rabbit jerked out of the hat ears and all immediately."

"The only rabbit left is the *sphere.* If George thinks it is OK, I'll call the Colonel and advise him of a potential détente; that a return to Miraflores is in the cards. I'll let you know tomorrow. If we are all on the same wavelength, George and I will fly east. You can spring it on the POTUS alone or we can all go into the oval office together and strap it on him. That OK?"

"Clive, you're a pal."

"Once we've reviewed Nixon's situation, can we get into the FUSAG thing?"

"Of course. We requested troops a few days back. I'll call the Secretary of Defense and pry him loose from his binoculars. Things are happening so fast we're going to have to juggle several balls. Clive, I appreciate your letting me in on your company policy. I know that is tight stuff."

O'Reith said, "See you tomorrow afternoon, Al. Ta-ta." His Rolex said it was six pm. McDonough would be leaving the studio. He said to Maxine, "Haig seemed close to panic. I think I'll call Carolyn."

"Clive, you are certainly on edge these days," Maxine chided. "There really is almost nothing you can do to solve these problems."

"I would if I could. Everything is going wrong at the same time." He picked up the telephone and dialed Cook's number. When she answered, he said, "Carolyn, I just got off the phone with Haig. He's upset because that committee still has the heat on Nixon. Ask George to call me when he gets in."

"OK. I will. See you tomorrow."

O'Reith was nervously rattling the ice cubes in his empty glass when McDonough called.

"Carolyn said you were on edge, Clive. What's the word?"

"Did you have a good day, George?" O'Reith asked.

"Things went swimmingly. If it keeps going at this pace, we'll have the *Miter* in the cans by mid-January."

"That's a bit of a slip, isn't it George?"

"We could have a delay. Cherry Cokeland is in jail?"

"Oh no!" O'Reith cried out. "What for."

"The cops at Echo Park caught her smoking a joint of marijuana."

"Stan into it?"

"Yes, he says he'll have her back on the set tomorrow. There will be a court appearance in a couple of weeks. We'll shoot around her inasmuch as she won't be released until around noon."

"George, Haig is about to panic. Nixon is slipping further into the quicksand. Al is ready to spring the *sphere* on him. Time to brief the Caudillo."

"What if you do and then it doesn't happen?" McDonough asked.

"I'll put it to him strong. Give him time to think how he will pull it off. I'll tell him to keep tight on it. We've got to do that, George."

"Put that way, I agree." McDonough said. "But no jumping the gun."

"Haig asked me to fly to DC for a chat. Be nice if you came along. Alice is with Helen. Ask Aztec Sam to take your place for a couple of days."

"OK, I'll do that. When do we leave?

"I'll call the Colonel right now. I want to see Helen in the morning and then go over things with Carolyn. Let's leave around noon."

"Very well. I'll see you at the airport unless I hear otherwise."

Sitting in the first class cabin on the TWA 707 headed for Washington, DC, O'Reith asked, "George, aside from the *sphere,* do you see any way to head off this disaster looming over Nixon?"

"The only thing that could save him would be a national emergency."

"Like an attack with nuclear weapons?"

"Something of that order."

"Christ, George, he's in negotiation with Brezhnev to end that possibility. Who else could drop an atom bomb on us?"

"The Republic of South Africa has the capability. A satellite photo revealed something that looked like a big blast in the Indian Ocean south of Cape Town. And who knows, Honduras may have the bomb as well."

"Whose satellite?" O'Reith asked.

"Israeli intelligence. They always keep London in the loop. I got the news a few days back. Meant to tell you. Forgot."

"That isn't much help," O'Reith said unhappily. "Fat chance the South Africans would attack us. Nixon would be laughed out of town if he declared a national emergency over Honduras."

McDonough said. "So where does that leave us? Nixon has already axed off all of the likely goats. Haldeman. Ehrlichman. Richardson. Kissinger is the only one still around powerful enough to be a burnt offering. What if it turned out that he was a rat, that he had leaked vital information to the Democratic Party, information related to the Nixon-Brezhnev Doctrine? What if the plumbers that broke into Democratic National Headquarters were there to retrieve state secrets? What if Kissinger went on TV with tears in his eyes saying he had betrayed the confidence of the POTUS and it was his entire fault?"

"High drama, but would he do it?" O'Reith asked.

"We would have to convince him it was in the national interest."

O'Reith snorted. "George, you know better than that."

McDonough looked at his wristwatch. "Well," he sighed. "We have three hours to come up with something that will work."

In the Watergate Hotel on the top floor in a corner suite, O'Reith was registered as 'Colonel Jack Drake'. Haig, with a wide grin and Kissinger with a suspicious frown appeared at the door on the dot of six, holding their rubber face-masks in their hands. O'Reith began mixing drinks. Kissinger, obviously in a pet, scowled at McDonough. Haig, cheerful and upbeat, told a World War II short-arm inspection joke as O'Reith handed round the martinis. Since it involved circumcision, Kissinger was not amused. After a long restorative swig of gin, Haig began, "Well fellows the chief is getting further and further behind the eight ball. If we don't do something he's headed for the corner pocket with the cue ball bumping his bottom. Sure as hell. How do we get him out?"

O'Reith, feeling mischievous replied, "George has a scheme that involves Henry here falling on his sword. Like to hear the details?"

Haig guffawed.

Kissinger growled, his mouth moving up and down with no words coming out. Finally he managed to say gruffly, "I am not going to commit political suicide."

"Not even for the chief?" Haig asked playfully, sipping his drink.

"Just kidding, Henry," O'Reith said. "On the plane I mentioned to George that Nixon had already axed off all potential fall guys. You were the only one of any substance left. You should take that as a compliment to your luminosity. George suggested you might confess to treason."

"Very funny, I'm sure," Kissinger responded dourly. But O'Reith thought that the portly German Jew was warming up a bit."

McDonough said, "Henry while you think of a scheme to save the chief, I will volunteer to lead our little group in prayer. What do you think about that?"

"We do not need a prayer. We need a miracle."

O'Reith said, "We could do a variation on a Kissinger suicide. Why couldn't Charles Colson fall on his sword?"

Haig guffawed again, slapped his knee. He said, "Colson doesn't have a sword. All he has is a pen knife."

"We could bump him up to a Deputy Secretary or something like that," O'Reith suggested. "Then when he was highly visible, call him in and tell him he had to make the supreme political sacrifice."

Kissinger finally emitted a faint, fleeting smile. He said in his heavy voice, "First of all, there's no time. Second, Colson would sing like a canary? Then where would we be?"

Haig made a face. He said, "Henry's right." He was pleased that Kissinger was getting into the spirit of it.

"O'Reith said, "Fellows, we have to come up with a national emergency that the public can accept as real."

"Such as?" Kissinger probed.

"How about a general uprising of all the Central American states south of the *sphere*? A grand conspiracy, bigger and more menacing than just Honduras and El Salvador. This would be a cabal going all the way down to the Panama Canal. Fidel Castro would be behind it with help from China."

Kissinger in a nervous sweat, growled, "Gentlemen, we spent all of that effort to establish a détente with China. The president visited Beijing. Everything now is OK between China and the U.S. Does all of that fine diplomatic work go up in smoke?"

"Henry, will diplomatic smoke help the POTUS escape the committee?" Haig asked.

"Why don't we put it to Nixon and see if he'll go for it?" O'Reith said.

"Let's leave China out of it," Kissinger suggested.

"It loses some of its urgency that way," Haig said. "Castro is not much of a threat without a foreign power behind him. It's difficult for

Joe Doaks to get worked up about a banana republic revolt. Nobody really thinks the canal is in danger."

"Why not India," O'Reith suggested. "They have nuclear weapons and are left-leaning. The average Indian with his turban and kooky get-up is a natural suspect. One of them could be guilty of the highest of crimes."

"And the Chinese hate them," McDonough added.

"That's a plus all right," Haig agreed. He looked over to Kissinger. "We go for that Henry?"

"I don't like it. Seems like a charade. Phony as all get out," Kissinger sighed. Then shrugging, a frown of resignation on his jowly face, he continued, "Together, we present it to the Chief," "I don't want to be the solitary author of this folly."

"It is not folly, Your Excellency," O'Reith said. "We have to put those rinky-dink republics down before we can drill."

"Could you not negotiate with them for oil and gas rights?" Kissinger asked.

Trying to conceal his exasperation, O'Reith carefully explained that negotiation would result in an expensive profit-sharing contract. Once the caudillo was in control, the costs of exploration would be insignificant. He made his final point. "Your Excellency, with all of those remaining mini-states down, the U.S. would exert complete hegemony over all of Central America. Only the rump Mexican Republic would remain. It is an American diplomat's wildest dream come true. And RMN is the hero."

Kissinger snorted.

Haig said, "I like it better every time we expand on it."

"So we go for it?" O'Reith asked.

"POTUS is in Key Biscayne," Haig said. "I'll call him later today. We'll try for a meeting this week. Do we still have the *sphere* as a fall-back position?"

"The Colonel is ready to go," O'Reith said.

"May I ask what is the *sphere* fall-back? Kissinger asked, suspiciously.

"I'll explain it you later, Henry. It is sensitive as mortal sin," Haig said.

"Al, we leave matters in your capable hands," O'Reith said. "George and I will get back to our motion picture project."

Haig brightened, saying, "Clive, I'm glad you brought that up. I read in *Variety* that George was completing Helen's film. Is she still ailing?"

"Yeah, Al. Keep this tight. She's under treatment for a recurring tumor. George volunteered to pinch-hit as the director until she is back up to par."

"You're the star of it are you not, George?" Haig asked, grinning.

"Eve Arden and I share the honors of being above the title," McDonough said modestly.

"I understand it is a remake of *The Shoes of the Fisherman*," Haig said. I hope it has a bit more pizzazz. The original; with Anthony Quinn was a bit heavy-handed. He put a messianic spin on it."

"This version is indeed more spirited," McDonough explained. "The 'fisherman' in this version is none other than Boris Godunov. After becoming Tsar of all the Russias, he aspires to become the Pope in Rome as well. *The White Satin Miter* is the story of his march from Moscow to Rome. It culminates with his being crowned as Pope and the recital of his first encyclical called *Casti connubii II*."

"I remember that encyclical," Kissinger said. A modern one. Isn't that anachronistic?"

"That's Hollywood for you Henry," McDonough said. "We all have to realize that motion pictures are a blend of fact and phantasy. Henry, you are correct. *Casti connubii* dates back to 1930 and it was not a success. Pope Paul VI put out *Humanae vitae* in 1967 and it too, failed. In his infinite wisdom, he is trying to overcome the misfortunes of both of these encyclicals by the promulgation of *Casti connubii II* which is just now hitting its stride. Having it recited in the movie is a device to give it greater circulation. The average movie-goer cannot distinguish the 15th from the 20th Century."

"I read *CC-2*," Kissinger said. "That political angle in its second paragraph caught my attention. Does the Pope intend to launch a diplomatic initiative in the Near East? If so, he is running a bit late."

"Actually, Henry, that was Clive's idea," McDonough explained. "Our company is presently running a million barrels a day of Asmari crude out of the Poghdar Field in Iran."

"I don't buy the notion that Poghdar is in Iran," Kissinger challenged. Even Jews can read maps. No matter what the Shah says, I say Poghdar is in Afghanistan."

"Keep that under your hat?" O'Reith said. "In our contract with Standard Oil the bill of lading for that crude stream reads Khuzestan, South Persia. We definitely don't want the State Department involved."

"It is proper that we be concerned by that bit of deception," Kissinger said haughtily.

"Why don't we keep cool on that one, Henry," Haig suggested. "After all, job one is to get RMN off the hook. We're among friends. Let's not rock a boat that has us in it."

"Good suggestion," McDonough agreed.

Kissinger grumped, fell silent, and looked surly.

"Before we adjourn George," Haig asked. "If it is not asking too much, could you shoehorn me into the movie in a cameo role? I've always wanted to appear on the silver screen. I'd be ever so appreciative."

"It will subtract from your authority as the president's Chief of staff," Kissinger objected morosely. His features were all gloom.

"Nonsense," Haig said. "The POTUS recognizes the need for his men to enjoy a bit of harmless frivolity."

"Remember the movie is about Boris Godunov, a Russian," Kissinger pointed out. "Our president is working on the Nixon-Brezhnev Doctrine. We don't want to be involved in anything that could be construed as offensive."

"Brezhnev could care less about the tsars, especially one of Godunov's ilk," Haig replied airily. Turning to McDonough, he asked, "How about it?"

"You could appear in the side-scenes where a pretty young woman named Cherry Cokeland is trying to buy a second hand Cadillac." McDonough said.

"What kind of a chick is this Cherry Cokeland?" Haig asked. "Nice looking?"

"Definitely pin-up material," O'Reith said.

Kissinger said, "Al, you're going to get yourself into the frog pond."

"Don't be silly, Henry."

"You'd be the official State of California emissions inspector," McDonough suggested. "With a snappy green and blue uniform and a yellow cap with a black plastic brim and a little doctor's kit with the bottles of chemicals and pieces of litmus paper that you attach to the exhaust pipe with a clothespin. You hang around the used car lot run by a Mexican named Aztec Sam. He's after you to get lost. Would that do?"

"Perfect!" Haig exclaimed. "May I appear in the Boris Godunov movie too?"

"Surely not, Al," Kissinger lamented. "Think of your dignity."

O'Reith said tersely, "Al, if you want to be in both movies George will do the necessary."

Haig said, "I'll ride with you guys back to National. We can talk about it."

As soon as the three men were in the back seat of his limousine, on the way to the airport, Haig said, "Well I didn't want Henry to know but I sprung the *sphere* on the POTUS. I told him that it was our last resort."

"What did he say?" O'Reith asked.

"He was staggered but slowly, very slowly, he began to see it would work. He likes it."

"When do we tell Kissinger about it?" McDonough asked.

"Nixon wants to leave him in the dark until the last minute. We must move a hell of a lot of troops around in a big hurry. Henry would get nervous about that. Can we do it?"

O'Reith said. "Al, get them to Central America, George and I can do the rest."

On the flight back to LA, McDonough said, "Clive, you look worn down. All that talk with Haig and Kissinger get you down?"

"No I'm OK. George. I wish Helen would wake up. It's the last thing I think about at night and the first thing I think about in the morning."

"Clive, I feel partly responsible for this miserable state of affairs. It was I who brought Kondratieff into the act. But beyond moral support all I offer is the power of intercession with our Lord. We can round up Max and Alice and Carolyn. I could lead the group in prayer."

"Good idea," O'Reith agreed. "How about a short session at Culver City tomorrow? Then get together in Long Beach. Cocktails and prayers. George I don't hold you responsible in any way for Helen's condition."

Ridley and the nurse attended a wakeful but mute Helen. At six o'clock, in the parlor with Parkinson and Cook, a pensive O'Reith, waiting for McDonough said, "You know, Helen and I are High Church but we only go for weddings and funerals. The last time Helen and I prayed was in the cathedral at Santiago de Compostela after that crazy pilgrimage. Over 10 years ago. We knew then she was up against it. I suppose the Good Lord was listening. She was cured. At least for quite some while."

"All of my scientific training militates against it," Parkinson said. "However I have come to realize from conversations with psychiatrists that there is something in the human psyche that is beyond medical understanding."

"Well, when prevailing on the Almighty for help," Cook said, "I would never sell George short. If a miracle worker exists, it is he."

A limousine rolled up in front. A dismayed O'Reith watched McDonough arrive with the entire cast of the movie. Eve Arden, Aztec Sam, Lynn Landury, Cherry Cokeland, Susan Shams and Meg Muffin-Driver. Seeing the look in O'Reith's eyes, a visibly worried McDonough said, "They insisted on coming."

O'Reith welcomed them into the house and led them to the parlor. McDonough introduced them to Parkinson. The butler rolled in the drink trolley and began mixing cocktails. For the Pentecostals, all members of the Foursquare Church at the Angelus Temple, he offered Coca Colas or 7-ups. When they had downed their drinks, McDonough suggested they go upstairs to Helen's bedroom for the prayer. Helen lay on her bed, her eyes closed, apparently asleep. Without a word, Cherry Cokeland, Meg Muffin-Driver, Susan Shams, Lynn Landury and Aztec Sam joined hands and formed a chain around the foot of Helen's bed. They began singing the spiritual, *Down in the Valley on my Praying Knees.*

O'Reith was annoyed and was on the verge of stopping the singing. But Parkinson took his hand. Cherry Cokeland took his other hand. McDonough linked hands with Cook and Ridley and the nurse and now they were in a circle around Helen's bed. When the spiritual concluded, McDonough began: "Dear Lord, we are gathered here tonight to pray that Helen O'Reith will awaken and begin to speak to us again." He begged the Lord for help. O'Reith thought that would be the end of it but Meg Muffin-Driver said, "General O'Reith, we are going to pray your wife through this crisis if it takes all night. When we finish, she will have recovered her wits." Then she began speaking in tongues and the other members of the church joined in the unintelligible murmuring. Each one in turn took up the challenge. O'Reith would have liked to disengage himself and go downstairs for another drink but that would be impolite. So he stayed in the chain of praying Pentecostals. Around midnight, when he was out on his feet, worrying that Maxine would be concerned because he had not called, he thought of all the ways he might excuse himself from this marathon of a prayer. Then Helen Simpson appeared in a gold go-go outfit and ballet slippers, her curls tied back in a red ribbon. She inserted herself between Cook and Ridley and slipped her prayer in.

Still O'Reith was the central figure so he continued to hold hands with the members of the chain, summoning inner resources to remain upright although his game leg had long ago gone to sleep. He became aware that Helen Simpson had said a prayer and it was Cook's turn. The praying was coming around. Parkinson would be next and then it would be up to him. He began thinking about what he would say.

Helen suddenly sat up, looked at her husband and asked? "Ace, what are all these people doing in my bedroom?"

Before he could respond, Cherry Cokeland shouted "Hallelujah! Hallelujah!"

Then all of the Angelus Temple members were shouting and they began a trot around the bed of a mystified Helen O'Reith. As Alice Ridley came near she said, "Honey you've been out for a spell. We've been praying you through."

"My word!" Helen said, putting her right hand to her breast. Then she spotted McDonough. She asked, "George, whatever are you doing here? I thought you were living in Rome with Carolyn. And where did you get that silly halo?"

"We're both here with you, Helen," Cook said. "That halo is the McCoy, Don't knock it"

McDonough said, "I've been directing *The White Satin Miter.*"

With a confused Helen watching open-mouthed, hands still linked, the petitioners continued to march. From time to time the Pentecostals would burst into song. They began: *In My Heart There Rings a Melody.*

Seeing Parkinson in the ring of celebrants, Helen realized that she must have been quite ill. As McDonough came around for the second time, she asked, "George, what the hell is *The White Satin Miter*?"

"It's your motion picture Helen," McDonough shouted above the din.

"I never heard of it George," Helen shouted. "One of us is nuts."

"We're all nuts!" O'Reith shouted, borne along by the happy carolers. At least his leg was functioning again. He felt the stinging sensation of returning circulation.

Finally the Pentecostals ran out of steam. The march ended. Each of them hugged Helen and wished her well. Parkinson and Ridley herded them out and down to the parlor. O'Reith took Helen in his arms and tears came to his eyes. "You've been away for some days, baby and it is wonderful to have you back again."

"Where have I been Ace?"

"I'll tell you tomorrow, baby," he answered. "Right now I'm going to take a shower and get in beside you. It's three o'clock in the morning."

Next morning at breakfast he explained that she been treated by Dr. Kondratieff on November 7, had fallen into amnesia and now on the 20th of December, she was back among the conscious.

"Ace I have no recollection whatsoever of that motion picture that George is directing. None."

"Don't you remember the screen test? Don't you remember that you were trying to get Jackie Gleason for the role? George wanted it and you thought he was too old and too fat. You insisted on a screen test. Then you tried to get Rod Steiger to play the part. Only after he declined did you let Alice talk you into giving the part to George."

"Don't remember any of that, Ace? Why was I under treatment?"

"Your breast cancer recurred. You refused radiation therapy and chemotherapy. George knew this faith healer in London. After the fourth treatment you lost your memory. You had had a tough day at Culver City the day before and you and I and Max and Alice had drinks at the regular hour. You had a double martini on the rocks and wet the ice a couple of times. Max thinks your metabolism was partly responsible. Kondratieff thinks you lost your memory because there was something that you wanted to forget."

"Well, I have certainly forgotten a lot of things. What was I doing at Culver City the day before the treatment?"

"Directing that farce of a movie."

"And now George is both the leading man and the director?"

"Alice has helped him a bit," O'Reith said. "My personal opinion is that it will not be a famous flick. We can scrap it since you have no recollection of it."

"Surely I must have a scenario."

"You do. It's in the study. But it has been tinkered with. You may want to see what it looks like. George has kept a work print. You could go out to Culver City and run the dailies through the movieola."

"Well we can't cancel it. Those poor Pentecostals would be out of a job. I owe them a great deal for bringing me around."

"What about getting a good check-up? Max can set it up. Check out the cancer."

"Ace, I feel as if I don't have anything. No aches. No pains. I feel like a slip of a girl again."

"Even so, Max should give you the once over. You should reconsider treatment."

"Never! I have not forgotten the misery of radiation treatment. And I sure as hell have not forgotten that all of my hair fell out." She reached up to feel of her bald head and exclaimed, "Ace! My hair is growing. Come feel of it." Sure enough her head was covered with a fuzz of a color somewhere between blonde and gray. "Remarkable!" O'Reith said.

The telephone was ringing and it was Parkinson. O'Reith said, "Max, Helen is in pretty good shape and hair has started growing on her head. Why don't you come out and have a look?"

"Say a prayer I don't get a speed ticket, Clive."

While Parkinson was giving Helen a physical examination, O'Reith called McDonough at Culver City and told him to finish the movie. Helen had no interest in it inasmuch as she didn't remember anything about it. O'Reith asked when it would be in the cans.

"Looks like mid-January, Clive," McDonough answered. Hal's comedy writer is redoing the final side-scene to include Al Haig. As soon as I see the revised scenario, I'll call him and we'll set up the shooting schedule."

"That sounds good, George. When Parkinson is finished, I'm going to the office and see what's going on around the world. I'll drift out your way after lunch. We can schedule a visit to see the Caudillo."

In the office, his telephone was ringing. It was Al Haig." He answered, "Al how's a boy?"

"OK, Clive yourself?"

"Ticking along on 16 cylinders Al. Helen came out of her sinking spell, a heavy weight lifted."

"That is indeed great news, Clive," Haig responded. "It makes asking another favor much easier."

"What can I do for you, Al?"

"Clive, can you imagine my surprise when I asked Nixon if it would be OK for me to play a cameo role and he requested that he be given one as well."

O'Reith laughed. "That's an easy one, Al. Does he know anything about the picture?"

"I filled him in to the extent that it was about Boris Godunov going down to Rome, getting himself appointed Pope and then sacking the place. He would like to come in as the Doge of Venice."

"I'll tell George, Al. He will fit that in. Could get the chief to read a foreign policy speech that more or less parallels what we're getting ready to do in Central America?"

"Why not? Nixon can emote like the devil when he's in the mood. We've got a fair country-boy speechwriter on the staff. Bill Safire. He's an eloquent SOB. What say we ask him to come up with something? We can frame it in the context that Boris traipsing around Rome upsets the Doge. It can be a warning for him to stay away from Venice."

"Sounds great, Al. I'll pass this along to George and he'll call you on it."

McDonough purred contentedly as O'Reith related to him Nixon's desire to play a role in *The White Satin Miter.* "Clive, if you were here you would see me beaming with delight. I'm beginning to think that we should remove the side-scenes and make them into a separate movie. That will allow us to expand on the original scenario and give Nixon a role with some real flesh and bones. What do you think of that?"

"Good idea," O'Reith said. "I was never in favor of those side-scenes. That was something you and Alice hatched out and Helen, in her distress, went along with it. I doubt if she would have agreed to that if she'd been lucid."

"No need to be judgmental, Clive," McDonough chided him. "It seemed like a good idea at the time."

"George you said some time back you were having trouble with Cherry Cokeland. She got caught smoking marijuana. Is that resolved?"

"Yes. We agreed to a misdemeanor plea with no jail time and paid a $50 fine."

"Good. OK, George, let me take a look at the lines for Nixon to read."

"Very well. This may cause us to run beyond the middle of January."

"I suppose it can't be helped."

"Clive, in that era, people who came to see the Pope kissed his foot as a sign of devotion. We'll have to ask Nixon if he will agree to do that if we wish to preserve historical accuracy."

"I'll put it to Haig. Just a guess but I say Nixon won't go for it. Politically damaging. Maybe Kissinger could come on ahead of him as his High Functionary and perform that act. What do you say?"

"Not in the ancient protocol but who would know?"

"That's what I say," O'Reith muttered. "Who the hell would know? Who the hell would give a damn?"

Chapter VI

FUSAG

In the first class cabin of a Pan American DC-8 on final approach for a landing at Aurora Airport, O'Reith, through low clouds, got a glimpse of the miniature Eiffel Tour. He genuinely missed McDonough. Bright, witty, insightful, always with a new idea about international politics and an intuition about forthcoming intrigue, he lightened up his business life. The Colonel's brand new Chrysler New Yorker that Nixon had sent down to him would be there to meet him. He would bypass all immigration and customs formalities. Since he was wearing a .45 Colt automatic in a shoulder holster and had a 7.25 mm 'society' Mauser strapped to his right leg, that simplified matters. He felt a twinge of regret that he would not be staying at the *El Camino Real* Hotel whose bartenders were perfect dry martini specialists. But he would have to stay at the *Palacio Nacional.* No getting around that or the compulsory, gnat infested, game of golf.

O'Reith, although he missed McDonough, was quite capable of dealing with the Colonel. After all, he had known him for two decades, had negotiated any number of oil and gas concessions with him. The Colonel would lay behind the log on Honduras and El Salvador. His long suit was secret police work, not revolutionary war. But it was inevitable if he wanted to keep his job. O'Reith was here to tell him the date of the invasion and the size of FUSAG. Haig had never come clean with him on that point. But no need for the Colonel to know that. He would tell him that it was The First United States Army Group. That implied at a minimum, four corps, enough to subjugate not only the isthmian states but all of South America.

After a twenty-minute drive down *Avenida de la Reforma*, the Nile green Chrysler crunched along the gravel path between the palace and a series of parterres of showy tropical flowers. Long arrays of reds, violets, blues and yellow blossoms. Avocado trees, heavy with fruit. The garden beckoned. When the big car stopped at a side portico, the Colonel, grinning broadly, asked, “How do you like the limousine Mr. Nixon sent me? I assume he wants something in return.”

“Nice smooth ride. A tangible demonstration of his friendship for you,” O’Reith replied. “Pity we can’t loll around in the garden.”

Climbing to the second floor, the Colonel asked, “How is *Pecos Lil*? Last time you were here she was under the weather. I trust she is better now?”

“Yes indeed, Colonel Jiminéz, she is much improved I’m glad to say. She would have come along but she is recovering from treatment and needs her rest.”

“I can well understand that.”

Soon they were seated in the luxurious second floor office. “The American newspapers are not being kind to President Nixon,” the Colonel said. “That congressional committee is pressing his testicles.”

“They are annoyed with him all right,” O’Reith agreed. “His recent foreign policy speeches were designed to tell the American people how important he is. It is a way of asking them to write their congressmen to call the dogs off. But none of that is going to work. That is why we are all agreed that you should return to Miraflores. Haig has promised an armored division. Can you make it with that?”

“But of course. How does this fit in with Honduras?”

“Haig said he would send us a complete army group. We’ll split off the armored division, send it to La Guaira. You can meet it there and march on Caracas. George and I will take care of Honduras. If the Committee forces Nixon out, we’ll fly him to Guatemala City and install him as president.”

“Why doesn’t Nixon round up those committee members and have them shot?”

O'Reith laughed. "He would if he could. But he'd really be in trouble then."

"He could send them down here on an investigation," the Colonel continued. "I would be more than happy to make them disappear."

O'Reith laughed again. "That is an unreasonable expectation. Those guys know we're stirring something up. Should he send them down for a look-see, they would dope it out that they would be liquidated and decline the invitation."

"Is there a possibility of a *golpe de estado* in the United States?"

"Impeachment is the more likely consequence. We are trying to circumvent that with FUSAG. In his next foreign policy address, Nixon will accuse the left-leaning Indians of stirring up trouble in Central America. Most Americans don't know anything about them and will readily accept them as enemies of democracy. They will associate them with the native Americans that we had to exterminate in the 18th and 19th Centuries."

"I have often wondered why you Yanks felt it necessary to exterminate the red men and replace them with blacks. We kept ours. It is true that Cortéz axed off a few Incas. And there were the other odd atrocities. But in the main, the native South and Central American indigenes are flourishing."

"To your great distress," O'Reith retorted.

"Heh heh," the Colonel said. "You have me there, sir."

"Back to India," O'Reith said.

"They will deny involvement, surely".

"It will be too late. The troops will be here. We will cross the frontier with a force of such overpowering strength that it will all be over before the Security Council of the UN can debate it. By the time they do, and issue some vague resolution, we'll be in there drilling up the best prospects."

"I sincerely hope it works out like that. When do we expect to start?"

"Middle of February. I'll confirm that to you once Haig sets a date certain for the arrival of troops."

The Colonel put on his horn-rimmed reading glasses, pulled a large National Geographic World Atlas from a shelf behind his desk, winked and said, "Let's take a look at the theater of war.

O'Reith came around to look over his shoulder. The Colonel flipped the pages until he found Central America. With a pudgy forefinger he pointed to Honduras. "See those three villages on the Caribbean, Ceiba, Trujillo, and Limon? Land infantry at the first two, say a division at each place. Then, at Limon, land the armored divisions, say two or three. At Puerto Cortés, a port town just across the line from Guatemala, you can set up your headquarters. Now looking at the Pacific side, *Golfo de Fonseca* is clearly the ideal landing site. You can land a division at La Union and another at San Miguel. Follow the river valley to San Salvador. Once the inconsequential Salvadorian Army is liquidated, then a thrust across the line to Tegucigalpa would finish that campaign. With both countries down, you could conquer Nicaragua."

"You speak as if it were I who will command these forces," O'Reith said.

"Who else could it be?" the Colonel asked. "You are a five star general. The forces involved are great. You think the Government of the United States will entrust an army group to an untested commander?"

The two men looked at each other in silence. After some long minutes, the boy came with coffee and mineral water. O'Reith, his hand to his cheek, slowly walked around the Colonel's desk and returned to his chair. He eased himself into it and sat contemplatively. As the boy poured the coffee, strong, black and aromatic, O'Reith said, "I had not looked at it in that light."

"It must be you," the Colonel said. "It must be you."

O'Reith sighed. "I get the heebie-jeebies just thinking about it."

"You'll be OK once the cannon flash."

"Haig pressed me to come up with an acceptable commander," O'Reith mused. I had planned on using David Penrose, the artillery officer during the abortive attack on Honduras."

"I remember him, but he is too junior for this assignment. You can still use him, of course. Artillery."

"Colonel Jiménez, I saw those beautiful flowers growing in the garden as the car came up. Let's go for a stroll. We can talk as we watch the birds and the butterflies."

"All right and golf tomorrow?"

"Yes. I look forward to that. We'll have to ride. My leg is not up to walking."

"I never walk anyway. It shall be as you prefer."

In the garden they took in the fine tropical flowers, winning smiles of approval from the head gardener. O'Reith pointed out a ruby-throated hummingbird, his beak thrust deeply into a honeysuckle blossom on the garden wall. Soon they spotted several varieties of hummingbirds, all gathering nectar. Butterflies flitted among the blooms; yellow-winged ones in profusion but here and there a Monarch in this floral largesse. The Colonel asked, "What is Sir George doing these days?"

"When *Pecos Lil* was sick, she asked him to direct as well as co-star in the movie she was making. He is still at that but it should be wrapped up shortly. I need his help when we get started down here."

"He's the man for it," the Colonel agreed. "General O'Reith is there a chance that I could play a small role in the film that Sir George is making? You said that President Nixon would appear as the Doge of Venice. I could be in his entourage. Or alternately I could be one of the Borgias. Cesare perhaps. You know that family originated in Spain. The name was Borja. In Italy it took the new spelling."

"The Borgias don't have a great historical reputation," O'Reith noted

"That doesn't matter," the Colonel replied. "Only scholars know that they were masters of the poisonous arts."

"I'll take it up with Sir George," O'Reith said. "When he schedules Nixon, you can come up too."

After 18 holes the next day, O'Reith gave the Colonel further detail on their plans, then departed after lunch. Arriving in Los Angeles late, O'Reith went directly to the Fullerton Building to cuddle up with Maxine. Early next morning he was on his way to Long Beach. Helen, in a yellow satin housecoat and matching mules, was having a bowl of oatmeal and toast. Mills had not yet arrived. "You look good without makeup, baby," O'Reith began. "The Caudillo sends regards to his dear *Pecos Lil*."

"How sweet," Helen replied sincerely. "Did you tell him about my adventures?"

"Just that you'd had a sinking spell but were on the mend. What does Max say?"

"Clean bill of health. Tumor has disappeared. Lymph glands clicking along OK. No swelling. My hair is growing out day by day. I was miraculously cured by those Pentecostals."

"Did you find time to read the scenario for *White Satin Miter*?"

"I did. Absolutely no recall. In Culver City yesterday George showed me the file with my notes and interviews and records of his screen test. I drew a blank."

"Did George tell you that both Haig and Nixon cadged out cameo roles?"

She laughed. "No. But why would I care? They are so vain."

"Caudillo hit me up for a part."

"What did you tell him?"

"I told him I would put it to George. The Colonel thinks he would make a neat Cesare Borgia. I like the idea of seeing him act alongside Nixon."

"I like it too," Helen agreed.

"So if you're OK, I'll visit George at the studio. When I know what he has lined up, I'll call Haig. Nixon will make a major foreign policy address from San Clemente, a convenient time to put him in the movie."

"By the way, George is having a problem with the final side-scene."

"Yeah?"

"That guy Aztec Sam is in the slammer on a hot check charge. Seems they also want him back in Corpus Christi, Texas for something. George cannot do the climactic finale without him."

"Stan on the case?"

"Not yet. I asked Jerry Geissler to get him sprung. Haven't heard back. If it were not for the Texas charge, he could be out on bail."

"Baby I'm on my way to Culver City."

"George, where do we stand?" O'Reith asked as he entered the director/actor's dressing room.

"Problem with Aztec Sam."

"Yeah, Helen told me yesterday. What did you think of her appearance?"

"A different woman."

"Yeah that's what I thought too. A great relief for me. Any word from Haig?"

"They arrive San Clemente on March 1st. Nixon, Kissinger, Rogers, Colson, Stans and a guy called Boniface Milhous Latrobe. They call him 'Heavy'."

"Milhous? Must be kinfolk. Wonder what he does?"

"Haig said he would get into it with you. He's expecting a call."

"I'll call him in a bit. Are we scheduled for shooting?"

"Yes. When they are settled in, Haig will invite us down. Officially we visit the POTUS to discuss the Arab oil embargo. During that meeting, I will give him his lines. From San Clemente that night, they helicopter to Culver City. We film them next morning. They'll go back to San Clemente and leave for Washington. That keeps the newspapers out of it."

"George, the Colonel wants to be in the movie too, as Cesare Borgia," O'Reith explained. "I told him it was OK if you agreed. Helen giggled when I mentioned it. She doesn't give a damn one way or the other."

McDonough rolled his lemon-colored eyes" Another anachronism. Cesare comes to the historical stage earlier than Boris Godunov."

"What difference does it make?"

McDonough shrugged. "Considering our audience out there, none really."

"OK, I'll tell him to plan on early March. You'll write some lines for him?"

"I'll think of something," McDonough said.

It was March 8, 1974. O'Reith had just hung up after talking to Haig in San Clemente. He dialed McDonough. "George, Al wants us to drive down this afternoon for cocktails with Nixon and party. You and I, Nixon, Kissinger, Haig of course, and that Latrobe guy. Can you get away around three o'clock? It's about an hour's drive. If we leave at three we'll arrive in time to freshen up and maybe Haig will brief us on what to expect."

"Be waiting for you to pick me up," McDonough replied.

Driving south, McDonough asked, "Haig tell you anything about Latrobe?"

"Ex army NCO. Quartermaster Corps. Nixon wants him to be a part of FUSAG. I suspect he is a rat man. He'll be the guy who tells them what we're doing."

All of the government men were dressed in dark suits, white shirts and navy blue ties. O'Reith was in his signature midnight blue tuxedo. McDonough was in white linen with perforated white oxfords. His huge, over-stuffed briefcase was on the floor in front of him and the butt of his .44 Webley-Fosberry protruded slightly from one corner attracting the attention of the secret service men. They were in Kissinger's apartment with a view of the Pacific. Stars twinkled in the sky. Here and there, on the water, yacht lights winked on and off. A T-man with a Police Positive .38 in a shoulder holster mixed the drinks. No one spoke. Nixon appeared grim, tight-lipped. Electric tension in the air. Nixon, a dry martini man, was served first. McDonough, a scotch and soda man took his drink tentatively, sniffed it suspiciously. O'Reith was third. He rattled the ice cubes waiting for the others to be served. When everyone had a drink in his hand, Nixon said, "Father George, would you kindly lead us in prayer?"

McDonough set his drink down, removed his breviary from his briefcase, found a prayer he had scribbled out years ago during the war.

He began:

> "O Lord, your humble servant George P. McDonough is here gathered in these parlous times with our valiant leader President Richard Milhous Nixon and his entourage. We seek thy divine protection against the evil winds blowing in our direction from the venomous House Judiciary Committee. Also, O Lord, we are here met to plan a great military undertaking to bring freedom and justice to the poor, oppressed people of Honduras, El Salvador and points south. We ask thee to bless this saintly crusade and bring victory to our gallant Supreme Commander President Richard Milhous Nixon."

Kissinger squirmed and cringed but sat up straight when the halo appeared and began to gleam brightly while McDonough recited the prayer. When McDonough closed his breviary, Nixon said, "Father George, that short, snappy prayer was just what the doctor ordered. I liked it and thank you for it. As a small token of appreciation I would like for you and General O'Reith to accept these autographed brand new $15 bills that, as you will note, have my picture on them. It is, in my opinion, a good likeness. These bills will go into general circulation next week. I have always thought that we needed a $15 bill, a bridge between the ten and the twenty. When I was a California Congressman, I was always finding $20s in my coat pocket. Then, they were large bills. It was a bother to change them. So the $15 fills that niche. What do you think of them?"

"This is a signal honor, Mr. President," McDonough said.

"Look at the back," Nixon continued enthusiastically. "See that picture of the lunar landing? That's Neil Armstrong and Buzz Aldrin in those space suits. See the little American Flag beside them? It is specially made, stiff, so you can see the Stars and Stripes. It was a great patriotic moment and marks the high point of my first term."

"Well it is a remarkable bank note," O'Reith agreed. "Yes sir!" He continued. There will be no worry about inflationary pressure exerted by this note. I will frame it and hang it above the desk in my den. I agree with Sir George. It is a great honor from a distinguished statesman."

"Originally I planned to put a picture of the San Clemente 'White House' on it," Nixon ran on. "I couldn't get Bill Simon to go for it. The lunar landing was probably the best idea he ever had."

"Certainly an event to commemorate," McDonough said, his halo fading.

Nixon basked in the luminous rhetoric, a man feeling good about the world and himself. Turning to O'Reith, he continued. "Clive, that is General O'Reith, I'm not a small talk man. I ignore basketball and it is too early in the season for baseball and the Superbowl is history. I'll get right down to it. My main worry, aside from this Watergate nuisance, is the Arab oil embargo. What do you think?"

"Mr. President, Standard Oil is taking a million barrels a day of our Poghdar light crude oil for the Far Eastern market but it could be delivered to their El Segundo refinery if we were in a crisis. We're running 10 strings in two fields near Poghdar and by the end of March we'll have another hundred thousand barrels a day on the line. Standard will take that stream too. By June 30, we'll double that. So embargo or no, we can count on 1,200,000 bopd. Our Exploration Department is optimistic about those structures in Honduras. Once that state is part of the *Co-prosperity Sphere*, we'll drill. If we go in there in May, we could be running half a million barrels by year end. That will take the sting out of the embargo."

Nixon drank deeply of his double martini. He said, "I like it." Turning to Haig, he continued. "Al, I want FUSAG to be a high priority operation. I'll make a major foreign policy speech on the dire threat of Indian Communists in Central America." He turned to Kissinger and continued, "Henry sit down with Safire and get us a good rousing address worked out. I want to scare the hell out of those pusillanimous democrats in Congress who are trying so desperately to put me down. Got that?"

"Yes, Mr. President," Kissinger rumbled.

Nixon continued, "Fellows, I'd like for you to meet 'Colonel' Boniface Milhous Latrobe. Friends call him 'Heavy'. He a was company supply sergeant for a while in the Quartermaster Corps at Fort Lee, Virginia. He had a bit of a run-in with the Judge Adjutant General's Department over some misplaced Jeep tires. But that is all behind him. I've had a word with the Governor of the State of California and arranged for him to be commissioned as a brigadier general in the National Guard. I was thinking of calling the 48th Division into federal service and making it the command division of FUSAG. General Latrobe would then be the commander in chief. General O'Reith, what do you think of that idea?"

O'Reith sized Latrobe up. He was an even five feet tall, tubular with a square block of a defective-looking, under sized head, He had angular jaws, oyster ears, nervous brown eyes, and a rat trap mouth. He wasn't quite a pinhead but it was a close call. His hat size could be no more than five and a half. Maybe just a five. Ruddy, he was wearing a tan felt hat with feathers in the brim, a shiny brown leather jacket and brown corduroy pants. He had on a black string tie with a brass elk's head clasp and his bronze belt buckle, the size of a demitasse saucer, had the letters BPOE embossed upon it. His shirt was tan with rhinestones around the pockets. Pencils and ballpoint pens filled his shirt pocket protector. Muscular with short arms but big hands, he would weigh in at about 220 pounds stark naked.

"Calling up the guard is a good idea, Mr. President, "O'Reith answered. "I'm sure that Colonel Latrobe is completely qualified to lead FUSAG. However Colonel Jiménez may not support a man who is unknown to him. He has strong feelings about military leadership. We can discuss it with him at Culver City. He will appear with you in the movie."

Before O'Reith stopped talking, Haig was on his feet, looking sternly at Nixon. He said, "Mr. President, We would have trouble with Congress if we appoint Heavy here. That run-in he had with JAG was a general court martial. He did six months in the stockade. We could not keep that secret. Some member of that congressional committee would jump on him like a duck on a June bug."

"Nixon shrugged, glanced over at the silent Latrobe, and said, "Heavy we'll find some other slot for you. Meanwhile, tomorrow buy 500 shares of Standard Oil stock for me."

Haig added, "Clive you may find this a heavy burden, but you are obviously the man of the hour. FUSAG will be a large force. With your record, the Congress will approve your being the Supremo." Haig turned to Nixon, "Mr. President, we want to give FUSAG every chance to succeed. I urge you to appoint Clive."

"Well if you think that is the correct move Al, what can I say?"

Kissinger rose, set his half-finished drink on the cocktail table and growled, "Mr. President, I too support the appointment of General O'Reith. At least he is a known quantity. And he is the architect of the *Greater Central American Co-prosperity Sphere.*" OK then," Nixon agreed. "Clive, you're in the cat bird seat."

"Yes Mr. President," O'Reith said. "You can depend on me."

Nixon turned to McDonough. "Father George, what role do I play in the *White Satin Miter*?"

"Mr. President, you are to play the part of the Doge of Venice, Lodovico Canatella. Boris Godunov has invested Rome with a Cossack army and has usurped the position of Pope. Worried about a possible realignment of political power in northern Italy, you have requested audience with the new Pope. You come to express your loyalty and simultaneously remind him of the great power of Venice. The lines you will read portray a man of presence, one unafraid to confront reality. In fine satin raiment with a glittering gold-hafted sword, you will inject high drama into the film. Boris Godunov has assumed the papal name of Alexander VI, which is exactly the same as the now deposed Borgia Pope that he has unceremoniously imprisoned and whom he will, in due course, execute for treason and blasphemy. Godunov has retained the previous Pope's name to sow confusion among his enemies, which are many. You will remark to him how clever that is. You will also express admiration for the hot-off-of-the-press papal encyclical called *Casti connubii.* Shooting time is estimated at ten minutes, which will include your remarks and the gracious acceptance of your loyalty. Also in that scene will be Colonel Jiménez. He appears as a member of the Borgia family. He has been at odds with his cousin the deceased Pope.

He is glad to see him put down. During the ceremony you will invite him to visit Venice and he will graciously accept." McDonough fished around in the briefcase on the floor and found the Nixon sub-scenario. He handed it to the president as the secret service man poured another round of drinks.

Nixon quickly scanned the document and putting it in his lap, said, "Piece of cake. Father George I look forward to appearing in this religious epic. It will attract a wide audience among Christians of all denominations. You are aware that I am a member of the Society of Friends. One thing is clear from our current political debacle. It is time to return to a regime of moral rearmament. MRA! If we can go forward from this day with an agenda oriented towards doing the work of the Lord then we will be entering an era of ethical leadership which I have always espoused from deep in my heart."

"Those are exactly my sentiments, Mr. President," McDonough echoed.

Kissinger said in his low, rumbling voice, "*Casti connubii* sounds rather familiar. Have I not heard of that?"

"Indeed, Excellency," McDonough responded with a wide grin. Pope Paul VI recently issued *Casti connubii II.* He is hopeful that it will reverse some of the negative publicity that emerged from his first encyclical in 1967. That ill-fated missive was titled *Humanae vitae.* As they say out here in LaLa Land, it bombed."

Nixon's expression suddenly became puzzled. He looked at the cylindrical Latrobe, who was struggling to fit into his sagging easy chair. Then he looked at O'Reith and asked, "What are we going to do with 'Heavy' here?"

"If he is inducted into the California National Guard, then we will utilize his talents as part of that division," O'Reith said.

Haig said, "Mr. President, maybe we had better not push on that one too hard. You know when a National Guard regiment is federalized, that automatically triggers a fitness check of all officers. 'Heavy' could have a reliability problem and because of his middle name, it could be an embarrassment."

Nixon rubbed his chin, leaned over closer to Haig. He said, "Al, I'll leave it to you to do the right thing for him. He's in a bit of a spot and I would like to see him settled in somewhere, preferably in Central America. Actually South America would be OK. Or Asia for that matter. Even Africa."

McDonough said, "Colonel Jiménez has an opening for a quartermaster type in the Guatemala City Armory. Most of the supplies were depleted during the Great War of Consolidation. But there remain some Sherman tanks with corroded mufflers and a few 90mm Long Tom rifles. When the Colonel comes up to take part in the movie, I could have a word with him about Heavy."

"I would be deeply appreciative," Nixon said.

Latrobe's chair picked that moment to give up the ghost. Splinters flying, 'Heavy' Latrobe found himself on the floor. Huffing and pulling, three Secret service men got him unsteadily to his feet."

"That is a $250 dollar chair," Kissinger said with dismay.

Nixon stood, rubbing his hands together. He said, "So we're all set. We remain here until you notify us to come to Culver City." They shook hands all around. Kissinger kicked at the debris from the chair, muttering.

O'Reith and McDonough were back in the limousine headed for Los Angeles.

McDonough said, "Clive, would it not be simpler to buy that House Judiciary Committee off?"

"It may be too late," O'Reith responded sleepily. He was beginning to nod off.

"But it is worth a try," McDonough insisted.

"We would have to be careful," O'Reith said yawning. "Surely Haig thought of that. After all George, Nixon would have thought of that. Should we try it and it goes agley, we could be in the dock. I say forget it. If we can't place Nixon in Guatemala, then that's tough titty. He will not be missed in the White House."

"We discuss it tomorrow when our minds are refreshed," McDonough agreed.

O'Reith dozed until the big limousine pulled up in front of the Fullerton Building. Maxine was in bed, breathing softly. She stirred when he kissed her. O'Reith showered and climbed in beside her. He took her in his arms and was immediately asleep.

Next morning after a visit with Helen, he proceeded to the Culver City studio. McDonough, recalling 'Heavy' Latrobe's tumble, was sitting in his canvas-back chair that had been heavily reinforced with side slats. It no longer creaked under his pressure. Mills was putting the finishing touches on his morning face. In an expansive frame of mind, he said, "Clive after a good sleep with my head clear, I've thought that we could help Nixon by papal intervention. What do you think? Paul could write a letter to the House Judiciary Committee pointing out how important it is to have Nixon firmly on seat because of his enormous burden as keeper of the flame. Good idea?"

"I don't think it is, George. If Nixon were a Roman Catholic it might make sense but he's a Quaker. The Judiciary Committee would resent papal interference. The letter would be released to the press. It would cause a racket. Besides, George, we really don't know for sure how deep his troubles are. Clearly Nixon is worried. What is he worried about? He can deflect almost any threat except that of impeachment. The committee wants to hear what's on his tapes. Nixon needs to get rid of them. If there is incriminating evidence on them, he's up the creek. Let me talk to Haig. Maybe we can find out exactly where he is vulnerable. Meanwhile, keep the Pope out of it. OK?"

"If you say so," McDonough responded.

"George I have the utmost respect for your political intuition. But this one I don't fully understand. Helen and I had a near fatal run-in once with a Congressional House Committee and I don't wish to be drawn into another one. Where do we stand on this great epic movie for which an eager American audience waits with baited breath?"

"We can't finish the side-scenes without Aztec Sam and he is in durance vile down in Texas. We were unable to get him out of the Los Angeles jail because of the Texas charges. Now they have extradited him. I'm trying to figure out a way to end that part of the movie without him. So the side-scenes are on hold while we finish up the *Miter*. We're scheduled to shoot Haig and Nixon and the colonel in ten days. March 24th. Everyone is notified."

"Do we have a work print of the side-scenes?"

"No but we could make one up."

"Do we still plan to remove them and make a separate movie?"

"We should, McDonough agreed. "Those side-scenes lack continuity and interfere with the flow of the *Miter*. Each one is a Cadillac joke with football, golf, and a few Pentecostal hymns thrown in. Their only virtue is that they distract from a rather colorless motion picture. Clive, a bloke named Edward D. Wood, Jr. dropped by the set the other day. He was digging around in the trash barrels, looking for discarded film. I struck up a conversation with him. Turns out he is a professional filmmaker as we are. He just finished up a so-called art movie called *Heads no Tails*. He said his forte is to work old discarded film segments into his pictures in a way that makes sense to the audience. It is similar to using archival material but much cheaper. We chatted for a bit. Wood has quite a repertoire of movies that he's made. It occurred to me that we could turn the entire side-scene movie over to him. Let him complete it with whatever material he has on hand. I told him we were having trouble because one of the main actors was in jail. He said that he would substitute someone else but never let his face be seen. I can't imagine why I didn't think of that. What do you say, Clive? Let's hire him to complete the side-scenes."

"George I know something about him. To begin with, he is a transvestite. He is not a famous movie director. Many of his films are pointless. No plot. His credits are not of high quality. Helen despises him. On the plus side, he is a decorated Marine Corps veteran. As far as anyone knows, he was the only gyrene to hit the beach in the battle of Tarawa with panties and a brassiere under his fatigues."

Apoplectically, McDonough heaved his bulk out of the chair. He sputtered, "My word! That is odd! Well, in his defense, he says he prides himself in staying within budget. Would Helen object? After all the side-scenes are unrelated to the *Miter*."

"That's something," O'Reith agreed. "I mean about him staying within budget. I don't know how Helen would react if she knew we had hired him. I'll ponder that overnight. By the way, I'd like to watch the filming of the scenes with the Colonel and the POTUS. Get a laugh out of it."

"Of course. Why not."

"George, let's connect those side-scenes and run the film strip through Helen's movieola. We'll take a look at it and decide if we want to bring Ed Wood in."

"Good idea. Do we wait until we film Al Haig as the EPA man?"

"Yes, that will be better. If we finish in one day, we can view the entire film on the 25th. I'll be glad to see the end of this. It is getting on my nerves."

The Colonel was already on the set when the presidential party arrived. Nixon greeted him effusively, slapping him on the back and posing with him and a fidgety Kissinger for photos. Nixon gave the puzzled ex-dictator an autographed $15 bill. After a quick makeup job by Mills to lighten up the president's darkling features, shooting commenced. From behind the camera, O'Reith watched the scene unfold. Nixon made his remarkable address which, with the time and location suitably altered to conform to present foreign policy dicta, would be broadcast that night. After filming the scenes for the *White Satin Miter*, McDonough led Al Haig to a second set for the side-scene. Grinning and gesturing, Haig donned his EPA uniform, picked up his fume-sniffer. Mills gave him a last minute dust-off, combed his hair and put his cap on at a rakish angle. As Haig came on the used car lot confidently, a snarling dun-colored mutt tried to chase him off. Haig shouted, "Jesus! Get that goddam stray out of here!"

"Don't pay any attention to that cur," McDonough muttered. "That's Aztec Sam's dog, Growler. He doesn't have any teeth. He lives on oatmeal and chopped marshmallows."

Filming complete, O'Reith invited the POTUS and his entourage to dinner in Long Beach, riding with Nixon in the presidential Lincoln Continental. Cook, at Culver City to watch the filming of the celebrities shared her black Cadillac with McDonough and Kissinger. The Colonel rode with Al Haig in O'Reith's limousine with Cherry Cokeland and Meg Muffin-Driver riding in the jump seats. Helen insisted that the Pentecostals be invited to the dinner. Nixon, even in the absence of secret service men was unconcerned about it.

Originally, O'Reith, Helen and their youngest daughter Helen Simpson occupied the tenth and top floor of the Pacific Condominium Building. Some years later, O'Reith bought the ninth and the eighth floors as well. Now after a fine dinner, Helen, Ridley, Cook and the Pentecostals were assembled in the projection room on the ninth floor to watch a religious movie, sing hymns and carry on.

O'Reith, the Colonel, Nixon, Haig, McDonough, Kissinger and Latrobe were gathered in the oak and leather den on the eighth floor. The butler poured brandy for the POTUS and Haig. Latrobe was a Jack Daniel's man. McDonough and Kissinger were drinking scotch and O'Reith had a club soda on the rocks. He was getting sleepy and was ready for this day to end. Nixon in a leather easy chair, swirling his brandy in a huge snifter, took a long swig and began. "You know politicians are proud people and I suppose I am one of them. I am quite distressed by this bad patch that we, that is that I, am going through. But I refuse to let it get me down. You know I have this dream. Yes, a dream but it is more than that. While I am a public servant, I aspire to a greater dimension. I want my place in the unblinking sun of history. My great hope is to bring the *Greater Central American Co-prosperity Spher*e into the Union as the 51st state." He paused, let a slow smile form fully on his jowled jaw. He turned to look into the Colonel's eyes. "Colonel Jiménez, I have the greatest respect for you. I admire the peace and tranquillity that you have brought to that once unhappy region. The people are prosperous. Crime has almost vanished and your military successes speak for themselves. I salute you as not only a patriot in the highest degree but also for your vast store of wisdom that has guided you through the treacherous political underbrush of Central America. Make no mistake, Colonel. You are the man of the day and even of the hour. You must be proud of all that. Who are we to demean your magnificent glories? Still, although you would be giving up your presidency, and no man wants to give up that which represents the apex of success, if my dream were to be realized, early in my third term, I would nominate you to become Chief of the Central Intelligence Agency."

"I would be honored, Mr. President," the Colonel said, bewildered.

Kissinger said, "Mr. President, are we not faced with a bit of a snag as regards your third term? Isn't there a prohibition against it in the XXIIth Amendment?"

"That is an annoying detail all right," Nixon agreed. "But you can walk on the political waters, Henry. As soon as we get back to the office, I would like for you to open an initiative to repeal that distasteful rider to the constitution."

"Well sir, strictly speaking, it's a matter for the Attorney General, but as a favor to you, Mr. President, I'll attend to it right away," Kissinger said. Nixon was well lubricated from martinis, wine at dinner and now cognac. Kissinger, not wanting the POTUS to become surly, kidded him along.

"What about me, Mr. President?" Haig asked. "In your third term, will there be a place for a simple soldier?"

"Al, you will remain my Chief of Staff, my alter ego. I plan to reward all of my lieutenants handsomely."

McDonough coughed slightly to gain attention. Nixon looked over at him and asked, "Yes, Father George?"

"Mr. President, while this may seem a bit indelicate, had it occurred to you that it might be possible to make well, some kind of an arrangement with the House Judiciary Committee? Clive and I have had some experience dealing with those people. You know how it goes: I will do something for you if you will do something for me."

Nixon's mood changed abruptly. From a happy warrior he was suddenly the pursued weasel. In the easy chair, he hunched down, his face in his hands, his fingers running through his disheveled hair.

He jerked his head up, faced McDonough and with a drawn face, rasped, "Fuck the committee!"

McDonough blushed. He said, "Mr. President I didn't mean to..."

Nixon cut him off. He repeated, "Fuck the goddamned committee. Feed 'em fucking fish. Fuck 'em all and the horses those cocksuckers rode into town on!"

Silence prevailed except for his sobs. Nixon was slumping, almost out of the chair. Tears were running from his eyes. "Those vermin!" he muttered.

McDonough clasped his hands together, and eyes heavenward, began:

> "God, this is Father George and we are asking you to look in on our little gathering here in Long Beach, California. We are asking you O Lord to infuse moral stamina into our beloved commander, Richard Milhous Nixon. We beseech thee, O Lord to hear us and bring our leader back to his placid, serene self."

And so they were sitting silent until Nixon recovered his poise.

Presently the POTUS sat up. He apologized, "Sorry about that outburst gentleman. This is a difficult time for me. Father George I should not have railed at you. Your question merits an answer. I'd like to make peace with them. No doubt about that. We could get the wherewithal, any amount. But of course, such a supplication would smack of subornation. I could not do it. As you are well aware, my principles are of the highest caliber. I could never do anything that might be interpreted as unlawful. Indeed I am a lawyer and a damn fine one too, if I say so myself, especially in prosecutorial matters. Also

I remind you that I once proudly served in those celebrated halls of the House of Representatives and at heart, as you are a simple priest, I am a simple lawmaker. As a practical matter, it is too late in the day. Had we acted early on when it was a fire in a waste paper basket, possibly it could have been contained. Now, alas, it is a roaring wild fire, burning out of control, sad to say." He looked over at O'Reith and continued, "You have had experience with things burning out of control. For that, I value your advice."

"Mr. President," O'Reith responded, "If those tapes were burning out of control on the White House lawn, you would not have to surrender them. Why not pile them up, pour gasoline on them and torch them off? After all, they contain many confidential conversations involving foreign diplomats and heads of state. Some would be embarrassed by their revelations."

"Such a course of action has been recommended to me by a noted Washington lawyer," Nixon responded. "The problem is that I would lose their content which I need to write my presidential memoirs."

"What if they were mysteriously stolen from the oval office?" McDonough suggested.

"Never get them past the Secret Service, damn their snooping eyes," Nixon answered bitterly. "To complete my response to your earlier question, Father George, just as an exploratory effort, I did commission a trusted friend to approach the chairman of the House Judiciary Committee. Not to attempt a bribe because that would have been immoral as well as illegal. His mission was merely to determine if grounds for a quid pro quo existed. Sadly there was none. As a matter of fact, my agent was asked to leave rather rudely. I was upset about it but what can one do?"

McDonough said, "I certainly understand that, Mr. President. Well I am confident that our plans for FUSAG will bear early fruit and all of these threats against your presidency will melt away like a scoop of vanilla ice cream on the Los Angeles sidewalks in the summer sun."

It was the middle of April. McDonough and O'Reith, sitting in the dark in the 9th floor of the Long Beach apartment watched the projectionist load the first reel of the *Miter*. O'Reith had invited Helen to see it but she declined. She was shopping in town with Alice Ridley.

McDonough said, "The movie may not be much good but we came in under budget. That's something."

"I'm pleased about that," O'Reith said. "With Nixon, Haig and the Colonel adding a bit of cachet, we may be surprised about its performance at the box office."

"Clive I managed to squeeze Kissinger in too as a spear-carrier. Not a significant role but at least he is there and recognizably so. I thought that since we were going to make a short subject out of the side-scenes, it would be good public relations to get him in the main picture."

"I'm glad to hear that," O'Reith said.

At the end, after the lights came up, McDonough asked, "What do you think?"

"It could be a lot worse, George," O'Reith said expansively. "I suppose people will get a kick out of seeing Nixon and Haig and Kissinger decked out in medieval finery. Few will recognize the Colonel, of course. But in Latin America, he adds a certain amount of class to an otherwise forgettable film. We have to bear in mind that some people really go for religious movies. But I'm not one of them. Your performance, as would be expected, was impeccable. You'll win an Oscar. Beyond that, we have to wait and see what happens at the box office. But it is clear that we have two movies, not one. Let's separate them."

"Very well. But I resent your calling it forgettable", McDonough said snootily. "Clive, not to change the subject, but I've given a bit of thought to Nixon. What if, in the final analysis, we can't save him? What if he goes down the tube?"

"Except for going to Guatemala, I don't know."

"Clive, one problem we have with the Colonel returning to Caracas is military support. If we control an army in Central America, we could move a division down there and help him get reinstalled. But it would be outside your mandate as Supremo. You could be subject to courts martial."

"I thought about that all right," O'Reith agreed. "I'm willing to chance it. I'm going to ask Haig for cover. We need to have the Colonel running things. We need new oil concessions."

"And putting Nixon in to run the *Co-prosperity Sphere* is icing on the cake."

O'Reith nodded. He continued, "Yes, but we have to make it stick. We don't want to install Nixon one day and have him hanged, drawn and quartered the next. How would that look?"

"Well it is worth thinking about," McDonough agreed. "Clearly we must have American troops in Guatemala before Nixon takes office. Clive, I've been studying the American political system. Should the House of Representatives impeach Nixon and if the Senate then convicts him, he will be turned out of office but not necessarily imprisoned. Is that correct?"

"Yes but he won't be rid of his tormentors. Good chance he will be indicted in a district court for high crimes and misdemeanors. Convicted too. So he may wind up behind bars. Too early to predict that, but the system leads in that direction."

"Say he's convicted. Does he have to appear in the Senate to hear the verdict?"

"Yes."

"And he just walks away?" McDonough asked his eyes deeply hooded.

"That's it. The Senate lacks power to put him in prison."

"So we could meet him as he emerges, drive to Washington National Airport and put him on a plane to Guatemala?" McDonough suggested.

"I believe so."

"And he begins his presidential campaign at that point?" McDonough probed.

"That is where it gets tricky, O'Reith replied, a worried expression on his face. "The troops should be in there before he begins his campaign. Otherwise there could be uncontrolled rioting. Nixon got pelted with tomatoes once in Caracas on a good will tour. Should that happen to him in Guatemala City, he might, well he might throw a shoe. We don't want him sore at us for getting him into a pissing contest with a skunk."

McDonough's eyes bulged momentarily at the thought of what might happen. He said, "I follow you, Clive."

O'Reith said, "An indictment could be issued against him within hours of conviction. I'll call Haig today. Our signals must be straight in plenty of time to strike while the iron is hot

That night O'Reith called Haig at the White House. "Hey Al baby, when can I count on having FUSAG on the water?"

"California National Guard has been activated. We're giving them some training. Half of 'em never had basic. They should be ready to go by the end of May. In the east, the Iowa National Guard is also in training. Ready the same time."

"That's two divisions. I'm expecting a reinforced corps, minimum of five divisions."

"Can't be. That would strip us down to nothing. I can give you a third division in 60 days and a fourth in 90. That's the best I can do."

"Not what we agreed to but I'll accept that. Now regarding our friend the POTUS, George and I were talking last night about him. What do you think?"

"Impeachment?"

"Yes."

Haig huffed into the mouthpiece, "Well it is almost a certainty."

"Will he fight it out to the finish?"

"He says he will. He'll use up all of his options. He's a spunky guy."

"If he did have to step down, we have to ponder his election campaign in Guatemala. Things could go wrong. He might not get elected. Of course if we already had troops on the ground..."

"In Guatemala City?"

"Yeah so he would have a fair shot at it."

"What happens to the Colonel without our support?"

"If he shows up in Caracas, they'll throw him in a military prison. Might even shoot him out of hand."

Haig was silent for a few seconds, collecting his thoughts. Then he began, "I thought he was more popular than that. Well, we can retain the American troops on standby in Central America. If Nixon steps down, there will be plenty of confusion in DC until the new government gets going. Gerald Ford is not in the loop on this. Being a slow deliberate kind of fellow, probably take him a few days to get control of everything. He is not exactly waiting in the wings to take over. He is merely there in case he is needed. We need a period of time when nothing is for sure, a fluid situation, as it is called. Keep matters murky. After the landings in Honduras, the troopships and support vessels can sail down to Panama for a long refueling. I'll see that they are combat loaded. Just before Nixon steps down, he can declare a state of emergency and name Venezuela as the aggressor. So the Colonel can get cracking. That keeps you in the clear too. We want to hit 'em as hard as we can, coming off the boats. We keep one division in Guatemala to help Nixon get started. I realize there may be riots if the locals know the Colonel is checking out. We don't want that and I'm sure Nixon would not either. Troopships return to Guatemala to move the remaining three divisions to La Guiara. With three divisions, it will be a romp. Let me kick it around with Kissinger. Get his take on it. You and George want to fly up here in a couple of days? We'll get down to the nitty-gritty on it."

"Sure. Call me when you're ready." O'Reith agreed.

It was Monday, May 20th. O'Reith and McDonough were in a corner suite on the 4th floor of the Watergate Hotel, checked in as Jack Drake and Father George. The vanilla-colored electric clock hanging on the pale ivory wall said it was five minutes until six, the appointed hour. As the bellboy brought in the drink tray, the telephone rang and it was Haig. As soon as Haig and Kissinger arrived and were out of their disguises, the four men shook hands and O'Reith, mixing drinks directed them to the soft seats around the cocktail table. For some moments the only sound was the clinking of ice cubes in heavy glasses.

O'Reith looked over first at Haig, then at Kissinger, raised his glass and said, "Success, Gentlemen!"

They echoed the toast. O'Reith asked Haig, "Where do we stand?"

"Embarkation set for June 1. One division coming out of Fort Stoneman, California destined for El Salvador. Another division coming out of Fort Dix, New Jersey headed for Honduras. Boats are not too fast but you can count on establishment of beachheads on or about June 20th. Your pal, Lieutenant General 'Howlin Mad' Mulheny, will land with the eastern force and will be in tactical command of the entire operation. Mulheny's buddy, Major General Albert Mason will land with the 48th Division in El Salvador and command that force."

"That sounds OK," O'Reith said. "I'll meet Mason when he steps foot on the land. George will greet Mulheny on the other side. What about Nixon? Is he OK to take over from the Colonel?"

Haig looked over at Kissinger whose dour face slowly warmed up into a ghoulish grin. He growled, "He recognizes that it may come to that. But at this moment, the Chief is not ready to face up to it. I romanced him along, just joking you know, trying to get a rise out of him. He fixed me with those dangerous-looking eyes and snapped, 'It is too soon for that! I am not a crook and I am not going down'. So I let it ride for a couple of days and then he invited me to the Lincoln sitting room one night for a cognac. I asked him, respectfully of course, I asked him what were his plans if worst came to worst. He said, 'I'm fucked if I know. Maybe go down to Tia Juana and run a Mexican whorehouse.' We got a good laugh out of that. I said, "Mr. President, Clive and George think you would really do a wonderful job running the *sphere*."

He laughed and replied,"you've got to be kidding."

"So I didn't say anything more. He poured us another jolt of cognac and I sipped it along. He was in a brown study. He got up and walked around the room slowly and said with a laugh, 'Henry, I don't speak a goddam word of Spanish. What the hell would I do if something went wrong? Like a riot or something like that?' I answered him softly, saying, "Clive and George would never let you get in a jam down there. They would give you some good men, men you could rely upon."

He said, "You know Henry I really like that Clive. He is a straight shooter. And Father George. My kind of sky-pilot."

I said, "Well Mr. President, they are true blue, not like some of those ophidian congressmen we know so well."

"Sounds like he may be coming around," O'Reith said.

"I'll try him out again in a few days," Kissinger said. "Do you suppose we could set him up to make a secret visit to Guatemala City? He could take Bebe Rebozo and Robert Ablanaplank with him. Al and I of course. You and George. The Colonel could give him a tour of the city."

"We could get up a golf game," O'Reith suggested. "The Colonel has a first class course out near the airport."

"That sound's great," Haig agreed.

Kissinger said, "Why don't you fellows stay over? Al and I can line up an appointment with the Chief in the morning. Clive, you can spring it on him and Al and I will cheer you along."

"Suits me," O'Reith said. McDonough nodded.

They were gathered in the oval office. Nixon seemed stressed but he was trying to appear cheerful. Not much of a small-talker, he was ready to get right down to it. O'Reith suggested a look-see trip to Guatemala City. If Nixon liked what he saw, then they could get into the details of taking over from the Colonel. Nixon, cagey at first, soon warmed up a bit. O'Reith described the beauties of the city including the miniature Eiffel Tour.

"I like that!" "Nixon beamed. "Since I was a little kid I wanted to live in Paris. Of course Guatemala City is not Paris. But it is not Sing Sing either."

"That's a plus right there," O'Reith said.

"Tell me more about how it would be," Nixon said.

"About the trip?" O'Reith asked, feeling his way along.

"No! About running the country," Nixon asked, a thin smile crossing his features.

Warming up to his task, O'Reith began. "You would have to throw your hat in the ring and become an official candidate for the presidency. Then the campaign."

"How long of a campaign?" Nixon asked nervously.

"Couple of days," O'Reith said. "Down there they settle the hash on elections pretty quick. We'll put out some posters with your picture on them. Colonel rounds up some voters. They vote. He counts the vote. You're in."

"Well that sounds just fine," Nixon responded with enthusiasm, his jowly face beaming. "I'll have some campaign posters sent down. I'm in no mood for a lengthy campaign. After I win the election, then what?"

"We leave the posters up for a while. Good public relations. Then sir, you would be the president of the *sphere*."

"Well I like that idea!" Nixon said, getting into the spirit of it all. "I would still be an American, albeit a Central one, heh-heh-heh. Plenty of time to write my memoirs. I need to come up with a solid, snappy title for them."

"The name of your new nation rolls easily off the tongue," McDonough added. "*The Greater Central American Co-prosperity Sphere*, a state that runs from the Yucatan Peninsula to the Costa Rica line, at least it will just as soon as we liquidate those two dens of *fidelista* iniquity, Honduras and El Salvador. You could call your memoirs *My Mastery of the Sphere*."

"I like it," Nixon said. "Would you write the introduction, Father George?"

"I would be flattered, Mr. President."

"Well it is settled then." Nixon turned to Haig. He asked, "How is the Honduras business going?"

Haig repeated the schedule for the departure of the two divisions.

Nixon looked to McDonough and asked, "What if we wanted to expand in the north? I'm thinking of liquidating the Mexican rump. We would be standing on the Rio Grande. That would give that House Judicial Committee something to think about. A threatening Central American Colossus on their very doorstep. In the navy we called that menacing grandeur."

"Easy as pie, Mr. President," McDonough assured him, using a familiar Americanism he knew Nixon would understand. "Texas could be next in line."

"The old domino theory," Nixon muttered. "Isn't that right, Henry? Isn't it?"

"It is sir but to think of Texas is premature, Mr. President." Kissinger said. He was nervous.

Nixon rubbed his shadowy chin, said half aloud, "Two divisions, eh? Al, are you comfortable with that figure? We promised Clive that FUSAG would be at least six divisions."

"It is a question of availability, Mr. President. We simply cannot strip the country bare. We'd have to pull in NATO troops. And from the Far East."

"Well, I think we should do it," Nixon said, pounding his left palm with his right fist. And send in the Marine Corps too. Don't forget naval and air forces. Al, to counter this terrible red threat, we have to meet force with force."

"Then, Mr. President, we could expand in the south too," McDonough suggested softly. "We could go all the way to the Panama line."

"Stand on the Colombian frontier?" Nixon speculated, fist pounding air. "Build a Maginot Line."

"Well, we could do that sir," McDonough confirmed gleefully, his yellow eyes dancing. "Grand Design." He was in his element.

Nixon turned to Haig and said, "Al, we'll need to put some nuclear weapons down there too. Just in case. I don't trust those Russkies one bit."

Henry Kissinger said, "Remember Mr. President that it is not the Russians who threaten the sphere. It is the Indians."

Nixon snapped his fingers. "Yes that's right Henry. It was just a slip of the tongue. Forget the nukes." Then to O'Reith he continued. "Well then sir, let's line that trip up. I'll be glad to see the Colonel again. You fellows have a nice trip home."

With time to kill they took in *Chinatown* at the Madison with Jack Nicholson and Faye Dunaway. O'Reith had read in The *Hollywood Reporter* that it was a flick about a 1937 water utility scandal in Los Angeles. He vaguely remembered a sensational murder case of that era when some local politico had been gunned down at City Hall. It was described as 'Chandleresque'. Afterward they checked out of the hotel, and rode to Dulles International for their flight west.

On the way back to Los Angeles, McDonough said, "We should brief the Colonel on all of this. Even though he dearly wishes to return to Venezuela, we'll have to assure him that he's not being kicked out."

"Yeah, I thought of that," O'Reith agreed. "I'll call him tonight. We can slip away tomorrow and fly down there."

The next morning O'Reith entered his office with the telephone ringing. It was Haig. He began, "Clive, Nixon has decided to make the trip to Guatemala a state visit. He will award the Colonel the Legion of Honor for his fine work in stabilizing the *sphere*. That sounds OK to you?"

"Sure. But it will have to be the equivalent of an oak leaf cluster. Ike has already awarded him the Legion of Honor. He's expecting us but not a state visit. I'll call him back."

"OK. Air Force One flies us into LAX. We will pick you and George up and then head south. The POTUS would like for you to go in uniform. You'll have orders today returning you to active duty. What about George? Will he have an official position?"

"He can be the Chaplain General of the armed forces of the sphere. There's an outfit here that makes military uniforms for the motion picture industry. I'm sure he'll want to wear a white linen get up with a silk kepí on a balsa wood frame. I'll take care of that. When do we go?"

"Day after tomorrow. That way, Nixon can make a major foreign policy speech tonight. He'll ramp up the aggressive nature of the Indian threat and say some good words about the Colonel's firm determination to keep the *sphere* in the free, democratic camp."

"OK."

"Clive, this is off the record, "Haig added. "Henry and I are basically patriotic Americans. We're not like the POTUS. He's a public relations patriot. We have talked about the Sword of Damocles hanging over him and while we will do everything we can to save him, if he goes down, we don't plan to go down with him. He's got it in his head that we are going to join him down there and it worries me. Neither Henry nor I can work up much enthusiasm about being big dogs in the *sphere.* We would like to stay on in government here in DC and help the new boy, get his feet on the ground."

"Any idea what kind of a guy the new boy is? O'Reith asked.

"No. Until he became the Veep, he was a solid, predictable Republican Congressman. Some say that he's a deuce or trey kind of guy. They say that's why Nixon picked him. He didn't want a hotshot to come in behind him. Ford is not too flamboyant, a guy from a small town somewhere in the Midwest, a football-playing, school-teacherly, Rotary Club type. Easter egg hunt kind of guy. He gets down on all fours and lets little kids ride around on his back."

"Well, Al, I understand your desire to stay in Washington."

"Clive, Henry and I are depending upon you. We're a bit concerned that Nixon wants to concentrate so much military power in Central America. While he's basically stable, he could go off on some wild-eyed tangent. Henry and I are both nervous about his plan to expand the *sphere* to the north. Not that we're thrilled about his plans for the canal. And on that point, would it be too much to ask you to cool George down? The Potus eats that stuff up. Neither Henry nor I think it is a good idea to egg him on like that."

"Al, for me it is just a practical matter. I'm looking for new oil fields. But I share your concern. Like you and Henry, I too, am a good American. The foreign policy that George and I pursue is fundamentally beneficial to the U.S. We control a stream of petroleum that can be diverted to the States whenever the need arises. As far as Nixon getting a wild hair, if I am the Supremo, you can count on my cooperation. I will take orders from you, not Guatemala City. Once we have the Colonel back on seat in Miraflores and once Nixon is in control of the National Palace, we'll do whatever the Defense Department tells us. And I will tone George down. You know how he is. His enthusiasm just wells up and he can't turn it off. That is part of his amazing charm. Al, what about James R. Schlesinger? Is he cooperative?"

"Not to worry, Clive. I'll attend Mr. Schlesinger. I'll get the National Zoological Garden to release a flock of prothonotary warblers in that hole in the Pentagon. They'll stop him dead in his tracks. Do your best and I'm glad to hear that you understand the position that Henry and I are in. Clive, I'm glad we had this talk. I feel much easier about it all."

"OK, Al. Let me call the Caudillo. We'll line the trip up. I'll call you back."

On the flight from Los Angeles to Guatemala City, Nixon, Kissinger, and McDonough were reviewing the speech that Bill Safire had written for him to deliver from the steps of the National Palace. They were in the huge cabin on Air Force One. Nixon wanted to deliver an *Ich bin Berliner* type of speech. The four of them were testing out various possibilities, hung up on how to translate *Co-prosperity sphere* into Spanish.

In a smaller compartment near the rear of the plane, Haig was saying, "Clive, I didn't mean to alarm you about Nixon getting grandiose ideas but he is sure as hell capable of them."

"Not to worry, Al," O'Reith said. "George gets them all the time. I'm used to it. Furthermore I monitor activities in the *sphere* closely. Here's the skinny on it. It is mostly a myth. The Colonel controls those oil fields up in the Yucatan with his *boys* from Tachira. It's the same in the city. Law and order derives from that same source. His *Guardia Nacional* consists of more Tachiristas. When he leaves the city for Caracas, his *boys* will go with him. As for those oil fields in the former Mexican provinces in the Yucatan, they are well along the road to depletion, making water. Oil production is marginal; barely enough to pay operating costs. Cigar money, that's all. Nixon can only control Guatemala City with troops that we supply him. We'll declare Aurora Airport to be the command post for the Central American Strategic Air Force. I've got a guy working for the company who rose to the rank of colonel in the Army Air Corps. He's a fighter pilot a decade younger than I am. He's married to Venezuelan red-hot. She keeps him on a tight leash because he is famous for his roving eyes. We can call him up as a lieutenant general to be in charge of all military operations in Guatemala City. Then, under him, you can install a contingent of marines to keep Nixon safe and out of harm's way. What do you think?"

"So Nixon will be in exile."

"That's it. Impotent."

"That's not the end of the world," Haig said, smiling.

They were returning from a successful visit to Guatemala City. The Colonel had been a splendid host. His bodyguards had sprayed the swamps to kill off some of the mosquitoes and *jejenes.* Their game of golf was pleasant with Nixon shooting in the low eighties. Drinks and meals at the *Palacio Nacional* had been sumptuous. Nixon had decorated the Colonel with a special Central American Medal of Honor. The Colonel, in return, brought out his best Bombay gin for the occasion. Nixon had basked in the light of friendly associates. His speech had been well received. Now on Air Force One, returning to San Clemente, surrounded by his friends, clutching his *Romeo y Juliette* box of Cuban cigars, a gift from the Colonel, he was smiling and radiant. Haig was on his left and O'Reith on his right. From a round table in the presidential lounge, Nixon asked, "What did you fellows think of my speech?"

A beaming McDonough said, "Mr. President, it was superlative. A stirring speech and one we will remember."

Haig nodded agreement, as did Kissinger. Nixon, in high spirits continued, "It was one of the best speeches I have ever made. You know when you have an expectant, enthusiastic audience; it makes all the difference in the world. It was a big gathering. Did you notice that? Did you notice how they smiled and clapped their hands when I announced that I was one of them? Their upturned happy faces said more than words could ever express."

"The Colonel is pretty good at drumming up a crowd," O'Reith said. "Besides, the word is out that you are to become their new leader and that generated much optimism. None of them ever imagined that the great *Presidente Norte Americano* would be coming down to run their country. It is a triumph for you Mr. President."

"I can see that," Nixon said heartily. "I pray that I can live up to their expectations." Turning to McDonough he continued, "Tonight after dinner would you lead us in prayer, Father George, a prayer not only for the people of the United States, and they need it, but also for the people of the *Greater Central American Co-prosperity Sphere."*

"You can count on me, Mr. President," McDonough said humbly.

Nixon was rubbing his hands together in happy anticipation. "You know fellows; I'm beginning to wish I were already installed. Not that I'm giving up the fight against those ravenous jackals in the Congress but I now know that, however things turn out in Washington, I still have a political future."

"One of the nice things about operating out of Guatemala City, Mr. President, is that you have a more efficient way of handling opposition parties," O'Reith offered. "You'll have no Watergate-type worries."

"How does one deal with opposition?" Nixon asked thoughtfully.

"Liquidation," O'Reith said. "Instantaneous Liquidation. The Colonel is a past master of that fine art."

They were all silent, looking around the table at each other. Finally, after some long moments, Nixon smiled and broke the silence. He said. "I like it. Another Saturday Night Massacre but with real tommy guns."

In McDonough's dressing room at funny acres, Mills was making him up for some retakes. Running the *Miter* dailies through the movieola, he had discovered some gaps in the continuity. These had to be corrected before the film could go into circulation. O'Reith was standing beside him. McDonough asked, "Clive what does it look like? When are we going to put the boot in?"

"It was set for June first but there have been the usual delays. Haig told me last night that we could plan on debarkations on both sides of the isthmus around the end of June. I plan to be dockside at La Union on the 28th of the month, a Friday, to meet Al Mason, Mulheny's pal. He's to be the C.O. Haig said that was about right. He'll let me know if the date changes."

"That's in El Salvador?"

"Yeah."

"What about the other side? Who will be there?"

The Iowa National Guard will be coming into La Ceiba. After that, an armored division will be coming in to Puerto Cortéz. But that will be later. Are you up to it?"

"I'll be there, Clive."

"Fine. Should be a good show, George. I've never been to either of those ports but I understand it never gets really hot. Humid but not hot. Not like Khuzestan."

"We thank God for his small mercies." McDonough concluded.

"I'm on my way to the office, George. When will you be finished here?"

"Couple of days, Clive. Then Carolyn and I will be off to Rome for a few days. Get a bit of rest before..."

That night at home with Maxine, O'Reith was surprised to get a call from Haig. There was an edge in his voice. He said, "Clive, can you come east? The chief is in a panic. We need to buck him up. Reassure him that all is well. Can you bring George along? Probably need to say a prayer. Maybe two."

"Al, I'll call George and be back to you in ten minutes," O'Reith said.

"Awaiting your call."

Cook answered his call on the third ring. She was giving McDonough a water massage in the Jacuzzi. O'Reith went to the point. "George. Panic in the White House. Haig wants us to come up tomorrow. We can charter a plane. Get out of LAX around seven in the morning. Bring your prayer-book."

"That bad, eh?" McDonough said gloomily.

"Yeah, Nixon is taking some heat from that committee. My concern is that we'll get half way through the campaign in Central America and he'll pull the troops. Remember we went through that once before when LBJ was on seat."

"That was dicey all right. I'll meet you at the airport at six thirty in the morning."

"See you George. Get a good night of sleep. Long day tomorrow."

They were in the air at eight o'clock and it was a smooth flight to National Airport. A government limousine with deeply tinted windows met them and soon they were in their suite on the 4th floor of the Watergate. It was a few minutes after three. Since their meeting with Haig was set for six thirty, they both napped until the appointed hour. On the dot, they arrived at the White House and were immediately shown into Haig's office. He was smiling vacantly. "Chief is in there pacing the floor," Haig began, nodding in the direction of the Oval Office. He picked up his telephone and said softly, "They're here, Mr. President."

Nixon greeted the two oilmen eagerly, shaking their hands vigorously, not smiling, not trying to put a good face on anything but once they were sitting, he broke into a shallow smile. "Those judicial bastards are turning the screws on me and there isn't a goddamned thing that I can do about it. I'm on the verge of getting the shakes. How about a drink?"

"Martini on the rocks for me, Mr. President, with a twist," O'Reith said.

"Johnny Walker Black for me," McDonough said. "Squirt of soda but no ice."

Haig requested the same and soon the four men were dipping their bills. "Where's Kissinger?" O'Reith asked.

"Holding hands with Golda Meir in Tel Aviv," Nixon said. He took a sip of his drink and arose. The others rose too. Nixon began pacing the oval office, his yellow legal pad in his right hand. "When are we going in?" he asked.

"Looks like the 28th of the month," Haig said.

Nixon looked at O'Reith. "You all set?"

O'Reith nodded, said "I'll meet the California National Guard on the West side. George will meet Mulheny across the isthmus."

"Sounds OK," Nixon said. "Are you expecting much resistance?"

"No sir," O'Reith replied. "I doubt if there will be any fight in them. I give the campaign five days to penetrate the two countries and another five to consolidate the gains. The Colonel will visit both capitals and proclaim them to be part of the *sphere* and that will be that. He will then announce that he is stepping down and set a date for elections. That can be whenever you want it."

Nixon put his legal pad on the edge of his desk and his hand to his jaw, looking downward. He said, "I really don't know what I'm up against. I'm still hoping for a miracle. Maybe I can hang in here for two or three months. It all depends on the Supreme Court. If they find against me and I yield all of the tapes, I've had it."

Haig said, "Congress is waiting on that decision. If it goes against you, Mr. President, they're whispering on the floor of the House that the Judiciary Committee is going to recommend a motion of impeachment by the end of the month. At the same time the troops go in to El Salvador and Nicaragua, the full House will be considering a vote. It could go to the Senate for trial in late July."

"Jesus! Jesus Christ!" Nixon said. He was sweating and took his handkerchief out to wipe it away from his brow. "Time for the tough to get going."

"This could be the time for a prayer," McDonough suggested.

"Let's have another drink first," Nixon suggested. "Get in a praying mood."

Later, ice melting in his glass, the POTUS said, "OK, Father George."

McDonough opened his prayer-book to a suitable page, his glowing halo flickered a time or two and then became robust, winked out fully circular. He began:

> "O Lord, this is your humble servant George P. McDonough speaking from the tiny planet earth and we are gathered in the Oval Office of the White House. Our Chief is in great peril from the Supreme Court of the United States and on our bended knees, we beg of you Lord to deliver him from the evil gaggle of corrupt congressmen who are pressing the court. O Lord, let the Supreme Court find in favor of our Chief so that we can all resume our patriotic defense of the country against our *fidelista* enemies. Thank you O Lord for your bounteous favors."

"That was a first class prayer, Father George," Nixon said, clapping him on the back. "Let's hope it works."

With time on their hands before their flight, O'Reith and McDonough decided to take in *Godfather II* with Al Pacino, Robert Duval and Talia Shire. It was showing at the Huntress Court Cinemaplex in McLean, Virginia, near Dulles International. Two and half-hours with a twenty-minute break. Touted as an 'epic vision of corruption in America', O'Reith sat through it but did not enjoy it. He had seen enough violence in the oil fields and in the sky over Germany. When they came out, O'Reith asked McDonough, "What did you think?"

"Boring. I've seen tougher thugs in rural France. The music was not too bad. I wish Nino Rota would set some of our classic hymns to music."

"Maybe he would if you asked him," O'Reith suggested.

"That's a thought," McDonough agreed affably.

On Sunday, June 30th, a cool breeze blowing across the *Golfo de Fonseca* found O'Reith in suntans and combat boots watching the debarkation of the 48th Infantry Division from the troopship MV *Banana Emperor.* Out in the gulf, as far as the eye could see, a string of vessels with soldiers, tanks, artillery, trucks and jeeps were waiting their turn to discharge. O'Reith counted forty vessels in all. Troops from the *Emperor,* were coming down the gangplank and lining up in company formations on the dock parallel to the ship. Faint, indistinct commands from the platoon sergeants caught his ears and he watched the soldiers come first to attention and then to parade rest. The sun glinted off the brass collar insignia of the NCOs. Company guidons fluttered in the soft air. O'Reith always got a tear in his eye and a lump in his throat when he saw American soldiers landing on a foreign shore. Not that he was sentimental about war. He detested it. Nevertheless he was moved by the occasion. He felt a thrill when a breeze lifted the American flag flying from the stern of the *Banana Emperor.* Seeing that a battalion was off the boat, he turned, got into the rear seat of the olive drab sedan and asked the driver to take him to the dock to greet General Mason. As he rode along the rutted red clay road, he wondered how McDonough was making out on the other side.

It was an occupation, not an invasion. These troops were the first of five divisions that would land on the two shores and if anything, both 'enemies' were glad to see them. The Yankee dollar was always welcome in these climes.

After two weeks of *war,* the only troops that were *hors de combat* had been felled by venereal diseases. O'Reith and McDonough were back in Guatemala City at the *Palacio Nacional.* Haig had sent Safire down to help the Colonel draft his Victory Address which he would present first in Tegucigalpa and after that, in San Salvador. As wars go, this was the best run one that O'Reith had been in. Haig had also sent a bundle of posters showing Nixon in a wide-brimmed sombrero. Below his smiling portrait was the legend: *Notre Nixon.* The posters would go up around town. O'Reith remarked to McDonough, "I wonder where Haig came up with *Notre Nixon*?"

"Perhaps his aide spoke only French," McDonough suggested.

"Could be," O'Reith agreed. "You suppose we could print up some *Nuestro* patches to cover the *Notre*?"

"We can check that with the Colonel," McDonough said absent-mindedly. "It may not be important." He was sitting across from O'Reith reading a stack of telexes. He sat up and said cheerfully, "Clive, a bit of good news. Aztec Sam is out of that Texas jail. He is on his way to Culver City. That means we can finish the side-scene movie. I'll catch a plane to Los Angeles tonight. That Pan Am DC-8 that comes up from Lima gets in here around midnight. So I can be at LAX early in the morning. I'd like to meet him when he arrives and we can go right to work. I'll telex Ed Wood to join us there."

"Well George that is good news! How long will it take to finish?"

"A couple of days. We have to shoot a few final scenes to tie it all together. The ones where Meg Muffin-Driver finally buys her Cadillac hearse. I can be back down here around the end of the week."

"A hearse?" O'Reith asked, somewhat taken aback.

"After all of the jockeying around, all she could afford is a signal red Cadillac hearse that was ordered for a funeral home in Sofia, Bulgaria. The Bulgars wanted to pay for it in zlotys and that killed the deal. So it ended up brand new on a used car lot."

"Some movie," O'Reith said. "I'll be glad to be rid of it."

The Colonel came in and saw the *Notre Nixon* posters. He asked, "What are those?"

"For Nixon's campaign," O'Reith asked? "What about that *Notre* business? Can we paste some *Nuestros* over them?"

"Quite unnecessary," the Colonel said. "He wins the election with posters or without posters. It's an unnecessary expense. When is he coming, by the way?"

"Haig says he wants to hang on in Washington as long as he can. He is hoping against hope, but possibly the Judiciary Committee will take pity on him and let him off the hook. My guess is that it will not happen. Haig thinks the full house will vote articles of impeachment soon. Should that occur, Nixon will be down here in a couple of days. He will never let the Senate try him."

"I would like to be back in Miraflores on *Cinco de Julio*, for a hero's welcome," the Colonel said.

"I'll telephone Haig early morning from Los Angeles," McDonough said. "I'll ask him to release a division of infantry to help you become re-established just in case the hero's welcome doesn't pan out."

"Ask for two," the Colonel suggested.

"Very well," McDonough agreed.

"Well here is a nice little message from Cherry Cokeland, "McDonough said cheerily as he continued riffling through the stack of messages. "She and the other Pentecostals are getting together to compose some Nixon hymns. Cherry says they admire him for his patent patriotism as well as his strong religious personality. His speeches reflect his beliefs in doing well for the people. They're coming down for his inauguration. They want to sing in his parade."

"Inaugural parades are superfluous," the Colonel said. "Dangerous too. They tend to turn into shooting galleries. If those people want to sing, they can do it right here in the palatial garden. Anywhere else is asking for big trouble."

"We can arrange a small inaugural party with a few drinks and the hymns and Nixon may want me to say a prayer to bless his administration," McDonough said.

The Colonel's round face suddenly became pensive. He looked first at McDonough and then at O'Reith. Then he began, "Gentlemen, to use an American idiom, may I ask if you have leveled with Richard M. Nixon?"

"Leveled with him about what?" O'Reith asked.

"When I leave for Caracas," the Colonel continued, "my Tachira troops leave with me. They cement this *Greater Central America Co-prosperity Sphere together.* Without American troops, Nixon's presidency extends no further than the gate of the *Palacio Nacional.* And then only with the gate closed and locked. Is he aware of that fact?"

"Haig and I have considered that it might not be a smooth transition. It is something I think about, all right," O'Reith agreed. Right now, I'm counting on Haig to be a powerful factor in the new U.S. administration. But it is complicated. No question about that. It is the timing that is so tricky."

Chapter VII

The Signal Red Cadillac

Although O'Reith had expressed optimism about the two movies, privately he considered them both to be write-offs. His main concern was seeing Helen recover. Nervous about the events unfolding in Central America, when McDonough said that he was calling for Ed Wood to meet them at the studio, a tiny warning bell began ringing at the back of his head. That night O'Reith telephoned Ridley in Los Angeles. She was in her own room.

O'Reith began, "Alice, did I wake you up?"

"Clive! Well it's nice to hear from you. Helen just had a glass of warm milk and went to bed. Everything is OK."

"Alice, George is flying back to LA tonight. They have managed to spring Aztec Sam out of that Texas jail and they are ready to resume filming. George plans to engage Ed Wood to help out. You know how Helen feels about him."

"She has no use for him and others of his ilk," Ridley stated firmly.

"Alice I have the utmost confidence in your discretion, your judgment and your concern for Helen. If Ed is to be a problem for her, we cannot have him involved. So I ask if you would join George, Aztec Sam and Ed at the studio and direct the meeting in a way that the outcome will not upset Helen. If she truly has lost interest in the films, then I see no reason why Ed can't take over. He's inept. As far as I'm concerned we can give him the side-scene movie just to get rid of it. George wants to shoot some tie-ins. I am not in favor of that. Maybe you can convince him to just unload it as is and let Ed complete it. There will be some legal formalities. We will have to deed the movie over. Check with Robert Walters. Use your power of attorney to shut off expenditures. Will you take on that responsibility? I want George to return quickly and help me down here. So in that sense, I agree on letting Ed step in. If that won't work, the only other solution is for you to complete the two movies. Does that make any sense?"

I understand, Clive. You can count on me. You can quit worrying about it."

"Alice, if any complications arise, phone me. In the morning you can tell Helen I called while she was sleeping."

"Sure Clive. Take care. Don't take any wooden *pesorinos*."

"I'll call again tomorrow. Alice, I'm counting on you and I appreciate it. Alice, before I forget, are you and my daughter speaking?

"Helen Simpson?"

"Yeah."

"We're OK, Clive. All a misunderstanding. Since she had already told that flake goodbye, it was easy."

"Alice, Helen Simpson is flighty. With her mother ailing, she needs… well you know."

"Clive, I understand exactly. I'll speak to her today. Tell her you called and asked about her."

O'Reith flew the Aero Commander to La Union. The advance was moving slowly because of guerrilla activity. While in conference with General Mason and his staff, Heavy Latrobe burst in upon him in the uniform of a corporal, angry and agitated. His little square block of a head was in constant motion. His eyes flickered from O'Reith to Mason as if he were trying to determine which of the two was responsible for his predicament. He said, "General O'Reith, I have been unfairly treated and demand that you rectify my position. I am supposed to be a general officer and look at me."

O'Reith said, "Well of course, Corporal Latrobe, I will look into it."

"That is not what I want!" Latrobe responded, red in the face and surly. "I demand to be removed from this insect heaven. You must take me back with you in the Aero Commander."

"Corporal Latrobe, the Aero Commander is fully laden," O'Reith replied. We have no room for another passenger. I will discuss your case with General Mason and we will advise you shortly what has been decided. You are dismissed."

"You'll never get away with this, General O'Reith. President Nixon will cook your goose." Latrobe fuming, refused to leave Mason's tent. Two military policemen were summoned and he was removed forcibly, ranting, frothing at the mouth, and waving his arms.

"What in the hell is this all about?" O'Reith asked.

"He is a victim of the classification system," Mason said. "If I take action, it would be highly irregular. I would have to report it back to the California Board and I would no doubt get a sharp note from them. They could take it up with the Judge Advocate General. Considering that Latrobe has been convicted by courts martial, I'd be on the hot seat."

O'Reith shook his head in disgust. "Tell him that you have requested authority from California. Maybe that will hold him for awhile."

After conferring with Lieutenant General Mulheny on the Caribbean side, O'Reith returned to Guatemala City fully expecting to find McDonough ready for duty. But all he found was a gloomy Colonel Jiménez, a stack of messages and last weeks newspapers from Los Angeles, New York and Washington DC. A letter from the White House had come by courier. The date on the red stamp was July 1, 1974. He opened it and read:

> Dear General O'Reith:
>
> I am concerned about the proper placement of my nephew Heavy Latrobe. He was treated unfairly by the California Classification Board. Inducted into the 48th Division as a corporal, he was assigned to duty as an assistant to a supply sergeant. This posting is far beneath his dignity and, as you can imagine, he is quite upset. Therefore I ask you to reassign him to a more auspicious post and confer upon him the temporary grade of brigadier general. I would like for you to consider him as a key man on your staff. He should

be entitled to dine at the Officers Open Mess and he should be invited to all social affairs befitting a man of his rank. I know that I can count on your cooperation in this regard.

Very truly yours,
Richard M. Nixon, POTUS

The second message, a note from the telephone operator said, "Urgent! Call Alice Ridley on the set."

O'Reith dialed Los Angeles and in minutes, had Ridley on the line.

She said, "Clive I am desperate. I don't know what to do."

"Where is George?"

"He's here, arguing with Ed Wood. Things are snafu if you will pardon the expression." Panic was in her voice.

"What's the matter?"

"Clive, I took both movies to Helen's studio at Long Beach and ran them on her projector. The *Miter* is so leaden that when released, it will sink out of sight. Not one person in a thousand will sit through the first five minutes. And after that it gets worse. The coronation scene, remember that was the screen test, it is terrible. But *Red Cadillac* is not too bad. It jumps with several really neat songs. I went goose-bumpy when those Pentecostals sang *Doin' it for the Pope.* They perform that number in Pomona College varsity jackets. They swing their hips and clap their hands. *I've got a Chancre on my Soul* brings the house down. Now that's a song with a moral message! Young people can identify with that one and with those players. Aztec Sam is a comic. He'll get some laughs. That football guy, Landury, with his dry humor, contrasts with the gaiety of the others. Cherry Cokeland was a cheerleader for the Dallas Cowboys for a couple of years. She's an eyeful in short-shorts. Even better, she sings like Ella Mae Morse, that Fort Worth canary. When she belt's out the *Bordello Blues*, it makes you want to cry in your beer. You remember Ella Mae don't you? She was Freddie Slack's hotshot chanteuse and wild as a Mexican go go girl. The golfing crowd will identify with Meg Muffin-Driver who has nice legs and of course, since they are all Pentecostals, the movie will attract a wide religious audience. Finally, with that one-eyed, three legged, yellow mutt chasing Al Haig as the EPA guy, we have a bit of political satire. In short, we should unload *Miter* on Wood and keep *Red Cadillac.* The several side-scenes fit together reasonably well. I can buy some archival material with a jumpy musical sound track and a few songs and dances seen from a distance in Hollywood Bowl. We'll have a moneymaker. *Miter* will never earn a nickel."

"Will Wood take the *Miter*?" O'Reith asked.

"Yes but he and George have locked horns because Ed wants to appear below the title as producer and director. George thinks he should be the director. Ed won't take it unless he gets to be the director."

"I better talk to George about that," O'Reith said. "Alice, another thing that worries me is what happens if Helen regains her memory? If she should remember that the *Miter* is her thing, she'll be enraged when she finds out that we've foisted it off on Ed Wood."

"Not much chance of that happening," Ridley said.

"You are probably right. But we ought to get an opinion from Max on it."

"I'll call him."

"Would you? Is George handy?"

"He's right here listening."

"Put him on."

"Clive, glad to hear your voice. How are things going in Central America?"

"George you know very well that things are screwed up. As usual I might add because of your gross dereliction of duty."

"Clive that is a monstrous accusation. I take umbrage."

"George, how did those Pentecostals find out that Nixon is coming down to take over from the Colonel? That is one monumental leak!"

"I suppose I accidentally let the cat out of the bag. But it doesn't matter. No one would ever take them seriously."

"Well it distresses me," O'Reith said.

"Not to worry Clive," McDonough said soothingly.

"George you were supposed to be gone a couple of days. Here it is a week and you're still tangled up in it."

"I didn't expect Wood would be so unreasonable. Worse, I never, never expected that Alice Ridley would dump the *Miter*! It's preposterous! She thinks those ridiculous side-scenes make a better movie. Clive I must say I am ticked about the whole affair."

"Good. All the more reason for you to take your make-up off, get on an airplane and come down here to help me out of a jam."

"May I bring Carolyn?"

"I don't care but you better bring plenty of mosquito repellent because where you are going, you're going to get punctured with some regularity."

"Clive, I am not really a strategic military thinker. That's your forté."

"Nevertheless, I rely on your judgment in political matters. Moreover I want you in charge on the Caribbean side because of our plans for the Colonel. I cannot order Mulheny to take a division to Venezuela. We have to work that through Haig and I don't want Mulheny talking directly to him. And that reminds me of something, George. I would like for you to telephone Haig today. Advise him that I have a letter from RMN asking me to promote Heavy Latrobe to the rank of general. Unless things have changed, all promotions to the rank of general officer have to be approved by the Senate. Tell Haig that Latrobe is upset. Right now he is in the stockade in La Union for insubordination and refusal to obey orders. But I can't keep him there very long. No point in having an angry Nixon pissed off at us. I haven't discussed this with the Colonel but we could make Latrobe a general in the Guatemalan constabulary or something like that. In due course, Mason will have to report Latrobe's situation to some guy in the pentagon."

"I'll call Haig; have an answer on Latrobe when I arrive tomorrow night."

"Great, George. I'll be expecting you. I need moral support."

"Yes of course Clive, I understand that. Very well," he sighed. "I'll let Alice do whatever is necessary. I'll be on my way in the morning. We can have dinner together in the palace tomorrow night. Now here's Alice."

"Alice, after you talk to Max, go ahead and make the decisions. Let Wood have the *Miter*. We'll doctor up the *Red Cadillac* and put it into distribution. Try to get our money back. Wood not too upset about getting the *Miter* instead of the side-scenes?"

"He has never seen the *Red Cadillac*. So he does not know what he is missing. As far as the *Miter*, he is tickled pink to get it for nothing. Since we stripped out the side scenes, it is not quite long enough to make States Rights Distribution. But he said he would lengthen it with his chase scene. After I get the go-ahead from Max, I'll call in Stan to take care of the legal work and we'll strap the *Miter* on Ed. I'll work on the *Red Cadillac* until it is ready for distribution."

"See if you can mollify George. He's upset because we're pulling the plug on him."

"Not to worry. I'll soothe his jangled nerves."

Within the hour his telephone rang and it was Parkinson. He began, "Clive, I just got off the horn with Alice. She wanted to know if Helen would ever regain her memory of the movie. You recall I told you about the fugue stage in amnesia. Helen possibly could have a double fugue. She could wake up and remember everything about the *Miter*. We can't predict what will happen. I told Alice I had no idea of what might occur. Funny things happen and often they are unpredictable. Anyhow we agreed to go for the money. So she's going to give Wood the *Miter*."

"Max, it's the right thing to do. We have to chance it. Thanks for the call."

He looked at his calendar. It was a Friday, July 5, in Venezuela it would be the great Bolivarian holiday *Cinco de Julio*. He went down to the Colonel's office to see him with his face in his hands, elbows on top of his desk. He seemed sad. O'Reith said, "Well it looks like the calendar ran out on us for 1974. We're not going to get you back into Miraflores as early as we wished."

"I am distressed about it. Flor was looking forward to rejoining the altar society and of course Margot is eager to return. How are things going with President Nixon?"

"He's still on the hot seat waiting for a Supreme Court ruling. If the court goes against him, the committee will vote out articles of impeachment. After Sir George talks to Haig today, he'll be on his way. At dinner tomorrow, he'll fill us in."

"What about my division of American armor?"

"On the way to Honduras. I don't know when it will arrive. Troop ships have gone to Aruba for fueling. Soon as Nixon makes up his mind to split out of the USA, we'll bring them back and you'll be on your way."

"I'm ready for it. I'll smite those *Accionistas*!"

"Colonel, you remember that Latrobe guy? He was at San Clemente when we met with Nixon."

"I do remember him, General O'Reith. Short tubular chap, maybe a pinhead. What about him?"

"Nixon wants him to be a general in the 48th Division but because of his past, he cannot pass the hard eyes of the California Classification System. Another difficulty is that the US Senate has to confirm all appointments to the grade of general officer and they may be reluctant to do that. General Mason doesn't want to get involved in a brouhaha that could hurt his chances for promotion. Could we appoint him to a suitably high post in the Guatemalan Army?"

The Colonel laughed, said, "He can be a field marshal for all I care as long as I don't have to put up with him."

"We don't have to go that far. But he will need a snappy uniform and a cap with scrambled eggs. He should appear in *gran tenue.*"

"My tailor can fix him up to look like the Emperor of Bangkok if that would help."

"I'll send the Aero Commander to La Union for him. Where can we put him?"

"*El Camino Real* on *La Reforma*. Until we decide his ultimate destiny, we put him in charge of obsolete ordnance in the armory at the soccer stadium."

"A perfect solution. I'll see you tomorrow."

McDonough and Cook arrived at six pm. on a Pan Am 747 en route to Bogotá. O'Reith met them in the green Chrysler. In the cushions with Cook facing them in a jump seat the big Limousine rolled off the tarmac.

O'Reith asked, "George, *Miter* unloaded OK?"

"All done Clive," McDonough replied. "Stan quit-claimed it to Wood subject to a waiver stating that I would accept him as producer/ director. My name as well as Eve's will appear above the title. RMN appears below the title as a 'featured actor'. The Colonel, Kissinger and Haig appear in the regular cast. Alice signed as Helen's agent. Inasmuch as Wood got the *Miter* as a gift, we charged all production expenses to the *Red Cadillac.* Total outlay of just over $900,000. Alice thinks we will recover that in six weeks."

"When does she plan to release it?" O'Reith asked.

"Ten days. She has to get it up to minimum length so States Rights will take it."

"Well, George, that chapter of our career is behind us. Did you talk to Haig?"

"About Latrobe?"

"Yeah."

"Haig said it was sensitive. Nixon owes him money. Worse, he's been indicted in Orange County, California for insurance fraud. He had to get out of town pdq. Haig knows we could never lobby him through as a general officer. Nixon could appoint him as a commodore in the navy. That's below flag rank, and wouldn't require confirmation. But he would never go for that. It would besmirch the navy, and by extension, make him look bad."

"So it is OK if the army looks bad?"

McDonough shrugged, continued, "I held the line while Haig talked to Nixon about your suggestion that he be commissioned in the Guatemalan Army. Nixon OK'd that. So if the Colonel will play ball, that problem is solved."

"The Colonel could care less," O'Reith said.

"Where is Latrobe at this moment?" McDonough asked.

"He should be on his way back from La Union. I sent the plane last night but they got socked in. Evening fog. No report today. We'll call the hotel from the palace and see if he's there."

"Geophysical crews arrive tomorrow," Cook said. "We need room reservations."

O'Reith nodded.

"Clive, another point as regards Latrobe," McDonough added. "Haig said that Nixon is now sure of his impeachment. It could come around the end of the month. He intends to negotiate a pardon agreement with Gerald Ford. He wants the U.S. government to recognize him as the legitimate president of the *sphere* with Latrobe as his vice president. Any problem with that?"

"No. We'll run that by the colonel. I can't imagine why he would object."

As they pulled into the gravel driveway at the palace, the Colonel, on the side stoop greeted them. One of the gardeners was picking avocados. A housemaid escorted McDonough and Cook upstairs while O'Reith waited below with the Colonel who asked, "Drinks in a half hour?"

O'Reith nodded.

Flor and Margot joined them for cocktails in the bar that adjoined the palatial dining room. As the butler mixed drinks, a freshened up

McDonough entertained the ladies with the niceties of film editing. Cook had changed into a pale blue pantsuit and she had a yellow ribbon in her hair. The butler served the oilmen their usual. But it was Johnny Walker Black and Coca Cola for the Venezuelans.

After an avocado salad with hot red pepper and lime juice they had barbecued chicken and brown beans. Vanilla ice cream came with the coffee. Then Flor and Margot excused themselves. It was time for coffee, cigars, cognac and plot.

In his den the Colonel asked, "What is new, Sir George?"

"Nixon figures the boot to come around the end of this month, depending on the whims of the Congress. He told Haig that he accepts the offer to become president of the sphere."

"That is good news, indeed," the Colonel rejoined, as he turned his *Claro de Havana* in his stubby fingers to even the ash. "May I plan on returning to Miraflores in August?" His black eyes sought O'Reith's crystal blue ones.

"George goes to Honduras tomorrow to line up the 34th Division for departure," O'Reith said.

"We expect a signal from the Pentagon to Mulheny tonight," McDonough added. "Haig said he would get that done right away. Troopships should be underway from Aruba tomorrow."

"Colonel Jiménez," O'Reith said, "Haig cleared Heavy Latrobe to become a general but only until Nixon arrives to begin his presidential campaign. He wants Latrobe on the ticket with him as vice president."

"Good idea," the Colonel said, sipping cognac and watching the ash grow on his Claro. "Those peasants get to acting up, Nixon may not like it as well as he now thinks. If he decides to split out of here, Latrobe's broad shoulders can take the load."

"I hope that does not happen," O'Reith said. "Nixon still has to negotiate the terms of his pardon. May we plan on a four year term for Nixon?"

"With a regiment of U.S. Marines guarding the palace and the city, he can make four years in a breeze," the Colonel opined.

"And without them?" O'Reith asked.

"I give him a half hour," he added gloomily. The ash on his cigar was over an inch long. He knocked it off into a conch shell ash tray.

McDonough said, "After you are safely ensconced at Miraflores with a loyal Venezuelan army to keep you on seat, the 34th will return to maintain the peace in Honduras, El Salvador and Nicaragua. The 48th will then patrol the border in both the north and south. Haig has agreed to that but has to get the approval of Gerald Ford after he takes office. A bit of uncertainty there. Colonel Jiménez, how long to bring the Venezuelan Army into the fold?"

"I can't say. I've been away quite some long time. I was hoping to keep the American troops in Caracas for six months. Maybe a year."

"That could be difficult," O'Reith said.

"If something goes wrong in Caracas, if there is a glitch, will I be again welcome in Florida?" the Colonel asked, looking at O'Reith.

"I can't answer that question. Haig can explore it with Ford, once he is on seat. Perhaps we can open negotiations with him while he is still the Veep. It would be nice to have it all set."

Cook flicked the ash off of her panatella and sipped her cognac. "Those geophysical crews start shooting along the cordillera in a matter of days. We'll have a prognosis hanging on the wall in the tower conference room in 60 days. If it looks good we'll put two strings on the water by Thanksgiving Day. They'll be turning to the right before Christmas. If we make a discovery, we'll need troops for a long indefinite future."

Next morning O'Reith caught a Pan American DC-8 to Houston and an American Airline DC-10 to Dulles International. He took a taxi to town. Sitting with Haig in his West Wing office, he suggested they discuss pardon terms with Vice President Ford. Haig thought that would be a mistake.

O'Reith asked, "Can we count on Nixon to issue a Red Alert before he checks out? Without that, we'll be exposed with American troops in Caracas."

"You're dead right about that," Haig agreed. I'll get on the POTUS to do that a couple of days before he resigns."

"OK, Al. I'll be on my way. You know how to find me."

"Clive one other small matter," Haig asked, When will *The White Satin Miter* be showing?"

"Al, I'll ask Alice Ridley to call you on that."

With that, O'Reith returned to Guatemala City. He and McDonough were alone in the Colonel's parlor. "Not a good trip, George," O'Reith began. "Haig does not think opening a dialogue with Ford will be useful. We just have to tough it out until he is installed as POTUS. The House of Representatives is deliberating articles of impeachment. We're down to days. What's worse my youngest, Helen Simpson, who runs with a fast crowd, called me while I was in Washington. That goofy singer Ray Stevens, you know the *Ahab the Arab guy*?"

"I never heard of him," McDonough said.

"Well, everybody in the USA has heard of him. He's organizing a national 'streak in' against Nixon."

"Egad, Clive. Just what is a 'streak in'?"

"It is a parade down a prominent avenue with everyone in the nude carrying banners saying: 'Let it all hang out for Tricky Dick Nixon'. Hanging out refers to the tapes among other things."

"And why would you be concerned about it, Clive?"

"Because my daughter plans to lead the parade down Hollywood Boulevard."

"My word! What did you tell her?"

"I told her it was OK with me if it was OK with her mother."

"What did she say?"

"She moaned. Her mother had already nixed it. But she may do it anyhow."

"The matter is not resolved. Helen Simpson has a mind of her own. If Nixon learns my daughter streaked against him, it could queer our happy relationship."

"It can't hurt much. The troopships have arrived on the Honduran coast", McDonough said. "Start loading tomorrow."

"Latrobe holding up OK?"

"Yes. He's waiting for Nixon, a bit irritated that we don't tell him anything. We asked him to inventory all of that junk in the soccer stadium. He's upset about that. But he knows it won't be for long."

"How's the invasion going?"

"So far so good. Those natives don't want to fight. A few guerrillas are acting up. No worse than what we have right here in the city. The seismic crews are working without interruption. Carolyn is looking at the surveys. She'll be back here at the end of the week."

It was Monday, July 16th. O'Reith asked, "George, did Mulheny get his clearance to send the 34th to La Guiara?"

"Not yet. We're still waiting."

"Haig said he'd get right on it. How long to load a division?"

"A week anyhow. Maybe longer."

"I'll telephone Haig tonight if we haven't heard anything," O'Reith said.

The Colonel had been advising his Tachira troops of their imminent departure for Venezuela and arrived late. He said, "General O'Reith, I have recalled my troops from the Yucatan. The oil wells are now shut in. The Casinghead Company bottom line will be little affected."

"Where are the troops now?" O'Reith asked.

"Quartered at the armory. General of the Artillery Latrobe would like to give them orders. I suggested that he not do that. He was upset. I made it plain that they would resist any instructions he gave them. So everything is OK for now. We hope to soon depart. The *boys* are lonesome for the homeland."

"It won't be long," O'Reith said. "How many must we accommodate?"

"Well sir, we have 30 at the airport, another 30 here guarding the palace; I brought 50 back from the Yucatan and we have 20 at the armory. Then the military police patrolling the city, say another 50. That makes 180. Could be a few more here and there. We should plan on berths for 200 men."

"Sir George and I fly to Puerto Cortés tomorrow in the Aero Commander. Would you like to come along? You can go aboard a troopship, see what it is like."

The Colonel was elated. He said cheerily, "That would be very kind of you."

Flor and Margot joined them for drinks and listened as the Colonel described how happy his *boys* were to be going home.

O'Reith asked, "Colonel Jiménez, will you go with the 34th on the troopship?"

"I prefer flying. Can you arrange a flight to *Isla de Orchila*? The government no longer maintains a garrison there. Once the troopships have departed and we have an ETA off the Venezuelan coast, I could fly to the island, await their arrival and then join the troops on the beach. Wade ashore with them. Be photographed with water dripping from my pants legs for *El Nacional*."

"What about your *boys*?"

"They can go on the troopship, of course. I'll just take two or three of my close associates."

"I'll call Los Angeles tonight, line up a B-17 for you," O'Reith said.

Next morning they flew the 200 miles to Puerto Cortés to inspect the 34th as it prepared to embark on the MV *Banana Emperor*, the MV *Banana Express* and the forty-odd other ships. O'Reith asked about the length of the runway to determine if they could transport the Colonel's men in a C-54. O'Reith figured 4 trips would get all 200 of them from Aurora to Puerto Cortés. After a squad of troops stepped off the airstrip, Mulheny reported that it was 6,500 feet long. That was enough.

After dinner with Mulheny and his staff that night, next morning they flew to La Union to confer with General Mason. O'Reith explained that the C-54 would deliver the Colonel's men to Puerto Cortés and then fly to La Union to bring American military policemen to Guatemala City.

Mason asked, "How many and for how long sir?"

"We'll need about a hundred men, General Mason; protection for the airport, the palace and the armory. And a patrol force for the city. The Pentagon promised a Marine Corps detachment to arrive in 3 weeks."

"I must report your request routinely to the Pentagon, General O'Reith," Mason said. "Does that complicate matters?"

"Not as long as you copy it to General Haig in the White House."

"Yes sir, I can do that with confidence. When may I expect the C-54?"

"I'm waiting a 'go' signal from Haig."

"Yes sir, I'll have the troops ready. Each man to bring his full kit?"

"Yes. Four flights for the Colonel's men to Puerto Cortés," O'Reith advised. "That should cover you."

"Yes sir."

After lunch, the travelers returned to Guatemala City, arriving late in the afternoon of July 25. The Nile green Chrysler took them to the palace. As they were having drinks, an urgent call came in from Haig.

"Yes sir, Al, How have you been keeping?" O'Reith asked when the Colonel passed the instrument to him.

"Like a one-legged man in an ass-kicking contest Clive," Haig replied impatiently. "Supreme Court ruling came down yesterday against us. House began impeachment hearings last night. Things are going to hell in a hand basket up here. Nixon sent an aide to canvass the Senate. Guy came back and reported the POTUS had three votes. He fell into deep depression. He and Henry are together right now praying for holy salvation. They've been at it for an hour or so. Henry won't be able to get up off his knees. Anyhow, looks like at least three articles of impeachment no later than July 31st. Henry has advised him to resign on more than one occasion but so far he's resisting. But realistically, he has to go and he knows it and he has to go before the Senate begins deliberations. With only three votes, they'll have him convicted before the first coffee break of the morning session. How soon can he be elected president of the sphere?"

"Hold on Al, I'll ask the Colonel.

The Colonel smiled and began, "We'll put up those *Notre Nixon* posters tomorrow. Margot will come up with a snappy slogan. We'll print it up and post it all around town. Once they're up, we can announce his candidacy and elect him two or three days later. He could be inaugurated August 3rd. How would that be?"

"Al, the Colonel says he'll be in on August 3rd. That OK?"

"I'll make it OK," Haig said.

"Al, we're moving his *boys* out of here in the morning. They'll be flying to Puerto Cortés to board the troopships. I asked General Mason for a company of MPs to replace them here in the city until you send me some marines."

"Marines?"

"Yeah, Al, remember we talked about that and you said it was OK."

"I may have Clive. In this crazy situation, I can never remember from one day to the next what I've said. Clive, I may, repeat may, be able to pry a platoon of military policemen loose. Say three squads. That's 33 men and a second lieutenant. They may not be marines. Can't guarantee that."

"A platoon! That's small potatoes Al. They are coming to protect Nixon, for Christ's sake! Either you send me a reinforced company or agree that I can hold on to Mason's MPs from the 48th."

"Clive, I'll join the POTUS and Henry K. just as soon as we're through talking. When the supplications run down and we're having a post-prayer nightcap, I'll put it to Nixon that we need troops in

Guatemala for the long haul. The problem is that once Gerald Ford becomes president, he can recall them immediately."

"We have to take our chances on that," O'Reith replied. "But we've got to get our Red Alert. We're up a creek without that."

"Yeah, I know," Haig said. He was ready to hang up when he remembered something. He said, "Clive, are you still there?"

"Yeah, Al, shoot."

"How long for the Colonel and the 34th to reach La Guiara?"

"It is about a thousand miles or so from Puerto Cortés to La Guiara. At 20 knots, they should make it in 3 days and then a couple of days to disembark a contingent large enough to march on the capital. The Colonel plans to meet them on Orchid Island.

"Why doesn't he go with the troops?"

"He wants to be here to turn over power to Nixon and I think it is proper that he should. It would not look too good if he had already decamped."

"That is certainly true," Haig agreed.

"So if he stays for the ceremonies, he can leave for the island in the evening after inauguration. How does that sound?"

"We need to do it that way," Haig agreed. "Instead of the 3rd, can we set it up for August 10? That's a Saturday. Nixon could make his resignation speech on the ninth, fly to San Clemente; get a bit of rest and on to Guatemala City. Get in around noon. I'll ask Bebe Rebozo to provide a Lear Jet. He'll want to come down for the formalities. Will you meet them at Aurora Airport?"

"Sure, I'll line up a motorcade to escort the presidential party to the palace. We'll have the Guatemala Army Band, an open-air car with pennants for the Nixons and the Colonel. Latrobe and Bebe Rebozo can follow. George and I will bring up the rear in the green limousine. We'll string military policemen along *Reforma*. It'll be a nice parade."

"Can Nixon make his inaugural address from the steps of the palace? Any problem with that?" Haig asked.

"There could be an unruly crowd. But we can close the gates. Everyone can still hear him but he'll be out of tomato range. Spanish or English?" O'Reith asked.

Haig chuckled. "English, we tried it him out *en espanol*. He sounds like a Tex-Mex hawking tamales on a street corner in San Antonio."

"For the average Guatemalan, it might just as well be Chinese. Are you and Henry coming for the event?"

"Can't promise it, Clive. Ron Ziegler is set up to escort Nixon to San Clemente. Certainly one of us should come down. I'll try to make it myself. POTUS in bad, bad shape. Pat is in a melancholy mood. Bad scene all around. We'll have to keep POTUS jollied up and out of depression long enough for him to make a good speech. How about that make-up girl you've got working for you, Sharon Mills? Can she come along to touch him up before he gets off the plane?"

"Sure, call Alice Ridley. She'll take care of it."

"OK, Clive, I guess that's it. By the way, Alice called me like you said she would. She explained about the *Signal Red Cadillac.* That's neat."

"Great, hang on one second, Al." O'Reith looked to the Colonel, asked," The 10th instead of the 3rd. That OK?"

"Why not," Jiménez answered.

"Al, we're on. Cheers."

The oil executives, the Colonel, Flor and Margot were in the presidential parlor planning the procession. O'Reith began, "With all of those marginals around, I'm a bit nervous about having those guys in open-air cars. Colonel Jiménez, will we be safe? We don't want some nut to take a shot at them."

"Well, a parade is part of the ceremony when a new president takes office. We can't have him skulking in unseen like a horse thief. With the military policemen stationed along the way, he should be safe enough. After all, the city is quiet right now. There are a few tigers on the loose but if we keep a low profile, maybe they won't bother us. The trouble begins once you get outside the city limits."

"You're sure of that, Colonel Jiménez? No need to worry about those tigers?" O'Reith asked.

"I doubt if there are a half a dozen in town," he said.

"Is the Guatemalan Army Band any good?" McDonough asked.

"I have no idea. "I can't recall a performance."

"Let's line up a rehearsal in the soccer stadium," McDonough added.

"Good idea," Cook seconded the motion.

"Latrobe can do that," the Colonel suggested.

"What tunes are they going to play?" O'Reith asked.

Flor Jiménez suggested, "The band could begin with *Marshmallows and Meadow Larks* as they get into the cars at the airport, a light airy melody."

"Followed by, *Honey bees to the Hive* Cook said.

"And then *Flowers of the Forest*, McDonough added. "Gets us up to the hotel."

"How about *Coronel Cortés, Conquistador* from the hotel to the gates of the *Palacio Nacional*," the Colonel offered.

"Just the ticket. And once inside the garden at the palace, as the gates swing shut, *Hail to the Chief*. Then he speaks," O'Reith said.

"Perfect!" Margot Jiménez exclaimed, clapping her hands in delight.

They all laughed gaily. The houseboy brought the drink tray and there was merriment all around.

The Pan Am clipper from Los Angeles brought the papers down on August 5th. Propped up in bed at the *El Camino Real*, O'Reith was looking them over when he spotted a headline on the front page of the *Yellow Peril*. It read:

> NIXON STREAK SNARLS TRAFFIC AT HOLLYWOOD AND VINE!
>
> August 4, Los Angeles. Ray Stevens the corn pone comic singer organized a nationwide streak denouncing President Richard M. Nixon after the Supreme Court ruled he had to turn his tapes over to the congressional committee. Nationwide, the streakers numbered in the hundreds of thousands. A masked girl with a fine figure led the crowd in the parade along Sunset Boulevard and we wish we could have seen her face. We counted about 5,000 souls in the parade, none of them with gray hair. No potbellies and no sagging titties. The youth of America spoke. We know who the masked girl is. But for once, our little newspaper is not going to name names. We will however, offer a clue. Her father is one of the powers that run this town. Some would say he runs the country. Some think he runs the world. Anyway, we are not going to pick a fight. Even if we were, we would be leery. Only fools would get involved in this madness.

But it was a headline in The *Washington Post* that immediately caught O'Reith's eyes. When he saw it, he breathed a great sigh of relief.

The *Washington Post*
August 4, Washington, DC

NIXON SAYS WOLF HUFFING AND PUFFING ON DOOR

From the White House lawn, a visibly worried President Nixon announced in a hollow voice that resonated in the hot summer afternoon, that the CIA had just uncovered a widespread and pernicious conspiracy against the U.S. This so-called *Axis of Evil* includes Mexico, Venezuela, Colombia and all of the Central American states except the *Co-prosperity sphere.* The evil masterminds behind this sinister threat include *fidelistas* and *mumbaistas,* these latter a dangerous radical religious cult from the area around Bombay, India. President Nixon declared a national emergency and a Red Alert. All military forces are being readied to repel an expected invasion of Florida and troops are preparing to launch pre-emptive strikes throughout Latin America as required. Nixon says this threat greatly exceeds the Cuban Missile Crisis of 1962.

At the State Department, a grim-faced Henry Kissinger spoke in calibrated words of this sudden menace, comparing it to the face-off in the Middle East. He said he would travel to Tel Aviv for discussions with Golda Meir immediately.

At the Defense Department, a shaken James Schlesinger, called back to the Pentagon from a bird-watching trip, declared the nation was prepared to meet all threats including the poisoning of crested kingfishers in the National Zoo.

As he put the papers aside and got up to get a bottle of soda water out of the minibar, the telephone rang. It was Helen. She began, "Ace, I want you to speak to Helen Simpson."

"What about?" O'Reith asked.

"She streaked down Hollywood Boulevard!"

"Helen I was just reading about that in the *Peril...*"

"The *Peril* didn't identify her but it was her all right. Ace she wore a ski mask and sneakers. There was this guy who was masked too. She couldn't see his face or his feet but she saw everything else."

"So what?"

"So she didn't come home after the streak. Ace, she fell for the guy! On the spot, that is on the street. She took him with her to the guesthouse in Holmby Hills. They shacked up. She only saw his face after they were in bed!"

"Rae rat on her?" O'Reith asked.

"No. She's had the key to that place for a long time. This is not the first time she has taken some guy out there. Rae Regan doesn't like it but she long ago quit paying attention to her. But when she didn't come home the next day I called. Phone off the hook, naturally. So I called Rae. Asked her to knock on the door. Big flap of course. Then Helen Simpson called, gooey sweet of course. She wanted to bring him home for me to meet."

"You should be flattered, Helen. After that racket with the beachcomber, she's met the love of her life and wants you to bless the affair."

"After almost 48 hours of continuous copulation she falls in love," Helen continued. "The idea of bringing him home to meet mother arose out of exhaustion. Ace the guy works in a shop that makes dresses for transvestites. He decks the drag queens out in their finery! What do you think of that?"

"Normal for Hollywood. So what?"

"Ace, he may be a bisexual! I asked her why she took up with him and she said there was something about the way he moved! What moved was his you-know-what. Up and down and from side to side."

"Helen, it may not be as bad as it looks. She's had odd boyfriends before."

"She wants to bring him in the house!"

"Au naturel?"

"Ace, be serious. I don't know if he's au naturel or not. I am not going to let him in."

"Helen it is inappropriate for me to speak to her over the telephone. Can't this wait until I return?"

"No, Ace. You have a responsibility."

"Where is she?"

"Sitting here beside me, tapping her feet, in a pout. I took the guesthouse keys away. She's pissed off purple as you would say."

"Where is the drag queen guy?"

"He's sitting out in the car on the curb. That's why Helen Simpson is in a snit. I won't let him in the house."

"Put her on," O'Reith said wearily.

"Hello, Daddy Cool." She purred musically into the mouthpiece, imitating her father's manner of speaking.

"So you're in the news and in the soup as well, sweetie pie," O'Reith began. "Your mother and I are of a more conservative era. Streaking was not *de rigeur* when we were your age. And you didn't pick a boyfriend based on the size of his…"

"Daddy Cool it was not like that at all! Not at all! Mother is making a big deal out of this. Larry is a wonderful boy and he has political aspirations and I'm really in love with him. We have the same ideas about social justice. We both believe in free love, sharing the wealth and…"

O'Reith interrupted, "Sweetie pie, men have always believed in free love. It is only since the birth control pill that women do. Put your mother back on the line."

"Yes sir! Daddy Cool!"

When his wife came back on the line, O'Reith said, "Helen, I don't see any way out except to invite the boy in and talk to him. See what kind of a guy he is…"

"I won't have that fag in my house, Ace! I won't!"

"Helen, as it happens, this is somewhat sensitive. As you know, George and I are working with Nixon. Trying to save him and it is iffy as hell. That isn't to say that if he finds out that Helen Simpson was the Hollywood Streak leader that it is the end of the world. I can take the heat if it comes to that. Going beyond that, refusing to meet the boy will just alienate her further. She'll stalk out and the next thing we know they'll be shacked up in a cardboard box on the sidewalk on Central Avenue next to one of those joints with a flashing red light over the door. So ask him in. Give him a fair shake."

"Ace you can be maddeningly right sometimes."

"Where's Alice?" O'Reith asked.

"She's here."

"Put her on."

When Ridley came on the line, O'Reith said, "Alice,Take one of my bathrobes, go with Helen Simpson and invite the boy in. Then you can introduce him to Helen. It will be smoother that way.

"Sure. I'll do it. Here's Helen again."

"Helen, Alice is going to run interference for you on this. I'll be home in a few days and together we can sit down and find a way out of this. What say?"

"Well, when you put it like that, I guess I have to agree. But I sure as hell don't like it. I suppose you heard that Nixon was on national TV. He resigns tomorrow."

"I hadn't but we all expected it. See you in a few days, baby."

Early on August 9th, O'Reith called Haig in his White House office. "Al, are we all set?"

"Everything looks OK, Clive. Nixon put the word out yesterday on national TV. He resigns at noon. Then he heads west with Ziegler. He has organized a counter-streak, a red herring, to take place while he's addressing the nation. Kissinger is in charge of it. He's going to turn the entire State Department out in the buff and lead them at a trot from the Reflecting Pool all the way to the Washington Monument. It's Nixon's way of saying farewell to all that."

"That's a good idea, Al. Good cover while he's making tracks. Henry can use the exercise. Very well, I'll meet the Lear Jet in the morning."

"Take care, Clive."

"Ta-ta, Al."

August 10, 1974, like most Saturdays in Guatemala City, was balmy and fresh, befitting its cognomen: Land of Eternal Spring. It had rained in the early hours, the cool drops washing the dust from the mimosas and bougainvillea trees that lined the sidewalks of *Avenida de la Reforma*. By noon, the sun was high, vying with the fleecy white clouds for dominance of the sky. The temperature was 80° F. Street vendors hawked their gimcrackery. Beggars clogged the sidewalks. Urchins milled about, cadging cigarettes. In the tonneau of the green Chrysler were O'Reith, the Colonel, Flor and Margot, these latter ladies destined for Los Angeles on the Lear Jet that, even now, approached Aurora Airport bringing the presidential party. Trailing were the two open-air cars, rear seats empty. As the procession rolled down *Avenida Hincapie*, a small gate opened on the taxiway across the runway from the terminal. A freshly painted Sherman tank was parked prominently near it. The rumble of four idling Cadillac V-16 engines drowned out the other noises of the street. The top hatch of the tank was open and the head and shoulders of a steel-helmeted 48th Division MP was evident. The tank's 76mm cannon gleamed in the soft sunlight. The gate swung open and the three cars edged around the tank, drove onto the taxiway and continued parallel to the terminal building until they reached the perimeter road around the 3,000 meter runway. The guards allowed them through and as they made their way, the blue and white Lear Jet touched down and began taxiing toward them. The three cars waited until it stopped, some hundred yards from the terminal. A taxi carrying McDonough and Cook joined them. Then, and only then, did the small caravan approach the aircraft. The engines of the jet idled, signaling that the pilots planned to take off again without refueling, quite soon. The door of the airplane opened, the ramp came down and O'Reith made his way aboard. Bebe Rebozo dressed in a gray and white seersucker suit, a white straw hat on his head, was reading the sports pages of the *Miami Herald*. Beside him sat a moping Pat Nixon smoking a filter tip cigarette. Her hands were unsteady. Next to her sat the disgraced former POTUS, RMN, scribbling on his yellow legal pad. His hands too, were a bit shaky. Sharon Mills, on a fold-up stool put the finishing touches on his face. Across from him, a smiling Al Haig, in a dark blue business suit, looked on with evident approval. O'Reith greeted them all, shaking hands around. He explained that the Colonel was in the car outside and that as soon as they deplaned, Flor and Margot would board. He asked of Haig, "Al, will you join us for the drive in, the presidential address and the swearing in?"

"Good God No!" Haig retorted. "I'd lose my job straight-away if Gerald Ford even suspected I was in this part of the world. I came along to help RMN with his speech."

"We better get a move on," O'Reith said. "We're already running late. As they deplaned, the Jiménez ladies took their place on board, followed by Cook with her bulging briefcase of Honduran seismic lines. A platoon of MPs from the 48th Division had surrounded the three cars. They had escorted General of the Artillery Heavy Latrobe, wearing his dazzling white silk outfit and lightweight general's hat decorated with silver scrambled eggs. On his feet were white, ankle-high boots of soft kidskin. His costume gathered the light of the day, reflected it like a silvered orb and gave him the aura of a religioso. Just before the copilot closed the main hatch of the Lear Jet, O'Reith stuck his head inside and said, "Sharon, look after Flor and Margot. You can put them in guest quarters in the Fullerton Building."

In the first open car, Richard M. and Pat Nixon took their places. Behind them, in the second car, General Latrobe and Bebe Rebozo sat. And in the green Chrysler, O'Reith and McDonough sat in the cushions. They awaited Jimenéz who had gone aboard the Lear Jet to say adios to his wife and daughter. He joined them, took the jump seat. Car doors slammed. Engines came to life. The three-car caravan snaked across the runway in a long U-turn and exited the airport just as they had entered. Outside the automobiles paused, engines idling, to allow the Sherman tank to edge out in front of them. Between the tank and the open car bearing the Nixons, the Guatemala Army Band fell in and brought their instruments to attention. In all they numbered forty with a goodly section, as one would expect, of brass. Two tubas, four trumpets, four saxophones. Then came the flutes and the fifes followed by a dozen reeds. The drummers brought up the rear. Two bass drums, four snares and a tambourine. The shrill whistle of the military police captain cut through the air; the band crashed into the opening bars of *Marshmallows and Meadowlarks.* The tank throttles were opened: automobile engines purred. The procession started.

Slowly, quite slowly, they went to *Avenida Hincapie* and away from Aurora Airport. They inched their way up to the intersection with Diagonal 12 where they jogged right to the roundabout at *Parque Independencia.* Now they were in *Avenida La Reforma* going north. As the line of cars straightened out and rolled along the broad avenue, the Colonel grimaced at his companions and muttered, " hope all of this comes out OK."

"You seem unduly concerned," McDonough observed.

"You can never tell exactly when some wild card will flip out of the deck, Sir George." The Colonel added. He looked at his watch. "Almost one o'clock", he observed. "What time do I depart tonight, General O'Reith?"

"Around eight. B-17 expected in the early evening. Not to worry."

"Well I do. I am on the pins and the needles. Have I got that right?"

"Just pins and needles," O'Reith corrected him.

The band had finished *Marshmallows and Meadowlarks.* Now it was playing *Honey Bees to the Hive.* The procession had covered several blocks. O'Reith noted a cross street sign that read *15 Calle.* As *Honey Bees* faded, the melodious strains of *Flowers of the Forest* floated back over the street noises.

Bystanders gathered on the sidewalks. A pair of American military policemen stood at parade rest at each intersection. On the left, stately gardened mansions of an earlier era blazed with the colors of violets and roses. It was warm in the limousine. The procession moved so slowly that O'Reith found himself nodding off. The lead car crossed *6a Calle.* He sat up sharply as president-elect Nixon stood and climbed atop the jump seat with his hands clasped above his head. He gestured in triumph to the ragged, bewildered peons along the sidewalks. "Nixon should not be doing that," the Colonel said nervously. "I should have warned him."

"Maybe nothing will happen," McDonough said.

"Maybe," the Colonel echoed, unconvincingly.

Then imitating his master, Heavy Latrobe stood on his jump seat as his car began to cross *6a Calle.* His brilliant white uniform gleamed pristine in the noonday sun. His short, thick arms were windmilling above his tiny head. He was basking in the glamor of the ceremonial parade, looking from one side of the avenue to the other, accepting his accolades. Suddenly from *6a Calle,* two snarling tigers, loping in parallel, bounded into the *avenida,* and leapt upon the rear of the open car. With perfect timing, each black and orange cat, mouth agape, bit deeply into Latrobe's shoulders. The cats jumped from the car carrying him, shouting, screaming, and dragging his heels across the *avenida.* On the other side, *6a Calle* terminated in a densely wooded area. Even before Latrobe had disappeared into the brush, four more man-eaters raced out of the hedges that fronted the side street. The animals were roaring with hunger. Latrobe screamed a time or two and fell quiet.

"Jesus H. Christ!" O'Reith exclaimed.

"Zounds!" McDonough said excitedly.

"Well, there goes Vice President Latrobe," the Colonel noted sadly. "I can't say that I am surprised. Guatemala City is a funny kind of town to be a vice presidential candidate in."

As the procession passed beneath *Torre del Reforma,* Bebe Rebozo disappeared from view, presumably hugging the floorboards.

"You suppose we should speed this show up?" O'Reith asked.

The Colonel said, "The tank engines are old and have been poorly maintained. It isn't much further now. Look, we're passing the hotel. Soon we'll be at the *Palacio Nacional.*"

When the tigers took Latrobe away, shouts and murmurs arose sporadically from the bystanders. Nixon, in the car ahead, unable to see what had happened to his erstwhile Veep, took the shouts to mean approval. He became more animated.

"Should we stop the procession and tell him what happened?" O'Reith asked.

"Better to go on. Get it over with," the Colonel said. "What can we do?"

"I guess you're right," O'Reith admitted. "But it seems bizarre."

They were transiting *Ciudad Olimpica*. The band broke into *Coronel Cortés Conquistador*.

"We're almost there," the Colonel said, relief in his voice.

O'Reith discerned the head of Rebozo peering over the top of the car door. He had lost his hat. Bolder, he sat up and began waving back at the green Chrysler. "He's trying to get our attention," O'Reith said.

McDonough said, "I suppose I should signal back at him that it is OK."

"Well, it is not OK but I guess you're right. Wave at him," the Colonel said.

McDonough rolled the car window down and gave the frantic Rebozo the high sign. It failed to calm him down. Rebozo continued to gesticulate wildly.

"We could do this indefinitely," McDonough said, rolling up the window again. "How long until we get to the *Palacio Nacional*?"

"Ten minutes maximum," the Colonel said.

The motorcade was slowly turning left into *8a Calle*, which led to the central plaza, and then, the *Palacio Nacional*. O'Reith, hands clasped in his lap, passed the time listening to the pounding beat of *Coronel Cortés Conquistador*. The melody dwindled as the motorcade arrived at the gates of the palace. The tank pulled out of the procession. The three big cars crunched onto the graveled parkway that ran between the palace and the garden. The huge wrought iron gates clanged shut once the cars were inside. A motley clutch of bystanders was gathering. Nixon got out the car, helping Pat. Together they ascended the stone stairs to the base of the portico. The band played *Hail to the Chief*. Nixon stood at attention with his right hand over his breast, a beatific smile on his face. The oilmen and the Colonel slipped out of the car, gingerly climbed the steps to stand beside RMN on the other side from

Pat. O'Reith spotted the New Hope Pomona Minstrels on the steps. Cherry Cokeland was swinging her hips. When the music wound down, he asked the Colonel, "Where are the crowds to hear my address?"

"On the other side of the gate," the Colonel said.

"Those ratty looking souls?" Nixon asked. "Why they're marginals! Where are the men and women dressed in suits and nice dresses? Like we had on my previous visit."

"Well sir, they saw you the first time. Once is enough," the Colonel continued. "What few there are, are here with us on the steps. That crowd milling around in the plaza is a different bunch of cats. They are your people. You might as well get started."

Outside, the gate, the crowd got larger and noisier. Scuffles broke out back in the plaza in the general direction of the cathedral. Several ripe tomatoes exploded against the iron grill work. Shouting occurred, as masses pressed against the gate. Inasmuch as the electricity was off, the public address system was not working. One of the aides held a megaphone for Nixon.

Speaking in stentorian English, Nixon began:

> "My fellow Central Americans, Vice President Elect Latrobe, members of the press and the military, diplo mats and friends, I appear before you today as the second regularly elected president of our grand and glorious *Greater Central American Co-prosperity Spher*e. Many of you have never seen me in the flesh before but surely you recognize me from television. I want you to know that it is my intention to be as good a president as Colonel Jiménez. I will emulate him in every way and continue his policies that have made the Co-prosperity Sphere a model of economic efficiency not only in Central America but also in the world. Let me affirm and reaffirm to you that I am a patriotic man. Always I place the affairs of state ahead of personal gain. Do not expect any significant legislative changes for the next few years. The Colonel has made all of the necessary adjustments to our society and it is enough that I continue his good work. I would not be complete in my address to you if I did not mention the gallant soldier who will presently become my vice president. I refer to General of the Artillery Boniface Milhous Latrobe. I am certain that when you get to know him and understand him, you will feel for him all of the love and admiration

that you feel for me. Finally, I declare tomorrow to be a national holiday and I urge all of you to have a good time, that is, after you go to holy mass in the morning. And I remind you that as Roman Catholics in a truly Catholic country we must take to our hearts the new papal encyclical called *Casti Connubii II.* Tomorrow, as you kneel in your pew, think kindly of Pope Paul VI and his encyclical and ask him to bless you."

The crowd hung on. Taking heart from their presence, he continued.

> "Richard M. Nixon will be the president that you remember when your children are grown and they too will remember him for his good works particularly in the field of education."

The faces at the gate registered disbelief not at what he said but because they could only guess at the meaning of his words. O'Reith, McDonough and the Colonel slipped away from his side and went inside the National Palace. Bebe Rebozo joined them. He whispered to O'Reith, "Back there in the motorcade I was signaling for you to stop. Didn't you see what happened to Latrobe?"

Just inside the foyer, Nixon's voice droned on:

> "One thing that I take pride in above all others is that I am an old line patriot in the spirit of our founding fathers. Always, yes, always, Richard M. Nixon has placed the good of the country above all other considerations. Let me remind you of the Alger Hiss case. Had I not nailed him when I did, the Hammer and Sickle would now be flying over the White House in Washington, DC. My fellow Central Americans, you may go to bed tonight without worry that communism will ever come here. Richard M. Nixon is proud to put his hand over his heart and recite the oath of allegiance to the flag and everything for which it stands. I would never sell out our subtropical paradise. I would never try to distort or twist our laws. Richard M. Nixon would never sell out his country for personal gain. Richard M. Nixon intends to stand fast against the forces of *fidelismo* and *mumbaiismo* that so infect Mexico, Venezuela, Honduras and El Salvador. Nixon stands you a dandy and long-lasting president."

O'Reith answered Rebozo. "Are you referring to the fact that he was carried away by those tigers?"

"Well it is no small matter, for Christ's sake," Rebozo rejoined. "We'll have to tell the president. You heard him talking about the new administration. He mentioned Heavy twice. We don't even know where he is. We don't know what condition he is in."

"We know what condition he is in," the Colonel muttered. "Dismembered. Eaten alive. Forget about Latrobe. He is history."

Rebozo looked at him with utter disbelief in his eyes. "Why didn't you stop the motorcade and send those military policemen after the tigers?"

"It was too late. Those babies work fast. We would have found nothing but bones and those well gnawed. It seemed better to push on to the palace before something worse happened."

"A couple more of those cats could have popped up from nowhere and gone after Nixon. Then where would we have been? No president. No vice president. Besides," O'Reith added. "Going after man-eaters is a dangerous quest. The captain of the military police now is surely aware of what transpired. He will by now have assembled a team of marksmen. We'll have a report from him presently. All we can do now is attend the swearing in."

"That's when Nixon will notice that Heavy is missing. They are supposed to be sworn in one after the other." Rebozo said.

"That's true," O'Reith agreed.

"It seems to me that you fellows are taking this rather lightly," Rebozo said.

Nixon continued speaking to the peons.

"Our new president does not seem to know when to stop," the Colonel said. "Perhaps we should suggest to him that he give it up. If he's waiting for all those marginal people at the gate to go away, he'll be there a long while. Let's ask him to come inside and get sworn in."

The Colonel stepped to the door, touched Pat Nixon's shoulder and motioned to her to shut her husband down. She nudged his ribs and tipped him off that he was wasting his breath. He stopped speaking, smiled and waved idiotically at the crowd at the gate. Rivulets of seedy tomato juice stained the driveway. At a signal from the Colonel, the palace fuglemen ushered RMN and Pat into the grand hall to take the oath of office. A wigged barrister with a bland expression on his face held a bible. A Spanish interpreter stood by. Nixon, all smiles, asked Rebozo, "What did you think of my speech?"

"Fine speech, Mr. President."

"What have you done with Heavy?" Nixon asked smiling and looking around the room for him. "We'll need him for the swearing in."

The Colonel answered for Rebozo. "Unfortunately, Vice President Elect Latrobe was borne from his car by a pair of man-eating tigers. Thus he will not be available to take the oath of office as vice president of the *Greater Central American Co-prosperity Sphere.*"

Nixon's jaw dropped. His eyes bulged out. He said "What! What's that you say?"

O'Reith said, "Those two babies shot out of *Calle 6a* and bolted across the avenue like racing cars at the Indianapolis Speedway. They must have been hiding out in those Acacia bushes in *Parque Centro America*. They grabbed him and headed off before anyone could react. That oversized cap with the scrambled eggs reflecting the sunlight caught the tiger's eyes. Most likely they made short work of him."

"Jesus Christ!" Nixon exclaimed.

"It is all so sad," Pat Nixon added, lighting a cigarette.

"Well, we have to get on with it," Nixon concluded ruefully. "Swear me in."

The Colonel snapped his fingers. The barrister stepped forward. The interpreter took her place and within minutes, Richard Milhous Nixon was sworn is as the second president of the *Greater Central American Co-prosperity Sphere.*

Although early afternoon, hands trembling, Nixon said, "I need a drink."

Pat nodded and lit a fresh cigarette from the butt of the one she was smoking.

The major participants in the drama retreated to the presidential residence and in the Colonel's private den the houseboys began bringing the gin and scotch. Rattling the ice cubes in his martini, Nixon said, "I can't get over what happened to Heavy. There I was accepting the tribute of my subjects and unknown to me, the tigers had whisked him out of the car."

"They came within inches of me," Rebozo said. "I could smell their breath. They sure as hell hadn't been chewing their Certs."

"Are we taking all necessary measures to find him?" Nixon asked forlornly.

"Probably not much left of him by now," the Colonel lamented.

Pat Nixon tossed off her scotch and lit another cigarette. "It is all so sad," she repeated.

Nixon was scribbling on his yellow legal pad. He said, "Well, we have to come up with a new vice president. Bebe, How about you?"

"Dick I am honored that you would think of me but my many business interests in Florida require attention. So I must graciously decline."

Nixon looked at the Colonel. He asked, "I don't suppose you would accept the position. I could surely use your vast store of experience."

"In just a few hours I depart for Venezuela to reclaim my rightful place as head of my country."

"Really!" Nixon said.

"Surely you knew about that, Mr. President," O'Reith said. "The Red Alert is in all the newspapers."

The Colonel stood. He began shadowboxing violently. He said, "I am off to unseat that scoundrel Carlos Andres Pérez. I will smite him. I will say, take that you vermin! Take that forever!" In the heat of anticipation, he became florid. His short arms windmilled wildly. Beads of sweat popped out of his forehead. His face became angry. He ranted, "All of them! All of those villainous *Accionistas*! When I appear, standing straight and proud on the steps of Miraflores, they will scamper. Like the muskrats on the deck of the Titanic, they will jump into the icy sea. And then I will find that base Romulo Betancourt. He lives in Mercedes in luxurious quarters, his imperial, richly adorned chambers. I will throw him into prison immediately. I will re institute the *Seguridad Nacional.* I will summon Pedro Estrada from Madrid. With a snap of my fingers, Venezuela will be a changed nation!" He became calmer, sat.

Nixon sighed, motioned to the houseboy to refill his glass. He said, "I guess you're right. So much going on these last few days, I vaguely remember the Red Alert speech. I'd had a couple of drinks. I didn't expect you to leave so soon. I was hoping you could help me get my feet on the ground."

"That's quite all right, Mr. President. Even a man of your high Excellency can't remember everything going on in this mad world. You will find your way quickly."

"Well I hope so." Nixon said with emphasis. "Well, gentlemen, what am I to do for a vice president? How about you, Clive?"

"I'm an officer in the Army of the United States on Red Alert."

Nixon looked at McDonough.

"I am a simple man of the cloth, your Excellency."

"You could do without," the Colonel suggested. "I managed for over a decade. Besides President Nixon, Heavy Latrobe would have been your third Veep. Word could get out that you were a tricky guy to be a vice president for."

Nixon looked at the Colonel with a mixture of amazement and despair. He took a swallow of gin and looked reproachfully at him. "Are you suggesting that men who become my vice presidents are unlucky?"

"Well, two out of three became croppers," the Colonel said.

Nixon, asked hesitantly as if expecting more bad news, "Colonel Jiménez, what about my Secretary of State?"

"What about him?"

"Who is he?"

"Mr. Nixon, that position is currently unfilled. We have no Secretary of State at the present time."

"And Secretary of Defense?" Nixon asked plaintively.

"I have been wearing that hat in addition to my others."

"Chief of Staff?" Nixon asked." His hands were trembling. "I cannot function without one."

"You're fortunate there, Mr. President, You have two finance ministers. You can convert one of them into a Chief of Staff."

"Two finance men?"

"One for external funds. Banana money, subsidies and oil revenue," the Colonel explained. "The other one is a local currency man, a quetzal guy."

The expression on Nixon's face was of utter dismay.

O'Reith said, gentlemen this is all becoming rather morbid. Let's drink a toast to the new president of the sphere."

"Here! Here!" Rebozo shouted.

"Here! Here!" they all echoed. Glasses clinked merrily. Nixon, ginned up, throwing off his melancholy, again feeling sure of himself, began telling a story about how he and Kissinger had outsmarted Golda Meir. Halfway through, the party was interrupted by a messenger who reported that the search party had found Latrobe's white uniform, shredded and bloodstained. His feet were still in his soiled white boots except for the toes, which had been bitten off.

"Jesus!" Nixon said. "Jesus H. Christ! He has two sisters. Beulah and Bertha. How can I tell them what happened to him? It is beyond belief." His eyes once again became sad.

"Politics is a dangerous profession, Mr. President," the Colonel said. "You could tell the sisters that he was assassinated; a frequent political fate in this paranoid place."

"That's a good idea," Nixon agreed. "Colonel Jiménez," he continued. "Have you any parting words of advice for me on how to run the country?"

"President Nixon, running this country is much simpler than running the United States. Remember these few things. About 10% of the people can fend for themselves. Street vendors, the feather merchants, the banana growers, the rum distillers and those who enjoy the benefits of government service. The beggars too, in their way. Of the remaining 90%, a small fraction, maybe 2 or 3% are agitators. They stir up the simple peasants eking a hard living off of the land. Unfortunately, peasants can be stirred up easily. And those that move to the city quickly become marginals, like those hanging around the gate to hear your speech. They will loiter out there all-night, pissing against the gate and defecating with abandon. Big mess in the morning.

The key to running a nice, quiet country is to find, round up and liquidate the agitators. Unhappily, new ones always come along to take the places of those just liquidated. Those peasants who have become marginal must go to prison. If not, they hang around the streets and beg for a handout. A prison construction program is a must because the population never stops growing. Every year you have more people who need to be locked up. Among those locked up, some become vicious and they have to be liquidated. We have here a *Congresso Nacional* of 55 members. In the decade I have been here, they do as they please and I do as I please. I take care that they are paid regularly. I veto all of their legislation. That's the quid pro quo. It seems to work out quite well. We have no problems, working together in harmony."

"Is there not some kind of social security system in place for those who are impoverished?" Nixon asked. "And what about Medicare and Medicaid?"

"We do not yet have those programs in place, sir. They were legislated and in due course, annulled."

"Colonel Jiménez, here we are three-quarters of the way through the 20th Century and you tell me that in the *Co-prosperity Sphere*, those who have fallen through society's economic crack have little or no recourse. Does that not erode the meaning of *Co-prosperity*?"

"Sir George suggested that name," the Colonel said. "You know how he is. He tends to over dramatize mundane events. The truth is that we have little prosperity. That's why we have the problems I just described. But in due course, you will get used to that and learn how to come to grips with it."

"Well I certainly hope so," Nixon said, somewhat abashed. He was flagging and he looked down at the floor. He said softly, "I wish there was something we could do for poor Heavy."

"Issue a stamp. Put his picture on it," the Colonel suggested.

"Or on a coin or even a new issue of banknotes," Nixon mused. "Yes. I plan to put out a new bill with my picture on it. We could honor Heavy posthumously."

"We already have quite an array of bills outstanding," the Colonel commented. "The highest note is already up in the millions of quetzals."

Rebozo said, "All the more reason to issue a couple more. In the United States, our highest note, the $100,000 bill has a picture of Woodrow Wilson. Down here, we could issue the NanoNixon and the NanoLatrobe. Why not that? Say a 5 NanoNixon Quetzal Note and a 3 NanoLatrobe Quetzal Note?"

"Christ," Nixon said, adding, "How much is a Nano?"

"A big, big goddam number," Rebozo explained. "Three or four gadzillions. We'd only have to put out a few of them. They'd never circulate."

"That is a really keen idea," Nixon agreed. "But I want something in circulation with my picture on it."

"Could be a coin," the Colonel suggested. "We have 5 quetzal notes but we don't have a 5 quetzal coin."

"Minted from pure silver?" Nixon asked.

"Not a good idea," the Colonel said. "Silver would disappear from circulation like snow on a hot plate. Stainless steel would be more practical. Or even pewter. Maybe plastic. Milk, when its available, comes in bottles with cardboard caps. You could collect them and convert them."

"O.K, we'll do that," Nixon said. "Can we whistle up the Secretary of the Treasury first thing in the morning?"

"Well, I'll be gone, Mr. President," the Colonel said. "But somebody around here ought to be able to find him. He is called the *Ministro de Financas para quetzales*."

"How about you, Bebe?" Nixon asked. "Would you try to locate him tomorrow?"

"Sure," Rebozo agreed. He was sleepy and ready for bed.

The Colonel continued, "That fellow, the *Ministro*, is named Higgs Bosun Brown. He's your candidate for the Chief of Staff position. General O'Reith knows him quite well. He was once an employee of the Casinghead Company."

Nixon turned to O'Reith, asked, "Is that so? What is his background?"

"Varied experience," O'Reith said. "He was in the automobile business for a while. He worked for us as a lobbyist both in Sacramento and Washington. His buddy, name of Newton B. Reno also works for the government down here."

"Oh?" Nixon responded.

The Colonel said, "Reno is chief cartographer, Mr. Nixon. He is also runs the geodetic office. And he assists *Ministro* Brown with the design of stamps, currency, seals of the republic. Things like that. He's a handy chap to have around."

"On the subject of currency," Nixon asked, "how do I get my hands on a few carrying-around Quetzals?"

"Higgs Boson Brown will get you what you want," the Colonel answered. "We have high speed printing presses. One final point, Mr. Nixon. In these tropical climes, a political leader can do most anything. But beware of the Church. If the Pope gets after you, the support of your people fades fast. Remember that."

O'Reith was tiring and beginning to feel the strain of the day's events. He and McDonough took leave of the presidential family and escorted by four of the Sherman tanks, drove to the *El Camino Real*.

"What time does the Colonel leave?" McDonough asked as they walked towards the elevators.

"As soon as the plane gets here," O'Reith replied. "After dark. Pilot will ring from the airport."

"Dine together, Clive?"

"All right, say eight o'clock?"

"I'll be in the bar about fifteen till."

"I'm going to take a nap, George. Ride to the plane with us?"

"Yes, I want to remind him of the encyclical and expansion of the College of Cardinals.

The telephone awakened O'Reith after seven and the sun had set. The pilot of *La Cruz de la Cañada* was on the line saying, "General O'Reith sir. We just got her chocked up on the parking stand. Fuel wagon coming round. We'll just have a bite in the airport restaurant and be ready. Say ten o'clock."

"We'll be there, Tommy."

"The Colonel?"

"Yeah and two or three aides."

"Still going to Orchid Island?"

"Yes. Tommy, we'll drive right up to the main hatch. Be there on the dot of ten."

"Yes sir."

O'Reith rose, dressed and telephoned the palace. When the Colonel came on, he agreed to meet them at the hotel. Over a dry martini on the rocks, O'Reith briefed McDonough.

Normally, on a Saturday night, traffic would be heavy on *La Reforma* but it was after nine and there were still quite a few troops stationed along the way which tended to discourage automobiles. The Colonel was sitting between the oilmen. His four suitcases were piled up on the seat beside the driver.

"So it is finally happening," O'Reith began. "After a long exile, you're on your way to reclaim your position as the Second Coming of Simon Bolivar. I assume you are in a suitable state of jubilation?"

"Actually, as a matter of fact, I have what you Americans call the 'butterflies of the stomach'. Still I do look forward to it. Of course I look forward to it. My future it is. I just hope... Well I don't want to run into any snags."

"With a division of armored infantry, how can you go wrong?"

"You are right, certainly. Nothing to worry about. Still, you know, one frets. You've been on the eve of battle General O'Reith. Surely you know the feeling."

O'Reith laughed. "Yes. Looking back it all seems so simple but at the time I was as nervous as you find yourself tonight."

McDonough said, "Colonel, you won't forget your promise to help me expand the College of Cardinals?"

"Of course not, Sir George. Just as soon as Flor rejoins me, which will be in a few short days, she will approach the Archbishop of Caracas. She'll get things going. I must advise you however that I have or at least I used to have a powerful enemy in the Church: one Monsignor Rafael Arias. In 1957 he was critical of my administration. I was spending money on roads and bridges and telephones and things like that. He though the money should have gone to feed the poor. We fell out over it. If he is still there, I'll have to have him sequestered. That is always touchy. One has to be careful with those churchmen. You can't put them in prison. You can't have them shot. And if they disappear there's always a hell of a racket from Rome. So I will have to look carefully into that. But not to worry. I will give you the help that you need."

"And our encyclical?"

"I'll do what I can of course," he continued. "That one is a bit stickier. First of all, I have to fully establish my position as president of the republic. That could take some weeks depending upon the degree of resistance I encounter. As you British say, I don't want to mix the oranges with the grapefruit. But once I'm in the clear, the encyclical will come into its own."

"I can ask no more," McDonough concluded with a sigh. "Any little thing that I can do for you, a message to No. 10 downing Street, a word with Mr. Wilson. All you have to do is ask."

"Well I'll ask it right now and General O'Reith I need your help as well. It is important that my government be recognized quickly by her majesty's government and also the government of the new American boy, Mr. Gerald."

"I'll speak to the Prime Minister by telephone instanter," McDonough said, snapping his fingers in the darkness.

"Tomorrow is Sunday, Colonel," O'Reith answered. "I'll telephone Haig early on Monday to get the wheels rolling. I assume you'll be able to take control of telecommunications quickly upon your arrival in the capital. I'd appreciate it much if you would let me know how things are going. Haig will ask me about that."

"I'll let you know immediately we get things organized."

"A final point," the Colonel said.

"Yes, of course," O'Reith replied

"A small matter," the Colonel continued. "There is not much money left in the treasury. I've had to draw it down quite some smart amount. Extra money if things don't go right. My other finance minister, Rafito Chavira, is in Switzerland even as we speak. I left enough to run the government for a couple of weeks. But our new president, Mr. Nixon, he'll have to have a care pretty soon. I didn't want to bring it up while we were celebrating. It would be like throwing cold water on the party, so to speak. Perhaps you could mention that when you talk to General Haig. Try for fifty or sixty million."

O'Reith bit his tongue to keep from berating the Colonel for raiding the treasury. But it was too late now. He said, "I'll see what I can do."

The Chrysler was edging up to the same airport gate where they had passed earlier in the day. The guard, with a flashlight, looked them over carefully, finally signaled that they could enter. The limousine slowly made its way to the main exit hatch near the tail of the ancient bomber. The Colonel boarded. His aides followed. The driver loaded his luggage. O'Reith had a quick word with the pilot. The hatch was closed. As the pilot started engines, the oilmen departed the airport as they had come. Both were nodding off before they arrived back at the hotel.

It was a blessed Sunday morning. O'Reith slept late. The telephone rang around eleven and it was McDonough. "Had breakfast yet, Clive?"

Sleepily, O'Reith answered. "George, you woke me up. I'll shower. Meet you downstairs in half an hour."

They breakfasted on mango, papaya and avocado all of it lubricated with fresh squeezed lime juice. Over coffee, O'Reith said, "George I expect a call from Carolyn later in the day. She was eager to get those seismic lines up on the wall. If she's seen anything interesting, she won't be able to sit still."

"So we don't go check up on our new president?"

"I don't. You may want to. He's in good hands with his wife and Rebozo. All I have to convey is bad news and I'm pondering if I'll even do that."

"He has to know the Colonel stripped the cupboard bare," McDonough said.

"You could tell him," O'Reith suggested.

"Then the remains of the late Heavy Latrobe, McDonough said. "Transportation back to the states."

"Why not a military burial right here in the city?" O'Reith suggested. "At the time of his demise, he was a general officer in the Guatemalan Army. Besides it is up to Nixon to decide what is proper."

"It is just a shoe box anyhow," McDonough sighed. "Well, I may go later in the day. Hanging around the hotel is boring. Dinner here?"

"Yes," O'Reith said. "If you get an invitation, feel free to accept it."

"OK if I tell him about the treasury?"

"George, it can surely wait until tomorrow. I don't care but if he offers you dinner and you accept, that will not be a particularly pleasant dessert item."

"Yes, you are right. I'll not bring it up."

Coffee finished, O'Reith summoned a pair of MPs to guard him as he stretched his legs. The city sidewalks were dangerous for a rich-looking white man limping along with an expensive-looking cane. With no exercise in a week, his leg was giving him hell. Since it was Sunday, he could limber up at leisure without worrying about business affairs.

When he returned to the hotel at five, the hall porter greeted him saying, "General O'Reith, a call from Los Angeles coming in."

CHAPTER VIII

FAMILY FEUD

O'Reith went up to his room, certain that Cook was on the other end of the line. But it was Helen."

"Helen!" O'Reith purred into the mouthpiece. "Didn't expect to hear from you but I must say I am pleased. I've been on the street getting some exercise. Are you well? Everything OK?"

"Ace, I'm well enough physically but inside I'm crushed. I've fallen out with Alice. A friendship of forty years gone just like that."

"We can't accept that, baby. You must make up with her."

"She betrayed me, Ace. She gave away my beautiful period piece movie to that no good transvestite, Ed Wood. Can you imagine such cinematic treachery?"

"Where is Alice now?" O'Reith asked.

"I have no idea and I don't care. She left here in tears an hour ago. I told her I never wanted to see her again. Ace, it is in The *Hollywood Reporter*, *Variety* and even the *Yellow Peril* picked up on it. Ace I am the laughing stock of Hollywood and I am absolutely miserable."

"Helen a Pan American DC-8 that comes up from Santiago, Chile lands here about one o'clock in the morning. It's a non-stop to LAX. Helen, I'll be on that plane and home shortly thereafter. Now listen to me."

It was the voice that had blistered many a lieutenant general over the years. "Helen, I want you to call Alice and apologize. Tell her that you have been speaking with me and there has been a grievous mistake."

"Ace, I cannot do that. We were near to tearing hair. We called each other names..."

"Helen!"

"All right Ace, I'll call her but don't expect me to..."

O'Reith interrupted. "Just apologize, Helen. Ask her over for a drink."

"It will be difficult for me, Ace."

"Helen, if you insist on being irate, you can be pissed off at me. I'm the architect of the deal with Ed Wood. Can we leave it at that until I get there?"

"You! I can't believe that! You rat! You Judas! Tend your knitting, Ace. And go…"

O'Reith's voice was merciful now. He said, "Helen, cool off a bit. You have just recovered from a lapse of memory. Amnesia plays tricks with one's mind. Max is in on this soap opera too. I'll bring him along. Now call Alice. I-m-m-e-d-i-a-t-e-l-y!"

"You know what you can do, you Judas Icarius!" She slammed the telephone down.

O'Reith broke the connection up and dialed Ridley. He said, "Alice I just got off the phone talking to Helen. Our worst nightmare. She is explosively angry with us. I tried to calm her down. No luck. I asked her to call you. Can you meet me at LAX in the morning and bring Max?"

"Yes, I'll come. Of course. Clive, she was hot under the collar. We said things that had lain buried for years. I don't know..."

"Are you two friends or not?"

"We're friends."

"Well let nature take its course. Anger eventually abates."

"I hope so. Thanks for calling. I'll meet you in the morning."

O'Reith dialed McDonough's room and there was, as he expected, no answer. He called the palace and asked for him. "How's it going babe?"

"Not too well. I shouldn't have come. He's been hitting the gin bottle pretty hard. We just came out of a prayer session. Rebozo is torqued up. Pat is chain smoking Pall Mall cigarettes. Carolyn call?"

"No but Helen did. George, we're twisted off over the *Miter*. Word of our deal with Ed Wood made the papers just as Helen recovered her memory. She's on the outs with Alice. I'm catching that Pan Am flight tonight. You'll have to hang on here and tend to Nixon until I can calm the waters."

"Zounds! Clive, are you going to call Haig?"

"Just as soon as I resolve the problem with Helen."

"Could you hit him up for a little something for the treasury here? I don't want to break the news that the government is on the brink of bankruptcy."

"Yesterday, you seemed eager to tell him."

"My thinking has changed. Nixon is no condition to get that kind of news."

"OK, George. I'll try for some emergency funding. I'll call you tomorrow."

"OK, Clive. Godspeed."

As he left the hotel, the sky was flickering fire and thunder rolled out of the mountains. Raindrops pelted the windshield of the taxi. The flight was turbulent from take off. The big jet vibrated, jittered and trembled as if it had the St. Vitus Dance. Only over the Chihuahua Desert did it smooth out. By the time they arrived in Los Angeles, a little after seven in the morning, he was rum-dum. Ridley and Parkinson met him at the baggage claim with long faces. It was Monday, August 12, 1974.

"Rough flight, Clive?" Parkinson asked, seeing the oil baron's worn features.

"Roller coaster all the way, Max." He glanced over at Ridley. "Did Helen call you, Alice?" She shook her head sideways.

"When did you last see her, Max?" O'Reith asked.

"Day before yesterday. I called early last night. Maid said she'd gone to bed."

O'Reith picked up his bag from the carousel and followed Ridley and Parkinson to the limousine waiting at the curb. He smiled at his chauffeur and piled into the tonneau. Parkinson sat beside him. Ridley took a jump seat. The big Cadillac pulled out into traffic, turned down Inglewood all the way to the Long Beach Freeway. There, the chauffeur sped up to the limit and shortly they were standing in the drive of the

Ocean Boulevard flat. O'Reith led his friends through the lobby and into the elevator. At the penthouse door, O'Reith nodded to the butler and pushed past him to Helen's bedroom. Helen's maid said, "She's just now waking up."

O'Reith nodded. When the maid let them in, Helen, propped up on pillows, feigned hopelessness. O'Reith saw immediately that it was an act. Parkinson solicitously felt of her forehead and then took her pulse. He said, "Helen, your heartbeat is normal. You look OK. How are you feeling?"

"Betrayed!" she said bitterly, refusing to acknowledge the presence of Ridley. To O'Reith, she said arrogantly, "Ace, please dismiss these intruders."

"We're not on a sound stage, Helen. No lights. No cameras. I walked out on important business to get this tangle straight." He glanced at the maid, "Please bring Mrs. O'Reith her breakfast and coffee for the rest of us." As the maid disappeared, O'Reith continued. "Helen do you recall putting Alice in charge of the *Miter*?"

"Yes. I gave her power-of-attorney. I trusted her and believed she would never do anything to hurt me. Now look what she's done! She's torpedoed me!" Her voice rose in anger.

O'Reith said, "Helen, it is not as you think. McDonough believed that injecting some humorous side-scenes would liven up the film and you agreed to that. Then you fell into amnesia. Against my better judgment, I allowed him to hire Ed Wood to finish the movie. It was a difficult decision. In the end, we wound up with two movies. Alice thought the second one; titled the *Signal Red Cadillac* was better than the *Miter*."

"Helen, this is the acid test. *The White Satin Miter,* produced and directed by Ed Wood Jr., is showing as the bottom feature of a double bill with *Let Me Die in Drag* at the Carleton Theater over on Fleet Street. The top half of the bill is also an Ed Wood flick. No problem getting tickets. *The Signal Red Cadillac,* produced and directed by Helen O'Reith is playing at Grauman's Chinese, sold out every day. But Alice can get tickets. I suggest that you and Alice attend both movies and then you can make up your own mind. After seeing the *Miter*, if you still want it back, I'll telephone Ed Wood. Is that a deal?"

"Ace, I would never watch a film called *Let Me Die in Drag*."

"Honey," Alice said, "We can always get up and walk out when it begins."

"I am not speaking to you Alice Ridley."

"If you won't speak to Alice, you won't speak to me," O'Reith said, rising from his chair and grasping his cane. "I'm going back to Central America."

"Ace, you can't leave me," Helen begged.

"I can and I will if you don't change your attitude." Then to Parkinson, O'Reith said, "Shoot her full of hop, Doc. She's beyond redemption."

"Oh Ace," Helen begged, "Don't go. You can't go!"

"Speak to Alice," O'Reith commanded.

Helen's face fell. Looking down at the bed cover, she muttered, "Alice honey, I made a mistake."

O'Reith sighed in relief. Ridley rushed to Helen and took her in her arms. The two women sobbed together. Parkinson closed his black bag, smiled faintly at O'Reith and departed. In his study, O'Reith called Haig at the White House. When the presidential aide was on the line, O'Reith began, "Al, howsa boy?"

"Things are still pretty hectic, Clive. POTUS Ford is feeling his way along like a snail creeping through molasses. Trying times. How about with you? How's the new president of the *Greater Central America Co-prosperity Sphere* getting on?"

"Not too good, Al," O'Reith answered in a steady voice. "That's why I called. Nixon inherited a little budgetary problem and he doesn't know about it yet."

"Needs federal funds?"

"Yeah. The *Co-prosperity sphere* is stone-broke. McDonough spent all day yesterday with them. Nixon down pretty low. Banging away at the bottle. Playing gin with Rebozo. Everyone on edge. That business with Latrobe hangs heavy over the scene."

"What business? What happened to Heavy?" Haig asked.

"Couple of man-eating tigers snatched him from the motorcade."

"Jesus! Jesus H. Christ!"

"Yeah, that's what I thought too. George was going to spring the bad news about the budget deficit but then decided it would be better to wait. What are the chances of getting an infusion of do-re-me, American money? Say $50 million?"

"How did you find out about it?"

"Colonel told me as he was getting on board the plane for Orchid Island."

"You think I can walk in cold turkey and ask the new POTUS who is still having trouble finding the can, to wire $50 million to the treasury of the *sphere*?"

"Al it is more than a request. It is a has-to-be."

"Clive I'm looking at a slip of paper. Written on it is all the money we're sending down there. Listen to this. Banana Subsidy. Ten cents a stalk. Save the Tiger Fund. Million dollars a quarter. Endangered rare snakes, turtles and plumed birds. Same amount. Volcano Ventilation Control. A million a month. Tropical Golf Course Development Friendship Fund. A cool million every month. Yucatan Resettlement program. That's a biggie. Ten million a month."

"Al, Nixon needs a quick shot. Call it a financial bracer. The Colonel looted the treasury. All the money gone to Switzerland."

"Gees. Jesus H. Christ," Haig said. He let out a long audible sigh. "OK Clive, I'll scout around here. There has got to be some kind of a slush fund we can tap for a few million. Let me go to work on it. I'll wire him some money before the close of business. Veterans Administration is usually sitting on some heavy sugar. Clive, how about Honduras? I assume we've won that battle."

"We've won it in the town of La Union on the Pacific side and at Puerto Cortés on the Caribbean side. That's about as far as we've got. Just a few troops left at Puerto Cortés. All that gang has gone to Venezuela. On the Pacific side, we've got all of the 34th Division except the military police contingent."

"You're expecting to find oil around there somewhere aren't you? Clive, it would help a lot if I could tell Ford we had struck it big. He frets the Arabs could put the embargo on again. Soften the blow for me babe."

"Al, Carolyn brought the seismic lines up on the same plane with you last Saturday. I'll call her now and ask her how it looks."

"Give a call back in an hour Clive. I'll tell you when the money can go out. Fill me in on the oil wells."

"You got it babe."

He called Cook at the office. "Carolyn, how does it look?"

"The lines are hanging on the wall. They don't look too promising. So I'm taking a longer look and they still don't look good."

"Structures?"

"Yes but they are nothing like what we see in Venezuela or the Middle East. What is more worrisome, the velocity surveys indicate denser limestone than we saw in the Yucatan. Put it all together and we come up with a so-so prospect."

"How deep to test the entire column?"

"Eight thousand feet, more or less. Volcanics below that."

"If we should find an oil column, what kind of producing rates?"

"Hard to say. Maybe five hundred barrels a day. The decline would be rapid."

"Carolyn, for political reasons we may have to put tools in there and drill a well or two. As long as we're drilling, we can keep the California National Guard. And without that, Nixon is a goner."

"Yes sir. You know best but don't get up high hopes for big oil."

"With the Colonel back in Caracas, we can make up for it on Lake Maracaibo." O'Reith said. "If all went according to plan, he has landed at La Guaira. If he got through the tunnel OK, he should be in Caracas now. He promised to call when he secured the telephone system."

"Yes sir. Do you want me to line up tools for Honduras?"

"Please do Carolyn. I'll call Haig back in a few minutes and I'll tell him we found some drill-able structures. I'll sidestep the size and quality. He can report to Ford that we plan a drilling campaign. We hang on to the troops."

"General O'Reith, Cook continued. "Why do we want to stay down there? Those Yucatan fields are depleted. The Guatemala surveys are negative. In Belize we drilled a couple of dry holes. Nothing there. We are not in the banana business. Nixon is not a key player in our little solar system. So what's the point?"

"Carolyn, I'm getting soft in my old age. We got Nixon into this and I feel bad about him being isolated. Especially after the tragedy during the parade."

"What tragedy?" Cook interrupted.

"Heavy Latrobe."

"What happened to him?"

"Couple of lightning-fast, man-eating tigers snatched him out of the open car. It happened so quickly that if you didn't have your eyes on him, you would never have seen it. Anyhow, he's gone. I mean, really gone."

"Gee, General O'Reith. Poor guy. OK, sir, I'll line up a Bell and Burden rig for La Union. Should have it on the water in a couple of weeks."

"Fine, Carolyn, I'll see you in the office tomorrow. After I call Haig, I'll bring George up to date."

"George OK?" Cook asked, concerned.

"Yeah, he's holding hands with Nixon and Rebozo."

"Give him my fondest, sir."

"I'll do that Carolyn."

He broke the connection and dialed Haig. "Al, I just got off the phone with Carolyn. She had the Honduras seismic lines hanging on the wall. Found several structures but we won't know how good they are until we drill them. She'll have a rig on the water within a couple of weeks. You can pass that along to POTUS Ford. We need to keep the troops in there while they're drilling. OK?"

"Should be OK, Clive," Haig answered. "With oil in short supply, he'll see it that way. Any word from the Caudillo?"

"No, that scamp is silent as the grave. He said he'd call just as soon as he had the communication system wired for sound. Maybe we'll hear today."

"Clive, in my talk with the POTUS, he said James Schlesinger reported a 'lost' division of armored infantry. He was referring to the 34th. I had to let the POTUS in on the scheme to put Jiménez back on his seat. He didn't like that at all. He wants to cancel the Red Alert. He wanted to know why the Colonel had left Guatemala. When I told him that Nixon was down there, he damn near went ballistic. So I had to level with him. Henry was there with me, moaning and shaking his head and calling it all a political disaster. POTUS wants the 34th out of Venezuela *tout de suite*." I told him that I would go to work on it. So I have to do it."

"Can you hold off for 24 hours?"

"Maybe, maybe not."

"Al, if we pull the troops, we may have to pull the Caudillo too. Have you got a place for him?"

"Hell no! Clive, nobody wants him. He's poison!"

"We wanted him when Guatemala was going down."

"That was over ten years ago. Clive, we have to face up to the fact that his record on civil rights is just so-so. The ACLU would string him up by the heels if they could get their hands on him."

"So would the *Accionistas*, Al. What are we to do?"

"How in the hell did I get into this, Clive?"

"Trying to do the right thing by Nixon. Have you got his $50 million lined up?"

"Yeah and it was not easy. I got it out of the Interior Department. Lakes and Rivers. I expect a reverberation from some functionary I'll have it on the wire within the hour."

"Al, can you wire it to the attention of Sir George P. McDonough?"

"Since when is he the treasurer?"

"He's not but after my next phone call, he will be. We can't trust the existing set up. The Colonel had two finance ministers. The one who handles the real money is a guy named Chavira. Right now he is in Zurich. If you wire it to his attention, one of his functionaries in Guatemala City will see it and send the funds to Switzerland straight away. Send it to George and we'll know it is safe."

"Who is the other finance minister?"

"American guy, his name is Higgs Boson Brown. He runs the printing presses. Puts out the local currency, the Quetzals."

"Where have I heard that name?"

"He used to work for Stan Ethering. He was our bagmaster on Capitol Hill for a spell."

"I remember now. He was the guy who tried to bribe Robert Byrd."

O'Reith laughed, said. "Yeah, that's him all right. We had to get him out of town in a hurry. He will more than likely become Nixon's Chief of Staff."

"Jesus wept!" Haig lamented. "I'll need some documentation, Clive. Ask Nixon to send me by courier a notification that George has been appointed treasurer and finance minister?"

"I'll do that right now babe," O'Reith said. "Dig around in your four star bag and see if you can find a spot for the Caudillo in case he goes down in Venezuela. Surely Henry could use him in the State Department. Maybe special representative to Havana?"

Haig laughed, said. "Don't count on that."

By chance, McDonough was in his room at the hotel and he picked up on the first ring. O'Reith advised him of the pullout of the 34th and the transfer of $50 million."

McDonough said, "Clive that is bad news about POTUS Ford pulling the 34th division. I feel terrible about jerking the rug out from under the Colonel. Even worse, Nixon has decided to make a major foreign policy speech on nationwide TV."

"When?"

"Tonight."

"What's he going to talk about?"

"The threat."

"Can you talk him out of it?"

"I doubt it. He's itching to do something. Palace is confining. He's bored."

"Ask him to steer clear of any pronouncements about Venezuela. If Nixon goes on TV in support of the Colonel, it could complicate matters. Can you call Harold Wilson? Surely in some corner of the British Empire he would fit in."

"No need to borrow trouble Clive. We really don't know. He may be OK. Calling Wilson would be a waste of telephone money. If we are forced to do something, I'll call Black Rod."

"Good point, George. I'll put in a call to Mandy Macabra in Maracaibo. She may have heard something."

"Good idea, Clive. Well, I'm on my way to the palace to get what Haig needs and then pop in on the central bank. If the funds have arrived, I'll sequester them so that rat of a Chavira can't get his paws on them. Call me later."

"Take care, George."

O'Reith broke the connection so he could call la Macabra in but immediately realized calling Maracaibo was not as easy as calling Guatemala City. He'd have to book it. It could take hours. At the same time, he became aware of how tired he was. He wanted to go to Maxine. He needed a bath and a shave and a massage. He caned himself to the elevator and when he was in the garage, let his chauffeur enclose him in the tonneau of his limousine. He dozed all the way back to town. Arriving at the Fullerton Building, it occurred to him that he could drop in on Flor and Margot Jiménez in the guest quarters. It was possible, even likely, that the Colonel had called them. As a good family man, he would do that first, before anything else. But even as his finger was out to ring their bell, the heaviness of his exhaustion overcame him. He returned to the elevator, went up to his floor, fumbled for his keys, found them, opened the door and met Maxine in the hall. She helped him undress and led him to the Jacuzzi. She whipped up lather from his shaving mug, and as he relaxed in the swirling hot water, whisked his face smooth. When he was soaked, shaven and dripping perspiration, she helped him out, toweled him off and led him to the massage table for a workout.

Limbered up, she took him to bed. After they made love, he collapsed into a deep, deep sleep. It was almost the cocktail hour, when he awakened. He dressed in an open shirt and slacks and well-worn loafers. The hot bath and the French dip and the long nap had restored him. He felt born again. Maxine awaited him. As the butler rolled in the drink trolley, she said, "The papers are on the table. The headlines are glaring. How are you feeling?"

"I'm OK, Maxine. Pressure can sneak up on you. Suddenly I was overwhelmed. The picture is so complicated. The timing is so close that I can hardly keep it all straight in my mind."

"What is your main concern?"

"The Colonel."

"Why him, he's basically a nobody?"

"He's supposed to be back in Caracas forcing entry into Miraflores, *a golpe de estado*. He was going to call me and he hasn't. Maybe something went wrong."

"His chances of regaining power in Venezuela are zero. Surely you know that."

"Well, it has nagged at me all right. I thought with a division of American infantry behind him, he might make it. And he may yet. He is determined. I'll grant you he is far from popular."

"Why not let him go down the tube?" Maxine asked softly. "Why is it important that he regain his dictatorship?"

"Venezuelan congress voted out a bill nationalizing the entire petroleum industry. We'll lose our concessions on Lake Maracaibo. With the Caudillo back on the job, he'll kill that legislation."

"Silver, you're 69 years old and it shows. You are a rich man. Oil concessions in Venezuela are no longer important. Throw in your hand. Let's return to Paris. Our place there stands empty. I'd like to replant my garden. Surely by now it has gone to weed and seed. Monique never cared for it. Clive, let's do that. It is time."

"I can't leave George to handle all of these problems alone."

Maxine laughed.

"Sweetie, if I walk away, George will never be able to resolve the mess. He would hate me for the rest of his life and I wouldn't blame him. Think of it. Nixon hangs by a thread. Goodness knows what has befallen the Colonel. Al Haig depends upon me to get things straight. What am I to do?"

"Walk out, Silver. Say to hell with it."

The butler had prepared the dry martinis. He served Maxine. Under O'Reith's piercing eyes, he carefully lowered ice cubes into the second heavy glass, surrounded it with a paper napkin and placed it into the outstretched hand of his master. Like a wraith, he quietly vanished.

"Sip it Silver. Nurse it along," Maxine said softly. "You're on the edge."

He smiled at her, said, "Cheers, Maxine. I'm not yet on the goofy list."

"You're getting close, Silver. Putting Nixon on seat in Guatemala was eccentric. Sending the Colonel off on a quixotic quest in Venezuela was lunatic."

"All of it seemed quite reasonable at the time," O'Reith mused, eyes vacant and staring at the wall. True, we were at the limit of political reality. But it seemed to be working. I sensed we were in trouble when Heavy Latrobe got it. I felt in my bones that it was all unraveling."

"Who is Heavy Latrobe? What was it he got?"

"Inaugural parade. Latrobe, a pal of Nixon, was to be his vice president. With Bebe Rebozo in an open car behind Nixon's, when Nixon got up to accept what he thought were accolades, Latrobe did the same. He is, he was, a short squatty guy. In a gleaming white uniform that the Colonel had dreamed up for him and a cap with silver trimmings, the soft morning sun reflected back like a halo. It was that glow that ruined him. If he had kept his feet on the floorboards, he would have been OK. But he got up on the jump seat. Two of the Colonel's man-eating tigers snatched him, bounded to the pavement and tore off into a side street that dead-ended into a wooded area."

"My goodness!" Maxine said. "Is that little detail in the newspapers?"

O'Reith found himself guiltily amused. He sipped his martini, said, "Well it is not funny. God, that came across like a B movie. Speaking of the papers..."

Maxine brought the *Los Angeles Times*, the *San Francisco Chronicle*, the *New York Times*, the *Washington Post* and the *Yellow Peril.*

He glanced through them saving the *Yellow Peril* for last, knowing their account would be the most pungent. Sure enough it was right on.

The Yellow Peril

Los Angeles August 12, 1974. Yesterday in Guatemala City, Ex-President Richard M. Nixon was inaugurated as president of *The Greater Central American Co-prosperity Sphere.* Colonel Marcos Pérez Jiménez who has been president of that political curiosity for quite a few years handed over power to him. It is not clear why he decided to relinquish power at this time but it is an open secret that he and his family have wished to return to Venezuela. Perhaps he has further political ambition to the south which may be revealed to us in the coming days.

The ceremony was marred by the disappearance of Mr. Nixon's running mate, one Boniface M. Latrobe, recently General of Artillery in the Guatemalan Army. 'Heavy' as General Latrobe was called, was snatched from his open touring car by two man-eating tigers and carried off to the bush. He was a small, compact man but of considerable girth. We can safely assume that he provided the tigers with a good meal. One might think that man-eating tigers would be a rarity in a place as large as Guatemala City but in fact they are something of a pest there, especially in the parks. Over a decade ago, with a grant from an American Oil company, Colonel Jiménez imported several dozen man-eaters and over the years, under the 'Save the Tiger' banner, they have multiplied and now threaten the entire population. If you are an affluent Guatemalan not only can you have a tiger in your tank but you can also have one in your front yard. Aside from the 'Latrobe' incident, the inaugural parade went smoothly and the ceremony attending the swearing in went off without a hitch. The presidential speech was extraordinary in that the new president, Richard M. Nixon seemed to be unaware of the fate of his running mate. He made reference to him at least twice before discussing a number of extraneous matters including an acknowledgment of the encyclical *Casti Connubii II* recently promulgated by Pope Paul VI. Oddly Mr. Nixon also referred to the Alger Hiss case and that he would never allow communism to come to Guatemala.

There is speculation about how the new administration will work out. Mr. Nixon was pointed in his declaration that no new legislation was contemplated and that he would follow in the Caudillo's footsteps. Colonel Jiménez was not a great success in Guatemala. He was able to stay in power because of his police state methods and his heavy political hand on the tiller of an economic ship that is far from seaworthy. The locals are restless and crowded around the big palace gate during Nixon's speech. Some scuffles took place and it was not a quiet afternoon. Tomatoes were hurled at the palace gate.

There exists controversy about the legitimacy of the election (the campaign lasted a mere three days) because there was virtually no electioneering. Posters were put up on lampposts throughout the city saying *Notre Nixon* but beyond that, it all seemed to come as a big surprise. One wonders at the origin of the posters.

We would expect some comment from President Gerald Ford in Washington but as of this date, nothing. In any event, we wish Mr. Nixon all the best in this, his third presidential term."

"Not a great endorsement," O'Reith muttered.

"All the more reason to say goodbye," Maxine said. "I can pack in an hour."

"We can't go just yet. Maxine, George has the idea that he can become the next Pope. He is fanatically working to that end, and of course, I have been helping him. Carolyn too. She has fallen in love with him. I don't know how long Pope Paul will last. Nobody does. But George has studied the longevity of the Montini family. Montini himself was a sickly youth. George knows this, of course, and he confessed to me that Paul had lasted much longer than he thought he would. Now Paul is 77 or so and George has the idea that he's only good for a couple of years. He's talked him into an expansion of the College of Cardinals. I think there are 120 or so right now, many more than the 80 that elected Montini. George figures if he can put in enough cardinals sympathetic to his cause, he can become elected. He would like to have it up to maybe 150 with over half of them favoring him."

Maxine laughed. She sat pensively for a while, put her drink glass down and came over to sit in his lap. She caressed his gray hair,remembering that it had been that way since their first meeting. He never told her that it turned gray overnight after 2nd Schweinfurt when he was 36 years old.

She said, "Silver, we should ask Sharon Mills to redye your hair. George's chances of becoming Pope are slimmer than the Colonel's chances of getting back to Miraflores."

"You are right," O'Reith sighed. "But it is important for him to have a run at it. He was once a simple parish priest in Northern Ireland. Unfrocked because he let his gardener hear confessions. While he was a counterintelligence agent during the war, he got another chance. John C. Masterman set him up as Bishop of La Roche Guyon and confessor to Rommel's Army Group B. Once he attained the rank of bishop, he couldn't let go. Since then his every waking moment has been dominated by his desire to move up the hierarchy. You remember how elated he was when he got his red hat?"

"Who is John C. Masterman?"

"Now he is provost at Worcester College,Oxford. Then he was head of the MI5 section in charge of counter-espionage. His claim to fame is invention of the double cross system."

"Is George really religious?" Maxine asked, giggling.

"He's about as religious as Joseph Stalin," O'Reith replied. "George has been a power broker for all of his adult life. Becoming Pope is the ultimate act of that profession."

"So how do we extricate ourselves from all of this?" Maxine asked. "I can smell the lavender and the pivoine in my little weedy garden. Next spring the cherry trees will be in bloom and then we'll have some delicious fruit. And figs in the summer."

"I'm ready for that," O'Reith murmured.

The telephone was ringing. Maxine answered and it was Flor Jiménez. She asked for O'Reith.

He said, "Hello Flor, any news?" Her voice, reedy and unstable, warning him that something was wrong. He continued, "Flor, you sound distressed. Have you heard from Marcos? Is all well?

In a trembling, halting voice, searching for words in English, she said, "He is in prison! Our trusted friend and personal lawyer called to tell me that Marcosito was in Santo Domingo military prison, in solitary confinement. They have him in chains and on bread and water. I don't know what to do. They may shoot him." Her voice broke and she began sobbing into the mouthpiece.

"Flor, take care," O'Reith said. "Maxine and I will come down immediately."

But as they made for the door, the telephone was ringing again.

"I'll go," Maxine said. "Come when you're finished."

As Maxine closed the door behind her, O'Reith picked up the telephone. It was Haig. He began, "Clive, a bit of bad news. We had to recall the 34th. They had already landed the 325th battalion at La Guaira. Luckily, we were able to halt the disembarkation. Unluckily, part of the battalion had already started towards Caracas. They were traveling the La Guaira-Caracas Expressway. Some jeeps and weapons carriers with a company of infantry including the Colonel were in that long tunnel that goes under Mount Avila. Accident of some kind. Tunnel blocked. The Colonel, a couple of jeeps and a platoon were cut off on the Caracas side. Those who could, reversed out, returned to the coast and we back loaded them onto the *Banana Emperor.* As things stand, we're short thirty or so men. No telling what happened to them."

"Al, they nabbed the Colonel. He's in irons in Santo Domingo. Bad scene."

"How do you know? What about our troops?"

"Flor just called. She's sobbing downstairs. The Jiménez lawyer in Caracas telephoned her."

"Clive, more bad news. POTUS Ford asked me to audit all of those grants and subsidies that Guatemala is getting. Specifically he wants to know what the hell the Volcano Ventilation Fund is."

"That was to pay for a seismic survey all across the country to look for weak spots in the earth's surface where a new volcano might spring up".

"Wouldn't you use that exact exploration technique to look for oil?"

"Yes. Why?"

"Well it is a hell of a coincidence if you ask me."

"Can we defer that to a later time?"

"Yeah, it is small potatoes. By the way, the POTUS is pretty sore about Nixon. The news of his inauguration, including the slip-up with Latrobe, made headlines in the *Washington Post* this morning."

"Yeah I know!"

"The president was considering a pardon for him but this blows it, I'm afraid. He asked me if I knew how this had happened and I just shook my head. He asked Henry. He clammed up too. But if we were under oath, we would have to come clean on it. You can understand that. We need to come up with a goat. Any ideas?"

"It could be Rebozo," O'Reith said. "He's down there now, with him, as you know. Things were not too good yesterday. Nixon was into the gin again crying, gnashing his teeth and wringing his hands. George thinks some of that may be theatrical. Pat is madder than a wet hen. She can't get out of the presidential residence for all of those peons milling around. The central plaza is full of 'em hooting and howling. She wants to go back to San Clemente where she has some friends. Rebozo wants out too."

"Clive, how will all of this will end up? Henry is nervous."

"Al, could we strap the disaster on Ron Ziegler? He and Nixon are pretty close. Why don't you put the POTUS up to that?"

"Ziegler doesn't know anything. Danger of a backfire there."

"Al, let me find out what happened. Flor can help. I know those cats in the government. I could negotiate release of our troops as a special representative of POTUS Ford."

"I like that. Think it will work?"

"We can pin the failed invasion of Venezuela on the disgraced Nixon. Get him to apologize for it publicly on the steps of the national palace. It will cost some money. Pay a multimillion-dollar fine. We'll have to decorate some of those guys. That would be President Carlos Andres Pérez and his foreign minister and the warden of Santo Domingo prison. Ford would have to make a conciliatory statement. You know, a 'sorry about that, chaps' type of address. Want to try it?"

"Yeah, I do. Let me run it by the POTUS. Henry will act up. He would dearly love to be the negotiator. Could he be a co-negotiator?"

"OK if he stays out of Caracas and doesn't send any funny messages. Leave him out if you can. This is my type of imbroglio. My command of the Spanish language is excellent. My local advisers think like government functionaries. We can read their minds."

"I'll point that out to the POTUS. This is not a job for tyros. Henry does OK in Europe and Asia. South America is a different kettle of fish."

"Al, you can say to Henry that by doing it this way, we can finesse it without getting ourselves into the meat grinder. He would like to keep his nose clean, surely."

"After I talk to the POTUS, I'll go to work on Henry."

"Al, as an extra, ask Ford to reconsider a pardon for Nixon. Without troops, he's a goner. Pardoned, he and Pat could go back to California. Happy ending. No reason for the poor bastard to go down the drain. Maxine is squeezing down on me. She wants to return to Paris. I need to clean up these odds and ends. Go with her"

"That may be the best idea you've had today," Haig said enthusiastically. "Give me a couple of hours, Clive. What time do you go to bed?"

"Usually around ten. But I'll wait up for your call."

"It will be before ten, Clive."

O'Reith polished off his watery martini and joined the ladies in the apartment below. Flor had stopped crying. O'Reith accepted a cup of tea from Margot. He began, "Flor, I just spoke with General Haig about a rescue. He'll review it with President Ford and we should have some news later tonight. Some American soldiers with Marcos are prisoners. We plan to negotiate the release of the soldiers and ask clemency for Marcos."

"Who would do the negotiating?" Flor asked.

"I would with the help of Mandy Macabra in Maracaibo. You remember that she attended the celebration at Punto Fijo terminal some years ago."

"The witch woman married to the missionary? The wife of the Eastern Rites priest?"

"Yes," O'Reith said, his eyes gleaming. "She has a way with government functionaries."

Maxine said, "Silver I find that an attractive idea. I could go with you and stay in Maracaibo while you were negotiating. I would love to visit *El Escondite* again. I could telephone Mandy tonight and tell her we're coming. You could commute from Maracaibo to Caracas."

"Be a couple of months, Maxine," O'Reith said. "Those guys don't get a chance like this but once in their careers. They'll make the most of it."

"That's OK with me," Maxine replied. "From there we can go to Paris."

"Can we get Marcosito out of irons?" Flor asked.

"First priority," O'Reith said. "Get him some decent meals too. And cigars."

"When will we know if President Ford will help us?" Margot asked.

"Haig said he'd call before ten o'clock. As soon as I know, I'll advise you."

"Even if it is after midnight, would you call me?" Flor asked.

O'Reith put his teacup to the side, rose and pulled Maxine up beside him. He nodded at Flor, gave her a good hug and started for the door.

In their flat, the aroma of roast pork filled the room. Maxine went to the kitchen to check up on it.

"Dinner at eight, Silver. Another martini?"

Although he was over his long-established limit, he said, "Yeah, I would."

Haig called as they were finishing a vanilla flan with ice cream. "You're on babe," he sang out gaily when O'Reith answered. Can you be here tomorrow to get into the details?"

"I'll be on a morning flight Al," O'Reith responded. "Get together in the afternoon at your convenience."

"Say six o'clock. We'll have drinks and dinner with the POTUS and Henry?"

"I'll check into the Watergate and you can send a car for me," O'Reith said.

"Colonel Drake?"

"Colonel Drake."

O'Reith hung up; decided that tonight he would have a cognac, his first in twenty years. He asked, "Maxine do we still have a bottle of Five Star Martell?"

She fetched the bottle and poured him a snifter. "OK if I book a call to Mandy?" she asked.

"Yeah and then dial Flor. I'll give her the news.

Just after six the next evening, they were in a vaulted antechamber to the Oval Office. Soft indirect lighting muted the gray walls. Henry Kissinger, Alexander Haig and Clive Colin O'Reith sat patiently awaiting Gerald Ford.

Haig said, "Clive, Ford has already had a word with the Venezuelan ambassador. They agreed that a negotiation is in order. The POTUS asked that our troops be properly fed and cared for. The ambassador assured him that they would be."

"I guess he couldn't get in a word for the Colonel?" O'Reith asked.

"Wrong time," Kissinger said.

"Hot Potato," Haig said.

As O'Reith nodded understanding, the POTUS entered. The three men rose to greet him. Haig introduced O'Reith. Gerald Ford beckoned them to their chairs. "You fellows like a drink?" he asked.

"Dry martini, Clive?" Haig suggested.

O'Reith nodded.

The POTUS spoke softly into a telephone on the deal table. A black bartender in formal dress rolled a drink trolley across the room.

Haig began, "Clive, the president is in agreement with your being appointed as a special negotiator. Inasmuch as you are presently serving as an officer of the Army of the United States on active duty, immediate retirement is suggested. The president feels that there should not be an inference to the government of Venezuela that you are acting in a military capacity. We don't want even the suggestion of pressure. We want a humble, sincere approach."

President Ford sipped his drink, nodded.

"Henry here will be available to offer you any advice or assistance that you require," Haig continued.

"I'm sure that I will need some and I appreciate it, Henry."

Kissinger said, "I'm pleased that I can support such a powerful personality in a difficult negotiation. I envy your command of the Spanish language. In a situation as we find ourselves today that is a priceless asset."

O'Reith said, "This one is touchy all right." He looked at Ford. He began, "Mister President, as General Haig may have told you, our company is well acquainted with Colonel Jiménez. We have negotiated oil and gas concessions with him over the years. I know him as well as his family. Flor is as nice a person as you could want to meet. It is true that the Colonel has not always lived up to our high standards in the field of human rights. Nevertheless, fully understanding your commitment to getting our boys back home, if I see an opportunity to mitigate his imprisonment, I would like to do that."

"If the Venezuelan Government shoots him, it is OK with me," Ford said.

"They don't have capital punishment," O'Reith replied. "They would only shoot him if he tried to escape and that is unlikely with him in irons."

"How do you know that?" Kissinger asked.

"His wife spoke to their attorney in Caracas," O'Reith continued. "Mr. President, my colleague is in Guatemala City now with Richard Nixon. I spoke with him on Sunday and Pat Nixon is not taking this well. She would like to return to California to be among friends. She's fretting and chain-smoking like an active volcano. Do you see any way that we could help out there?"

"Richard Nixon has been a naughty boy, General O'Reith," the POTUS answered.

O'Reith became calm, sipped his martini gingerly.

Haig said, "Clive we discussed that. If Nixon will publicly read the statement that Henry here has prepared, then President Ford agrees to pardon him."

"I think he'll read it," O'Reith said. "Fully dressed or in the nude."

"On the steps of the national palace with reporters from the *Washington Post* and The *New York Times* on hand," Kissinger stipulated.

"Yes and we'll have reporters from *El Nacional* in Caracas and *Panorama* in Maracaibo as well," O'Reith added.

"*Los Angeles Times* too?" Kissinger suggested.

O'Reith laughed. "They'll be there without invitation. And the *Yellow Peril*."

So it was agreed and after a splendid dinner in the White House dining room, O'Reith, slept in the Watergate Hotel and returned to Los Angeles the next day. Maxine had arranged the visit with Amanda Macabra. She and O'Reith would travel on the Pan-American Boeing 707 flight that stopped in Guatemala City enroute to Lima. O'Reith had the speech that Nixon was to make from the front porch of the National Palace. Kissinger had roughed out the key demands and Safire wrote it. Ford had signed off on it. O'Reith also had the details of the proposed Nixon pardon. It would be up to McDonough to remain with Nixon, help him rehearse his speech and then make sure he delivered it soberly and sincerely. The U.S. Army Signal Corps would control extensive press coverage. Nixon had to perform flawlessly. Anything short of total piety and atonement would clang like a broken bell, fatally defeating the message. In his mind's eye O'Reith could see McDonough, dressed in white linen with his Montecristo on his head stoically standing behind the orating Nixon with his Fosberry-Webley .44 tickling the former president's rib cage. Nixon was going to make a good speech. Of that, he was sure.

He was now quite nervous about the situation in Guatemala City. McDonough had not called. Here it was Friday, August 16 and he had heard nothing since the previous Sunday.

He dialed the number for the *Palacio Nacional.* A recording came saying the call could not be completed due to technical problems. An hour later he got the same message. So it went all afternoon and soon the cocktail hour was upon them.

O'Reith scanned Nixon's 'goat speech' as Kissinger called it. The butler rolled in the drink trolley and Maxine joined him. A half-hour later, sipping a martini and discussing the dinner menu, McDonough called.

"Glad to hear from you George. I've been trying all afternoon to through. What's going on down there?"

"Guerrillas keep cutting the line. The only international links are the CIA lines in the national palace and the hotel here. The residence is cut off. They may cut us off at any minute."

"Can't those military policeman control that, George?"

"Clive, the situation here is deteriorating. Those MPs are keeping the streets open and the palace protected and not much else. The Colonel's men knew where all those troublemakers hung out. They could keep them in their holes. Now, with him gone, several gangs have popped up and they're causing trouble all over town. Even worse, we've had a rash of tiger incidents. You know those cats are night animals. They've been showing up in the city parks around midnight. Just about put finis to the puppy-lover trysts. City services are going downhill too. No mail. Electricity is erratic. One minute the lights are on and the next minute they are off again. No trash pickup. Many shops closed. Gasoline stations closed."

"How's Nixon?"

"Not good, Clive. Legs are swollen. Phlebitis. He's popping pills, green, yellow, and some purple. He wants to call his doctor in Washington but he can't get a line. He's really upset because the telephone comes and goes. Mostly goes. The palace is a favorite target. Peons prowl around day and night. Throw tomatoes. Try to climb over the walls. MPs stay after them but it is a chore. Nixon wanted the soldiers to start shooting the peasants. But I put the kibosh on that idea. That would really stir them up. Pat Nixon is close to being a screaming meemie. Rebozo sulks around. Wants to leave but most of the flights have been canceled. Worse, getting to the airport is no easy task even with the MPs."

"How are you getting around, George?"

"Four tanks and the green Chrysler. Tank in front, tank behind and one on each side. Some noisy caravan. It is a pity that Latrobe didn't fix the mufflers on those tanks before..."

"George, I just returned from a meeting with Haig, Kissinger and the new POTUS, Gerald Ford. I'm on my way to Caracas to negotiate the release of captured American troops taken prisoner in the tunnel."

"The Colonel?"

"Santo Domingo. They've got the little bastard in chains."

"Egad."

"I was planning to come through Guatemala City with Maxine en-route to Panama. We were going to catch that Pan American DC-6 prop job that flies into Maracaibo. But I'll change that. Maxine can go via Miami. I'll fly down to see you in the B-17 with a speech that the administration wants Nixon to give from the steps of the palace. Haig is lining up transportation for the American press corps. A Venezuelan airplane will bring reporters from *El Nacional* and *Panorama*. We'll have extensive coverage including newsreels. If Nixon says his speech the way he is supposed to, he will get a pardon from the POTUS and a free trip back to San Clemente for himself, Pat and Bebe. But I'm not going to stay for that event. I've got to hot-foot it to Venezuela."

"What about the Caudillo?"

O'Reith laughed. "George he is *persona no grata* in spades. The administration doesn't care what happens to him. But in the meeting, I advised the POTUS that I planned to help him for old time's sake. I didn't mention oil concessions as you may well imagine. I don't dare bring that up in the same session where I discuss the American prisoners. I'm going to wire work it through Mandy. She knows all those cats."

"When can I expect you, Clive?"

"Sometime tomorrow. Could be late in the afternoon. The B-17 is in Maracaibo. I'm going to call down there and get it headed to Mexico City. I'll catch a Pan Am jet and change planes there. I'll buzz the *Torre del Reformador*. You'll hear it and you can come to meet me."

"I'll be there, Clive. Have a care. Regards to Maxine."

The *Cruz de la Cañada* was waiting for him at the Mexico City airport. He boarded and napped on the flight down to Guatemala City. He awoke as the old bomber rolled to a stop halfway down the long runway and turned around to taxi back to the terminal. A bank of fleecy white clouds that hugged the horizon dimmed the glare of the sun, low over the Pacific. It was after six and O'Reith was ready for a drink. When he saw the green Chrysler enter the side gate and start across the taxiway, he signaled the pilots to stop the airplane. No point in announcing his arrival to whomever might be watching from inside the terminal. Minutes later, he was deplaning. Over his shoulder he told the pilots to refuel the aircraft, file a flight plan for Panama City and Maracaibo and wait for him in the pilots lounge for a midnight take-off. The big green car idled near the main exit hatch. McDonough sat placidly in the tonneau. O'Reith caned himself to the ground, joined him and they shook hands in the limousine. "How's it going, George?" O'Reith asked.

"I just came from the palace," McDonough said, breathing heavily. Nixon knows you are arriving."

"Is he sober?"

"Yes. I locked up the booze cabinet last night. I told him if he was a good boy, he could have a cocktail with us tonight after he heard what you had to say."

"It is a ten minute speech. Nixon takes responsibility for the failed *golpe de estado* and many other sins of the world. It is a clever speech. Kissinger wanted to touch on all of the sore points that exist between the U.S and Venezuela. The *Accionistas* are annoyed about the Colonel getting asylum during the Eisenhower Administration. They're pissed off about the Bay of Pigs fiasco because Fidel Castro provides free cigars to the politicos. They're upset because the American oil companies are resisting nationalization. And they are howling mad about the Colonel being set up in Guatemala by the CIA. Needless to add, an attempted *golpe*, backed with American infantry is the final indignity. So Nixon is going to apologize for all of that and if you can get him to weep and wail, it would help. The Venezuelan newspapers would pick up on that to our advantage."

"Too much to ask," McDonough said mournfully. "He's not likely to cry on cue?"

"If he wants his pardon, he has to put on a performance. He's got to be dried out and convincingly contrite with a sobbing Pat Nixon at his side and he has to sound like he really means it. You could put a slice of onion behind the handkerchief in his coat pocket."

"At what hour of the day will this transpire?"

"A light colonel in the Signal Corps arrives tomorrow on an Air Force 747 along with all the stateside reporters and cameramen. Work out the details with him. A second plane will bring their equipment. Coordinate it with the Venezuelan Press Corps that comes up from Caracas. After the speech, the Nixons, Rebozo and you fly to California on one of the 747s."

"Clive, do we just let this place blow apart. Abandon it?"

"When it is all set up, withdraw the entire military police force to the palace except for those guarding the route to Aurora Airport. Tell the commander of MPs that as soon as the Air Force 747 is in the air, he can form up his troops and march them back into Honduras to rejoin the 48th Division."

"Clive, this town will go crazy with no central authority."

"George, there is little enough now. If we leave Guatemala to the Guatemalans, they may sort it all out. To be honest with you, I could care less."

"We write it off," McDonough said glumly. "What about Honduras?"

"Troops will stay until we drill a well or two. Carolyn is gloomy about it."

They were crawling down *Avenida de la Reforma*. Ahead was a freshly painted Sherman tank. The tank behind, as well as the two flankers, were old olive drab clunkers peeling paint with dirty black exhaust spewing out of corroded exhausts with shot mufflers, a noisy procession. With the roar of the V-16 Cadillac engines pounding their ears, the two oilmen talked with their heads together. O'Reith said, "George, let's stop at the hotel and have a drink. You can read the speech. Do we dine with the Nixon's tonight?"

"Yes."

"Phones working?"

"They were an hour ago."

"While we dip the bill, we can call them."

"Nixon expects that you will have a drink with him and Pat and Bebe."

"OK. I'll save space for an extra. George I've fallen into some bad habits here lately. Drinking twice as much as I should."

At the hotel marquee, the tanks rumbled up alongside the Chrysler sheltering them from the horde of swarming street urchins. When everything came to a stop, the driver helped O'Reith and McDonough to the concrete. The doorman held the door for them. At the bar, sipping his martini, O'Reith asked for a telephone. Presently Nixon was on the line. O'Reith asked, "Mr. President, how are you holding out?"

"I'm OK General O'Reith," Nixon responded. "Looking forward to our visit. Where are you now? At the airport?"

"No we're at the *El Camino Real.* I need a shave and a shower before dinner. We will be at the palace within the hour if the tanks don't break down."

Nixon laughed fitfully and they agreed on dinner at eight.

"George, he sounded a bit hysterical. Let's hope he doesn't blow a gasket before he makes his speech."

"He won't," McDonough said. "He can concentrate just fine when he's for it."

"George, when you get back to LA, call on Helen. Hold her hand. Reassure her that we did not try in any way to undermine her movie. Let Alice brief you before the visit. The morning I got back, we had quite a flap. Me. Max. Alice. Sharon. Helen. Bad scene for a while. It is patched up but it would be a generous gesture on your part to see her and atone for our collective sins. Maybe you can pick up a few tips from the Nixon speech. Then, call Black Rod and tell him you want a letter from Franco to Carlos Andres Pérez, president of Venezuela. Letter introducing Father Antonio, confessor to Franco as well as the King of Spain. Letter says Father Antonio arriving Caracas as religious envoy from Spanish Government. Letter requests Venezuelan Government allow Father Antonio to visit Jiménez in Santo Domingo military prison to attend his spiritual needs during this period of anguish and travail. Blah blah blah. Make sure it is well stamped with wax seals and tied in purple ribbon. You know. Heavy stuff. Letter to be placed in the Pérez hand by Spanish Ambassador in Caracas. Soon as you get your copy, round up your priestly garb and catch a plane for Maracaibo and meet me at Mandy's place."

"OK. What then?"

"By that time, Mandy will have stroked the warden of the prison, whoever that merciful soul may be. She'll have him sugared up. You can go to work on him straight away."

"Clive, if you had taken Holy Orders, the Church would not be in such a deep pit today," McDonough said solemnly.

O'Reith sighed. "I may yet." He finished his drink and stood up. As they went out to the marquee, the tanks started their engines.

The evening started out pleasantly enough. McDonough unlocked the liquor cabinet. Bebe Rebozo took over as bartender. The drinks were good and generous. Nixon looked at his martini lovingly for quite some long moments before taking that first ambrosial sip. Then he said, "General O'Reith, Father George told me about the misfortune that has befallen the Colonel and I am distressed. In the short time that I was with him I became rather fond of him. Can we do anything to ease his misery?"

"I don't know, Mr. President," O'Reith answered. "I'm going down to Maracaibo tonight. We have many contacts with the government because of our oil concessions. I plan to explore that matter."

"Well, I hope for the best."

Pat Nixon, overjoyed at the prospect of returning to San Clemente, chain-smoked Pall Mall cigarettes. Nixon became jubilant as O'Reith explained that his pardon would be comprehensive covering whatever crimes he had committed or could, in future be charged with. He would spend no time in the courtroom and no time in jail. He would even be able to collect his $50,000 annual pension. As O'Reith talked, Bebe Rebozo nodded his approval. He too, was ready to as he put it, "to get the hell out of this forsaken place".

After the first sip, Nixon downed his entire drink and rattled the ice cubes at Rebozo for a refill. O'Reith opened his mouth to object but McDonough, rising from his chair, frowned a warning at him. McDonough followed Rebozo to the liquor cabinet to delay Nixon's refill, to give O'Reith time to talk.

O'Reith took the 'goat speech' from his briefcase and handed it to Nixon who was looking over his shoulder at Rebozo wondering why it was taking so long to bring his second drink. O'Reith began, "Mr. President, as you read through the address you are to make, you may find parts of it offensive. Let me assure you that the text was carefully negotiated. President Ford told us what he needed; Henry Kissinger prepared the outline and William Safire wrote it out. You may think it harsh, but that is the price of your full and complete pardon."

Nixon began reading. From time to time he muttered "lie!' That's a crock! The nerve of that guy! I won't make this speech! I refuse!" Henry Kissinger wrote that speech! Safire can do a hell of a lot better than that. Who do they think I am? A goddamned jailbird? He looked back at the liquor cabinet, said, "Bebe where the hell is my goddam drink?"

McDonough brought it. Nixon tasted it and made a face. "Goddammit, there's no goddam gin in it. For Christ's sake, give me a decent goddam drink! What kind of a guy do you think I am? A corporal in the fucking Salvation Army?"

"Dick!" Pat Nixon objected. "Mind your manners. These men are helping us."

Nixon let the speech fall to the floor. He put his head in his hands. McDonough returned with a fresh drink with plenty of gin in it. He said softly, touching his shoulder, "Mr. President. Taste this one. See if it is to your liking. We all know of your troubles. Be assured that we would like for all of this to be finished."

Nixon retrieved the speech from the floor and after a long swig of gin, began to read it more carefully. When he got to the end of it, he smiled. He said, "Fellows, out in the garden this morning, the chauffeur was hosing off the limousine. The guy speaks a little English so we struck up a conversation. He told me he knew of a chap that wanted to take Heavy's place, to be vice president. Maybe we should whistle him up. After all, if I am to leave, somebody has to run the country."

"Something to think about," O'Reith agreed, not wishing to ruffle Nixon's feathers. He was ready for dinner so he could leave McDonough to finish up.

"What is the bloke's name?" McDonough asked.

Nixon put his glass on the cocktail table and fished around in the pocket of his suit coat. "The chauffeur wrote it down for me. I can't pronounce it." He located the slip of paper, put his reading glasses on and said, "General Kjell Langerud Garcia." He mutilated the 'Kjell' and the 'Langerud' but the 'Garcia' came out all right.

"Do we know anything about him?" O'Reith asked.

"He was one of the many generals in the Guatemalan Army," Nixon said.

McDonough said, "I remember him vaguely. The Colonel had all of those chaps under house arrest. Every now and then one of them would act up and the Colonel would liquidate him. This one kept his head down. He's probably running one of those guerrilla gangs that prowl the city at night."

"It might be a good idea to check the guy out with the CIA," O'Reith suggested. "Just to make sure they don't have anything against him. They have an office over a bar next to the U.S. embassy."

"They've all packed up," Nixon said bitterly. "With the tigers kicking up a fuss and the gangs on the loose, the embassy, the CIA, and *Alianza Para Progresso*, kit and caboodle, they said to hell it with and took a plane back stateside."

"Well, it is late in the day," O'Reith continued. "In the morning you could try to get a call through to Al Haig. But if that doesn't work, about all we can do is plug the poor guy in and see if he lights up."

"I agree with that," Nixon said. "We'll get him in here tomorrow and see what he looks like. He'll probably need a bath and a shave and a haircut and a new suit of clothing. We can't have a hippie-looking guy running the country."

"Is the Colonel's tailor still around?" O'Reith asked.

"Yeah, he's around here somewhere," Rebozo said. "I saw him out talking to one of the gardeners."

A major domo in black and white livery appeared and summoned the party. They dined on roast beef, *platanos* and diced carrots flavored with fresh tropical peppermint from the Colonel's garden. Over coffee, O'Reith looked at his watch, preparing to take his leave. McDonough said, "Clive, would it be all right if we introduced Garcia as the new vice president in the speech?"

A tiny red warning light came on in the back of O'Reith's head, but anxious to be on his way, he ignored it and said, "Why not? Could be a good idea."

"I'll attend it, McDonough said. "Just a couple of lines. Maybe three."

Nixon asked, "Father George, does General Garcia assume control of the country just as soon as I finish my speech?"

McDonough said, "In your speech, you announce that you will resign the next day at noon. So by then of course, you'll be back in California. Garcia can sleep late, have breakfast, when the clock strikes noon, he becomes president."

"O'Reith said, "It would be prudent to keep Garcia in the dark. After you fellows look him over tomorrow, if he fits the bill Mr. President, tell him you will announce his election as vice president when you make your speech. No need to tell him you will announce your resignation. Don't give him much time to get his act together. Don't invite him to hear the speech. He could be unpredictable as hell."

"I agree with that 100%," Nixon said.

O'Reith rose, thanked his hosts and said his good-byes. McDonough lead him out to the Chrysler. The four tanks rumbled to life and escorted him to the *El Camino Real.*

He checked out of the hotel and noisily rode, tank escorted, to the airport. The pilots stood beside the main exit hatch. O'Reith ducked his head and was quickly aboard. As the *Cruz de la Cañada* rolled down the long, long runway, O'Reith looked out through a plexi-glassed waist gun port. The lights of the city ran together as the aircraft gathered speed. From the air, the city appeared tranquil even though it was on the brink of chaos. His thoughts ranged far and wide. He wondered how Helen was getting along; wondered if Maxine had made it OK and would be waiting for him at *El Escondite.* He wondered if he could spring the Colonel. He wondered if Nixon would make a good speech. He did not worry about the captured American soldiers. In this crazy jigsaw puzzle, that was an easy piece.

They refueled in Panama and then it was just a couple of hours until they were on the ground at *La Chinita* near the Perija Highway, much closer to Macabra's place than *Grano de Oro,* now closed for conversion to a university campus. It was near dawn on August 18, a Sunday. He hoped Maxine had arrived and would be waiting for him at *El Escondite* which dated back to the 1950s when Dictator Jiménez offered new concessions on Lake Maracaibo. To take advantage of the increased oil field activity, Mandy Macabra built *El Escondite* (the hidden place) adjacent to an 18th Century Spanish limestone fort converted to a villa by a Venezuelan grandee. Next to it was a walled garden, 15 meters high with shards of broken beer bottles set in cement along the parapet. The ground floor of the inn had a bar, a dance patio, a restaurant and servant's quarters. The second and third stories consisted of bedrooms with suites at each end. One such suite was set aside for O'Reith.

O'Reith spotted Macabra's ancient black Cadillac as he left the arrivals lounge and got into the rear seat. The mulatto driver started the powerful V-12 engine. The big car rolled out of the taxi rank and soon was on the highway to Maracaibo. Just before reaching the main *alcabala,* the driver turned left into a small rutted dirt road which inclined upward at a steep grade. The automatic transmission growled as it shifted down to a lower gear. As they climbed higher, the engine began to ping. With each curve, more of the city lights came into view and then suddenly, atop a knoll, Maracaibo appeared aglow in neon. Traveling along a ridge at the crest, lake tankers came into view. Then appeared the string of lights along the cables of the bridge that crossed the narrows to Cabimas.

Downtown Maracaibo was a galaxy of flashing lights. Then, directly ahead the blinking green and orange sign announced *El Escondite.* In the glare of the headlights, Maxine stood beneath the marquee, Amanda Macabra at her side.

Widow Macabra-Schaeffer, a Ciudad Bolivar witch was, in her youth a dangerous woman. Her husband, Theodore, dead of lung cancer, had been crony of Harvey Holmes Halliday, founder of the old Calitroleum Oil Corporation. Over the years he had tangled with O'Reith, fallen from favor and when Halliday finally became exasperated with him, exiled him to Maracaibo where he met and married Macabra. In his later years, Schaeffer and Mandy, ran an orphanage for the stray children of Maracaibo of which there were always many more than they could take care of. Schaeffer's little Chapel, built with funds donated by the Casinghead Company, was known as St. Sulphide. She was Maracaibo's answer to the fabled *Dragon Lady* of Saigon.

As for 'la Macabra' there had been a time when if she didn't like you, she could be bad news indeed. Her large luminous black eyes projected menacing evil. Long ago, while they were courting, O'Reith scoffed at Maxine's description of Macabra's purported powers. When he met her, she jolted him with a shot of optic energy so intense that it took all of his willpower to look away. He nearly lost control. Now age had taken its toll and her magic powers were diminished. But this was not readily apparent and her reputation still frightened those who knew of her. Government functionaries feared her reputation as an axe lady. To compensate for the decline in her supernatural talents, she had made it her business to maintain useful relations with every significant personality in the Federal Government. And she kept tabs on those lesser lights that might some day rise above their contemporaries. In those days, Venezuela had many fixers, but none as consistently persuasive as Mandy Macabra. She and Maxine had been pals for thirty years, as close as Helen O'Reith and Alice Ridley.

When the romance between Maxine and O'Reith blossomed, Macabra guaranteed its success with an incantation. Over time, O'Reith became friendly with her but it was the affection one had for the black widow spider in the web in the corner of the garage.

O'Reith bussed Macabra, as Maxine lead him, weary and travel worn, up the stairs to their suite. As he undressed, he saw through the window the eerily gas-lit garden with its phosphorescent frogs, sinister fruit bats, luminous snails and flickering glow-worms. Water from the fountains still gushed up from the dragon's mouth and the gargoyle's nose. A bat was flying an ominous ellipse around the obscene red tassel of a banana tree in bloom. He fell asleep with Maxine in his arms.

Next morning after breakfast, O'Reith explained to Macabra that while he negotiated the release of the American prisoners, it would be her job to improve the Colonel's situation. McDonough would soon arrive in the guise of 'Father Antonio' to attend the Colonel's spiritual needs and determine what was required to obtain his freedom.

"First I must learn the name of the warden of Santo Domingo prison," Macabra said. "Once I know who he is, I will find a way to see him."

O'Reith said, "Highest priority is to get him out of irons. Make sure he is in a dry, healthy cell and that he is has three square meals a day."

"Of course," she agreed. "A matter of money and not too much of it either."

"I leave it in your hands then. We can exchange information each evening."

On August 20, traveling through the tunnel under Mount Avila, he looked for signs of an accident. About halfway through, a newly painted section appeared. The road below was freshly repaved. That must have been where the troops ran afoul.

This morning, traffic moved normally and he was soon at the American Embassy near Miraflores. Presently he was ushered in to the office of the American Ambassador, one Robert McClintock, who told him that a satchel bomb in one of the weapon's carriers had accidentally exploded and set off a series of smaller explosions. Several soldiers were killed and 31 were trapped on the Caracas side of the tunnel. The Colonel, in the lead jeep, was nabbed immediately. Expecting a triumphal entry to Miraflores, he wore his spectacular white uniform and a white pith helmet. His get up plus the escort of U.S. troops attracted the attention of the Venezuelan police. Quite soon he was identified as the notorious ex-dictator and taken straightway to prison. McClintock handed O'Reith his copy of the official letter appointing him Special State Department Plenipotentiary. The Americans read through the letter simultaneously. It was clear and straightforward. McClintock told O'Reith that he had personally put the original into the hands of President Pérez. In turn, Pérez gave McClintock the names, ranks and serial numbers of the Americans. McClintock passed that along to the Defense Department. Presumably all next of kin were notified.

Departing, O'Reith said, "I'll keep you advised, Excellency."

At Miraflores, he sought an audience. After a half-hour wait, a functionary named Lucio Peralta Ibanez explained that the president would be unable to see him. Ibanez produced a document, which outlined the damages suffered by Venezuela as a result of the failed *golpe.* Troops coming ashore damaged the beach. The tunnel explosion stopped traffic for 24 hours. Emergency repairs entailed overtime payments. There was the cost of prisoner upkeep, food and lodging, etc.

Ibanez advised that the 31 enlisted men and two-second lieutenants were under guard in a barracks at *La Carlota* military airfield in the Mercedes District. O'Reith requested permission to visit them. Ibanez said he would see to that. O'Reith asked about the fate of the dead soldiers. Ibanez told him they had been given Christian burial at the military cemetery near the airfield. Ibanez suggested they meet again in 30 days. O'Reith objected. They finally agreed to meet again in ten days. Ibanez summoned a sublieutenant to take O'Reith to see the prisoners. Back at Maiquetia that afternoon at the Maracaibo gate, a ragged newsboy hawked an extra edition of *El Nacional.* The headline screamed: NIXON HABLÓ! O'Reith brought a copy. Settled in his seat on board the DC-9, he read what Nixon had said from the portico of the national palace in Guatemala City on August 19. He translated the speech as he read it. More or less, it said:

> "My fellow Central Americans, members of the press, officers and men of the California National Guard and assembled diplomatic personnel. I am pleased to stand here before you to let you know that the government of Venezuela has stood strong against the machinations of the evil ex-dictator Colonel Carlos Pérez Jiménez. His attempted *golpe de estado* failed and the Colonel, now resides in a dank military prison in Caracas where in all probability, he belongs. Unhappily I must confess to you, that through a misunderstanding, I am somewhat to blame for this misadventure. I allowed him to use American troops. Traveling from Guatemala City to Caracas is a perilous trip. I thought having Americans as escorts would ease his anxiety. Never once did I imagine that he planned to use these soldiers to attack his native Venezuela. Heaven Forbid! It was never my intention that he would mount an invasion, which is, as everyone knows, anathema to a man of my high moral principles and precepts. The Colonel had assured me that his return to Miraflores would be welcome, and of course peaceful, and I had no reason whatsoever to doubt him. Now he must stand for judgment by his fellow Venezuelans and it is possible that censure against him may be severe. Also, during my time as President of the United States, some of my actions were not welcome in Venezuela and I take full responsibility for them and formally apologize. Let me assure everyone that my intentions were good and it was never my desire to cause pain or suffering for the Venezuelan people for whom I have a high regard even though they once pelted me with tomatoes. As a final point, although I was not directly involved in the notorious Bay of Pigs incident, I am aware that cigar supplies to Venezuela were interrupted by this unhappy event. I wish to make a full apology on behalf of the Central Intelligence Agency of the United States Government.
>
> At this time I wish to announce the appointment of General Kjell Langerud Garcia as Vice President of the Central America Co-prosperity sphere. I feel sure that when you get to know him as I know him, you will come to admire him and look to him as your

natural leader. Let there be no doubt about it. Kjell Garcia is a person of absolute integrity with charisma and intellect. He is a patriot of impeccable credentials. He will give you proper governance and lead the *Co-prosperity sphere* to even higher plateaus of success and prosperity. Considering that the country will be in splendid hands, my intention is to resign as president tomorrow at noon. At that time, General Garcia will become your new president and I know you will support him as you have me. We all wish him well. I also take this opportunity to announce that beginning tomorrow; special masses will be said throughout the sphere for the Pope's new encyclical *Casti connubii II*. Like all loyal Central Americans, I know that you will respect the Pope's words and take them to heart. Now I bid you goodbye. I will remain in your hearts and in your minds for as long as free people cherish democracy.

Richard M. Nixon.

O'Reith muttered, "George, you overstepped your authority." He wondered what Haig, Kissinger and importantly, Ford would make of that address. In Maracaibo, he hoped to buy a copy of The *Miami Herald* with an English language version. But when he arrived, the Miami papers were sold out. But *Panorama*, the local equivalent to the *Yellow Peril*, was on the stands. It, no doubt, would have a different take. He read their blistering comments aloud while having drinks with Mandy and Maxine. When finished he added, "Kiddos if these fellows had it their way, the Colonel and the Americans would all be shot. Our work is cut out for us."

The oil boom of the 1950s had long ago faded. And after the death of her husband, Macabra had converted part of *El Escondite* into a house of assignation. Girls occupied half of the rooms on the second floor and after midnight, the place became quite active. But at this early hour, the trio had the place to themselves. They were drinking Ron Pampero. O'Reith liked his with a dash of Rose's Lime Juice. Maxine and Mandy mixed theirs with Coca Cola. Macabra said, "General O'Reith, the warden of Santo Domingo prison, a colonel of Military Police, is named Raul de Cizancourt. His assistant arranged an appointment for tomorrow afternoon. Even today, Colonel Jimènez has a certain level of support in the country, particularly Tachira. I will bring this to the attention of Cizancourt. So by tomorrow night, I should have some news."

O'Reith went with her to drop by the U.S. Embassy and read the *Miami Herald*. By now the White House would have reacted to the Nixon speech. So next morning it was the Avensa DC-9 again, the tunnel and a taxi through clogged streets to the embassy. Macabra let him off and then continued on to Santo Domingo prison.

At the embassy, yesterday's *Miami Herald* carried the full text of Nixon's speech. It was comparable to the one in *El Nacional* except reference to the new vice president and the encyclical was omitted. White House comment on the apology was guarded. No mention of a presidential pardon. The speech was not linked to the American prisoners. With time on his hands, O'Reith called Ibanez and asked to visit the graves of the four American soldiers killed in the tunnel accident. Ibanez volunteered to pick him up so he went to the street and waited at the curb. At *La Carlota*, Ibanez flashed his *cedula* at the guard. Minutes later in the small manicured cemetery they stood over the freshly flowered graves of the dead soldiers. O'Reith noted their names. By five o'clock, he was back at Maiquetia. Macabra was there and they departed at six sharp. In the air, O'Reith asked, "Did you get to see him?"

"I did and it is a sad sight. His cell, two floors below ground level has a tiny light hanging from the ceiling which he says never goes off. Moths and mosquitos bang into it and are killed by the heat. Their incinerated bodies rain down on him. He can't sleep because of some strange-looking click beetles that crawl around in the mildewed bedding. Water-termites have burrowed into the walls. Sewage seeps from the crumbling mortar between the bricks. It accumulates on the floor. Scurrying rats drink from the puddles. I saw several wicked scorpions in the cracked mortar between the decaying bricks. The smell is terrible. The Colonel hasn't had a bath since he was locked up. He has sores on his arms and legs from the manacles. His hair is grown out and matted. He can't comb it. I wanted to cry..."

"What about the warden, Cizancourt?"

"No saint," Macabra said. "A lecherous-looking bird with spidery limbs, bony head and a raspy voice. He smokes those malodorous Barinitas cigars."

"Cheapest in the country," O'Reith muttered. "Just a cut above horse manure. Did you suggest we could improve his smoking supplies?"

"That and other things," Mandy continued. "He didn't seem impressed. He said he wished he could find the way to help me but the Colonel was a special prisoner and he had to keep him totally sequestered for fear he would escape. Maybe a few *Claros de Havana* will soften him up."

"You didn't get anything at all?"

"Cizancourt told me he would consider moving him to a dryer cell," Mandy continued. "But that is all."

"When can you visit again?"

"A week from today. Same hour."

"Mandy, we cannot accept that. The Colonel requires immediate relief. I can't telephone Flor and tell her what you just told me. What if you reappear in the morning with an envelope containing 10,000 bolivars and a box of Havanas?"

"Worth a try. That's $2,500 American money. I could tell him there was more where that came from."

"Let's try it and see what happens," O'Reith said.

Back in *El Escondite* with a restorative Pompero in his hand, he booked a call to Cook's office in Los Angeles. Four hours later as they were finishing dinner, it went through. It was McDonough.

"George," O'Reith began. "What's going on?"

"Clive, this is not a famous connection. Your voice sounds odd. Are you OK? Anything to report on you know who?"

"I'm OK George. I've been to the government and got things started. Slow going. You can tell Haig we'll be lucky to have results by Christmas. Our guy's condition is just so-so. We're working to improve that. What about Nixon's speech? Was it OK?"

"Haig said it was far from perfect. Nixon ad libbed more than they liked. To be completely candid, Ford thought parts of it seemed insincere. But Haig said that Nixon would get his pardon anyway. Ford feels strongly he must heal the Watergate wounds. The last thing the Republican Party wants is a former president in the dock for high crimes and misdemeanors. Haig says the pardon is set for September."

"I'm glad to hear that. When may I expect Father Antonio?"

"Maybe next week. I'm off to Madrid tomorrow. I pick up my letter, go to Rome. See if my house is still there and get my alb and surplice. Of course, I must call on His Holiness. One has to attend the niceties of religious life. He'll want to know how the encyclical is doing and

I want to brief him on the expansion of the College of Cardinals. So let's say two days for documents in Madrid and then a couple of days in Rome. Make it a week from tomorrow, ten days maximum I should arrive in Maiquetia ready to do the necessary."

"George every day of delay is another day in chains for the Colonel."

"You need not over dramatize it, Clive."

"See Helen?"

"Yes. I think we're OK. Alice went with me. Not to worry."

"How'd she look?"

"OK. A bit frail but she is in excellent spirits. She and Alice were going to see the *White Satin Miter*. It is showing at an art theater in the Mexican district, with Spanish sub-titles."

"That's a tough part of town. But with the chauffeur, they will be safe enough. I'm glad they're pals again. See Max?"

"I did. Her symptoms are in remission. That's all he would say. He has been counseling Alice to deal with Helen's outbursts."

"So she's still a little flighty?"

"Yes, but not to worry. Max is attending her regularly."

"George, Mandy will see the Colonel again tomorrow. Call Flor and tell her we're working on it. No alarming news. Carolyn moving tools into Honduras?"

"On the water, Clive. Turning to the right in about 30 days. She's here. Would you like a word with her?"

"Yes, put her on." When she responded, he asked, "Carolyn, how's everything going? All wired together?"

"Problems in Poghdar, Clive."

"Gas?"

"Crestal wells, Clive. We shut them in last week. Fifty thousand bopd down."

"Well, we knew it was coming. How about those smaller structures?"

"We put two of those wells on line to make up for the loss at Poghdar. With a steady drilling program, we can hold a million a day for quite some while."

"That rig headed for Honduras, radio the skipper to take it through the canal, across the Atlantic, double the Cape of Good Hope and up into the Persian Gulf to offload at Bandar Shahpour. Telex Scotty to get the papers lined up. Then call Bell and Burden. Amend the contract. Carolyn, we better brief the Shah on what's happening. Might be a good idea to curtail Poghdar all the way back to say, 750,000 bopd until we get a better idea of future performance."

"OK. I'll request audience with the Shah. I've already explained it to Hamilton. Standard Oil is relaxed about it now the oil embargo is a dead letter. Everything else is OK. Seems certain that Venezuela will nationalize concessions in the next few months. We have to estimate what ours are worth and open negotiations for a settlement with Mines and Hydrocarbons. That's it. We don't expect to get much, if anything. Here's George."

"Anything else, George?"

"No, that's it. I'll call from Madrid."

"George, what about the legalities regarding Poghdar? Has the Shah properly annexed it like he said he would?"

"Nothing has happened. It remains as it was when we went on the line."

"Can we jack him up on that, George? O'Reith asked. I promised Hamilton we would stay after him until we had a clear title to the oil field."

"I'll go with Carolyn to Teheran and remind him of it."

"O.K. George. Take care."

Chapter IX

Santo Domingo Prison

On August 25, the *Miami Herald* reported disturbances in Guatemala City. That night the Maracaibo radio station, *Ondas del Lago* confirmed the story with more detail. Trouble had broken out in the Yucatan as well. General Efrain Rios Montt of the National Opposition Front challenged President Garcia's legitimacy. Garcia put police squads in the street to shoot the tigers. General Montt, supported by the Guatemalan Society for the Prevention of Cruelty to Animals, sent rival gangs out to shoot the police. A week later, O'Reith got a package of newspapers sent down by courier from the tower. Included were The *Los Angeles Times*, the *San Francisco Chronicle* and importantly, the *Yellow Peril.* O'Reith went quickly to it.

> *CO-PROSPERITY SPHERE COLLAPSE*
>
> Los Angeles August 25, our correspondent in Guatemala City reports that a state of anarchy exists in this sub-tropical paradise where the national anthem is "Blessed Guatemala". When it was learned in the provinces that the popular president Richard M. Nixon had decamped, the highland peasants marched on the city. The police, occupied with roving tigers and countless gangs of varying insurgency, were unable to cope with the marching

indigenes. As of last night, the electricity was off, water was erratic and no telephones were working. Most of the shops were closed.

In Mexico City, President Luis Echeverria Alvarez announced that his armies were on the march to recapture the Yucatan provinces taken by force a decade earlier. Banners denouncing the vicious Guatemalan Dictator Carlos Pérez Jiménez were paraded through the streets by streaking university students. All over the city, strains of the martial national anthem *Mexicans, at the Call of War* could be heard over the clamor of traffic.

In Washington, President Gerald R. Ford announced on national TV that the United States had nothing to do with this but was sympathetic to Mexico's desires to have its southern provinces back. A representative of the CIA announced that it now appears that the *Greater Central America Co-prosperity sphere* was the black widow spider at the center of the Axis of Evil.

By day under a soft tropical sun, the garden at *El Escondite* was a beautiful place to behold. Mango trees leafed out in dense green foliage were heavy with fruit. A cluster of colorful Hacamayos announced raucously that they were ready to make more parrots. The papaya trees were bearing. A line of lime trees graced the long flagstone path that ran the length of the garden from the gargoyle fountain to the dragon fountain. Jacaranda trees around the perimeter with their showy clusters of purple flowers rose half way up the walls. A towering mimosa tree and a gaudy bougainvillea added to the panoply of color. Neatly arranged plots of African violets were planted between the trees. Water bubbled noisily from the fountains into catch basins. Open channels diverted the water into the irrigation system. Such a wonderland on the Tenth Parallel.

But by night, it was not the same. Above the high, stone wall could be seen the glow of Maracaibo's lights. Inside, this daytime paradise was an ominous, ghostly garden. The steady hiss of the gaslights, the melancholy tinkling of water in the runnels, the phosphorescent-eyed frogs hopping across the flagstones made this shadowy plot a place of impending evil. An occasional puff of smoke from one of the bug-zappers made the point that death was near. Treacherous even for a mere insect. The parrots sleeping in the mango trees had fallen silent.

Slithery fer-de-lances were on the prowl; active, aggressive, hissing in the underbrush, looking for trouble. At night, O'Reith wore boots that came halfway up his legs and his machete was handy.

In the corner of the garden next to the villa, mosquito netting covered a tiled patio making it safe and comfortable. In its center, stood a stone table with six lawn chairs. Overhead a gas light hissed softly. Entering from the villa kept out the bugs, snakes, bats and poisonous frogs. On the last day of August, in this secluded sanctum, the threesome were having evening cocktails. The sun was low and shadows were long. Minutes earlier McDonough had telephoned from Rome that he and Cook would arrive Maiquetia on an Alitalia 747 on Monday, September 2. La Macabra had now arranged for the Colonel to be moved to a ground-level cell that was dry and vermin free. A small window looked out on the prison courtyard. His fetters were removed for an hour each day so that he could take a walk. He had taken a shower.

On her latest visit, Cizancourt had assured her that the Colonel's irons would be removed at night so that he could sleep in comfort. So far, Cizancourt was U.S. $10,000 richer than when the Colonel was first incarcerated.

As they talked, the sun sank behind the garden wall. Night fell immediately. Here and there a star twinkled. The garden's night denizens stirred noisily. Fruit bats flew weird ovals around the banana tassels. Centipedes worried their way through the glistening moss. The eyes of the hopping frogs made phosphorescent tracery across the sleeping flowers. A gardener adjusted the flames of the gaslights. Darkness brought mosquitoes to seek blood. Many found the bug-zappers and crisped off.

O'Reith began, "Mandy, Ibanez told me today that the government will free the Americans early on Christmas Eve. They will arrive at Maiquetia before noon, to board a chartered Pan American Boeing 727 destined for Miami International. We've agreed to a fine of $35 million plus another $15 million for tunnel repairs. POTUS Ford will speak that day thanking Venezuela for freeing our troops so they can be home at Christmas. To paper it all over, the White House will release a statement saying the soldiers were sent down to reinforce the Panama Canal garrison but they were diverted by RMN and the Colonel. I will present this in writing to Ibanez when the embassy gives it to me next week. Venezuelan Government approval expected immediately. Ibanez told me that Pérez would sign it. I don't expect any White House flak. Haig has agreed to the fine, the damages and the presidential statement. So within 15 days, my work will be finished. The agreement calls for a down payment of $10 million, due within five days of signature. I'll stay until that payment clears. When McDonough arrives, we can discuss springing the Colonel. I foresee a long, difficult negotiation."

"Cizancourt has been pretty reasonable so far," Macabra said. "Perhaps we can persuade him to allow the Colonel to escape."

"Not a chance," O'Reith returned. "Too risky for him. He'd be charged with gross negligence and dereliction of duty. Be in the lock-up for life. No, we have to let the judicial process go forward, slow as that may be. As of today, he is not charged with anything. It could be months before an indictment comes down, longer for a certain trial date. The trial itself could drag out for months if not years. But once the verdict has been rendered, we can do something. It boils down to you and George looking after the Colonel until it is all over. Maxine and I are returning to Paris to our flat to lay low, maybe forever. This affair has rattled me. As you know, in Caracas, we have three vacant flats where our executives lived until the 96% tax regime went into effect. Flor and Margot can move into one of those flats. Another one will be for George and Carolyn and the third one will be for you. Can you arrange to live in Caracas until this matter is settled?"

"Yes, of course," Macabra said. "The man who brought you here, Cansor's nephew, is completely reliable. I'll put him in charge."

"That reminds me," O'Reith continued, "I was not prepared for your new chauffeur, the chap who picked me up at *La Chinita*. What happened to Cansor?"

"*Muerto, mi amor*,"La Macabra said dolorously. "Heart attack."

"How long ago?"

"It was after dear Theodore died. We had such a time getting the *Jefe Civil* to take over the orphanage. Cansor collapsed under the stress."

"That's a shame," O'Reith lamented. "The string is running out for all of us."

"General O'Reith," La Macabra continued, "With the certainty of nationalization, the Casinghead Company could be out of business in months."

"Yes. I'm aware of that. While George is helping the Colonel, Carolyn will negotiate with *Hidrocarburos* to get the best settlement. I'm pessimistic. But there is no turning back. For us, in Venezuela, the game is just about over."

"You won't come to see us anymore."

O'Reith laughed. "We'll come. And you can visit us in Paris. Next week we'll have the utilities turned on. I'll telephone Flor. She and Margot can come to Caracas. Will Cizancourt allow them to visit the Colonel regularly?"

"I'm sure."

O'Reith and Maxine departed Caracas for Paris late in November, the same day that the Colonel was indicted for high treason. Negotiation for release of the Americans had dragged out longer than he thought. But finally it was over. The deal was signed, the down payment was made and all that remained was for the soldiers to kill time until Christmas Eve. McDonough and Cook were installed in Caracas, as were Flor and Margot. La Macabra was settled in. She had introduced 'Father Antonio' to Warden Cizancourt. The Colonel, no longer in irons, had a comfortable cell, hot meals, plenty of cigars, new clothing, and a radio; he was content. *El Nacional*, *Panorama* and The *Miami Herald* were delivered daily. Flor and Margot came for tea every afternoon.

In theory, upon indictment, the Colonel should have been transferred to a maximum-security cell but in fact, as long as 'Father Antonio' and La Macabra took care of Cizancourt, Cizancourt took care of the Colonel. In early January 1975 he would appear in court to make his plea. McDonough, already screening criminal attorneys, would have a defense team in place long before then.

Before leaving Caracas, O'Reith, Carolyn and McDonough talked about the dismal future facing the company. Loss of the concessions in Venezuela, though regrettable, was long foreseen. O'Reith was alarmed about the speed with which the crestal wells in Poghdar had gone to gas. He also worried about the Shah's inability to settle the political question. Poghdar production would soon be down to 900,000 bopd. Honduras was a write off, a casualty of the recent fiasco. In Sumatra, production was falling. The government refused to discuss new concessions. What was to be done? Of the many possibilities they considered, in the end, they always came back to Gulf Oil.

It was the middle of May 1975. Maxine in a ragged white shirt and blue jeans was chopping weeds in her garden. One of her trees had ripe cherries and she knew where she could get a kiss for a bowl of them. Maybe even some high class stud service. O'Reith, working in his study, had just returned from a two-week trip to visit Helen in Los Angeles. Concerned because she was frailer now than when he had seen her in the fall of 1974, he also worried about her two recent memory lapses; one of three days and another of a full week. Worse, her memory of recent events was sketchy. She, with Ridley ever at her elbow, had taken in the *White Satin Miter* at the Pantages Art Deco Theater. Next day she had forgotten all about it. Parkinson, attending her regularly, prescribed several drugs of questionable utility. While in Los Angeles, Parkinson nagged him to get an examination. Reluctantly he agreed but rejected all of the sophisticated tests. He refused to be needled, X-rayed and threatened mayhem when Parkinson suggested proctology. He did agree to a urine specimen. Whatever testing it was subjected to, apparently it was OK but not potable.

Nixon, down in San Clemente, was restless. His fund-raising to establish his National Library was running slow. He was feeling isolated. None of his old Washington comrades would return his calls. In short, as he put it to Ethering, "I need to do something. I've got a ream of yellow note pads and plenty of pencils but nothing to write." He bugged Ethering for a job. Reluctantly O'Reith agreed to put Nixon out as an apprentice bagman. If he did well, advancement would follow. Nixon, eager to begin work, fretted because Ethering had to check the terms of his controversial pardon with DC. Haig told him that Nixon was *persona non grata* in the capital. Ford did not want him underfoot, prowling the halls of Congress, making mischief. Technically, he was forbidden to bribe any politician but if he were in Sacramento he was probably OK. California Assemblymen had little or no standing. Bribing one of them wouldn't even make it as a misdemeanor. Thus Nixon was placed on the payroll of Mineral Extraction, LTD, a wholly owned subsidiary of the Company with headquarters in Vaduz, Liechtenstein and offices in Sacramento and Washington. Company accounts were closely guarded secrets.

With his California affairs in good order, O'Reith enjoyed Paris and Maxine's charms. But aside from that, if the international oil and gas business can be compared to a game of seven card stud, and there are many who do just that, then O'Reith, it can be said, was looking at his hole cards. Those face up were a motley collection, a pair of deuces, a trey, and a seven. In addition to his other woes, a telex just in informed him that the entire first line of eight wells on the huge Poghdar structure had gone to gas. Last year's gassers had now been re-completed deeper in the limestone. But they were producing 10,000 bopd, not the 25,000 bopd of the original completions. Now they faced the work over of eight more. Even worse, the first line of wells on one of the small structures had gone to gas. Within months they would lose the crestal wells on the second small structure. By the end of 1975 total oil production would fall below a million bopd. Among its other consequences, this would distress the Shah mightily.

The Shah had still not annexed Poghdar. Afghanistan was certain, in time, to kick up its heels. As long as the Shah maintained a powerful army on the frontier to support the Gurkhas, things were OK. But Standard Oil wanted it fixed and Hamilton frequently reminded Cook of it. If the Shah should falter, well, it was something O'Reith did not like to think about.

Of course his was not the only international major with problems. Gulf Oil Corporation was in far worse shape. Their management had been caught up in a financial scandal. Some of their smartest executives had been forced to resign and the company was in turmoil. O'Reith thought it possible the company could be up for sale. Casinghead company treasury held over $2 billion in cash with no debt on the books. Income measured in millions of dollars per day, O'Reith was ready to move. Lines of credit existed with JP Morgan and Chase Manhattan in New York and with British Linen in London. Ethering and his accountants had made shrewd estimates of Gulf's oil and gas reserves in the ground both in the United States and worldwide. In the Middle East, the Kuwait Government was threatening a takeover of the fabulous Burgan Field, of which Gulf owned a half interest. Venezuela was a goner. These two blows could be crippling. Ethering's lieutenants had calculated that the weakened Gulf Oil was worth less than $2 billion. O'Reith was thinking about offering one and a half.

McDonough and Cook were now in his villa on Lago Albano, having just arrived from Caracas the day before. O'Reith awaited a call from them. It was decision time. Just as a muddy, smudged Maxine appeared in the door with a basket of cherries, the phone rang. It was McDonough.

"Clive," he began. "We're booked out of here on Monday, May 19 in the afternoon. Be in Paris in time for dinner. Do we go out?"

"Let me check with Maxine, George. Probably better to dine in. We have a superb cook. In any event, I'll meet you. Charles de Gaulle?"

"We'll be on Alitalia. Arrives at five o'clock. How long should we stay?"

"George we can cover the waterfront in one day."

"Very well. We'll book tickets to Caracas for Wednesday, the 21st."

"Are things heating up down there? How's the Colonel holding up?"

"He's OK. I'll give you a complete rundown when we arrive."

Next afternoon, comfortable in O'Reith's parlor, Maxine began mixing drinks. O'Reith asked, "How's the Colonel doing?"

McDonough sipped his Scotch and replied with a long sigh. "Complicated affair, Clive. He sat in durance vile until the government presented a bill of indictment. They included everything, of course. Lese Majeste for openers. Added to that, the usual: criminal corruption; malfeasance in office, police brutality in connection with activity of *Seguridad Nacional.* They accused him of murder in connection with the disappearance of certain political enemies."

O'Reith smiled and said, "Well at least they didn't charge him with mopery on the high seas."

"They may yet," Cook said, giggling. Maxine tittered. McDonough continued, "Once he was indicted, the government wanted him out of town. We delayed it a few weeks but in due course he was transferred to a high-security prison in *San Juan de los Morros,* some distance away. Goodbye to Cizancourt, an expensive bloke off the payroll. The Colonel has a garden in a private courtyard attached to his five-room suite. Nice bedroom, bathroom with hot water, parlor for guests and a private den where he can consult with the defense team. The kitchen has a refrigerator and a hot plate. He has a TV set. A secretary comes every afternoon at six with a portable typewriter. She takes dictation, brings messages and takes his mail to the post office. The flat has wall air-conditioners in bedroom, den and parlor. Hot meals are brought in.

He has cigars and a well-stocked bar. This costs us $500/day. In short, he is comfortable. But they keep a sharp eye on him."

"What about Flor and Margot?"

"The government provided them with an apartment in town. They can visit with no restrictions. Other guests limited to three hours in the afternoon. Defense attorneys can see the Colonel whenever they want to."

"Good treatment for a guy charged with all of those crimes," O'Reith said.

"There are reasons." McDonough continued. "First off, the Colonel has challenged the indictment and there is a fair chance he'll prevail. He has written a *declaracion indagatoria*, his side of the case. We presented that to the government in January. Lawyers expect a ruling this autumn."

"Snail slow," O'Reith said.

"The law's delay," McDonough said grimacing. "Slower in South America than in North America I think. The Colonel argues that when he departed Venezuela he was the president and when he returned of his own free will, he was still the president. He says Betancourt, Leoni and now Pérez are all impostors, illegally elected. From that point he challenges just about everything else except what they call malversation, peculation and related felonies, in his words, *lucro de funcionarios.* The prevailing legal wrangle goes all the way back to 1963 when the then U.S. Attorney General, Robert Kennedy negotiated an extradition plea with the Betancourt government. At that time, the U.S. ruled out all crimes related to brutality, murder, and corruption other than financial. All that remained were the financial charges. That petition, presented to the U.S. Supreme Court was affirmed. So at the time the CIA installed him as President of Guatemala, hanging over his head was an extradition order approved by the Court, narrowly defining the crimes with which he could be charged if he ever returned to Venezuela. Betancourt accepted that then and the Colonel believes it is still valid. To put it another way, the U.S. Court becomes his friend in the Venezuelan Court. This is reinforced by the fact that POTUS Eisenhower awarded him The Legion of Merit. While his offenses may be serious, they are not the stuff of firing squads. Our lawyers believe that we will win. If that happens, then the case will shift to determination of a trial date. Based on previous cases, it could drag on for two or three years."

"OK with us as long as he is well-treated. What happens if he is convicted?"

"He'll be sentenced and locked up in an ordinary slammer. Not good news."

"Does he get credit for time already served," Maxine asked.

"He does indeed. The best solution would be for his case to drag on and when sentence is pronounced, it would be equal to time served. That way he would be a free man."

"So what are you going to do when you get back to Caracas, George?"

"I will stay until we have an indication that our view prevails. I also plan to add an American constitutional lawyer to the defense team, one who has experience before the US Supreme Court. The US extradition order is paramount to our defense."

O'Reith nodded. "Call Stan. He'll fix you up." Then his face became serious. He began, "Without going over all of the bad news that Carolyn carries in her head, I propose that we open negotiations to buy Gulf Oil. Our reserves are falling fast. Gulf is on the ropes. The worst that can happen is that we open a bidding war. If the stakes get too high we will withdraw. In the meanwhile, before we approach their management, we will quietly acquire up to 4.9% of the shares; just short of the mandatory declaration required by the Securities and Exchange Commission. Stan says we have in the Vaduz account right now enough cash to buy about 3% of Gulf stock. We can double the amount of money from the Poghdar stream that we send to Vaduz. So in addition to the 3% which we can buy immediately, we'll have a steady income for more purchases until the effect of it drives the stock price up. With funds in the bank in LA, we'll buy stock until we go over the 5% limit in the U.S. That will bring out the SEC dogs and we'll have to file. The fat will be in the fire. The vultures will begin to circle. Just before the filing hits the papers, I'll telephone the chairman of Gulf. What do you think?"

Cook said, "I like it."

McDonough said, "OK by me."

"Very well, I'll start the ball rolling today. We'll nibble, keeping the price low as long as we can. The shares are trading around $25. Going beyond that, we must find new reserves to replace Poghdar. Carolyn, where do we look?"

"Has to be Africa, Clive. Middle East is one big powder keg. Sumatra and Java are rapidly becoming bad news. Besides that, nationalistic pressure will cap profits. I say we go to Nigeria, Gabon, Congo-Brazzaville, Angola and perhaps Equatorial Guinea. If we buy Gulf Oil, we're automatically in Angola or at least Cabinda which is almost the same thing."

McDonough said, "Africa puts us beyond the pale as far as the Raj is concerned. I suppose we still have influence in Nigeria but not much. And they're far from recovered from that disastrous civil war. Equatorial Guinea puts us in the Portuguese domain. The others are under the sway of France. Can we induce LeBel to come out of retirement long enough to establish a government liaison?"

"Well, he will help," O'Reith said. "All that will be required are a couple of phone calls. He'll do that."

"Like for me to call him, Clive?" Cook asked.

O'Reith nodded.

"Then there is Colombia," McDonough added.

"Colombia!" O'Reith exclaimed. "I like that one. When I was pushing tools for Calitropical Oil before the war, we drilled a couple of dry holes in the Magdalena Valley. Good shows. Just not big enough for commercial production. Since then Shell has found several prolific fields."

"Country is a mess," Cook said.

"That's right," McDonough agreed. "Warlords. Drug Cartels. Insurgents."

"We would have to straighten that up all right. Good job for the Colonel," O'Reith said. "Well it is a thought for the future. Maybe a couple of years from now we'll have a shot at it."

"General O'Reith, there is one other place we could consider."

"Such as?"

"North and east of Kettleman Dome. Block 36-C"

"Isn't that the block that legally is a can of worms?"

"Yes. An Act of Congress awarded it to the Southern Pacific Railroad in 1869. You remember the notorious bribery scandals that made Collis P. Huntington, Leland Stanford and Mark Hopkins fabulously rich men before the turn of the century? Southern Pacific was their railroad. It started in New Orleans, crossed the west to LA, went up through the San Joaquin Valley and terminated in San Francisco. The land must have been pretty close to worthless for congress to give it away so freely.

For every mile of track that was laid, the government gave them 20 square miles of land. Block 36-C is part of it, a complete township, and 36 square miles. Remember the San Joaquin Exploration Company?"

"Vaguely," O'Reith answered. "The name sounds familiar. Was that one of the tiny independents that went broke in the 1930s; one of the companies that Harvey Halliday bought for a song?"

"Right on both counts, sir," Cook replied. "San Joaquin Exploration leased it when the titles were not so screwed up. They ran several seismic lines in 1928. Geophysical exploration was in its infancy and the lines are primitive. But the structures show. The maps were in our files. Nobody paid attention to them."

"How did you come upon them?" O'Reith asked. "My recollection is that we always had much larger fish to fry."

"Remember that day you told me that Standard Oil was buying Calitroleum? You invited Hunter and I to join you in a new company?

O'Reith grinned broadly. "I do. With my heart in my mouth, I wondered if we were going to make it. The Colonel made us sweat blood for those Lake Maracaibo blocks. I really got to know that scamp. Indeed, I remember that all too well."

Cook continued, "Well, sir, shocked at starting over, searching the files, I found Block 36-C. One structure looks to be as big as Kettleman North Dome. I would have mentioned it then but you were set for Venezuela."

"Have you seen the seismic for Kettleman?"

"Standard Oil swapped it to us for some lines across the San Andrés fault down south in Orange County."

O'Reith nodded. "I can't recall the circumstances but it seems to me that there has been continuous litigation for the last 30 years. I know that Standard Oil, Texas Company and Shell have all tried to lease parts of it. The difficulty lies in the clouded titles."

Cook said, "The only solution is eminent domain. We can delineate the parts of the block that are interesting. Then induce the State of California to condemn them, seize them and lease them to us."

"In theory, if they do that, they have to put them up for auction. Given the climate of today's politics, it would be tough for us to win out," O'Reith said.

"We'd have to bribe the complete Assembly," McDonough said. "The biggest bag job in the history of the company."

O'Reith rubbed his chin thoughtfully remembering Richard M. Nixon walking the legislative halls of Sacramento. He said, "Carolyn, I'll think that one over. Tell me again the number of that block."

"Block 36-C. Vidoga Springs is just about in the center of it."

O'Reith noted it in his diary just as the chef tinkled his bell. The foursome took their places at the dinner table. McDonough passed judgment on a Bordeaux from the Rothschild's winery, nodding to the waiter who poured as they attacked the paté de fois gras.

When the Crepes Suzettes had disappeared, O'Reith asked, "George, what's new with His Holiness?"

"He is not a happy man, Clive. *Casti connubii II* is a dead letter. In spite of all the promotion, it goes nowhere; totally rejected. Worse, His Holiness is upset by the notoriety of the *Miter*."

"I was unaware that it had attracted any attention whatsoever," O'Reith said. "The last I heard, Ed Wood was going to stretch it out to 110 minutes with his famous chase scene and then release it into distribution."

"Clive, this is a bit indelicate, but I suppose there is no getting around it. Not only did Wood put in the chase, he also put in some material that borders on flagrant pornography. Some scenes between Godunov's mistress and the Count of Castiglio are, well, openly erotic. Nudity, concupiscence and carnality, while quite stimulating, definitely subtract from its substance as a religious film. You recall, in the original, we made a strong case for *Casti Connubii II.* To the dismay of His Holiness, Wood followed that with a graphic description of what the Pope promulgated. Paul was nauseated by it. Now, inasmuch as he deems me the architect of that monstrosity, he is unhappy with me. You said that Helen and Alice went to see it. Did they say anything?"

"Helen could not remember it the next day," O'Reith said morosely. "All Alice said was that it was pretty bad. I didn't ask her about it and to tell the truth I had forgotten all about the inclusion of those *Casti Connubii II* scenes."

"The movie was shown in an Italian art theater in Rome," McDonough said. "Paul got wind of it, had it shown in the Vatican projection room. Big racket. I was for it in spades."

"I believe it," O'Reith said. "On that subject, George, how are you coming with your plan to pack the College of Cardinals?"

McDonough simpered, squealed eerily. He said, "Well, Clive I can report a modest success. Yesterday before leaving Rome, I had the pleasure of putting four names before the Pope for his consideration to be elevated to the altar."

"Like who?" O'Reith put on his general's face, suspicious and unbelieving.

"Flor."

"George, surely not. She is the wife of one of the more notorious dictators of the 20th Century. Does the Pope know that?"

"In her dossier, which he has on his desk, certain details of her pedigree will emerge, McDonough said defensively."

"What are the chances of his reading it?"

"Well, he has aides who vet the candidates for elevation."

"Do they level with him?"

"Presumably."

"George, whom besides Flor?"

"Alice."

"Alice Ridley!" O'Reith exclaimed. "George she's a Bible Belt Baptist and an astrologer to boot."

"Actually her bona fides are within the criteria," McDonough countered. "There was a time when the Popes depended heavily on astrological prognostications. In the Middle Ages, the astrologers helped the Pope predict the arrival of Easter."

"And the only way Paul will find out any of her qualifications will be if he or his aide reads the dossier. Am I right?"

"Well, Clive, that's a given."

"You said four, George, who are the other two? Carolyn and Mandy?"

"That's it, all right," McDonough admitted.

"So the Pope will now have in the College of Cardinals an oil company executive, a Venezuelan witch and necromancer, a Los Angeles Astrologer and the wife of a dictator; four women who will vote for you, if and when it comes time to choose a new Pope."

"Clive, you don't have to put it so bluntly."

Cook said, "General O'Reith I for one, think that George would make a peach of a Pope. I don't see much of anything wrong here."

O'Reith snorted in her direction. Then he turned his face to look McDonough in the eye. He said, "One final question George and we'll move on."

"Yes, Clive."

"Have you bribed the Pope's aide?"

"Well, of course not. But I did indicate that an elevation to the position of bishop could happen depending on certain events taking place."

"What about Stan, George? Once you were of a mind to promote his candidacy?"

"I did that some time back. He will become a cardinal along with the others. The announcement will be made later in the year."

O'Reith sighed. He said, "Well good luck George. How long will you and Carolyn stay in Caracas?"

"We'll confer with the Colonel. See that he is OK. Mandy has a new confessor to take my place. Chap who was her husband's assistant at St. Sulphide. I hope the Colonel gets on with him."

"George I was unaware that the Colonel went to confession," O'Reith said.

"PR, Clive. We put pictures in the paper of my arrival at his jail. To continue, I have to go over the defense strategy with the American lawyer. He arrives today. After all that, Carolyn and I will return to Los Angeles and work out of the tower until we accomplish our various goals."

O'Reith and Maxine said goodbye to McDonough and Cook at the departure terminal. That night they went to see *One Flew over the Cuckoo's Nest* at the *Theatre de Dix-heures.* The line-up of stars included Jack Nicholson and Louise Fletcher. The film depicted the lunatic goings-on of a bunch of wackos in a state mental institution run by a sadistic matron. As they departed the cinema, O'Reith said, "But for the Grace of God, I would be in that goofy place." Maxine tittered and hung on his arm.

By October of 1975, the Casinghead Company had purchased 4.9% of Gulf Oil common stock at prices ranging from $24 to $26 per share. Mineral Extraction Ltd. in Vaduz had acquired 6% of the common stock and a parcel of bonds. It was time to make the move. Having once served with him on an API committee, O'Reith was acquainted with the chairman of Gulf Oil, one Kingwood DeGeneras Brock so he telephoned with a request for an audience. They agreed to meet in Pittsburgh on November 2nd. He then telephoned Cook and Ethering requesting that they meet him there. Cook told him that McDonough had flown to Rome to call on the Pope. O'Reith then called McDonough. "George," he began. "How are things going for the Colonel?"

"Not bad Clive. Our defense team prevailed. The major charges have all been dropped. The courts agreed that the Colonel could only be charged for the crimes accepted by the US Supreme Court. So he is not going to be shot."

"Do we have a trial date set?"

"No, our next move was to challenge the integrity of the Venezuelan Supreme Court on the grounds that a majority of the judges were members of *Accion Democratica*. Thus the Colonel was unlikely to get a fair trial. The government disagreed but they admitted some of the magistrates were tainted. We have a shot at picking independent judges but it will take awhile."

"Why are they treating him so gently, George?"

"Clive, there is a bit of a recession. The Colonel is becoming increasingly popular with the men and women in the street. The oil business is in decline because of nationalization. The economy is in trouble. Lots of people are out of work, especially oil field workers. Sugar prices are too low. But for some essentials like bread and meat, they are too high. The paradox of every downturn. People remember that when the Colonel was running things, the economy ticked along OK. So there is that. Another reason is that many of those top dogs can see into the future and may very well find themselves some day in the dock."

"Got any idea when they will set a date?"

"Could be in February of 1976. After local elections. No date will be announced until then. Some of the candidates are Tachiristas. The government does not want to give them any free publicity."

"George, I'm going to Pittsburgh to talk to King Brock with Gulf. Carolyn and Stan will meet me there. You're welcome to come if you like."

"I have plenty to do here, Clive. With Paul, that is."

The Gulf Building in Pittsburgh, of pale gray limestone is an impressive Art Deco tower of 44 stories located at 439 Seventh Avenue. Inside, the walls are of hand cut Italian marble. In the high speed bronze elevator cage headed for the top, O'Reith in his midnight blue tuxedo stood beside Stan Ethering in a dark gray serge suit and Carolyn Cook in an olive drab matronly maxi skirt that fell to her ankles. She had pearls in her ears; a beige blouse buttoned up to her Adam's apple and a black cloche with a veil. Her brown slippers more or less matched her clothing. A secretary met them as they exited the elevator and led them straight into the huge penthouse office where 'King' Brock presided over the ailing 'Sister'. His view of the city was panoramic. He could not see the broad Pacific as O'Reith could from the tower, but his view of the junction of the Allegheny and Monongahela rivers, was magnificent. Brock was a beefy man not quite six feet tall. His head was squarish, his eyes slate gray and his full head of silver hair was combed back. With his gleaming, white teeth, he bore a striking resemblance to Warren G. Harding. He was wearing a dark business suit and an immaculate, heavily starched, white cotton shirt. His oxfords were jet black and reflected the fluorescent light from above. He greeted O'Reith heartily as he vigorously shook the taller man's hand, clasping his shoulder with his left hand and giving him some good vibrations as he kept on pumping his right hand as if they were long lost brothers.

Brock could be described as affable in the extreme. He gave the impression of a mental lightweight. That assessment would be dead wrong. From a noted political family in New Orleans, he was a graduate in petroleum engineering from Louisiana State University and a member of the honor fraternity Tau Beta Pi. He had been a battalion commander in the 101st Airborne Division and earned battle stars and decorations in Normandy and Bastogne. His career with Gulf was a classic study of an intelligent, capable man with good connections, moving steadily to the top. Brock was 4 years younger than O'Reith, which made him 65, the compulsory retirement age. He said, "Jesus Christ Clive! How long has it been? I know. It was an API meeting in San Antonio. Must have been about 1950. Right?" He laughed loudly as he awaited O'Reith's reply.

O'Reith nodded agreement and presented Cook and Ethering. He identified their positions in the company. When the pleasantries were completed and the three Casinghead Company executives were sitting across from Brock at his huge glass-topped desk, the Gulf Chairman chuckled and said, "I suppose you all didn't fly up here just to see the river. Am I right?"

"King, we're grown up boys and girls. Our industry has some severe problems. And it is no secret that Gulf Oil, like our little company is wounded. How seriously, and what and can be done about it, is what we're here to talk about."

"Well you have that right Clive. Did you know we set a record last year for wells on fire? Christ Clive we had six burning simultaneously; one in West Texas, two in Lake Maracaibo, Two in Mozambique and one in the Neutral Zone. Tie that, pal."

O'Reith laughed. "King I saw one of those Lake Maracaibo fires. It was Ceuta No.1, a Mene Grande well, a torch you could see from Machiques."

Brock laughed. "That's right. It was a bad fire, Clive. One of the worst I've seen. We got Red Adair on it and it took him forever to put it out. Those offshore fires are t-o-u-g-h. I was so shook up about it I demanded we set up a blowout prevention section in our drilling department. We've got some of our best engineers on it."

O'Reith listened carefully and when Brock paused for breath, with narrowed eyes and speaking in his listen-to-me-carefully voice, he began, "King, would you believe me if I told you we were Gulf Oil shareholders?"

Brock's eyes opened wide. O'Reith detected a slight tremble in his hands. A bit of color faded from his florid features. He muttered, "No kidding?"

"King, we own 4.9% of the common stock and half a billion dollars worth of Gulf bonds. Today our purchases will drive us over 5% which means we'll have to file with the SEC dogs."

Brock switched his speakerphone on and signaled his secretary. When she answered he spoke sharply. "Katy, get me Lanny Molloy over at Lehmann Brothers. If he's on another call tell him to get off. I want to talk to him right now. OK?" Then to O'Reith and company he said, "Mums the word. I don't want him to know there is anyone in the office with me."

The three visiting executives nodded.

When the stockbroker came on the line, Brock purred into the speakerphone, "Lanny, how you are?"

"I'm OK King, what's on your mind so important? I had to get off of a call with a good customer?"

"Good as me?"

"Well no."

"Lanny, who's buying crippled up ole Gulf Oil today?" Brock asked slyly.

"King it is up a bit. Last trade was at $26 and three eights. Almost a buck. We hear rumors that a buyer in Europe keeps nibbling away at it."

"What if a poor country boy wanted to buy, say 10,000 shares? What do you figure he'd have to pay?"

"King we could spread that order out. Buy a thousand here, a thousand in San Francisco, some more in Dallas. St. Louis. Milwaukee. You know. Keep' em guessing. I'd say we could do that for under $27 a share."

"Lanny, do that and give me a ring when it is done."

"OK. King and thanks."

"You bet Lanny. Regards to mamacita and those little Molloys." Brock switched off the speakerphone and grinned broadly at his visitors. He said, "You know I've got to retire at the end of December. My retirement fund needs to be pumped up." He swiveled around to face O'Reith directly. He asked, And?"

"What would Gulf Oil consider a fair offer?" O'Reith asked.

"Board meeting next week. I can put it to them then. If you're in a hurry, I could put it to them by telephone right now."

"No hurry, King. We'd like to buy as much as we can under $30 dollars. Word of this is going to leak out fast enough as it is. Next week will be fine."

Brock said, "Coming up on noon. How about a drink and a good steak dinner in the company dining room?"

When they were served their cocktails, Brock looked hard and long at Cook. He said, "Carolyn, ever since Clive introduced you this morning, I've been trying to figure where I saw your name. It just came to me that some years back you wrote an article that appeared in the *Journal of the American Institute of Mining Engineers*. It was a discussion of a gold mine accidentally discovered while drilling for oil up on the Malheur River in Idaho."

"That was little old me, all right," Cook replied. "My humble claim to fame."

O'Reith laughed. He said, "Don't let her fool you, King. She got her fifteen minutes of fame for discovering the Tidikelt Field in French North Africa. That one saved Calitroleum from bankruptcy when the Shah went down in 1951. Harvey Halliday, bless his long departed soul recognized her intelligence and promoted her. She became vice president of the Exploration Department."

"Clive, that reminds me of something," Brock answered, twirling the stem of his champagne flute. "I saw a picture of the Casinghead Tower in the *Oil & Gas Journal* sometime back. It sure looked like the old Calitroleum Tower. I remember it had 39 stories, five fewer than what we've got."

"It is, King," O'Reith confirmed. After Mr. Halliday passed on, Vince Blake and I and Halliday's widow sold Calitroleum to Standard Oil. Gwyn Follis spearheaded that deal for them. The tower was part of the deal but they didn't have any use for it. It stood vacant for three years. Our new Casinghead Company struck it rich at *Lago Poniente* so we bought it back. At the last count we occupied five floors. Rest of the building is vacant except for an astrology shop in the lobby. You know King, when Halliday built that skyscraper in the thirties, he flaunted the building codes that required earthquake design specifications. But he built it hell for stout and covered it with an Austin Chalk facade. It has been through dozens of quakes and there isn't a crack in it. It was pink for many years and people would stop to look at the fossils embedded in it. Now it is faded and some of the fossils have been eaten away by the smog. But it is still an impressive tower. And it has that huge clock. When the smog is up high, you can look up from just about anywhere and see what time it is."

Brock looked at Ethering and said, "Stan aren't you the fellow with the reputation for making more federal law than the last dozen or so congresses?"

Ethering laughed. "Well I was a lobbyist for the Pure Oil Company back in the good old days. I guess you could say I've bent an elbow or two over the years with various and sundry DC politicians."

"The way I heard it," Brock said laughing, "it was arm twisting, mainly that of old Senator Quigleyson of Nevada. That scamp worked wonders attaching riders to existing legislation. He amended the Mann Act and the Spooner Act, the Smoot-Hawley Act and god knows what else. Always, I might add for the benefit of the Casinghead Company."

"King, you flatter me," Ethering said. "But the Quig took good care of Nevada too."

"No doubt about that. We should have somebody on our payroll with your perspicacity. One of our problems as you well know is that we have had some top management in the past who were naughty boys. You know, the bribery scandal."

"Stan keeps up with that stuff," O'Reith said. "I don't pay any attention to it. Christ, King, if every oil company executive that bribed a congressman were in jail, you couldn't put gasoline in your tank."

Brock laughed loudly and slapped his knees. He asked, "Any truth to the rumor that Tricky Dick is on your payroll? We hear he's haunting the halls of the California Assembly in Sacramento handing out hundred dollar bills."

"It's true," Ethering said. "Except for the hundred dollar bills. That has gone out of style. He passes out $15 bills with his picture on them. I don't know if they are any good. He works under my supervision. We need permits of one kind of another with great regularity. Drilling permits. Permits to cross state property. Easements. Rights-of-way. You name it. We have to have them and we have to have them in a hurry."

Brock chuckled. "Funny world we live in. Any of that stuff you need permits for in Block 36-C?" He roared with laughter.

O'Reith said, "Can't reveal military secrets, Brock. You know that."

Brock laughed.

After a fine lunch, the three oil executives returned to the Steel City Hotel on Ballagh-Cynwyd Boulevard. They were booked on an Allegheny Air Boeing 727 back to New York. Cook and Ethering had a late TWA flight to Los Angeles. O'Reith was on an Air France Boeing 747 destined for Charles de Gaulle. As he was packing, the phone rang. It was Parkinson calling from Los Angeles. He said, "Clive, wish I didn't have to disturb you like this but Helen has had a sinking spell. She's fallen back into amnesia. Three days now. She was out of it a couple of weeks ago for about the same stretch. You and I need to talk about this, face to face. Think you can squeeze a trip in?"

"I'll be on the same plane with Carolyn and Stan."

"I'll be awaiting your call, Clive."

When they arrived mid-afternoon in Los Angeles, O'Reith, still on EST, was weary. He said goodnight to McDonough and Cook at the Fullerton Building. After a long, lonely soak, he toweled off and looked at the telephone. What had been planned as a three-day trip now looked like it could be longer. He called Maxine and explained to her what had happened. Then he called Parkinson. He began, "Max, I just got in and I'm shot. What say we wait until the morning?"

"Sure Clive. Where and when?"

"Here in the Fullerton Building? I'm alone. Maxine stayed in Paris this time. Say ten o'clock?"

"May I bring Alice? She knows a lot more about Helen's state than I do."

"Yes do bring her," O'Reith replied. "How is Alice holding up?"

"OK but, well, you know there's plenty of stress and strain to go around."

"See you at ten Max."

O'Reith rang the tower dining room and asked them to send him a meal. Then he mixed a double dry martini on the rocks, loosened his bathrobe and slumped into an easy chair, too whipped even to watch KTLA. After dinner, even though it was still early, he went to bed and fell asleep immediately.

Next morning, he had breakfast delivered and read the papers as he awaited his visitors. In the *Wall Street Journal* he saw that Gulf Oil stock had closed at $34.50, up almost six dollars. The bell rang. Parkinson and Ridley were at the door. When they were seated, he offered them coffee from his breakfast thermos. O'Reith asked, "Max, what is the prognosis?"

"Short term, Clive, Helen is out of it. She's been out of it for five days as of right now. She's awake and takes care of herself. But she doesn't recognize anyone, not even Alice. She pecks at her food. She's listless; takes a morning nap for couple of hours; takes an afternoon nap that lasts until dark. Maid gets her up and to the table for dinner but her food intake is close to starvation rations. She's down ten pounds in the last week. Long term, she'll probably come out of it. But who knows when? It looks like we're going down hill and I don't know what to do. Clive, you're looking at a medic who was born with the century. I'm 75 years old. I don't practice anymore except for Helen. She needs special help, which she will not accept; a comprehensive physical examination with a cat scan, electrocardiogram, encephalogram, and the works. If we knew what was wrong, possibly we could treat her. Maybe even cure her. Age of course is a factor. You realize that."

"Is her hair still growing?" O'Reith asked.

"Fine, white hair, wispy, baby's hair, but she'll soon have a headful of it."

"Well, that's something," O'Reith said solemnly. "Alice, what do you think?"

"I think she has a physical problem in her head. Maybe a tumor."

"Is she having headaches?"

"She says she has a perpetual hangover," Ridley said.

"What do you say we send an ambulance around this morning and put her in the hospital?" O'Reith asked.

"An ambulance would frighten her," Ridley said. "We can get her into a limousine, especially her own. How about that?"

"Max?"

"She wakes up in a hospital bed it will be hell to pay but we need to do it."

O'Reith rose, put his hat on, said, "Let's go."

She was feather light in his arms as he carried her down the stairs and through the parlor to the limousine. Her eyes were open but she didn't recognize him. She said nothing. Parkinson led the way, O'Reith in the middle carrying Helen and Ridley behind. With Helen in his lap, Ridley beside her and Parkinson in the jump seat, they went directly to Century City Hospital and O'Reith stayed with his wife until she was admitted and sedated. Then the three of them returned to the Fullerton Building where O'Reith had arranged for lunch. Seated in the sumptuous parlor, the three sat while the waiter popped the cork on a bottle of Mumm's and poured three flutes. O'Reith was rarely a champagne drinker but he didn't refuse this one. Neither did Parkinson and Ridley. O'Reith said, "Max, she's dying, isn't she?"

Parkinson, grim-faced, said softly, "Clive we're all dying. We begin to die the day we're born. That's the way of Mother Nature."

"Not particularly reassuring in the present circumstances," Ridley said. "Clive, you have your affairs. And of course, you have Maxine. Max, you have your profession. I have nothing when Helen is gone."

Parkinson said, "Let's hold off on the crepe and candles until we get an accurate prognosis. We will now, you know. This time next week, we'll know exactly what we're up against. Maybe sooner."

O'Reith asked, "Alice, you say you have nothing without Helen. Don't you still have Star Signs?"

"It is functioning but I rarely go there. My assistants run it. I don't even know if it is making money. I have been totally absorbed with poor Helen these last several months."

The champagne lifted some of the gloom. Lunch was tasty. Pacific sole sautéed in butter, baby lima beans and Persian long-grained rice.

By the time they got to the ice cream, they had run through a second bottle of Mumm's and were laughing and telling jokes.

Late that afternoon, he awoke from a champagne nap with a slight headache. The telephone was ringing and it was Ethering. He asked, "General O'Reith, are you coming to the office while you're here?"

"Well, I wasn't Stan but I can. What's up?"

"President Nixon would like to see you. He just called from Sacramento. He asked about you and I told him you were in town. It is no secret. The news about Helen is on TV."

"Christ, Stan, we just admitted her to the hospital this morning. I can't imagine word would get out so quick," O'Reith said. He was genuinely astonished.

"Hollywood, sir. She's a star. What else could you expect?"

"You're right of course. I should have thought of that. To tell you the truth, my mind is not functioning properly. Stan, call Nixon back and ask him to fly in tonight and we can get together at ten o'clock in the morning. That OK?"

"Should be sir. I'll do it now and get right back to you."

O'Reith entered the tower through the basement garage. As he got out of the limousine, he noticed a green Chrysler parked down at the end. It rung a bell. He had seen it before somewhere. He made a mental note to ask the garage super to whom it belonged. Normally he would have taken the express to the penthouse. But today he stopped off at the lobby just to take a look at Ridley's shop, 'Star Signs'. It hadn't changed. It still had the chrome-plated cocktail-table-sized astronomical circle with the signs of the zodiac around the perimeter. Musical half and quarter notes in chrome steel, scattered here and there, gave it the impression that the world of astrology was a cheerful, happy one. The door was ajar and he could see nice-looking young women in basic black moving about with spirit. The place was obviously doing a good business. Giving it a parting glance over his shoulder, reminding himself to ask Ridley about those pretty girls, he re-entered the elevator and zoomed to the top of the tower. His secretary, Lauren, met him in the anteroom wearing a yellow blouse with a light green skirt that came just above her knees. A soft-spoken brunette with an oval face and brown eyes, she waited for him to speak. O'Reith said, "Hello Lauren. Long time no see."

"Yes sir, General O'Reith sir, it has been awhile. Mr. Ethering and President Nixon are waiting. I can ring them when you're ready."

"Ring 'em, Lauren," O'Reith said with his magnetic smile.

O'Reith walked to one of the clerestory windows, his favorite thinking site. He looked out at the yachts coasting along the Pacific shore. He turned at the rap on his door. Lauren was escorting his visitors. He approached Nixon warmly and shook his hand, slapping him on the back at the same time. "Mr. President, you're looking good and I'm pleased to see you again," he began. "Stan tells me we're getting our permits faster than ever before. You must have a knack for what you're doing. I am proud to have you on our team. Keep up the good work."

"Well, General O'Reith, it is good work and I am glad to have it. A man needs honest employment to ward off depression," Nixon said as O'Reith released his hand and greeted Ethering. Nixon continued, "I feel like I am useful and being with a group of politicians is right up my alley. It is like being at home. I heard the news about Helen on TV last night. I wanted to let you know of my concern. If there is anything that Pat or I can do...? And I certainly hope that whatever is wrong will soon be right."

"Thank you Mr. President," O'Reith responded. "Helen resisted treatment for a long time but now she is where she belongs and with Dr. Parkinson looking after her, I am not worrying."

"Could I ask how the Colonel is doing? Nixon continued.

"He is in a maximum-security prison several kilometers outside Caracas but his living conditions are fine. He has a suite with a few amenities. Flor and Margot are living in the little town nearby and visit him every day. His spirits are high and he is not suffering. His legal position seems to be improving. We have the best lawyers money can buy. But we can't predict the outcome. We're sure he will not be shot as a military prisoner."

"That's heartening. I'd like to send him a note of encouragement."

"Give it to Stan, Mr. President. We have an American constitutional attorney on the defense team. He often goes down there to confer with the Colonel. He will be glad to take a note for you."

"And Father George?" Nixon asked.

O'Reith laughed. "He has been playing the role of 'Father Antonio' here lately, confessor to the Caudillo and organizer of his defense. But he's back in Rome now in conference with Pope Paul. The Pope is pissed off at him because of the movie that you had a cameo role in, the *White Satin Miter*."

Nixon chuckled. "I went to see the movie, of course. I was in it and I couldn't resist. Pat went with me. It was showing at the Roxy in San Clemente. I was surprised to see that Ed Wood was the producer and director. I knew that could not be. Anyhow, Pat was alarmed at the pornographic description of what *Casti Connubii II* was all about. Quite a shocker, I must say."

"That is a sad story, Mr. President. Stan can explain it to you. Suffice it to say that the *White Satin Miter* showed in Rome at an art theater, attracted some notoriety with the result that the Pope ordered it shown, to his dismay, in the Vatican cinema. Father George is trying to get himself off the hook."

The trio laughed heartily.

"General O'Reith," Nixon continued. "How much of a strain would it put on our relationship if I asked for a little help in getting my boys sprung? Several of them are doing time and it is my fault."

"Stan will do whatever he can, Mr. President. I agree. If the top dog doesn't go to jail, then the little people should not either. You two get together on that. Let us know if you need any help. George will help too. Just give us the word."

"Well sir, I do appreciate your attitude. Another thing sir, is there anything to the rumor that the company is out to buy Gulf Oil?"

O'Reith winked, "No comment Mr. President."

Nixon laughed. "I know what that means. How often did I make that exact same statement? If you don't object, I may take a flier. Buy a few shares of Gulf."

"Go right ahead. It should be a good investment. O'Reith looked at the wall clock across the room from his desk. It was 12:30 PST. He pushed on his inter phone button. He said, "Lauren, the New York Stock Exchange is open. Call our broker at Merrill Lynch and get us a quote on Gulf Oil. Find out how many shares were traded at the opening."

When she rang back a few minutes later, O'Reith had the speakerphone on and the three men heard her say. "Gulf opened on a fifty thousand share block at $41 and three eighths."

"Thank you Lauren," O'Reith said and turned the speaker off.

"I say it is a $75 dollar stock," Nixon said.

"Well, you could be right, O'Reith agreed."

Nixon asked, "Do you think the big boys will stay out of it? Jersey and Standard Oil and Shell?"

Ethering said, "You can bet their legal departments are studying the Sherman antitrust legislation. Much depends upon the SEC dogs. If they are sleeping, the deal should be relatively uncomplicated."

O'Reith said, "Mr. President, up north near the beginning of the Sierra Nevada there is a township that originally belonged to the Southern Pacific Railroad. In the U.S. Geodetic Survey of 1878, it is labeled Block 36-C. Titles are far from clear and subject to litigation. Much of it is in legal limbo. Stan has all the details. You remember Carolyn Cook, our chief explorationist. Well, she thinks there could be a structure of some consequence there. Would you give some thought to how we might get the Assembly to condemn those properties under the right of eminent domain? Once that is done, we want the state to lease the mineral rights to us. I realize it could take awhile but we need to be looking for new reserves."

Nixon grinned slyly. "In theory it is impossible. They'll have to put it out for bids. In practice, we may be able to circumvent those laws. Let me look into it. On another matter, if I do a really bang up job in Sacramento, and I assure you General O'Reith that I will and you will be proud of me, what are the chances of my getting back to the capital? I long for the big leagues of politics."

"They are good, Mr. President," O'Reith said. "That's a lobbying job I'll have to do. President Ford would have to be consulted. I'll have a word with Al Haig when the time is right."

Nixon chuckled. "You think I need to let things cool off for a while."

"We need to let the ink dry on your presidential pardon." O'Reith said.

The three men laughed heartily.

That afternoon, O'Reith asked his three children to meet him for drinks at the Long Beach penthouse. He wanted to bring them into the picture about their mother. Here it was November 20th. A trip originally set for three days had stretched on for almost three weeks. But he could see the end. Parkinson was going to meet with them tonight bringing news of Helen's diagnosis.

So there were five of them in the parlor waiting for the butler to serve the drinks. Parkinson had the laboratory reports in his coat pockets. When the butler departed, O'Reith said, "Max, I guess we're ready. All three of the children wore worried faces. Rae Regan, her brother 'Little' Clive Colin and Helen Simpson sat quietly.

Parkinson began, "Clive, we might as well face up to it. Helen is suffering from severe osteoporosis. It has affected every bone in her body including her skull. Her metabolism has gone haywire. The food she eats is not properly converted into the essentials for good health. Her lapses of memory appear to be related to the defects in her metabolic functions but no doctor is able to give a firm prognosis. What is certain is that her periods of amnesia are occurring more frequently and lasting longer."

"Is there anything that can be done for her, Max?" O'Reith asked.

"Tomorrow morning, we'll bring her home. No point in keeping her in the hospital any longer. She will have a nurse around the clock. The dietitian has set out a nutrition regime for her which we hope will arrest the bone degeneration. Beyond that, nature must take its inevitable course."

"Is my mother still out of it? What do you mean by 'inevitable'?" Helen Simpson asked.

"Yes. This is not her longest stretch. But it soon will be. Almost three weeks now. She has no idea that she was subjected to laboratory procedures. I suppose we can thank God for small mercies. One of my greatest fears was that she would wake up and find herself in a hospital room. You asked about nature's inevitable course. We have to prepare ourselves, Helen Simpson."

"Yeah," O'Reith added. "That's what it looks like to me."

The bell rang downstairs. Presently Ridley was shown into the parlor. She said, "I called the hospital an hour ago and they told me Helen was to be released tomorrow morning. What's her condition?"

Parkinson went over the same ground with Ridley nodding her head. She said, "Well, I volunteer to move in and stay beside her as long as it is necessary."

"Alice, that would be kind," O'Reith said. "It would take a burden off of me."

"I'll bring my things in the morning. What time will Helen arrive?"

"We can set it up for noon, Alice. That OK?"

The same day that Helen returned home, Cook called O'Reith in Long Beach. She said, "Sir, King Brock telephoned. He wanted to talk to you urgently."

"I'll call him right now, Carolyn. Is he in his office?"

"Yes sir."

"When the call went through, O'Reith purred, "King how'sa boy?"

"Great Clive! Sitting on top of the world. You're talking to a man two weeks away from retirement. Mama and I are making our plans to move to Florida. No more shoveling snow for the Brocks. That little investment in the company stock looks better every day."

"Stan called me earlier. It was over $50 a share," O'Reith answered.

"Clive it is going higher. That is why I called. The board of directors decided to put the company on the block. That should muzzle the antitrust dogs. Some of us think Gulf Oil is a $100 stock."

"Could be, King. Got any idea when the auction will take place?"

"Early in 1976. I can't put a date on it. After the exchanges close, we'll put out an announcement. Next week we will set up an information room for interested bidders."

"King, we now own over 25% of the company. I suppose all of the majors will bid. I'm looking at my hole card. We are going to watch this closely. I thank you for filling me in and we look forward to being invited to bid."

O'Reith then called Cook back, explained matters to her and told her to bring Ethering current and buy stock up to $65/share.

O'Reith and Maxine flew to Rome to attend midnight mass at the Vatican with McDonough and Cook. After dinner in McDonough's apartment, he said, "Colonel's trial set to begin June 15, 1976, Clive, in Caracas. Probably put him in the city jail at La Planta. Not good news. They keep the addicts and screaming wackos there. If we don't provide him with one, he will be the only inmate in that place without a knife."

"Well, at least it is six months away. Time to work on it. What can we do to soften the blow?" O'Reith asked.

"Mandy will do what she can. The Colonel thinks the new magistrates favor his case. But they are just now getting organized. Could delay trial on into 1977."

"Is that what he wants? Maxine asked.

"Similar cases in past years have resulted in sentences in the range 3 to 7 years," McDonough said. "The Colonel has an idea that *Accion Democratica* won't win the next elections. The other political parties in the country are more sympathetic to his cause. He's taking some long chances, but he knows the terrain. In any event, with Mandy looking after his needs, he'll be comfortable. At least he will be as long as we can keep him out of the Caracas jail."

"Well that's something. She's pretty resourceful, "O'Reith said. "In a way it is good that he is out of circulation. What would we do with him if we sprung him?" He was sleepy and now wished he had not agreed to attend mass. But it was too late now and Maxine was actually looking forward to it. His mind was drifting too. He had spoken to Parkinson earlier in the day. Helen, still comatose, was slowly losing weight. Ridley was downhearted, near exhaustion, resigned to a long vigil. As McDonough continued talking, his thoughts were with Helen and he decided that at least he could say a strong prayer for her. If the Pope were listening, maybe God was too.

McDonough interrupted his chain of thought saying, "Clive, Carolyn and I are going at eleven. We'll be sitting with the cardinals and we need time to don our robes. I'll send the car around for you and Maxine at a quarter of."

"Christ George it is only a couple of blocks. We can walk."

"Cold out there Clive. Wet too. Misting steadily all evening. Clive I plan to pray for Helen during Mass."

"I'm in favor of walking," Maxine said. "Give me a chance to clear my mind and pray for Helen. I don't know why exactly Silver, but I am ready to be done with this year of Our Lord, 1975."

It was a cloudy day in early March of 1976 with the wind blowing down from the north. Snow dusted the higher reaches of the Los Angeles hills. He had walked to the tower from the Fullerton Building with narrowed eyes because of dust blowing down the drafty streets. Mills was waiting for him. She brushed his tuxedo to remove the grime and then she washed his face, touched up a few liver spots on his cheeks, fixed his hair and adjusted his monocle. When she was finished, he looked neat. She walked with him to his desk and held his chair for him. When he was seated she said, "You're all set, General O'Reith. If you don't need anything else I'll be on my way to Long Beach to attend Helen." He smiled, thanked her and waved as she went out the door.

He had returned to Los Angeles unexpectedly a week before. Parkinson had telephoned him in Paris that Helen had emerged from her long disconnect and she was asking for him. It occurred at a time when Monique, pregnant, was in Paris for regular prenatal check up. Maxine wanted to be with her and was thus unable to accompany him to the states.

He had been seeing Helen every day and was clearly relieved that she was gaining weight and if not cheerful, was at least realistic. Parkinson had explained to her that a complete physical examination had revealed a number of problems. Helen had agreed to occasional hospital visits as long as she could be back home in the evening. Ridley, worried about her deteriorating condition, was relieved that her old friend had returned to the world of the sane.

O'Reith sitting behind his desk, rose as Cook, Prescott and Holland were at his door. Cook was wearing an emerald green pantsuit with a Nile green blouse and matching high-heeled shoes with rhinestones around the toes. Holland was wearing khaki trousers and shirt open at the neck. On his feet were brown slip-on loafers. Prescott had on a dark blue, pinstriped suit, a blue tie and black elevator shoes. He was several inches shorter than Holland and with elevator shoes, came eye to eye with Cook.

O'Reith began by asking, Carolyn, what's up?"

"General O'Reith, Poghdar Field is down to 700,000 bopd and the two smaller structures have declined as well. We can no longer hold a 1,000,000 bopd."

"So what do we do?"

Prescott said, "General, we have the potential to keep the rate up but we'll have to increase the draw down. The only solution is to go to gas lift. That means a deepening program. We'll drill down to within fifty feet or so and squeeze cement above the water. Then we set gas lift equipment with the operating valve near the top of the cement plug. We can double production and hold it for quite some long time."

"Costs money?" O'Reith asked.

"We'll need four more strings in there right away," Holland said. "In addition to those already there. Of course we can deepen with tubing instead of drill pipe. But we'll have to go to three stages of separation to remove all the liquids from the gas. Then we're looking at $10 million for the gas-lift valves, meter runs and monitoring equipment."

"Are we all in agreement that this is the correct solution?" O'Reith asked.

"Yes," Cook answered. "We'll have to curtail our monthly purchases of Gulf Oil stock."

"What happens at auction time, when we make a bid for the entire company?" Holland asked.

"We'll have to explain all of this to JP Morgan and Chase Manhattan and the Linen Bank in London," Cook said.

O'Reith said, "Carolyn, line up meetings in New York and London. I'm going back to Paris. He turned to Prescott, asked, "Alan when will the first of the new rigs arrive in Poghdar?"

"Ninety days if we get high behind."

"Holland," O'Reith said. "Catch a plane to San Francisco. Take Bill Hamilton to lunch and explain what we're doing. While the oil markets have settled down for the moment, we can never tell when something will come up to throw things off the track. Standard Oil must be confident that we can keep delivering crude."

"I'll call him today, general."

After the meeting as they approached the elevator, O'Reith said, "Carolyn, I'm having second thoughts about Gulf. The company is not worth what some of the big dogs will bid. Jersey or Standard will bid high just to kill them off. Wiser to take our share of the profit and invest it in Poghdar."

"That suits me just fine, General O'Reith. "It would take us forever to find all the buried bodies and straighten things out. We'd have to fire half of the staff. Drive both of us nuts. I would never again get a good night of sleep."

O'Reith laughed said, "Carolyn you probably won't anyhow. What about drilling engineers? I can't imagine that we have enough on our payroll?"

"Prescott will begin recruiting today. By the time the rigs arrive, we'll have the personnel. We'll need well-site geologists too," Cook added.

"Make a list of what it takes and put a price tag on it. Let me see it. But don't let me slow things down." O'Reith rode down to the garage where his limousine waited.

That evening with Helen, O'Reith was having a dry martini with Ridley. Helen was having carrot juice with a dash of Angostura bitters on the rocks. She said, "Ace, I hate this goddam stuff. I'm going to tell Max that I'm not going to drink any more of it. It tastes like rat poison. I want some gin. That's g-i-n."

"You better follow his instructions baby, or you'll find yourself back in the soup," O'Reith said. "Helen, I'm going to New York day after tomorrow to see the bankers. Production problems in Afghanistan require some heavy sugar to get things fixed. After that, I'm off to London and then back to Persia. Then I have to visit the Colonel in Venezuela. I'll be gone for several weeks. Think you can hold yourself together?"

"Not with this fucking carrot juice," she snorted. "I suppose I'll be all right. I get visitors more often than I like. The kids hover over me like I was a candidate for cremation and maybe I am. Max comes every day. He carts me off to the hospital once a week for those ghouls to punch holes in my arms. As long as Alice will put up with me, I can make it."

Next morning in his office he asked Parkinson. "How does it look now, Max?"

"She's gained a few pounds and she has been her normal self now for three weeks. She follows instructions. As long as she does that, she'll be stable."

"She's ready to rebel against that carrot juice," O'Reith said. "She wants a shot of gin in the evening before dinner."

"Risky, Clive."

"How about an alternate schedule? Carrot juice one night and gin the next. Give her something to look forward to."

Parkinson thought about it for some long moments with a pensive face. He smiled and said, "Considering her condition, it's worth a try. See how she does."

O'Reith picked up the phone and dialed the penthouse in Long Beach. His daughter answered. He asked for Helen.

Helen Simpson sang out, "Mother, it's Daddy Cool."

When she came on the line he said, "Baby I'm with Max. I've got him to agree with an alternate schedule; carrot juice one night and a martini the next. If every thing goes OK, he'll make it permanent."

"Ace, you're a saint, a goddamned saint."

"How are you feeling baby? Like to get out of the house? Dine at the Limejuicer Club and then take in a movie. They're showing *All the President's Men*. Good cast. Robert Redford. Dustin Hoffman. Jason Robards, Jr. Martin Balsam. Hal Holbrook. Touted to win an Oscar for best picture. What do you say?"

"Ace, you've got a date. I'll be ready when you get here. I'm going straight to the bar and order a double martini on the rocks with a twist. If I were thirty years younger I would climb Redford's bones!"

O'Reith laughed. "You'll have to settle for mine, baby. I'll join you for martinis. We can pretend it is the good old days."

But it was a so-so evening. Helen lost her appetite before they got to the entree. Home early and O'Reith slept on the day bed in the guestroom.

Next morning in the tower, he was again looking at a wall map of Afghanistan and beyond that, Central Asia. He had not kept up with oil and gas exploration in the USSR. He made a note to ask McDonough to call Anastas Mikoyan to discuss the possibility of joining the Soviet Government for exploration in Kazakhstan and Azerbaijan. It would require setting up a company under Soviet law. As he was pondering that, it occurred to him that Mikoyan, who was 81 years old, might not be around much longer. O'Reith had never queried McDonough about a backup for him. Now might be a good time for that. Rubbing his chin he suddenly remembered that right down the street at 10889 Wilshire Boulevard, up on the 16th floor, Armand Hammer of Occidental Petroleum was probably sitting there reading the *Los Angeles Times*. He picked up the telephone and called him. As it turned out, Hammer was free for lunch. O'Reith invited him to join him at the Catalina Club.

"Dr. Hammer," O'Reith began as the two men were sipping Perrier on the rocks at a window table with a view of the harbor. "We have in our company an executive by the name of George P. McDonough who is on friendly terms with Anastas Mikoyan."

Hammer rattled the ice cubes in his drink, smiled slyly and whispered, "Father George?"

O'Reith laughed. "Well going beyond that Dr. Hammer, we're thinking about commercial connections in the Soviet Union. Also, I'm concerned about the age of Mikoyan. We may find ourselves without his valuable input. So knowing that you had many friends in Moscow, I called to see if we had mutual interests."

"If it involves oil and gas production in Russia, we are on common ground," Hammer said tersely. "None of us are getting younger. President Mikoyan and I are friends. I've known him since the 1920s.

We share an interest in fine art. His health is a matter of some concern to all of those who like and admire him. Can you be more specific about your proposal?"

"We have an oil field in the province of Poghdar..."

"I know about that," Hammer snapped. "Go on."

"We pay the Shah a royalty for allowing us to run the oil through an Oil Company pipeline at Bid Boland. It is an irregular arrangement and one that concerns our only off taker. We work with a gentleman named Scotty Trevelyen."

"Brave man. Military Cross," Hammer said tersely. "Go on."

"The Shah has tried to incorporate Poghdar Province into Khuzestan. Afghanistan objects, as you might imagine and even the Shah's Majlis has reservations about it. When we discovered that field in 1972, we considered running a pipeline to Vladivostok but it was too costly. Now I am having second thoughts."

Hammer nodded. "As well you should sir," Hammer said. "Let me tell you something. When I see a tyrant like Reza Pahlavi going nearly berserk about adding more crude oil capability, I wonder. The market cannot support that much more oil. And when I see him buy, buy, buy American arms and ammunition, I become suspicious. He has more tanks and military aircraft than any other regime in the Middle East. Where is the threat? There is no external one. It is strictly from the inside. A man does not behave like that unless he is extremely worried. I think the Shah of Persia, the Monarch of the Peacock Throne is either paranoid or he sees his destiny rapidly overtaking him. A long shadow."

O'Reith continued, "My concern, Dr. Hammer, is that there could be a resurgence of violence in Khuzestan that the Shah would be unable to quell. Father George will telephone Mikoyan to explore the feasibility of a pipeline to Vladivostok. Take the Shah out of the picture so to speak. It will be an expensive project but our treasury is in good shape. Still we will need added financing. So there could be something there for Occidental."

"Let's discuss it further after Father George speaks with Father Anastas," Hammer said smiling. He added, "They're both seminarians and by extension, philosophers. I suppose you know that."

"I knew George was. I know very little about Mikoyan except he has a brother who helped to design the MIG fighter."

"The 'MI' is for Mikoyan," Hammer continued. Anastas graduated from a seminary in Armenia in 1915 and became a priest but he was immediately swept up in the war and then the revolution and after that, the civil war. So his deep religious inclinations were squelched by political upheaval. But his wit did not suffer. He has one of the finest brains in the Soviet Union if not the entire world."

O'Reith made a tight smile. He said, "Father George can match him IQ for IQ. He likes power. But his background is similar. World War II cut his priestly service short. Father George is younger than Mikoyan, maybe ten years or so."

"I enjoy working with intelligent men," Hammer said.

"Dr. Hammer it occurred to me that Poghdar would make a tidy little SSR. How does that sound to you, the Poghdar Soviet Socialist Republic?"

"I like it. Let's carry that idea forward. I can help. And don't forget that Kazakhstan is lightly explored. Azerbaijan has seen much land drilling over the years but offshore, in the Caspian, we might find something. If we have the right connections, and we do, we can work out a profit-sharing plan on which we can all agree. Have you surveyed the pipeline right of way?"

"Yes. Two possibilities," O'Reith continued. Go straight to Vladivostok through Russia and China: the short route, say 3,800 miles. If going through China is a problem, then we can go to Samarkand, Tashkent, Alma Ata, skirt the northern reaches of the Pamir Mountains, then to Zyryanovsk, Kyzyl and Irkutsk. We'll have to cross Lake Baikal to Ulan Ude and then to Chita, Tyoda, Khabarovsk and finally Vladivostok. That route keeps us out of China but adds 550 miles."

"We'll have to get a reading out of Mikoyan on that," Hammer said, nodding his comprehension. "My guess is that he'll want to keep the line in the Soviet Union. Going through the Gobi would be all right but those heavily populated areas near Beijing and Harbin are causes of concern."

"That is my feeling too. I'll call Father George tonight and bring him current on this conversation. Then we see where it leads."

Hammer smiled. "It leads to a conference in the Kremlin. Let me know what Father George says."

The waiter was serving poached turbot in a white wine sauce with rice and fried zucchini in a lemon-parsley sauce.

That night, O'Reith telephoned McDonough in Rome and advised him that Dr. Hammer was in the picture. O'Reith had the feeling he was a bit miffed that another expert on Mikoyan was in the act. The truth was that O'Reith was extremely worried about events taking place in Persia. He remembered when the Shah got into trouble in 1951 and had to be reinstalled by the Raj and the CIA. It had been a trying time for Calitroleum Oil and in fact, Harvey Holmes Halliday, Chairman of the Board became a nervous wreck over it. O'Reith needed that not at this stage of his life.

The Colonel's trial has to stand as one of the juridical curiosities of the 20th Century. For one thing, being gone for so long, 18 years in fact, placed his crime into dim distant memory. Indeed, over half of the population of Venezuela were not born at the time he left Miraflores in January of 1958 in such a rush. Of course most of the other half knew something about him, especially his supporters, some 26% of the adults. After all, he was the constitutional president from 1953 to 1958 even if his election was of cloudy authenticity. They think he is the cat's pajamas. Another 26%, perhaps more, members of the *Partido Accion Democratica*, regard him as a pariah. They considered him to be a more of a rat and would shoot him if they could. What restrained them was that summary execution of the Colonel would without the shadow of a doubt, lead to public outcry, riots, disturbances and demonstrations. To put it another way, shooting the Colonel in the name of *Accion Democratica* could very well topple President Andrés and he was only half way through his term.

Former President Romulo Betancourt, principal architect of *Accion Democratica* was his most vindictive enemy. Once political allies, when they fell out, the hatred was enduring and insurmountable. Betancourt, the first democratically elected president after the Colonel departed, presided over the revision of the Venezuelan constitution. As he labored with new law, the Colonel was never far from his thoughts. As a consequence of his pondering, in 1961, the Supreme Court was divided into three tribunals. The first dealt with crimes related to the political and administrative branches of the government. This was aimed directly at the Colonel. The second addressed malfeasance in the realm of torts, labor and civil crimes. The third dealt with matters related to penal abrogation. Each tribunal had five judges who were elected by the Legislative Body. Thus the Supreme Court was highly politicized. By far the most dangerous provision of the new constitution required that when a president or former president of Venezuela was on trial, the three tribunals would convene as one body to consider the charges. Conviction would occur with a simple majority of eight. With *Accion Democratica* again in power, congressmen of this party had appointed most of the judges. The chances of Colonel Jiménez 'beating the rap' were slim to none.

The Colonel hailed from Tachira, as we know, and the populace there was far more sympathetic to him than the jaded Caraqueños, who had seen many a dictator come and go. Near the center of San Cristobal, the capital of that mountainous province, a square was once, briefly, called Plaza Jiménez. Briefly, because its dedication occurred on December 2, 1957, the 5th anniversary of his presidency and on January 23, 1958, the Colonel was gone; at least as far as Venezuela was concerned, he was gone. Caracas suffered a loss, but not a complete loss. In his haste to get away in the early hours of that melancholy morning, the Colonel left behind a suitcase filled with money, deeds, negotiable securities and several pairs of socks. Still in all, what Venezuela lost, Miami gained.

In the center of the square hurriedly renamed Plaza Commercial in January 1958, stands a bronze statue of the Colonel that few eyes have seen. At the time of the dedication, the crated statue was en route from the port of Barquisimeto where it had been delivered off a freighter that came from Florence, Italy. Rains in the Perija Mountains had flooded the roads so the statue didn't make it in time. But the 15-meter stainless steel plinth did, and it was the plinth that was dedicated on that gray thunderous day in the closing month of 1957. The statue arrived some days later and, shrouded in a green tarpaulin was hoisted atop the plinth. The Colonel intended to return to the land of his birth on Cinco de Julio of 1958. On that great national holiday dedicated to the memory of Simon Bolivar, he would unveil, or as his detractors would say, unfrock the statue. But as we know, on July 5, 1958 the Colonel was playing golf in Coral Gables, Florida with his new friend, POTUS Dwight D. Eisenhower.

The statue was crafted in 1941 at which time he was a newly minted captain in the Venezuelan Army, an idealist, as young army officers often are, and a bridegroom as well. The young army officer could see that there were problems within the Juan Vicente Gómez administration. Income was distributed inequitably. That was clear. Venezuela had many poor but in that era they would never have been described as 'marginals'. Only in later decades would that now fashionable word come to denote society's rejects, no-goodniks, drifters, and the useless. Prostitution existed, of course, but it was not seen as a great social problem unless a brothel happened to be located, as was often the case in Maracaibo, near a school for young girls. Then it provoked outrage, which cooled off as soon as the offending whorehouse was removed to another location. Captain Jiménez was sure that he could address some of these problems and make Venezuela a happier place for everyone. At that point of his career, he had imprisoned not a single protester; had not liquidated even one marginal; had driven no one into exile, temporary or permanent. But it is true that Captain Jiménez attributed some of the ills to Gómez, the 'old fox' as he was called.

Then 27 years old, Captain Jiménez had recently wed Flor Chalbaud Cardona, daughter of an army general who would presently reward his new in-law with promotion to the grade of major. Over the coming years she would bear him three daughters and help him in many ways.

Jiménez was already thinking about a new political party for Venezuela quaintly named the New National Ideal. As a soldier, his mind was disciplined and he scorned the masses because of their tendency to act up or riot, often for reasons not clear to anyone, although some said that empty stomachs were at the root of it. Major Jiménez was sure that when he exercised power under the banner of his newly created party, he would be able to cope with these disorderly elements of society. Inasmuch as public order was paramount and crowds often became rowdy, he would prohibit political activity, which included riots. Labor unions, which tended to foment trouble, would definitely be banned. Venezuela could do without strikes. He would eliminate freedom of expression, which meant closing down the newspapers and carefully controlling what was said on the air waves. In fact, most of what one could hear on the radio was music; loud, over-modulated, blaring music of a nationalistic, martial nature. The Colonel was not given over to popular songs that reflected the decadent mores of Mexico and Brazil. In those days, television was not a consideration.

He would build great skyscrapers, wide roads and expressways, elegant hotels, long bridges and major thoroughfares in Caracas and across the nation. He would double the number of ferries crossing from Lagunillas to Maracaibo and would authorize the construction of a bridge over the lake. He would increase the budget for the notorious Guasina Prison located on an island in the Orinoco River delta; strengthen the walls; add several new stories of cell blocks, and put more watch towers on the parapets. It was clear in his mind that social quietude and economic development would take precedence over political evolution. In fact, he hardly conceived of the notion that politics would ever change one way or the other. What he desired was that the people would unite under a charismatic leader. Thus, over time, benefits of the economic projects would reach them all, including the poor. The poor had plenty of time to wait for progress. But he didn't. He was impatient.

In 1941 Benito Mussolini, El Duce as he liked to be called, was the dictator of Italy and close crony, or so people thought, of Der Fuhrer. To reward Mussolini for his help in the dismantling of France, Hitler put one of his favorite sculptors to the task of converting a bronze block into a strutting likeness of El Duce. He was at that time 58 years old and moping because the Royal Navy had smashed up his beautiful fleet of sleek warships. Hitler hoped that the gleaming bronze likeness would lift his pal's sunken spirits. The 10-meter bronze block was cast in the winter of 1940 from obsolete cannon captured by the Wehrmacht in Austria, Poland and the Sudetenland. In the summer of 1941, with German legions driving into Russia, the sculptor converted the alloy into a passable Benito Mussolini complete with jutting jaw, dressed in *gran tenue* and forage cap that somewhat resembled an outsized fez. And that explains the 15-meter plinth in San Cristobal. A government functionary thought that if the statue were high in the air, its face would be difficult for someone on the ground to recognize.

When the statue was new, bright and shining, Mussolini often went to gaze upon his heroic likeness in the Royal Piazza of Rome. But in 1943, after Italy was invaded by the American Vth Army, Mussolini fell from favor. Along with many other statues of him, the one destined for San Cristobal found its way to a Roman scrapyard. In 1945, it was purchased by a Florentine junk man, who was handy with a blowtorch. When the Venezuelan ambassador in Rome got word that Colonel Jiménez was to be honored in Tachira with a statue, he saw a chance for profit. He notified Miraflores that the finest sculptors in the world were from Florence and that the Colonel deserved nothing but the best. A price was proposed which although quite high was acceptable. The Florentine junk man got the commission. Thus the Mussolini statue had its forage cap blow-torched off and a regular military cap with scrambled eggs installed in its place. The jutted jaw was suitably softened to conform to a photograph of the Caudillo. The statue, *mutatis mutandis*, if it did not look much like the Colonel, didn't look much like Mussolini either.

Now, the tarpaulin, which shrouds the statue is faded and torn and covered with dirty-white, bird droppings. Through rents in the fabric, rain has found its way onto the bronze. The stainless steel plinth, once glittering in the Andean sunlight has turned green, coated with a mixture of copper carbonate, oxide and phosphate. So has the concrete circle on which the plinth is erected. It has become something of an eyesore. Even the pigeons eschew it. Of high priority to the Colonel once he had the Miraflores Palace organized, was to put his name back on the wrought iron grill that spans the entrance to the plaza and to remove the tarpaulin and to clean the statue so that it glistened like new. But, as we know, that did not happen. Nor was it likely.

From time to time there is talk in the city that the *Accionistas* are coming for the statue to melt it down for coins. But as the date of the Colonel's trial has now come, the statue is still there and many in San Cristobal, particularly the young, don't know that it is, or at least is supposed to be, the Colonel.

Now, in June of 1976, the Colonel, in the dock for financial crimes and misdemeanors, if found guilty, could get seven years in prison, the maximum for crimes of this nature. However, as we know, he has been incarcerated in one jail or another since August of 1974 so two years of whatever sentence is imposed, has already been served. Until now his imprisonment has been a mere inconvenience in comfortable confinement. If convicted, he will have to serve the balance of his time in a regular cell in a standard Venezuelan prison and that is not an easy thought to contemplate. Venezuelan felons are for the most part, disagreeable people. They carry knives. They lack the civilized approach to life. They are dangerous.

The Colonel is not overly worried about that prospect. As a Venezuelan politician with an exact understanding of the system, he is confident that the *Accionistas* don't particularly want to have him imprisoned. The ex-dictator in the dock is one thing, an asset perhaps. The ex-dictator in prison with a large following among the public at large is a threat, a liability for certain. His lawyers have laid down a vigorous defense founded on the old South American political principle that 'he who steals from the public robs no one'. The defense, citing a political vendetta has succeeded in removing the most dangerous personalities from the court. Now it is composed of younger judges who see themselves as having prosperous futures. Not a man among them desires to be consigned to the scrap heap of judicial history, which is a common fate for an injudicious magistrate in this part of the continent. More importantly, the offenses have been reduced to mere misdemeanors. In short, the Colonel is ready to stand up like a man; receive his due.

His calculations were correct. He was sentenced to time already served, released from custody and the chief magistrate suggested that he seek solace outside the country for a while. Let matters cool off, as it were. The Colonel and Flor departed for Madrid that night with the ink on his prison discharge not yet dry.

But *Accion Democratica* was not through with him by a long shot. A series of new laws were rushed through the Parliament forbidding former presidents convicted of misdemeanors from holding office. And with no political base, the Colonel is a cipher. In effect the new laws condemn him to perpetual exile. He is 63, in good health and needs further employment. He knows that once he and the family are settled in, he must telephone General O'Reith in Paris. Surely there will be a spot for him somewhere. The Casinghead Company is a vast international organization and will always have the need for an astute statesman. As regards his shrouded statue in San Cristobal, it faces a bleak and uncertain future. The blast furnace beckons.

Chapter X

A Death in the Family

Usually, in a large family, when a member dies, there is a great deal of weeping, hand wringing and eventually, mourning. But this is not your average family. These are the *Sette Sorrelle* so named by the Italian oil mogul Enrico Mattei head of *Ente Nazionale Idrocarburi*, a competitive contemporary of the Casinghead Company. In this period, the 'Seven Sisters' were the largest oil companies in the world. Among their number were The Standard Oil Company, New Jersey, The Standard Oil Company of California, The Texas Company, Royal Dutch Shell, British Petroleum, Socony Mobil Oil Corporation, and finally, the moribund Gulf Oil Corporation. As noted, there was not only no mourning but the other six sisters were in fact, eager to put their unhappy sibling out of her misery. The sad part of it was that Gulf was an avuncular oil company. American motorists felt comfortable driving in under the huge orange and blue circular signs. Pulling into a Gulf station was a lot like pulling into your own driveway. The service was quick and courteous. The attendants were properly uniformed and friendly. The gasoline and lubricating oil were as good as any in the industry. A Gulf credit card was an enviable possession indeed. Many people, remembering its unsavory origin, did not like the hard-nosed

Standard Oil Company, New Jersey. But everyone liked the easy-going Gulf Oil.

That distinction aside, the petroleum industry has been in a state of consolidation since John D. Rockefeller waged war against his many competitors in the 19 & 20th Centuries. With every passing year, oil companies perish; usually the smaller ones. But from time to time a big one like Superior Oil Company goes down. This latter one gulped down by Texaco. Carnage is greatest during times of economic stress. In 1930-31, small oil companies dropped like flies as the price of crude oil fell to ten cents the barrel. This trend slackened as business improved but after World War II, as the American economy slowed in the 1950s, the failure of the smaller independents resumed its dolorous course.

When a major international oil company the size of Gulf Oil fails, that is news. Gulf's troubles began with the nationalization in 1975 of their half-owned Kuwait Oil Company. A second blow fell in 1976 when *Accion Democratica* nationalized their half-owned Mene Grande Oil Company. So after losing a quarter of its oil reserves in a matter of months, the management of the company was in a daze made worse by lurid revelations of illegal political contributions to US politicians. Who could imagine such a nice, friendly company like Gulf Oil doing a disreputable thing like that?

The plight of Gulf Oil did not go unnoticed. Still the other six sisters were leery of the antitrust dogs. But the tiny Casinghead Company, in comparison to the international giants was hardly visible. As O'Reith relentlessly bought the stock of Gulf, driving the share price higher and higher, it became clear that something important was about to happen. And indeed it did. The board of directors of Gulf put the company up for sale, effectively muzzling the antitrust dogs. After all, if a company voluntarily decides to go out of business, in a free America, how could it be stopped? And that is why representatives of the majors spent weeks poring over the data on exhibition in the information room of Gulf's Pittsburgh skyscraper.

So now on this muggy July day in 1976, the players have assembled in the huge 34th floor art deco conference room of the Gulf Tower which happily, is air-conditioned. Chief executives of the six interested sisters plus half a dozen other international oil companies were ready to make an offer. The Casinghead Company now held 35% of the stock, which was trading that day at $74.50/share. Cook's petroleum engineers had pored over the oil and gas reserve estimates for long 18-hour days. Their conclusion was that the estimates were too high. The company's eagle-eyed accountants, merging reserve data with financial information, concluded that Gulf was worth perhaps $60/share. When the time came to announce the winner in the grand conference room, O'Reith, an interested non-bidder sat in the back of the room.

As King Brock announced to the assembled oil barons that the Standard Oil Company of California was the winner with a bid of $80/share, O'Reith smiled. His long shot had paid off. The company's treasury would soon be filled to overflowing. These funds he sorely needed to revitalize their fortunes so that, for a few years at least, their company would not suffer the fate of Gulf Oil.

Upon his return to Los Angeles he found, not to his surprise, that he had been subpoenaed by the Senate Energy Committee under the aegis of Senator Lazlo Gimmeit Lagniappe, Republican of Illinois. O'Reith smiled, sure that he would not be alone.

The oil company executives were assembled at a long mahogany table in the Huey P. "Kingfish" Long Memorial Chamber of the United States Botanic Garden at 245 First Street SW, Washington, DC

Beside O'Reith sat Stan Ethering and next to him, Bill Hamilton and H.J. Haynes of Standard Oil of California. Further down the table sat Clifton Garvin and Lou Rawl of Jersey and next to them King Brock of the soon to be defunct Gulf Oil Corporation. Al DeCrane was there for Texaco. Executives from Amoco and Atlantic Richfield flanked him. Then came Armand Hammer for Occidental Petroleum Corporation, Sir David Barran of Royal Dutch Shell and Sir Eric Drake of the British Petroleum Company. These distinguished oilmen face an array of senators on an elevated dais next to the wall. They had to look up.

The clerk of the court entered and said in a monotonous voice, "Will you gentlemen rise and raise your right hand and swear to tell the truth, the whole truth and nothing but the truth?"

"Not I," said O'Reith.

Senator Lagniappe awoke from his nap, sat up straight, gaveled the murmuring executives to silence and asked defiantly, "General O'Reith is there some reason that you will not testify?"

"I'll answer questions. But I will not raise my right hand and I will not swear to anything," O'Reith said.

"Do you realize, General O'Reith, that you could be held in contempt of Congress?" Lagniappe said scornfully.

"Not likely, Senator Lagniappe," O'Reith replied. "I brought my file covering the payments I have made over the years to you, and many other members of the Congress. If I go to jail, you too, go to jail. The penalty for contempt is a year plus a small fine. The penalty for corrupt congressional behavior is seven years and a ruined career. Odds of seven to one appeal to an old wildcatter."

Laughter from the oilmen at the table was muted and tentative.

"General O'Reith, you have testified before the Congress of the United States on other occasions and this difficulty never arose. Why it is different today?"

"On all previous occasions, Senator Lagniappe, I was serving as an officer of the Army of the United States and I was testifying on matters of which I had the facts. I also had a soldier's responsibility to give good and accurate advice on a subject in which I was competent. That is not the case today. I have no facts regarding the questions you are about to ask. Furthermore I am not in the service of the United States of America. I am a private citizen. I have no responsibility to the government. So I take no vows. I frame no oaths. Sorry about that Senator Lagniappe."

"Very well, sir. We will today waive the requirement for sworn testimony. This is, after all a closed hearing. But be well warned that open hearings are in the cards. You gentlemen will have to reappear at a later date and be sworn in. The people of the United States have a right to know the facts surrounding the destruction of Gulf Oil Corporation. Gentlemen today we are talking about SORORICIDE! The truth is that you gentlemen have killed your homely but loving sister! Why did you do it? To ask the question is to answer it. Greed! Pure greed! You were not putting a beloved family member out of her misery. You killed her for her dowry.

Bill Hamilton of Standard Oil interrupted, "Senator we didn't kill her for her dowry. We married her."

Laughter filled the chamber. Lagniappe's face became red. He pounded the dais with his gavel, saying, "You are out of order sir!"

"And you, General O'Reith," he continued. "You are the architect of this heinous act. You sir, sitting in your ivory tower in Los Angeles, California gazing out of your high window at the boats on the Pacific Ocean conceived of this grisly homicide. At a time when our nation faces severe shortages of gasoline and lubricating products, the demise of a major oil company calls into question the integrity of the remaining entities. You gentlemen, collectively, have made a bad energy situation worse. Shame on you! General O'Reith! Without being under oath, will you agree to give answers that are as accurate as possible to the questions that we ask? After all, we are all interested in the same thing, that is, the safety of our oil supplies. As you know sir, we are all engaged in 'The Moral Equivalent of War'.

"Speak for yourself, Senator Lagniappe," O'Reith said. "Our company is not engaged in any kind of war, moral or immoral except the eternal *guerre du petrol*."

"General O'Reith, the entire nation is concerned about oil coming out of Iran. Those supplies are critical to the welfare of the nation. Your company is producing oil from that region of the world and we would like some of the details. As a starter sir, just exactly where is Poghdar Field, from which your company is producing almost a million barrels per day?"

"Poghdar, Senator Lagniappe is north and somewhat east of the Baluchistan Basin which is directly north of the Gulf of Oman."

"In what country is it located?"

"Persia, as far as I know, sir."

"By Persia, I assume you are referring to Iran."

"That's it. The Shah renamed it. I don't know why."

"General O'Reith we have evidence that suggests that Poghdar, in fact, is in Afghanistan."

"We get our information from the Shah, Senator Lagniappe. If he says it is in Iran, we just let it go at that."

"But in fact, General O'Reith, if indeed Poghdar were in Afghanistan, then oil royalties would have to be paid to the that government."

"To my knowledge, sir, there is no competent government there. What little administration that does exist is under the control of a notorious warlord named Duad Khan but I've never met him. Our oil field is under the protection of the British Government. That is public knowledge. And as regards oil royalties, that would be a matter between contracting parties and would be confidential."

Lagniappe continued, "Putting that gem of wisdom aside for the moment, why sir, would the British Government protect an oil field in Afghanistan?"

"Two reasons, sir. The oil generates revenue to pay for the Gurkhas who guard the field. Secondly, they think Poghdar is in Persia. Or so I'm told. They may not give a damn one way or the other as long as the production holds up."

"Could I ask who buys the crude oil?"

"You could but you won't get an answer. At least not from me. Contract terms are confidential."

"Is it true that the oil is sold to the Standard Oil Company, General O'Reith?"

O'Reith looked around the hearing room. O'Reith said, "Senator Lagniappe, there are Standard Oil men present. Why don't you ask them?"

"I prefer to ask another question of you sir. What is the role of Sir George P. Cardinal McDonough in the affairs of your Company?"

"He is an executive in our foreign operations."

"Is it not unusual to have a man of the cloth working for your company?"

O'Reith laughed. "Not if it is a man talented like Sir George is."

"Could I ask you what does Sir George do?"

"He is a top executive with various duties. Perhaps his most important function is to conduct the diplomacy, which results in oil concession agreements. His ties to the Roman Catholic Church as well as the Russian Orthodox Church and the Eastern Rites have proved invaluable to us over the years."

"Could you describe for the committee the relationship between your Company and the Iranian Oil Exploration and Producing Company?"

"That's the consortium, Senator. We call it the *Oil Company.* We pay them to use a section of their 30 inch pipeline which runs from Bid Boland to Bandar Shahpour. We pump Poghdar crude oil to the loading terminal."

"And is the Shah involved in that?"

"You would have to ask him," O'Reith said.

"This committee is aware that on more than one occasion, you yourself and Sir George have held meetings with the Shah in Teheran. Sources in the American Embassy have information about that," Lagniappe stated confidently.

"Yes that is correct. At one time we produced large volumes of crude oil from the Kavir Dome oil field located in the Persian Gulf. But today that field is in decline and accounts for a small fraction of the Shah's oil output."

"We are given to understand that you have conferred with the Shah recently."

"We stay in touch with him, Senator Lagniappe," O'Reith said. We pay courtesy calls from time to time. Keep the lines of communication open so to speak."

"Are you not aware, General O'Reith that it is diplomatically incorrect for you to personally negotiate with a head of state? When you have some matter for discussion with the Shah of Iran, you should take that to the U.S. State Department and ask them to intervene in your behalf."

"Senator Lagniappe," O'Reith said smiling, "That is a good idea whose time has not yet come. Nor is it likely to."

"Do you not realize sir, that by negotiating directly with the Shah, you leave the Federal Energy Department out of the linkage with the result that we in the government do not know what is going on?"

"I am acutely aware of that circumstance, Congressman Lagniappe," O'Reith said, keeping his face straight.

"How can our government wage the moral equivalent of war against petroleum privateers if we don't know what is going on?"

"I had not considered that, sir. I personally have no knowledge of petroleum privateers."

"Don't you think you should?"

"I will Senator Lagniappe, starting today. You can make book on it."

Muted laughter rose around the table. Lagniappe, clearly miffed, turned his attention to King Brock. Looking at him with a sympathetic visage, he began, "Sir, we would like to have your thoughts about the untimely and premature death of Gulf Oil Corporation."

Brock said, "Senator Lagniappe, it was murder in the first degree. That's what it was. Like a pack of Nazi U-boats, they ganged up on us. They bought up our stock and discounted our bonds. They got the ratings agencies after us. Senator Lagniappe, it was a terrible thing they did to us. When I think about it, these old eyes fill with tears. They tore us limb from limb and threw us to the wolves. We didn't have a chance. Old John D. Rockefeller, pious Baptist that he was, must be looking down from heaven's gates and sobbing his saintly heart out."

"Mr. Brock, is it true that General O'Reith made the first move that tilted Gulf Oil into the arena?" Lagniappe pressed.

"Well sir, I couldn't rightly make that accusation," Brock responded. "All of 'em knew we were wounded. They could smell blood. Kuwait crippled us in the Middle East. *Accion Democratica* hounded us to death in Venezuela. The political scandal here in the capital a couple of year's back hurt us. That bribery business didn't help matters at all. You remember Senator James..."

"That's all right, Mr. Brock," Lagniappe interrupted. "We'll pass over that."

O'Reith said, "Save that for the open session, Senator Lagniappe."

Laughter broke out again. The clerk had to call for order. Lagniappe, livid with rage, banged his gavel. He shouted "Silence! Silence! You! General O'Reith, you, sirrah!" Then, regaining his poise, he pounded the dais with his gavel. "This meeting is adjourned!"

Clifton Garvin of Jersey came over to O'Reith, shook his hand and said, "Clive, good to see you again. Where are you staying?"

"We're at the Watergate Cliff, even with notoriety, is a comfortable hotel and I am ready to be there after this circus performance."

"That's where Lou and I are staying. How about a drink tonight? We're going to ask the San Francisco lads and King Brock and the boys from London. Everyone. Call it a wake."

O'Reith laughed. "Accept with pleasure. Stan and I will be there."

Ethering at the elevated dais had whispered with Lagniappe. Returning, he nudged O'Reith, said, "Clive. It's all over. No open hearings. They don't want us back. But Lagniappe needs a new Lincoln Continental with a couple of cases of Jack Daniel's Old No. 7 in the trunk."

O'Reith brightened. "That's good news. Make that four cases. That car has a big trunk. Maybe a blonde in the tonneau. And don't forget a blow job curtain. See what Frederick's of Hollywood has in that line. The government can go ahead with the moral equivalent of war while we attend the wake tonight."

Ethering laughed. After drinks and oil field jokes at the Watergate that night, it was early to bed and next morning the two Casinghead Company men were on a jet headed west.

Helen was still responding to the gentle care of Parkinson. With the hearings finished, O'Reith had no reason to stay in Los Angeles but he continued to visit her for another week to keep her morale up. Then he took a TWA 747 to New York and another to Paris. He was ready for some loving from Maxine and she was ready to have him back in her arms.

In one of its many acts of infinite wisdom over the 200 odd years of existence, the United States Congress passed a law in 1869 giving newly organized railroad companies crossing the western United States, sections and in some cases, townships of land along the rights of way. These blocks were parceled out in a checkerboard array, one township on one side of the right-of-way, the next on the opposing side but displaced by one block. Block 36-C was one of hundreds of such awards. Over the years it had witnessed several gold rushes, a quest for water rights, oil exploration permits and many other dreams, mostly now vanished. In the fall of 1976, it was a sloping tract of land in the foothills of the Sierra Nevada on the eastern side of the great San Joaquin Valley. Much of the valley is covered with volcanic ash, or loess as it is known locally. On the slopes adjacent to the mountains, other soils have washed down and the mixture of loess and quartz and loam has created a soil where sagebrush, cactus and other flora eke out an existence. It is sparsely populated except for the town of Vidoga Springs, which has a modest claim to fame as an arthritis treatment center for members of the American Association of Retired People. Some of the springs are hot and soaking in them seems to bring temporary relief to aching joints. While people are few and far between now, it was not always thus. During the famous gold rush of 1849, many claims were staked, filed and granted by the State of California. Squatters followed the disappointed gold miners with their sheep and goats and they too, filed claims, which invariably were recognized. The goats and the sheep quickly denuded the limited vegetation. Many of them died of so-called *loco fever* thought to be induced by eating tumble weeds. So the squatters moved on to more promising parts of the valley. Then in the 1920s came the legion of oil explorers which filed mineral leases on top of the gold mining leases on top of the squatter's leases, many of them overlapping on land that was improperly surveyed to begin with. Like the dot com companies of the late 1990s, the oil explorers were largely cut down by the crash of 1929.

This grand debacle more or less coincided with the opening of the great American oil fields such as Yates in west Texas, East Texas in east Texas, Huntington Beach and Long Beach in California and Oklahoma City in the Mid-Continent.

So Lobbyist Nixon, stalking members of the Assembly in Sacramento, had his work cut out for him. Carolyn Cook gave him a map of what she wanted to lease. Eager to please and with his sights set on a return to the nation's capital, Nixon worked steadily to convince the Assembly of his mandate. Nixon and Ethering conferred regularly and made crucial decisions about the doling out of $15 bills. His first chore was to organize several dummy companies, all owned by the European subsidiary of the company. Then Nixon approached key legislators and persuaded them to attach riders of condemnation to the many legislative acts that went through the mill during the year. That done he further persuaded them to pass an act limiting the companies who were eligible to bid on these properties. It was known as The Equal Opportunity Oil Act. Only tiny explorers with little capital could bid on these properties. The propaganda that went along with this scheme was that if they allowed the majors to bid, they would scoop the properties up and sit on them. The wisdom of the Assembly was that the small operators would go to work immediately, thus creating new jobs for California. When the dust cleared on this famous auction in the fall of 1976 the winners were the dummy companies created by Stan Ethering.

Drilling commenced immediately. Several good-sized oil fields were discovered. The Oceanic Sand was productive, as was the deeper Stevens Formation. By the time of the November elections, the company was running 15,000 bopd of gasoline grade crude oil to steel storage near their recently purchased teakettle refinery in Fresno. O'Reith was in Los Angeles when Prescott called to give him the good news.

Even though O'Reith didn't regard Gerald Rudolph Ford highly, he considered him a better bet than James Earl Carter and accordingly, voted for him. But most Americans had seen enough of Ford. He was considered to be a nice guy but out of his element. Perceived as ineffective, often at sea, he seemed confused as regards economic issues. One unkind political cartoon showed him riding the back of an alligator in the Okefenokee Swamp, guided by two baffled-looking economists from the Department of Commerce. The hallmark of

Ford's campaign against inflation was the 'WIN' button. Republican functionaries handed them out generously to be worn proudly on coat lapels of the valiant warriors. The acronym meant Whip Inflation Now. But nobody did. Nobody even tried. Add to all that, his pardon of RMN in September of 1974, was the final nail in his political coffin. His administration, fatally flawed by events largely outside his control, went down to defeat at the hands of a reborn, evangelical Jimmy Carter who touted himself as the champion of the 'little people'. Oddly his religious fervor caught on with the public. And eschewing a limousine, when toting his carpetbag, he walked with his wife, Rosalyn Smith up Pennsylvania Avenue, he was cheered wildly. An honest man from an honest party was now in the White House. The millennium was upon us. Corruption in government had forever ceased. Or so it was believed. To the dismay of the oil and gas industry, Carter's first thrust was the establishment of a politically charged, highly vindictive, Energy Department at the cabinet level. A scholarly bird-watcher named James R. Schlesinger was chosen to run it.

For ex-POTUS RMN, the departure of Gerald Ford from the White House in January of 1977, was a signal that he could return to the nation's capital. To be sure on the eve of inauguration day, Nixon reminded Ethering of this and the word went out to O'Reith. Even as Carter was delivering his inaugural oration, the Nixon's were flying east. Soon he would be haunting the halls of Congress in his new job which privately, O'Reith called 'Bagmaster General'.

He would soon ascertain the mood of the new Congress. Price controls on oil produced in the United States were coming. A Sears Roebuck catalog of oil and gas regulation was in the offing. Domestic producers, large and small were going to take it on the chin. O'Reith reacted quickly. Before other oil companies figured out what was hidden beneath the thicket of the proposed new legislation, O'Reith sold off the Block 36 properties. He sold the Fresno refinery as well and took a solemn oath never to run another barrel of American crude oil to anywhere. Sure enough the Energy Department was born on August 4, 1977 and the voluminous 'energy package' was destined to be passed sooner or later.

By early December of 1977, POTUS Carter was pounding hard on the domestic producers. He was bad, bad news. But if his election over Gerald Ford was a signal defeat for the Republican Party, it was a bonanza for Chief Washington Lobbyist RMN as his official title read. He set himself up in New York City but commuted daily via the Eastern Airlines shuttle, to Capitol Hill. Even though the productive Block 36-C leases were sold, the company retained several excellent prospects on federal land. Nixon was charged with getting the required legislation passed so that the company, at some time in the future, could profitably sell these undrilled leases. Even worse, some of the proposed rules of the new Federal Energy Agency related to foreign production and were aimed particularly at the Casinghead Company. These onerous rules represented the venomous revenge of one Senator Lazlo Gimmeit Lagniappe. Even as he tooled around in his new Lincoln Continental with the titty-pink blow job curtain pulled down, drinking his Jack Daniel's whiskey in the company of his blonde floozy given him as a bonus, he was dreaming up ways to attack the oil industry. And why not? In this world, you had to go where the money was. Oil may not have been the moral equivalent of money but it was fungible. Nixon compared Lagniappe to an asp in a den of snakes and was working closely with Ethering to defang his proposed new legislation.

During most of 1977, O'Reith was in Paris but now in the winter of the year, he was back in Los Angeles to see his family and attend other matters. Helen had suffered a minor stroke followed by another sinking spell. He was spending time with her and Ridley and seeing his children and grandchild, Elaine. On Helen's only good night, he took her to the club to see *Saturday Night Fever*. John Travolta, the leading man, played against a new starlet, Karen Lynn Gorney. The music was by the three Isle of Man brothers called The Bee Gees. Barry, Robin and Maurice Gibb were sensational falsettos. All about disco dancing, it gave O'Reith a new insight as to what his youngest daughter was doing when she disappeared in the evenings. In his youth, before his leg got shot up, he was an excellent dancer. No longer. Clearly, times had changed.

Right now he was in the map room on the 38th floor of the tower. He had watched KTLA keenly during the Shah's November visit to Washington. POTUS Jimmy Carter wined and dined him and praised him fulsomely. At a formal dinner, he patted him on the back, telling him that 'Iran is an island of stability in one of the more troubled areas in the world'. O'Reith became suspicious when the police had to tear gas the anti-Shah crowds that gathered around the White House. When he saw tears in the eyes of Carter and the Shah on the South White House lawn, he calculated that the latter potentate was near the end of the trail. And by extension, the days of the Oil Company could very well be numbered. When Carter announced he was paying a return visit to the Shah in Teheran in December of 1977 because Rosalyn wanted to spend New Year's Eve with the Shah and his wife, O'Reith became more than suspicious. He became alarmed, concluding that the Shah's affairs were skidding downhill even faster than he originally believed. He shared his worries only with McDonough as he didn't want to appear cynical.

That is why he was sitting at a light-table, looking up at the huge map of Eurasia that completely covered the interior wall. Specifically he was studying a blue, dotted line that began at Poghdar Production Station No.1 and crossed into the USSR at Kushka on its way to a terminal at Vladivostok. From Kushka it went northwest across the Oxus Stream to a pump station at Samarkand; then to a second station at Tashkent and then it followed the local railroad to Alma Ata. A third station was set where the local line joined the Trans-Siberian. Building a pipeline along the right of way shown by the dots would require 6,125 kilometers of 30-inch pipe. This reflected McDonough's thinking in 1972 when Poghdar was under exploration. Even then he was leery of Persian politics. In the event, Persia won out because of the enormous expense of laying a TransAsiatic pipeline. But if the Shah were headed down the tube, big trouble would immediately arise throughout Khuzestan. Besides, the economics were different now. To begin with, crude oil was going for \$14.20/bbl, a far cry better than the \$2.35/bbl they were getting in 1973. And if the Shah went down, Poghdar, an orphan province would no longer be a part of Persia and only tangentially a part of Afghanistan. It could be easily detached. So there would be no further royalty paid to the Shah. Another factor was the decision to test the Bangestan formation, which in Khuzestan was productive in some (notably Ahwaz) structures. At Poghdar, where oil was originally found, the top of the Bangestan was at 11,500 feet and the first completion tested 10,000 bopd of 27° API crude oil with 2.5% sulphur. Unfortunately, the gas associated with this crude stream contained 5% hydrogen sulphide, a toxic gas. But treatment systems existed and after stabilization, Bangestan crude could be blended with Asmari and exported to Vladivostok. It was a good-sized oil reservoir and with 10 wells on gas lift could easily produce 150,000 bopd. Finally Cook had located a fourth structure to the north of the main field. There could be others, albeit much smaller, beyond that. Studying the long blue line, moving his game leg around to restore circulation, O'Reith drummed his fingers against the light table. After some long moments of contemplation, he asked his secretary to get McDonough on the line. It was almost six o'clock in the evening in Los Angeles. So at Lake Albano, it would be a morning hour. When the call went through, he began, "George, what are you up to these days?"

McDonough laughed lustily into the telephone. "Clive! How good of you to call. As a matter of fact, what I'm doing is what you Yanks call mending my fences."

"With whom, George?"

"Paul VI of course."

"Are you in the dog house?"

"Nothing serious. Paul is a bit annoyed at the failure of the great encyclical. And to complicate matters, he's heard some totally and absolutely false rumors from that idiot nephew of the late Cardinal Grannito Battista Girolo that I have used my high church position for gain outside the ecclesiastical realm. So I have to work on that. I have to dress up my image. What's on your mind?"

"Do you know that the Shah has been in Washington rubbing shoulders with POTUS Carter?"

"In a TV news clip, I saw them crying. I couldn't imagine why. You would think such an epochal meeting would be a happy occasion. I asked Carolyn about it and she said it was tear gas that the police used to control the agitators, people who don't like our lovable Shah."

"George that is why I am calling. I watched all of that on KTLA. It upset me. I think the Shah is getting shaky on his Peacock Throne. I'm sitting here in Carolyn's map room looking at that conjectured pipeline from Poghdar to Vladivostok. George, I'm ready to call in the welders and start burning rod."

"That bad, eh?"

"George, Carter is making a return visit to Teheran in January. That's cutting it pretty close for diplomatic exchange. If he's going to visit him again that soon, somebody at State is worried. Thus, I too am worried."

"Would you like for me to call Mikoyan?"

"I would, George. Tell him of our concern. Let him know that we would gladly give the contract for the line pipe to Russian steel mills. Tell him we would like to use five construction spreads; a British spread working from Afghanistan; two American spreads working from Vladivostok and the two Russian spreads working out of Omsk and Alma Ata. We should think in terms of a combination line composed of 30 and 28 inch. That way we can telescope one in the other and reduce transportation charges. Think he'll go for a deal like that?"

"I expect he will," McDonough agreed. "He will want some detail on the American and British contractors."

"On the American side I was thinking about Bechtel International out of San Francisco and Houston Construction Company. We should consult Trevelyen about the British Company. I like Wimpey International and Costain Construction but I would defer to his judgment In fact, maybe we should go for six spreads."

"I'll call him," McDonough said.

"George, it occurs to me that with the Shah down, Mikoyan might like to have Poghdar as a new Soviet Socialist Republic. We could plug Nixon in as the Sultan. Call for a referendum on independence Take no chances on the outcome. The Colonel could attend that matter in the role of chief of the secret police. What do you think?"

"That would make a nice package all right. Poghdar will need some leadership. We need to crack down on those warlords. At least we could rely on RMN and the Caudillo to obey orders. What about the pipeline? Have you given any thought to how much it would cost?"

"We estimated $5 billion back in 1972. Carolyn can get us a better estimate."

"I'll ask her to do that, Clive."

"George, bring Carolyn completely into the picture on this and after you get a reading from Mikoyan, call me back."

"How long will you remain in Los Angeles?"

"Another week anyhow. Could be longer. Depends on how Helen gets along."

"How's she doing, Clive?"

"She's been out of it for almost a month now. I visit her every morning. Max has been under the weather. We've got a couple of younger doctors looking after her. The prognosis is that she is not going to get any better."

"Sad story, Clive. Well, should she rally round, give her my best. I'll call you in a couple of days."

It was January of 1978. O'Reith had been back in Paris with Maxine for three weeks. Monique was there too. She was with child again and with her first born, Veronique Claire, now a tot of two had flown up from Hassi Messaoud to consult the doctor in Paris. O'Reith was somehow annoyed that she was pregnant again. He didn't know why. He hadn't liked it the first time and he didn't understand that either. After all that was a completely normal consequence of marriage and he was tolerant of, if not fond of her husband, Jean-Louis, now steadily climbing the corporate ladder at *CFP*.

McDonough and Cook were in Rome. Problems with Pope Paul VI had not gone away. Despite the lavish attention that McDonough gave to His Holiness, the rift remained. O'Reith did not enjoy listening to McDonough's tale of woe, all the more so as he was becoming repetitive. But in the interests of harmony within the company, he continued to lend a sympathetic ear.

One evening as the three of them were finishing the evening meal the telephone rang and it was Rae Regan, on the line. She said, "Daddy, you have to come home. Mother took a fall and she's broken several ribs. Dr. Max is not well. Those two young medicos are treating her here in Long Beach. She refuses to go to a hospital. We are all at our wits end. She is calling for you and she needs you."

"O.K. Rae, I'll catch a plane tomorrow. Is Max there with you?"

"Yes."

"Put him on."

When the doctor answered, O'Reith began, "Max, what does it look like?"

"Not life threatening Clive, at least not yet. We've got her taped up and she's sedated. My concern is that the new X-rays don't offer us too much encouragement. Her ribs have loss mass. I'm afraid to check out her arms and legs. She's frail, Clive. No getting around that."

"O.K. Well, I told Rae that I would catch a plane tomorrow. I'll call when I get in. Where are you staying?"

"I'm sleeping on a daybed in your parlor. Alice is here. So is Sharon. And your youngest. We have three nurses attending her and Rae Regan has been sleeping here too. Kind of crowded."

"Rae said you were ailing. What's wrong?"

"Arthritis. Takes me forever to get going in the morning."

"Go sleep in your own bed. Let the young docs handle it."

"Helen depends on me to be here."

"OK. I'm on my way."

O'Reith sat behind the Mach meter on the Concorde next noon and watched as the aircraft went supersonic somewhere over the Atlantic Ocean. A Lear Jet was standing by at JFK to take him west. Upon arrival at LAX, O'Reith spotted his limousine as soon as he came out of the arrivals gate. He fell into the cushions and dozed while the chauffeur tooled the Cadillac out onto Sepulveda Boulevard for the drive to Long Beach. When they arrived at his penthouse, he entered the foyer, nodded to the concierge and took the elevator up. Helen was in bed. O'Reith took her hand and asked, "Baby, how's it going?"

"Not famously Ace, I'm all broken up inside."

O'Reith remained at her side for several hours until one of the medicos ordered her sedated. When she was out, O'Reith went to the Fullerton Building and to bed. It had been a long, long day.

O'Reith and Parkinson were together in his clinic on the tenth floor of the Tower. O'Reith was looking at the X-rays of Helen's upper torso. It meant nothing to him. Parkinson said, "Clive, I didn't want to tell you this over the transatlantic telephone but look at her shoulder blade there. Notice the erosion. That is pretty bad news."

"Where and when did you make those pictures, Max," O'Reith asked.

"About ten days ago at UCLA Medical Center."

"Why is it such bad news?"

"Looks like multiple myeloma. I have suspected that for months."

O'Reith stiffened. "Max that is hard for me to take. Does she know?"

"No. But Rae Regan does."

"She'll tell little Clive Colin and Helen Simpson," O'Reith said.

"I think she already has," Parkinson said.

"How long has she got, Max?"

"Maybe just weeks. Once that stuff gets going, it is destructive as hell. The bones melt away. And she's pretty far down the road right now."

As a boy McDonough, quick to learn, realized at an early age that if were to have his way, he would have to learn how to manipulate his mother, a widower before his tenth birthday. The family was in modestly prosperous circumstances. His father had made money in Calcutta and his mother was from a family of means. When he was four, the family moved to Bombay where his father died of cholera. Returning to Northern Ireland, the land of both his parents, his mother settled his father's estate and they found a proper house in Belfast. McDonough, although not bad looking was not yet ready for a permanent liaison with the pretty girls around town. With an ear for language, by the time he finished at Beaumont College he was fluent in French, German, Spanish, Italian and importantly, Latin. So although he had no religious inclinations, he spoke the languages of the high Roman Catholic churchmen and as he became friendly with them over the years, he fathomed their patterns of thought and behavior. Being devious himself, he grew to expect it in others and found it aplenty among the bishops, archbishops and cardinals of his ken. Indifferent to the religion of his ancestors, he allowed his mother to push him into Holy Orders. Although he could never have been described as a fervent Christian, he was something of a fanatic and a great admirer of H.H. Kitchener, T.E. Lawrence and Charles 'Chinese' Gordon.

McDonough could hardly be described as a successful parish priest. He was disgusted with his slothful, lustful flock. He became bored by their repetitious sins of gluttony and lust. Worse he could hardly tolerate their onion breath. Thus he induced his often drunken gardener to hear confessions. For quite some time this worked all right but in the end, he was caught, unfrocked and dismissed. His mother already in failing health, horrified by the scandal, died shortly thereafter. In the Year of Our Lord 1937 with a resurgent Germany and a troublesome Italy, the British Government needed intelligence men badly and McDonough was perfectly qualified. MI5 snapped him up, no questions asked. He was proud of his accomplishments and figured that at a minimum, he had saved a dozen divisions of infantry from destruction and perhaps half of the ships in the Royal Navy.

The British Government agreed with his assessment. He had been on good terms with every Prime Minister since Neville Chamberlain. By the end of World War II, McDonough had become an expert manipulator of both government officials and high churchmen. He found that the higher their station, the easier it was to use them. His first big catch was Eugenio Pacelli, Papal Nuncio to Berlin who would become Pope Pius XII. He met Pacelli in Rome prior to his being appointed as Bishop of the See of La Roche Guyon, France, headquarters of the German Army Group B in 1943. In 1944, he became acquainted with the future Pope John XXIII who was at that time, Papal Nuncio to the recently liberated France. Since that era he had handled them both and now Paul VI. Rising steadily through the ranks of the laity as a result of his many favors to the Popes, McDonough became a Prince of the Church in 1965.

Everything was going roses for him until the publication of *Casti Connubii II.* McDonough had touted it as the savior of the Pope Paul's regime. But like *Humanae vitae*, it had become a cropper and now Paul VI had not one failed encyclical but two. Worse, the notoriety became pronounced with the showing of the *White Satin Miter* and *Signal Red Cadillac* right in the cinemas of the Holy City, as it was ironically called. Both movies extolled the virtues of *Casti Connubii II* in a rather glaring, some would say pornographic, way. Paul VI was taking some heat over this and when he finally got around to reading the encyclical that he had authorized but never reviewed, he was aghast. He was ready to disown it and McDonough.

McDonough was not so naive as to think he had never made enemies but his conceit was that his friends in the curia were far more powerful than his foes. Up to a point this could have been true. But with Paul VI's health flagging, many a cardinal was sizing up his chance to succeed him. Any calculation had to reckon with Sir George P. Cardinal McDonough so the papal knives were out. The late Cardinal Girolo had many weaknesses that McDonough exploited. For example there was the affair where Amanda Macabra's husband was made a priest of the Eastern Rites. There was the scandalous affair of a red silk chastity belt worn by Genevieve Ste Jacqueline when she made the pilgrimage to Santiago de Compostela. And although, presumably Girolo had gone on to paradise, he left a lurid diary. He also left a nephew whose exploits in the fleshpots of Rome often made the tabloids. The nephew had his diary.

McDonough and the Colonel had contrived, as a favor to the old Cardinal to spirit Nephew Girolo, a young sporting blade, off to the provinces of Guatemala where he became an unhappy auxiliary bishop.

With his august relative gone to heaven, there was no reason for him to remain in Central America and he didn't. Now returned from his long exile in the Guatemalan boondocks, young Girolo, resentful and vindictive, was back in Rome. All in all, it added up to trouble for one Sir George P. Cardinal McDonough.

One evening in May of 1978 around midnight while O'Reith and Maxine were watching *Murder My Sweet* on TV-1, the telephone rang. It was McDonough. His voice was confused and O'Reith suspected he had been into the brandy. He asked, "Clive would it be such a great imposition if I came for a visit? Just for a day."

"You are always welcome, George," O'Reith answered. When?"

"Tomorrow?"

"Sure. I'll send a car to meet your plane. Carolyn coming?"

"Of course, I don't travel without her."

"See you tomorrow, George," O'Reith said.

After the movie, as they were preparing for bed, O'Reith said, "Maxine, George was on the sauce. He's depressed about something, perhaps a religious matter. After dinner tomorrow night, I'll invite him to my den and find out what's eating him. Think you can find something to talk about with Carolyn?"

"We can always watch a movie. I would like to see *Grease* with John Travolta and Olivia Newton-John. It is playing at the *Berlitz*".

"Good idea," O'Reith said. "It is a musical. If you enjoy it we can go together in a day or so if you don't mind seeing it twice. Eve Arden is in it, her first appearance since *White Satin Miter*. I'd like to see it for that reason alone."

"Fine with me," Maxine said.

McDonough and Cook arrived around four o'clock in the afternoon and by the time they were through customs and immigration and drove from Charles de Gaulle to O'Reith's flat, it was the cocktail hour.

After dinner, O'Reith directed McDonough to the spiral staircase that went down to his den. He said, "George, watch your step. Hold the railing."

When they were down and seated, he continued, "Calvados or Armagnac, George?"

"Armagnac, if you please," McDonough said.

O'Reith fixed the drinks, handed McDonough his and slumped into his easy chair. "Cheers, George," he said holding his glass of sparkling water aloft.

"Clive, I'm on the edge of a cliff. Good chance I'll fall off. May even get pushed."

"Paul VI?"

"Girolo the younger. Remember him? Grannito kept a diary and in it are detailed references to the bargain I made with him to get Carolyn appointed as a Dame of Honor and Devotion," McDonough said.

O'Reith grinned. "Frederick of Hollywood's red satin chastity belt?"

"Exactly. Do you recall that you sent me three of them; two for Carolyn and one as a sample for Girolo to inspect?"

"Some things one does not forget, George," O'Reith said, chuckling.

"Girolo the younger showed the chastity belt to Paul VI along with the diary entry. The Pope is incensed to put it in its best light."

"George now could be a good time for you abandon your religious persona," O'Reith suggested. "Sell that place on Lake Albano. Unplug your halo. Move back to London, the center of the world after all. Forget the *Urbi*. Dedicate the rest of your days to Carolyn. A world of diplomatic activity awaits you on behalf of the company. You would be out of that mare's nest of a curia, let alone the College of Cardinals. George, those old prelates exert a negative influence on you. Piss on it. Get out from under it."

"Clive, I just can't. I can't skip out. Paul must hear my explanation."

"Explain then and fuck off."

"He won't speak to me."

"Really George. Call him on his hot line."

"You think I have not done that? Well I have. Several times. I get one of his toadies who informs me that now it is not convenient for me to see the Pope."

"Write him a letter," O'Reith suggested.

"Clive, be serious. What am I to do?"

"Drop in on him. Sit outside his office until he relents."

"I suppose I could try it," McDonough agreed in resignation. "Clive, the last time I called, a pip-squeak of a monsignor answered the phone, a new boy, one that I have never met. He told me the Pope was distressed by one of the songs sung in *Signal Red Cadillac*."

"Which one?"

"Do you recall 'Doing it for the Pope'?"

"Yeah that is a neat little ditty," O'Reith remembered. "Cherry Cokeland sang it. Her doctor in San Francisco had just advised her that she was with child. It was a lament for unwed motherhood as I recall."

"Exactly. Paul saw it," McDonough explained. "The chorus goes like this 'I lost my cherry on the Oakland Ferry. I was doing it for the Pope'. Lynn Landury was trying to cheer her up. He told her the Pope has said OK on fornication. Incidentally Clive that word is from the Latin *fornicatus*. It means 'arched'. I suppose it is a description of the female aperture. Anyhow Paul found that offensive. I must sit beside him and explain the circumstances of the movie."

"You could give him the lowdown on *fornicatus*."

"This is no occasion for levity, Clive. I must make him see things in a clearer light."

"Why would that make any difference? George, if he's pissed, anything you say will just make it worse."

"Clive, I simply do not know what to do." McDonough sighed heavily, daubed at a tear on his cheek. O'Reith poured him another stiff jolt of brandy.

"George, you suffer from a fixation," O'Reith said. "You have it in your mind that being elected Pope would elevate you to the highest pinnacle on this earth. Have you ever stopped to consider the duties of a Pope? George, in 30 days you would be bored out of your mind. And another thing, how would Carolyn fit into that scenario? Popes are attended around the clock, 24 hours per day. No more kissy-kissy. No more sudsy-fudsy in the Jacuzzi. George, your character disposes you to becoming a medieval Pope, a Borgia or a Girolo or an Este. When you are a modern Pope you can make no plans. Others do it for you. You would be trapped like the Colonel when he was in Santo Domingo prison. You would be worse off than when you were a humble parish priest in County Clare."

"It would not be like that at all, Clive. If I were Pope, I could snap my finger and the mountain would move aside."

"George, when you get back to Rome, insist upon an audience with Paul. Tell him that you have sinned and will have no confessor but himself. Then, examine your conscience and rid your soul of the accumulated sins of four decades going back to World War II."

"Clive!"

"I'm serious George. To be the Pope, you have to clean up the slate. Level with him about Girolo. Level with him about the litany of political lies that you have told the so-called statesmen of the world since the end of the war."

"Clive, if I were to make a full and complete confession, Pope Paul would excommunicate me! Besides it would take several days."

"George flash your halo at him. That would soften him up in a hurry. You are a repetitive sinner. You only commit a few sins but you do them over and over. List each one on the back of an envelope and estimate the times committed. He cannot excommunicate you George. If you make an honest, truthful confession, he has to absolve you. If he doesn't, then the system is broken. He may raise an eyebrow from time to time. Why would you care? You don't have to confess to him that you schemed to get a shot at election. You can fudge that. Nevertheless, for the record, that's Pride, George and you have committed the hell out of it." O'Reith poured him another snifter of Armagnac.

"I've already had too much brandy, Clive."

"Drink it anyway!"

McDonough's hands were twitching. He was wearing his signature white linen suit but for some curious reason, he had on a red felt fez with a black tassel. O'Reith asked, "George, why the fez?"

"I've always liked the way I look in a fez, Clive. A fez gives a man, especially a portly man, an added measure of distinction."

"You've seen too many Sydney Greenstreet movies."

McDonough smiled, sipped his brandy. "Clive, what you suggest that I do creates a great deal of turmoil inside my breast. I'm like the white rat caught in the gaze of the cobra. What you suggest is an enormity I would have never considered. But now that it is out there, on the table so to speak, I have to wonder if Paul would give me absolution? I have not been in the state of grace since 1936. You have struck a sensitive chord. To become Pope, one should be in the state of grace. It does not make sense otherwise. Would he absolve me?"

"He might strap a penance on you that would choke a horse but he damn well would steer clear of a possible backfire. How many Popes over the ages have had halos flashed at them? You are standing on firm ground, George, give it up."

"There's the rub," McDonough sighed, his eyes narrowing. He peered mole-like at O'Reith, repeated, "Flagellation is still in vogue in some quarters. The Vatican has its dark cellars."

"George, don't overdramatize." O'Reith rose as the teleprinter abruptly clattered. He was tired and sleepy and ready for bed. "Think about it George. And sweet dreams." O'Reith ripped the message off the machine and the two executives climbed the spiral staircase into the parlor.

Maxine and Carolyn had returned from the movie. O'Reith read Trevelyen's report of more trouble in the Middle East.

Maxine said, "Clive, *Grease* is truly a delight. Eve Arden plays the schoolmistress looking after all those horny high school kids. Guess who else is in that flick?"

"Can't," he laughed."

"Joan Blondell."

"No kidding. Christ I remember when she was a Wampas Baby. Must have been 1930 or 1931. She and Helen and Alice Ridley used to pal around together.

CHAPTER XI

TROUBLE IN PERSIA

Late in the afternoon of August 6, 1978, gathered in the penthouse in the rue de Surene. O'Reith, Cook and McDonough were listening to Scotty Trevelyen. He was saying, "MI6 has accumulated quite a bit of personal data on Mohammed Reza Pahlavi these last few months. Tracked his trips to Switzerland, phone lines tapped and his Alpine villas bugged. Doctors abound. The data suggests treatment for some variety of cancer. You remember how outspoken and demanding he usually is when we discuss oil matters with him. Well, now he seems tranquilized. Doesn't act up like in the good old days. Medicos have him on painkillers. Another alarming thing is that this fanatic Khomeini, keeps stirring the pot. He would like to return to Teheran. Add to that, the Teheran Bazaaris are beginning to lose faith in the Shah. Quite a bit of activity in the foreign exchange market. They're selling Rials and buying Sterling. Not a good sign. Once word of that filters down to Ahwaz, we could see some difficult problems in Khuzestan."

"Is the Oil Company still running six million a day?" O'Reith asked.

"Struggling to hold it. Gas gaps are giving us the dickens. A dozen small rigs do nothing but set gas exclusion liners. The reservoir engineers are predicting we'll be down to 5.5 million by this time next year. We're running 40 strings looking for Bangestan oil. That gives you an idea of the severity of the production decline."

"It's the same in Poghdar," Cook said. "We're installing gas lift as fast as we can. We've stopped the decline but not for long."

"If we can't keep the Shah on seat, it won't matter," Trevelyen said.

"What are the prospects of continuing to operate under a new government? Maybe this Khomeini guy will be reasonable," Cook suggested.

"We've been down that road before, Carolyn," Trevelyen answered. "When the mullahs take over, we're gone. Over half of the population of Persia hates us anyhow. With a crazy like Khomeini stirring them up, we don't have a chance. They'll force us to shut in and with all of the hands running amok, it will be a year or so before they get any production back on the line. This is a severe crisis. We will be standing short over a million bopd."

Trevelyen was interrupted by the telephone. Maxine answered. She said, "George it is for you. From Rome."

McDonough took the telephone, listened in silence and then his mouth fell open and the color drained from his face. His lemon yellow eyes became as pale as bananas. At length he hung up. He looked at Cook, then O'Reith, then Trevelyen and finally Maxine. He said in a weak voice, "He's dead. Heart attack. A few hours ago."

"Who, George?" O'Reith asked. But he already knew.

McDonough said, "Carolyn, pack our things." Then to O'Reith he said, "Clive, help us with bookings? We have to fly back to Rome tonight. I just don't know how I'll cope with all this. Such a great tragedy."

"I assume from the posturing George, that Pius VI is no longer with us. Am I correct?"

"Yes Clive. How can you be so callous at such a solemn moment?"

"Jesus Christ, George," O'Reith said. "You're gloating. You think this is a windfall don't you? George, did you take the advice I gave you in Paris in May?"

McDonough's nose went up. "Matters of the confessional are not to be discussed with laymen. Particularly with Episcopalians who are just a cut above heathens." He wore an injured expression on his face.

"Great acting George, but this is not cinema," O'Reith insisted. He was not listening. Hands clasped with Cook's, they had fallen to their knees. McDonough droned out a turgid prayer, his halo flashing reddish orange.

O'Reith and McDonough sat in the cushions while Carolyn and Maxine rode the jump seats to Charles de Gaulle. McDonough moaned, "Clive, I simply do not know how I will ever get through these difficult days. Who can predict how long it will take to assemble the College of Cardinals? They come from all over the world; the Metropolitans from the East; the lay princes from Europe and the Americas. Then we have those who come from China and India. You can imagine my long hours on the telephone. That reminds me. I must call George Bauman in St. Louis, Missouri. Paul named him a Knight in 1983 and I consider him a key ally."

"What is his claim to fame?" Cook asked.

McDonough appeared surprised. "Carolyn, everybody knows that he was the publisher of the *St. Louis Globe-Democrat*, a distinguished newspaper indeed. Not like that scurrilous *Yellow Peril* that Clive admires.

"George," O'Reith admonished. "You can read the *Globe-Democrat*. I will continue reading the *Peril*."

McDonough continued, "In addition to Bauman, I have many other solicitations to make. Many phone calls."

O'Reith asked, "George, exactly whom must you telephone?"

"Well, all of the cardinals that I recruited. Flor. Mandy. Stan. Then there is Mikoyan. He promised to help me assemble those red hats from the Soviet Union. I wish he were not so fragile."

"How many of those?" O'Reith asked. "Russian delegates."

McDonough sighed audibly. "I don't know for a certainty. There will be metropolitans from Moscow. Leningrad. Kiev. Vladivostok. Omsk. Odessa. Baku. Alma Ata. Murmansk. Archangel. Samara."

"And they are all in your camp?" O'Reith asked.

"Well I would expect so," McDonough said. They were pulling up under the marquee of the departure lounge. McDonough got out and then Cook and finally O'Reith, aided by his cane and Maxine's hand. Maxine abandoned her jump seat for the cushions and waited for the final good-byes. O'Reith shook hands with his guests. He wished them good traveling. When they disappeared inside the terminal, the chauffeur helped him inside and they returned to Paris.

On August 24th, a telex from the Oil Company in London brought more disturbing news from Persia. Although he knew that McDonough was preoccupied with the conclave of the College of Cardinals, he deemed the news so alarming that he called his villa near Lago Albano. Cook answered. O'Reith began, "Carolyn, I got a wire from the Oil Company in London. A Queen's Messenger came in from Teheran. The Shah is slipping further into despair and lethargy. Things are getting worse all the time. Is George around? I want him to make a call."

"He's dressing for a function at the Vatican. I'll call him."

When the papal candidate answered, O'Reith continued. "George, MI6 report. Shah is losing his grip faster than when Scotty told us about him earlier. He is attended around the clock by medicos flown in from Geneva with stuffed black bags. They're shooting him full of morphine. He is not taking care of his business and it looks like he is not going to get any better. So something is going to spring loose. George, I'm worried about Poghdar. How about calling Mikoyan. Urge him to OK that trans-Asiatic pipeline? Ask Carolyn to fill you in on those several smaller structures to the north of the main Poghdar Field. She thinks we could probably develop 300,000 bopd from them and run it for three years without decline. So if Mikoyan will OK it, let's go for it."

"Clive, as you know I am completely overwhelmed by the social and religious functions that attend the selection of a new Pope to replace dear departed Paul VI. Even now, as we speak, I am running late for an important soiree. Many of the metropolitans from the Eastern Rites are now here and it is important for me to greet them and ask them to consider me in the coming conclave."

"George, tonight call Mikoyan at home and get a reading."

"You insist?"

"I do."

"Clive the Vatican is a hotbed of activity just now. All of the important prelates in the world have gathered to lobby for their favorites."

"Mandy show up yet?" O'Reith asked.

"She met Flor in Madrid. They came together. Flor brought a note from the Colonel wishing me success. It made my day."

"George, like the Colonel, I wish you success too. But be realistic. You don't have a Chinaman's Chance. Those Italian cardinals will choose the new Pope and you might just as well get prepared for it. George, ask Mikoyan to line up clearances for a couple of company airplanes to resurvey and photograph a pipeline right-of-way. Tell him to line up a contract with a Soviet steel mill to supply the 4,000 miles or so of 30-inch and 28 inch line pipe. Then call Black Rod and explain it to him. With the pipeline operating to Vladivostok, even if the bubble bursts in Khuzestan, with British troops, the Oil Company can run that Asmari crude north as well. Call me back tomorrow night."

"Clive, I don't appreciate your dismissing the idea that I might prevail in the conclave. That is a totally unwarranted assumption on your part. You have given me several onerous tasks at a sensitive time. But I will follow your instructions as I always do. Have I not always been your loyal and obedient servant?"

"You have George, but the rhetoric is unnecessary."

McDonough made a series of more or less unintelligible sounds ending with 'Coo Bob'. Then he continued, "Clive, if we assume that both Mikoyan and the Queen agree on the Russian pipeline, where do we get the money? How much will it cost?"

"George, we have over $3 billion in the treasury from the sale of our Gulf Oil stock. We still have lines of credit with JP Morgan, Chase Manhattan and British Linen. Money is not the problem. With Oxy in the loop, we have $5 billion behind us. Political sway is the immediate concern."

"I'll have something for you tomorrow night," McDonough replied.

The next night as O'Reith and Maxine were finishing the baked linguado and waiting for the crepes, the telephone rang and it was MacDonough. "Clive, we have a green light from both Mikoyan and Black Rod. One of us will have to sign the protocol in Moscow. Black Rod will keep troops in Poghdar Province and put a battalion into Khuzestan if Shah gets chopped."

"Carolyn in the picture?"

"Of course."

"Has Stanley Cardinal Ethering showed up for the conclave?"

"He's here with us. Dinner party tonight. Flor and Mandy and Stan and Scotty."

"George I predict that your dinner party guests are your constituency. In toto."

"Clive you are a cruel, cold-blooded man. Besides, you forget the Russians."

"Indeed. I forgot about them. George I say 15 votes maximum out of how many? A hundred and twenty?"

"Something like that. I made it 123 yesterday but Cardinal Contreras from Mexico is in bad shape. He may not last through the final vote."

"When does the voting begin?"

"Tomorrow."

"Well good luck and keep me in the picture."

"Of course, Clive. You'll be the first to get the news."

O'Reith laughed. He said, "Let me talk to Carolyn."

"Yes, General O'Reith?" Cook answered.

"Carolyn, George did a neat job on Mikoyan. Will you have time to coordinate all this while the conclave is in session?"

"Yes sir. It's telephone work and of course, Stan is here with us."

"Do we know when the Moscow Protocol will be ready for signature?"

"A week or ten days."

"If we get a new Pope within that time frame, you and George can go to Moscow. If the document is ready before the conclave ends, I'll go. Maxine can go with me. She has never been there. Be a nice trip for her."

"OK sir. We'll do it that way."

"Carolyn, I'll have another word with George if you please."

"Yes sir."

"George, after the conclave ends are you game for another trip to Poghdar?"

"If I am elected Pope that would be a complication."

"Let's say that worst comes to worst and you're not."

"In that case I might go to Poghdar and stay."

"As long as you retain your sense of humor, George, you're in good shape. I should speak to both Mandy and Flor." O'Reith said pleasant words to the two Latin ladies and hung up.

It was a Wednesday, the 30th of August 1978. O'Reith had tried on several occasions to speak to McDonough in his Lago Albano villa. Cook always answered. The cardinal was indisposed. Crushed by the election of Albino Luciani, McDonough was suffering from daily migraine attacks. He was in his room in bed and a nun from the Vatican was attending him.

But this time, O'Reith was determined to speak to him. When Cook answered he said, "Carolyn, Scotty called me last night. The demonstrations in Teheran are turning into lawless looting. Buildings have been torched. There are casualties. Scotty worries that the Shah could go down in a matter of days. He has leukemia and is no longer rational. Scotty thinks we should see him urgently to get a feel as to his ability to stay on seat. As you well know, George is the only one of us who can get inside the Shah's skin. George has to go with us."

"Hold on General. He is in his bedroom with a cold compress over his brow trying to shake his migraine. I'll tell him this is important."

Presently a moaning McDonough answered in a weak, whining voice. "Yes Clive, as you know I am a sick man."

"You're going to be a poor one as well if the Shah packs up," O'Reith said sternly. The conclave is finished. You have no pressing affairs in Rome. Get over that. The Shah is reeling. You and I and Scotty have got to prop him up."

"Clive, you are heartless. When do we go?"

"Scotty is in London. I'll telephone him and set it up. I'll meet you and Carolyn at Fiumicino. When Scotty arrives, we'll travel together."

"Yes that's fine but Clive I must tell you that I had a phone call last night from Sergio Mikoyan. He said his father was quite ill and under treatment in Kuntsevo Hospital. He is 82 and quite frail. I would like to go to Moscow and pray for him. What if we delay the trip to Teheran long enough for me to call on Mikoyan and sign the protocol?"

"Well the protocol is certainly important," O'Reith answered." We should sign it while Mikoyan is still in the picture to avoid delays. George I'll call Scotty back and explain this. We'll go see the Shah when you're finished in Moscow."

It was an Alitalia 747 that got into Teheran late in the afternoon of Wednesday, September 27th. The Oil Company Zim met O'Reith, Cook, Trevelyen and McDonough at Mehrabad and went directly to the Hotel Caspien. Trevelyen went on to his quarters in the Oil Company building on Takte Jamshid. Next morning they set out to call on the Shah at his Saadabad Palace in Shemiran. In his Rolls-Royce limousine going up the hill, Trevelyen said, "Tension has relaxed a bit. Shah seems to be doing a little better. But he needs help. No doubt about that. My idea is to give him an assistant. We'll have to wait and see how he looks but at first blush, I think we need to install a deputy. Any ideas?"

"We need a tough cookie," O'Reith said. "Scotty if he's full of hop, how do we negotiate with him?"

"He's dried out for the moment," Trevelyen asserted. "We put some of our Harley Street medicos on his case. He was practically out of it and didn't realize we were stacking the deck. So our chaps pulled the plug on the morphine. They're giving him sugar water instead. They say he's more or less normal for now. What's the Colonel doing?"

"Temporary asylum in Madrid," O'Reith said. With Franco gone, Prince Carlos is reluctant to make any waves. Permanent asylum would get the newspapers and the TV on his back. So he gave him a one-year visa. He's ready to make a move."

"He worked with the Shah before in Guatemala, didn't he?" Trevelyen asked.

"He did briefly. They didn't mesh too well. As deputy to the Shah...?"

"What's Dick Nixon doing now?" McDonough asked.

"Bag work on Capitol Hill," O'Reith answered. "He could be our guy."

"They are acquainted," Trevelyen said. "If we get a break when we're talking to the Shah, let's spring that on him."

"That's for you George," O'Reith said.

Trevelyen said, "Fellows, SAVAK is weak as water. Why couldn't the Colonel be plugged in there? With Nixon as deputy Shah, the Colonel could work for him. No conflict there."

"I like that idea," McDonough agreed.

"They are a pair to draw to, all right," Cook said giggling.

It was Thursday morning at ten o'clock in the huge, baroque study on the second floor of the palace in Shemiran. The Shah in his sparkling, white suit with all the trimmings was seated behind his glass-topped deck smoking a fat Turkish cigarette with a golden filter tip. Curlicues of smoke from the cigarette between his large fingers revealed his tremors. His complexion was ashen, his hair, getting thin, was obviously dyed and his features were drawn. No doctor required to see that he was not in good health. His eyes lacked their old fury. If not yet finished, he was well along the way. He was not in a good mood. He glared at his visitors now seated before him, O'Reith in a tuxedo, McDonough in white linen, Trevelyen in a dark business suit and Cook in widow's weeds with a veil.

The Shah lifted a yellow telegram from his desk and showed it to Trevelyen. "This, gentlemen, comes from Sir Eric Drake. If not for this message of 'high import' as the legend reads, I would have found it quite difficult to squeeze you three gentlemen into my busy schedule. I'll just read you the text:"

> 'Esteemed Excellency: I cordially request that you give audience to Brigadier Trevelyen, General Clive O'Reith and the reverend Sir George Cardinal McDonough. As you know these men share my most private thoughts about matters in which we have a common interest and I beg that you listen well and carefully to the somber message that they bring.'

"Somber, Indeed! Is it is the perceived unrest in the streets that brings you? Am I right?"

"Just so, Shah," McDonough said softly. "It seems that your remarkable White Revolution is hitting a bumpy spot in the road. Shah, it was always ephemeral. Like the will-o'-the-wisp, now you see it, now you don't. As of today, you don't. Remembering some of the threats we have seen from earlier times, we wanted to assure you of our strong allegiance. Even if some of your own subjects find time to dishonor your noble self, be advised that the Raj stands behind you as he always has."

"Sir Eric is hardly the Raj," the Shah said snappily.

"He is the chairman of Anglo-Persian," Trevelyen said. "That is much the same."

Without waiting for the Shah to respond, McDonough smoothly picked up the train of thought. "Shah, Sir Eric speaks with as much authority, indeed he speaks with greater authority than Harold Wilson. If Sir Eric thinks things need fine tuning, then we should pay attention to his wise counsel."

"All right," the Shah snapped. "What is this 'wise' counsel that you fellows bring me?"

"Ah Shah," McDonough continued. "For one thing, we've noted that if SAVAK were hitting on all sixteen cylinders, these disgraceful outbursts of civil disorder could not happen. The demonstration on September 4, marking the end of Ramadan was extraordinary in view that the march contained thousands of unhappy people. These were your loyal subjects with whom you are in partnership in the White Revolution. The secret police let too many marginals fall through the cracks. And those 'unauthorized gatherings', Shah, they're still taking place."

"You think I don't know that, Sir George?"

"Well you are not doing anything about it," McDonough declared with a hint of exasperation. "You seem rather lethargic in the face of civil disobedience if I say so myself. You imposed martial law during the night of September 7th, and when the sun came up on the 8th, one of the worst riots of your reign occurred. Hundreds of people were killed. *Le Monde* called it *Vendredi Noir.* The *Times of London* referred to it as 'Black Friday'. One or two more disturbances of this nature and you may well question your relevancy. I might add that things are no better in Khuzestan. One strike follows another. If it were not for the expatriate supervisory staff, we would not be running crude oil today."

"Sir George," The Shah interrupted, "You overdramatize. At no time has our army lost control of the state machinery."

"Shah is it not true that from time to time you must go to Geneva for medical treatment?" McDonough asked.

"Everyone gets sick once in a while," the Shah declared defensively. "Even your ample, religious self."

"No cause for personal remarks Shah. Indeed I rose from my sick bed to make this journey, arduous in the extreme for a man of my age."

"Get to the point, Sir George. We're wasting time. "What medicine does Sir Eric prescribe for me?"

"Shah," McDonough continued in a soft voice. "Sir Eric makes no prescription. He leaves that to us. We were thinking that it is now the time for you to install a deputy. You can use a good strong assistant to help you cope with these disruptions."

"And just whom would that strong person be?"

"We were thinking of Richard M. Nixon." McDonough spoke unctuously. His charm was dripping sweet now that he had the Shah's attention.

The Shah gazed at McDonough with utter contempt. He said scornfully, "So I am to take on the disgraced American ex-president as my lieutenant? Is that the drill?"

"Ah Shah. Just so, Just so, Shah."

"That is absolutely preposterous, Sir George," the Shah snorted, wide-eyed now. "What credentials does Ex-president Nixon bring to my humble principality?"

McDonough said, "You will recall that his first term as POTUS was quite successful. He was re-elected by a landslide. He had to deal with the USSR. Brezhnev was no pansy. And then, Shah, there was the Vietnam affair. He handled that remarkably well. He opened a détente with China. That is the stuff of which operas are crafted. Of course we all remember his outstanding performance as president of the *Greater Central American Co-prosperity Sphere.*"

"He lasted a week," the Shah snorted.

"Circumstances beyond his control, Shah" McDonough went on. "His vice presidential candidate was killed in a tragic accident. The people were upset."

"And rightly so," the Shah snapped back. "Only a fool would lose his vice president to a man-eating tiger in an inaugural parade. That motorcade should have been traveling 60 miles an hour. When I land at Mehrabad and enter my limousine, we make tracks until the complete caravan is within the palace walls. The people of Guatemala were upset because of all those tigers running loose. They didn't care one way or the other about Nixon and his outré entourage. Another thing, Sir George, my understanding is that Mr. Nixon is a Christian. This job requires the incumbent to be a Moslem."

"Not to worry, Shah. We'll line him up for a religious training course, a Madrassa. He'll be a good Moslem quick as a wink."

The Shah snorted. "I should laugh," he spat out. He looked out at the steely faces of the oil executives, sighed audibly. "Well, I suppose I have little choice in the matter," he muttered with resignation. "This is, after all, East of Suez. The Raj reigns supreme. Who am I, the mere Shah of all Shahs, to resist?"

"Well spoken, Shah," McDonough agreed.

"And when may I expect the celebrated Mr. Nixon to appear?"

"No cause for sarcasm, Shah," McDonough said softly. "We are merely trying to do the right thing for everyone concerned."

"We can have him here installed by the middle of next week, Your Excellency," O'Reith said. "All he will need is a visa."

"I'll attend that," the Shah said wearily. Where should I send the telegram?"

"If you send it to the Casinghead Company in Los Angeles, we will forward it to him by courier." O'Reith said.

"Forward it to him where?" the Shah asked.

"Washington, DC" O'Reith said. "He is presently assigned as our legislative liaison officer there."

The Shah lit another cigarette and slapped his desk as if to signify that the session was concluded. "It was good to see you gentlemen again," he said, not with much sincerity.

"Ah Shah," McDonough spoke up. There is one other small matter."

"What now?" the Shah asked doubly exasperated.

"We would like for you to sack your SAVAK chief. We would like to replace him with a stronger personality, one who has great experience quelling rioters."

"Who would that be?" the Shah asked sarcastically.

"Ah Shah, we were thinking of the Colonel," McDonough suggested. His reputation for running a secret police force is impeccable."

"For a change, I agree," the Shah responded. "I never cared much for him but he certainly knows that line of work. Well that is OK. I was thinking of replacing General Zahedi anyway. When may I expect him?"

"He is in Madrid at present as a guest of Prince Carlos. You may send his visa to the Spanish Foreign Office. I'll see that they attend it."

"May I offer you gentlemen lunch?" the Shah asked.

"Well that is kind of you sir," Trevelyen replied.

"Indeed!" McDonough agreed.

"I have a good appetite," O'Reith said.

The Shah was as good as his word. Although he merely pecked at his plate, his guests enjoyed broiled sturgeon, Caspian rice with fresh dill and string beans in lemon butter. The wine, a pale Isphahani rosé, went down leaving no trace.

That evening McDonough and Cook caught an Iran Air flight to Rome. O'Reith returned to Paris. Trevelyen stayed on in Teheran to watch the scene unfold.

Weary from his trip, which was delayed by bad weather, it was after midnight when O'Reith arrived at Ruc dc Surenc. Grccting Maxine in her dressing gown, he kissed her, showered and fell into bed. They slept late and were awakened by the telephone. A reedy-voiced McDonough was calling from Rome. He began, "Clive I'm for it."

"What now George?"

"Albino Luciani, Clive. Surely you've heard?"

"Heard what?"

"He died in his sleep while we were in Teheran. His secretary, Father John Magee discovered him just minutes ago. The nine days of mourning begin. You realize this gives me a second shot at it, don't you?"

"Forget it, George. It won't happen. Now's a good time for you to drop out."

"No Clive, I'll take my chances. After all, I am better known this time. Perhaps my previous lobbying will carry the day."

"Don't get your hopes up." O'Reith hung up the telephone and said to Maxine, "Well I have to admire his tenacity. But he'll be disappointed again."

"Poor chap," Maxine said. "Hungry?"

"Yes. How about some bacon and eggs?"

They played golf that afternoon and had dinner at a pizzeria in Trocadero. He was glad to be back in Paris and looked forward to spending days, if not weeks with Maxine.

But it was not to be. Next morning, the telephone rang around 4 am. waking both O'Reith and Maxine. When he was in Paris, he always answered the phone because most of the calls were for him. So he sleepily got up and felt his way into the parlor. As he picked up the instrument, he saw Maxine standing beside him. She said, "Clive, I feel that something has gone really wrong somewhere."

O'Reith lifted the instrument and said, "Hello."

"Dad!" He recognized the voice of his oldest, Rae Regan."

"Yes Rae?"

"Dad, you must come home. Mother is deathly ill."

"All right Rae. The Concorde leaves around noon in the morning. Find out what time it lands at Idlewild and line a Lear Jet up to bring me straight to LA."

"Idlewild?"

"I meant JFK. I'm still asleep. What time is it on the coast?"

"It's a little after seven in the evening, Dad. Mother drifted off an hour ago. I called Dr. Max. He's here and says it is just a matter of days if not hours."

"Rae, let me speak with him, please," O'Reith said.

When he heard the doctor's voice, he asked, "End of the line, Max?"

"Looks like it Clive. Nothing else we can do. All of her bodily functions are shutting down. Pulse is too weak to find. She's barely breathing."

"I'll be there sometime tomorrow."

Maxine said nothing. She led him back to bed. Then she began to pack a suitcase for him. She let him sleep, checking up on him from time to time. He was tumbling and tossing. Finally at nine o'clock in the morning she called him to breakfast. With little appetite, she knew that his thoughts were far away, across the wide Atlantic. When he finished eating and poured himself a cup of coffee, she said rather timidly, "Silver, I know how difficult this is for you. Would you like for me to go with you? You know how shy I am. I feel so out of place... But I will come if you wish me to."

"Maxine this is going to be a bad scene. No getting around it. As much as I would like your company, we would not be together often. Better for you to remain here. I'll get through it as quick as I can and be back before you know it."

She rode with him to Charles de Gaulle. As they approached the departure entrance she said, "The garden is in ruins. I let it go to seed these last few months. Starting this afternoon I'll begin cleaning the weeds out. By the time you return, it will be neat and tidy and the fruit trees will be pruned and we will be all ready for spring." Her voice was failing her and tears rose in her eyes. O'Reith kissed her, picked up his small bag and let the chauffeur help him out. He didn't look back.

He'd be in the air about ten hours; three and a half across the Atlantic by Concorde and then another six in the Lear Jet. If the Concorde was on time and departed at straight up noon, he would arrive in Los Angeles in the early afternoon. He assumed that someone would meet him. The plane zoomed off on schedule and when the stewardess came around with champagne, he asked her for a dry martini. He had long ago stopped drinking during the day but today was different. Shortly after he downed his drink, lunch was served. Persian caviar to start was followed by a langoustine in tomato and basil sauce, sautéed breast of chicken with morel mushrooms and white rice with Artichoke hearts on the side. He finished up with mango slices in lime juice and a cup of coffee. He began to nod and slept until the captain announced they would be landing. As he cleared Customs and Immigration he saw his name held aloft by an uniformed man wearing a cap with a pair of wings on the crown. O'Reith approached him and the thick-necked, stocky man said, "General O'Reith, "I'm Nick Lepage, your cabin attendant for the flight to Los Angeles. If you'll follow me, we'll be in the air in fifteen minutes."

Rae Regan met him at LAX and together they rode to Long Beach. It was almost three o'clock in the afternoon. For the first several minutes they were silent. Finally Rae Regan said, "Daddy, she died about four hours after I telephoned. She had been in anguish for several hours and Dr. Max had given her a shot of morphine. It didn't do much good. So we were up with her and he said, 'Rae I'm going to give your mother another shot, stronger this time. You should call your father.' And so I did."

"Funeral lined up?" O'Reith asked.

"Wednesday at the Angelus Temple."

"Jesus! Jesus H. Christ!" O'Reith exclaimed.

"Daddy, there will be a big crowd. The temple has seats for 5,300 people. They'll overflow into the streets."

"Yeah I know. I guess it has to be. Were you able to find George?"

"I called Carolyn. She said she would find him and that they would arrive together. He telephoned later and asked me to make arrangements for him to deliver the funereal oration. So I called Rolf McPherson. He graciously agreed. He said it would be the first occasion where a Roman Catholic clergyman spoke from the stage of the temple. Daddy those Pentecostal singers are going to be the choir at the service. Mother wanted that."

"It's OK by me. How's Max doing?"

"OK. Like the rest of us. Out of it. He's home, resting up. The last couple of days..."

"Who will we find at home, Rae?"

"Alice is there. Helen Simpson. And Mr. Blake."

"Vince is in town?"

"He called this morning. He wanted to know when you would arrive. He'll say hello and then return to San Bernardino this evening. Virginia is not well. He offered to help out with the arrangements. Said it was the least he could do. I thanked him. Told him we were all set."

"Rae, I want to stop by the Fullerton Building. I need a shower and a change of clothing. Where is Sharon?"

"Home. Like the rest of us, she's been through the wringer."

"Well I can't see anybody without getting my face fixed. While I shower, will you call her and ask her to come. I know it is an imposition..."

"Daddy, you're so vain. Mother was vain too. Must be a reason for it."

"Rae, in this town if you don't look good, you're no good."

The hot shower and a change of clothes elevated his spirits. He called Maxine to let her know of his safe arrival and told her of the arrangements. He promised to be in the air on Thursday morning headed east. Mills rode with them to Long Beach and the three of them took the elevator up to the penthouse. Helen Simpson had tied a wisp of black crepe around the door know. Inside he found her weeping. He kissed and embraced her; kissed Alice and then turned to Blake. He said, "Vince thanks for coming. I'm glad to see you even if I'm non compos mentis from all that travel."

Blake was 77. When he and O'Reith worked together at Calitroleum, he was a hefty two hundred pounder with a wide, gruff, and often menacing face to accompany his apoplectic method of operation. He was much thinner now and had a slight, but perceptible cough. He was bald on top with a ragged fringe of wispy white hair. Blake had on a black suit that fit him loosely, white cotton shirt with French cuffs and ivory cuff links. His shoes were black and highly polished. O'Reith sized the older man up quickly, noted his nicotine stained fingers and concluded that he, like his wife Virginia, was ailing. Blake said, "It is good to see you again Clive. It has been a few years. How's Maxine?"

"She's fine, Vince. She's working the garden. She said she was too shy for this trip. I didn't press her. Rae said Virginia was under the weather."

"She's in the Cedars of Lebanon in San Bernardino, Clive. She's lost weight. The prognosis is just fair."

O'Reith nodded, said nothing but looked steadily at his friend while holding his hand. Both men's eyes were filled with tears. Some say that grief is a universal emotion and that everyone, that is everyone not psychopathic, feels it more or less the same way. But for men like Blake and O'Reith, men whose lives had been lived in danger's terrible and constant shadow, grief was mostly a collective memory of companions, employees and colleagues that had been killed or died in the line of duty. Even today, the memory of the falling derrick man, flailing helplessly as he burned up in the flames of the Holly No.1 haunted O'Reith's dreams. And from the war, there was a long list of men he'd flown with that did not return; a few of them killed sitting beside him in the cockpit of a B-17. Blake, could count more than a dozen men whom he had seen die in fires, blowouts and crown accidents.

After a while, O'Reith looked into Blake's eyes and said hoarsely, "String running out, Babe."

Blake nodded, said nothing.

The minutes and the hours had slipped away and the cocktail hour was nigh. The cadaverous, lantern-jawed butler sloped in as unobtrusively as he could. Looking at O'Reith, he asked, "Will you ladies and gentlemen be having refreshments?"

"Yes Oliver, roll in the trolley. A double martini for me. On the rocks with a twist." He turned to Blake and asked, "Vince?"

"Yeah. The same."

It was high noon of Wednesday, October 4. The mourners were gathered at the Angelus Temple across from Echo Park. O'Reith, family and friends, entering through a side entrance, occupied the first row of seats in the huge, circular auditorium with its tall dome. As predicted, it was a sellout. Helen's black coffin rested on a flower-covered bier, flanked by a dozen tall candles. From the pipes of the enormous organ came a mournful, muted rendition of '*Let me Cross the River Jordan, Lord*'. O'Reith sat, Rae Regan on one side and his son Clive Colin on the other. For a reason unknown, his mind brought up a memory. It was the summer of 1945. He was readying the VIIIth Far Eastern Air Force for movement to Tinian Island. He and Helen had flown up to New York from Bolling Field for the weekend. They were second honeymooning in the ballroom of the Waldorf Astoria. Xavier Cugat was leading his band and Abbe Lane was singing *The Breeze and I.* Indistinctly the lyrics came to him; "Ours was a love song that seemed constant as the moon...ending in a strange mournful tune". Near tears, somehow, through the grace of God he pulled himself together and maintained his composure. The organ's tones faded away. The lights under the dome were dimmed until a single spot shone on the bier.

Over the pastor's dais, a goose neck lamp illuminated the prayer book stand. Breviary in hand, McDonough in surplice and alb, wearing a red skullcap, came under the soft glow. He began:

> Ladies and Gentlemen, we are gathered here this day to pay our final respects to a grand actress, loving mother and dedicated wife. Helen Huntington Simpson O'Reith was every woman's woman. She was the Airwac in *Women at War*. She was Stella the battered wife in *Neon Lights*. She was Lily Langtry in *Pecos Lil*. And in the *Golden Lane* she was Lady Talbot. Helen O'Reith was Rosie O'Grady and the colonel's lady. Indeed, she was the general's lady and she stood by his side from the day he became a skinny lieutenant until he became what she called 'a round general'.
>
> When we go to see a motion picture, we expect to be entertained. How are we entertained? If it is a good movie, we quickly fall into the role of the hero or the heroine, carrying that persona out of the cinema and being it for hours until our worldly duties call us back to drab reality. Even a boy, who has seen a Western Movie, comes out wearing a white hat, ready for a game of Cowboys and Indians. My own experience in life leads me to believe that in every heart there is a strong desire to be someone else. No man, no woman, on this earth, is satisfied with the character, which God hath bestowed. We want to have an alias, be someone more beautiful, richer, more powerful. Each of us hopes for our fifteen minutes of fame. Plain girls dream of being fetching beauties. Ugly men imagine themselves as dashing, handsome heroes. In the dark of the movie theater, such dreams come true. Now our grand actress, our heroine of the 20th Century has crossed over to paradise where she must now star in movies where only angels tread the boards."

McDonough's face was now puffy and tear-streaked. His voice was becoming faint. He grasped the podium for support. Then pulling himself together, he began again.

He continued:

> "A decade ago we were dining in the Prince DeGalle in Paris. It was a celebratory occasion. Helen had flown from Hollywood. Several of us were sitting around the table and I said, when she

entered, 'Lo now comes the beauteous sylph from across the wide Atlantic'. Her husband, the general, looked across at me, smiled and said, 'George. She is all that, indeed, but for me, she is the girl from the other side of the mountain.' "And so she is. Fellow mourners, today the bell knells for Helen O'Reith. It will toll again tomorrow for thee and for me."

McDonough was visibly spent. He was trembling. His heavy trappings were wearing him down. His voice was gone. Instead of tears, his face was awash in perspiration and as he attempted to wipe his brow, he staggered, at the point of collapse. As if by magic, Carolyn and a matronly Sally Prescott appeared at his side and helped him out of the pulpit and off of the stage.

O'Reith had planned to go from the Angelus Temple directly to the airport. Seeing Sally Prescott, he realized he would have to speak to her. He rose, caned his way to the wooden steps leading to the stage. Upon it, he went across to the door through which McDonough had been escorted. Sally saw him right away and she was in his arms. She had been his friend and secretary for many long years. They spoke together for quite some long time. A refreshed McDonough joined them. When the visit was over, McDonough said, "Clive, I have to hot foot it back to Rome. When are you traveling?"

"I was going to New York today but after the long visit with Sally, I think I'll wait until tomorrow. Besides I have to confer with Stan. Estate matters. Would you two like to join Helen Simpson and I for lunch in Long Beach?"

"That is kind of you," McDonough said. "Carolyn?"

She nodded her assent and they left the temple. A Nile green Chrysler Imperial limousine was at the curb, engine purring. O'Reith said, "So that explains it. I saw that car in the tower garage and wondered about it. It's the Colonel's car, the gift from Nixon."

"Yes, I bootlegged it out of Guatemala City on one of those huge transport planes the Signal Corps sent down for Nixon's atonement address. I told the government man that it was Nixon's car, a bit of a little white lie if I do admit it. I'm going to have it sent on to Rome."

After lunch, Cook and McDonough returned to Los Angeles. The penthouse apartment was deathly silent. The doctors and the nurses were gone. Ridley and Mills were not there. It was the butler's day off.

The maid had gone for the afternoon. Helen Simpson faced her father in the parlor. O'Reith sensed that she was distressed. "What's the matter, sweets?" he asked.

"Daddy Cool, while we were in the temple, Brother suggested that I move to the Summit Street bungalow. He and Ellen Mae would like to move in here."

O'Reith smiled. "That's an easy one," he said picking up the telephone. He dialed his son's number and when he heard his voice, he began," Son, it is in times like these that we have to sort our legal matters. I've read your mother's will. She had the same idea as I about estate distribution. As her executor, I am quit-claiming the Summit Street property to you. Rae Regan will get the Holmby Hills place and Helen Simpson will get this place."

"Dad! That is not fair. I should come before her. Ellen Mae and I want to live there. Helen Simpson can move to this run-down address."

"Son it is settled. Helen Simpson considers this to be her home and I agree. You are hardly a pauper. Your mother left you a large inheritance. Stan Ethering will be calling you this afternoon. He will bring the documents you need. If Summit Street is seedy, fix it up or move out."

"What about your den, Dad?"

"The movers will be around tomorrow to move my things to the Fullerton Building. Do with it as you please."

"When are you leaving Dad?"

"Tomorrow son, George and I are returning to Europe. You know how to reach me." O'Reith hung up, looked at his daughter and asked, "How's that?"

She came over, sat in his lap teary-eyed, embraced and kissed him.

It was early on Thursday morning, October 5th, the day after Helen's funeral and the seventh day of mourning for the late Pope John Paul. McDonough, Cook and O'Reith, in the cabin of the Lear Jet were strapped in for the takeoff. McDonough was saying, "Clive I have to be in Rome for the weekend. Deliberations will begin next Monday."

"No sweat George, O'Reith answered. "We're booked on the Concorde out of New York. It gets into Paris around midnight tonight. You'll be home on Friday."

"Clive, do you remember Nicholas Breakspeare?"

"Vaguely. He was a tout at Santa Anita. Jailed for a doping incident."

"Clive, for shame! Breakspeare was Pope Hadrian IV."

"Oh! Must be a different guy. So what about him?"

"He was the only English Pope. I expect to be the second. I've picked the name Hadrian VI."

"Lotsa luck, George."

And so on October 11, 1978 while the Sacred College of Cardinals in Rome was deliberating, getting ready to go into conclave to find a successor to Pope John Paul, Richard Milhous Nixon became the first Deputy Shah on record. Colonel Marcos Pérez Jiménez was appointed bashaw and became the first South American to head up the notorious SAVAK. O'Reith, in Paris with Maxine, was struggling to come to grips with the great change in his life. He had no news from McDonough. He didn't have a clue as to who the new Pope might be. He didn't care either.

During the first few days of October, students began rioting at the University of Teheran. Looters set the British Embassy afire. The Oil Company headquarters was under siege. It was rumored that the former SAVAK chief was behind these events. Nixon asked the Colonel to look into it.

On October 16, around ten o'clock in the evening, McDonough telephoned O'Reith from Rome. He was sobbing and was clearly crushed. He muttered, "*Habemus papam*, Clive."

"And I can tell from the tone of your voice that it is not you," O'Reith said mercilessly.

"I always wonder how you can be so cruel," McDonough moaned.

"It's the times, George. Since Helen passed away, I can't seem to get into a normal frame of mind. I say the first thing that comes to me. Forgive me. Nevertheless George, I must be candid with you. I am quite pleased that you did not become the Pope. You would have been an abject failure."

"The College of Cardinals obviously came to the same conclusion," McDonough muttered.

"Why don't you and Carolyn hop a jet and come to Paris. Maxine and Carolyn will see us through this difficult period of bereavement, if that is the proper word."

"Well it is not," McDonough moaned. "All Roman Catholics must rejoice in the selection of a new spiritual leader. And though we mourn

Helen's removal from this earth, we rejoice in the knowledge that she is with Him. It is just that I am overwhelmed by the dolorous succession of deaths. Paul VI. John Paul. Mikoyan at death's door, Helen. I am stunned."

"All of them Christians too, George. Pack your bag again and come see us. Some good Paris cooking and vintage wine and we'll both see things through rosier glasses. We let the clock run. Time heals all wounds, they say. Besides we have a lot going on. We need to talk about that pipeline."

McDonough's voice became cheerier. He said, "We will come tomorrow, Clive."

"We'll meet you at the airport," O'Reith said.

After an early dinner, Maxine was showing Cook the Japanese lanterns she had installed in the garden below. McDonough in the downstairs den with O'Reith, was praising the choral performance of the New Hope Pomona College Pentecostal Minstrels. He wanted to do something for them. He began, "I wish they were here tonight. I wish we could hear them sing those spirituals again; such mournful, moving music."

O'Reith nodded.

The two men sat saying nothing, looking nowhere in particular. O'Reith saw that McDonough had something serious on his mind. He asked, "George, what is it?"

McDonough wore a long, sober, reflective face. He began, "Clive I am finished. Washed up. On the morning of the 17th with the ashes of his election still smoldering, the Pole's nuncio telephoned me, a brisk summons delivered with grave formality. I was to appear at the appointed hour at the Pope's office. I was given no options about the hour or the date. The nuncio, a pip-squeak of a Croatian monsignor met me promptly at eleven o'clock and showed me to his small, ornate office decorated with papal reliquary. He told me that the Pole had read my dossier and he was displeased with what he saw. Then he opened a manila folder and read out a litany of what he called interference with ecclesiastic matters. Much of them had to do with the late Girolo and his idiot nephew. The Pole wanted me out of Italy before his coronation. Can you imagine that, Clive! A man from Poland evicts me from my adopted homeland! He desired that I sell my villa on Lago Albano.

Immediately! He gave me thirty days. He said if it were not sold by then, the Vatican would buy it and convert it into a home for aged cardinals. He advised me that the lock on my Vatican flat had been changed and that my chattels would be packed and sent to any destination I selected. Can you imagine Clive; I furnished that tiny place with artistic curios from around the world. Now some lowly Italian clods will handle those artifacts with grimy, garlic-smelling hands. In what condition will I find them when once again they fall under the vision of my eyes? The Pole also wanted Carolyn out of the country. He demanded, mind you, demanded that I cease and desist all further participation by my humble self in affairs of the Church. To put it mildly, I was dumbfounded. After all, I was one of the three tellers at his election. I gathered into these hands that you see before you the scraps of paper with Karol Wojtyla written on them. In my small way, I contributed to his victory."

"Did you vote for him, George?" O'Reith asked, archly.

"I did on the 7th and final ballot," McDonough said, almost smiling.

"Was the handwriting on the wall, George?"

McDonough shrugged. His face became contemplative. He let out a long, audible sigh, said "Well it was. Of course."

O'Reith laughed. He said, "Well, you were not excommunicated. That's something."

McDonough's face became judgmental and some of the fire returned to his yellow eyes. "Aye, lad but the implication was clear."

"So you have been sacked. Railroaded out. I never thought that Rome was worth a mass. Paris perhaps, but not Rome. You are a wealthy man with a splendid companion, no quirkier than yourself. You are still a power in British Military Intelligence and in the Soviet Union. George, the world is full of work for you. Accept it. You can deed your villa over to the Company. It will be there when you want it. They can't keep you from visiting. Since they booted you out of Rome, where do you plan to set up shop?"

"London, of course. Where else could I go?"

"That's a good choice. George," O'Reith continued. "Well, sir. We have extraordinary problems in Persia. We need to check up on our management team. See how they are coping. Are you ready for a trip to Teheran?"

"I have no other business on my calendar."

They planned their trip for Monday, October 23 but on the Saturday before, Mikoyan died in Moscow. Armand Hammer in Los Angeles telephoned O'Reith in Paris. He and Frank Ashley planned to attend the funeral. They were traveling by Lear Jet and had room for two passengers. Hammer agreed to stop in Rome for McDonough and Cook. En-route to Moscow, they could discuss the progress of the Trans-Asiatic Pipeline.

On November 5, 1978, the Colonel arrested the former SAVAK chief and had him shot in Evin prison. But that settled nothing. Persia remained in a state of turmoil and people were being killed with astonishing regularity not only by the Shah's soldiers but also by the religious groups that were solidifying their positions on a daily basis. The oilmen put off their trip until things settled. A Kurdish Revolutionary Army had popped up out of nowhere and was causing trouble. Even the Bazaaris were in the act. Khomeini's return seemed certain. The Shah was of a mind to invite him back. His closest counselors advised him that such a move would be disastrous. Nixon was dead set against it. The Colonel wanted Khomeini to be brought back from France in a box on board an Iran Air Boeing 747. Then by truck to Evin Prison and once there, the Ayatollah, as he was called, could be shot in one of the soundproof cells below ground level. The Shah, turning virtuous in his declining years, snorted at the idea and waved him away from that dangerous subject. Khomeini remained a threat. Curiously, the Shah and his deputy, RMN became fond of one another and the Shah, more and more, delegated to him tasks that he considered unpleasant. Nixon, whose motto was, famously, 'When the going gets tough, the tough get going' grasped those tasks. The Shah's revered White Revolution was rapidly unraveling.

Both the Shah and Nixon believed that the constant application of pressure would calm the noisy hordes that flocked the streets of Teheran almost every night. But such was not the case. By mid-December, matters were in a bad way both in Teheran and in the southern oil fields. The acting manager of the Oil Company, one Paul Grimm, a Texas Company man was shot down and killed in his car while on the way to his Ahwaz office. Immediately, all oil field operations ceased. Wells were shut in. Drilling rigs stopped work. Barricades blocked traffic everywhere. Plans were made for the immediate repatriation of American and European employees. Consternation reigned among the many Persian and Pakistani employees whose jobs stopped. When December 31 rolled around, there would be no paymaster and thus no payroll.

O'Reith was in Paris on December 11th when Ridley telephoned. Ed Wood, Jr. had passed away. Under terms of the sales contract, his death triggered a clause giving Helen O'Reith the option of buying back the *White Satin Miter.* Since he was the executor of her estate, Ridley wanted to know what to do. He told her to buy the movie back and take it out of distribution.

Trevelyen met them at Mehrabad on the evening of December 20th[th] in a Rolls-Royce limousine with bulletproof doors and windows, escorted by a platoon of Gurkhas from Ahwaz in Oil Company pickups. Slowly, they made their way to the Hotel Caspien through streets full of noisy rioters. Roman candles pierced the night sky. Cherry bombs were exploding everywhere. The front windows of the Caspien were boarded up. The Gurkhas forcibly pushed people out of the street. The big car rolled along in low gear at five miles per hour. At the hotel, Gurkhas stood guard through the night. From the roof, having a nightcap in the garden, O'Reith and McDonough gazed down on the bedlam in Takte-Jamshid below. Neon signs in Farsi were winking and blinking above the hordes moving like aroused ants. The din was deafening. They were praying, chanting, singing and shouting. It was an insane asylum of the streets.

Next morning at ten o'clock, Trevelyen returned for them. Again Gurkha escorted, they inched their way through moiling masses to Golestan Palace at 15 Khordad Square in front of the Ark Mosque.

O'Reith hoped they could get their business done in a day or two because he wanted to spend the holidays with Maxine, Monique, her husband and their daughter, Veronique-Claire.

They found Deputy Shah Richard M. Nixon occupying the tall, bejeweled Peacock Throne in the formal reception chamber. But he was not dressed in white finery. He wore a dark blue business suit with the flag of the U.S. on one lapel and the Red Lion of Iran on the other. Although freshly shaven, his jaw appeared in a bluish cast from the stubble of his gray-black whiskers. His eyes were keen and piercing and his features were set in an iron grimace. He said, "Fellows, things don't look too good."

"Where is Shah?" McDonough asked.

"Upstairs, sedated," Nixon answered. "He is trembling from his palsy or whatever it is he's got. Nurses attending him. I think he is ready to leave the country. He needs expert medical attention, which he cannot get here. He should be in Geneva."

"Think you can take over as full Shah?" Trevelyen asked.

"I'm ready for it," Nixon answered gravely. "We have to turn this situation around quickly or it is keeno for the Peacock Throne. The Huns are at the gate."

"Can we rely on the Shah's pilots to get him out of here? Are they still loyal?" O'Reith asked.

"I think so," Nixon answered. "Clive, I want to say that I share your grief for Helen..."

"It was inevitable Mr. President. I thank you for your kind words."

"Shah travels in a Boeing 727 doesn't he?" McDonough asked.

"Yeah. He likes to drive it himself but he's definitely not up to it right now," Nixon continued.

"Well, he needs to get out while the getting is good," O'Reith said.

"I'll ask his nurses to prepare him for an audience tomorrow," Nixon continued. You fellows can explain the gravity of the situation. You may be able to persuade him to leave. I can't. He would suspect me of usurpation."

"Where is the Colonel?" O'Reith asked.

"Ahwaz. He is in the process of liquidating or placing in durance vile those Arabs suspected of killing Paul Grimm."

"He is well protected?" O'Reith asked.

"Army armored regiment. Tanks. Bazookas. The Works. He called in this morning. He said he had shot about 50 of the offenders. He's got another 50 or so lined up for imprisonment in Abadan," Nixon went on.

"Abadan!" Trevelyen exclaimed. "That my friend is one terrible place of incarceration. The prison consists of holes in the ground with iron grills over the top. No sanitation. No food unless you have a friend that brings it. A clean-up coolie appears every three or four days to shovel accumulated excrement out of the hole but only if he's paid. In the summer time, the temperature exceeds 135° F. A prisoner is only good for two or three days. This time of the year I suppose it is not too bad in that regard but it gets cold at night. The Shah set that up especially for drug dealers. It is not intended for other types of prisoners. It is usually full. What's the Colonel going to do? Put two men in each hole?"

Nixon said. "The Shah describes it as a model prison. But then I doubt if he's ever seen it."

"The Colonel holding up OK?" O'Reith asked.

Nixon laughed. "He is in his element. He brought in a couple of dozen of his Tachiristas. He told me over the telephone this morning that when he returned to Teheran, he expected to find a throng of screaming fuzzy-wuzzies in Evin Prison. He said they all need to be shot. He is definitely the kind of guy you need to deal with an off-the-wall situation like we have here today. I'd never make it without him."

O'Reith asked, "With the Colonel's help, how long can you hold it together?"

"Indefinitely," Nixon said grinning. "One thing is for sure. There is no shortage of ammunition here and no shortage of people to use it on."

"We always have to consider losing it," O'Reith said. "Since November, Father George and I have been working against the clock to build a pipeline from Poghdar to Vladivostok. We have clearances from the Soviet Government. Two Russian pipeline spreads complete with back-hoes; bulldozers and drag lines are working out of Omsk. The Pearson Syndicate is offloading equipment at Khoramshahr as we speak. I assume the Colonel has troops there to escort them north. An M.W. Kellogg spread crossed the Pacific from San Francisco last week. They offloaded at Vladivostok. Men and equipment, even now, are traveling across the USSR by way of the Trans-Siberian Railroad. Mikoyan Sovietsky Machino is rolling steel on a 24-hr/day basis. Costain Construction out of the UK and Houston Contracting out of Texas are mobilizing. The several spreads working night and day should have that 4,000-mile pipeline completed no later than June 30, 1979. Once that pipeline opens, as far as we are concerned, Persia can go down the tube. Gurkha troops in Khuzestan can guard the oil fields but the rest of it is finito. When that happens, you will take over as Sultan of Poghdar with the Colonel as your deputy. But make no mistake about it, holding this place together until then will test your mettle."

"Piece of cake, General O'Reith," Nixon said, smiling broadly. "The Colonel and I will keep the doors open. What kind of a place is Poghdar?"

"Desert country. Reminds me of the San Joaquin. Right now it is primitive but once we get organized we will build you a palace as grand as this one."

"That sounds fabulous. May I tell the Colonel of those plans?"

"By all means," O'Reith said. "When will he be back in town?"

"Toward the end of the week. He wants to make sure every thing is clicking along OK down south."

"Who is holding down the SAVAK fort here in Teheran?" O'Reith asked.

Nixon said, "Colonel has a couple of helpers. Weird guys if you ask me. One of them is a Major Flaco Graffitto, a fat, avuncular, round-faced guy with yellowish skin. He's a cross between Charlie Chan and Oliver Hardy, complete with black mustache, dyed, I think. He grins all the time and they say he is as dangerous as a snake. Other one is Captain Anthony Anthrax, a thin guy with a long chin and tiny reptilian eyes who resembles Stan Laurel. He grins a lot too. Both of them make my flesh crawl. I assume their names are noms de guerre. No mother would give their children names like that. Would you like to meet them?"

"Some other time. I vaguely remember Anthrax. He came in to see the Colonel one night in Guatemala City. Colonel described him as his 'night man' in the secret police. A scary guy from any angle you looked at him. I knew he had a 'daylights' guy too. That one must be Graffitto. He's had those birds for some years," O'Reith said. "They're Orinoco River rats. My younger daughters would call them 'heavy dudes'. I don't remember anymore what Anthrax looks like. I don't want either of them to know what I look like."

Nixon continued, "He has another creepy guy too who is with him in Ahwaz; a Captain Teddy Taupe. He looks a bit like Peter Lorré, except he has a roving glass eye. He lisps and carries a Luger equipped with a silencer. He likes to play with it, aim it at pictures on the walls, things like that. Could be a bit of a psychopath. The Colonel told me that he was the illegitimate half-brother of Pedro Estrada. Do you remember him? He was head of *Seguridad Nacional*."

"I remember them both. Estrada was then and is today, wherever he is, extremely dangerous. Taupe had a different name then and I can't remember it. He used to hang around the Mara Bar in the Hotel Del Lago in Maracaibo with a .25 Beretta tucked rather obviously into his belt. We were then getting acquainted with the Caudillo. He was holding up the publication of our *Lago Poniente* Concessions in the official gazette. Taupe was tailing one of his men who worked in the *Ministerio de Hidrocarburos*. Colonel didn't trust him." O'Reith lamented. "Maxine knows him too," he suddenly remembered. "And Mandy Macabra."

"The woman who helped the Colonel while he was in stir?" Nixon asked.

"Yeah. She ran this girlie joint downtown," O'Reith explained. "Pretty high class place for the time. The name of it was *El Techo Rojo*. Teddy Taupe lost his eye there in a brawl with one of the girls. A red-hot Colombiana from Tibu took a frog-sticker to him. Hell of a good-looking piece. I used to know her name. But I've forgotten it. Memory is shot. Could have been Maribel. Taupe is a lucky guy. She could have taken out his appendix by way of his esophagus."

They all laughed at the gallows humor.

Nixon suddenly smiled broadly and a light came into his dark eyes. He said, "Say fellows, before I forget. I have some of those Guatemalan Nanonotes in my briefcase. Remember the NanoNixons and the NanoLatrobes?"

O'Reith laughed. "Yeah, how do they look?"

"Great," Nixon replied. "While we were at it, we printed up some NanoJiménez notes too." He reached into the briefcase leaning next to the huge desk and brought up an envelope. From it he took out the bills, gave a set to O'Reith, another to McDonough and a third to Trevelyen. He asked, "What do you think?"

O'Reith said, "Two Nanoquetzales! A deuce note. Well the Colonel really looks good. And you do too Mr. President on that fiver."

"Yes I agree. But Heavy looks odd on that trey ball note. With no photo, we used a snapshot I took several years ago. He was not as heavy then. The Nanonote does not do him justice. Still we honored him. It's the spirit that counts. I sent several of the bills to his sisters. I hope they recognize him."

Next morning at ten o'clock on December 22, 1978 the Shah, in white occupied the throne, which yesterday had been occupied by his deputy. O'Reith looked him over carefully as the three oilmen and

Nixon were greeted and shown their seats. The Shah was pale. His hands trembled beneath the white tunic that he had spread across his middle. His widow's peak had greatly receded. There was no fire in his eyes and he was listless, as if in a hurry to get this interview over with. McDonough began, "Ah Shah. We've just been having a word with your medical staff and they are recommending a new treatment that has just become available. It appears to be just what you need. Of course you'd have to go to Geneva for it."

"For how long, Sir George?" the Shah asked weakly adding, "I am needed by my people. The White Revolution is faltering. My people require my steadfast leadership." Then he turned to O'Reith. "I share your grief, General O'Reith. Although I never met your wife I have seen her often on the silver screen and I feel as if I know her."

"I thank you for that, your Imperial Highness. We have difficulty understanding the ways of the Almighty. Her suffering ended, she dwells in a happier place."

"That is a good way to put it," the Shah said.

"Excellency," McDonough, eager to press ahead, continued, "We would expect you to be gone for quite some long indefinite time. But you need not worry about the Peacock Throne. Your deputy, Richard M. Nixon will attend every problem, every complication that arises. And Colonel Jiménez competently assists him. Shah, you have to face up to it. The White Revolution has gone a glimmering. Not to return. Ever. Still, you are not gone. You can fly to Geneva confident that when you return, all will be well and you will be greeted with cheers by what few of your loyal subjects are still around."

"I didn't sleep a wink last night," the Shah muttered. "Those hordes howled and wailed from sun down to sun up. Listen, they're still at it. I may not want to return. If that madman Khomeini is here, I'll be greeted by a firing squad," the Shah lamented, shaking his head in despair. "Gentlemen, I know that your intentions are good but this place is coming apart. The White Revolution is a dead letter. Without my personal attention, my deft and sure hand, it cannot be revived."

"Shah, it cannot be saved. We must find a new formula for governance. The oil alone..." McDonough continued.

The Shah interrupted. "You can forget the oil. Once the wells are shut in, those crazies will keep them shut in until we run out of money and Teheran starves to death. You gentlemen underestimate the insidious nature of the threat. This insane mullah Khomeini has poisoned the minds of the faithful. They are blind to the prosperity that I have created for them. They think that they will go on forever with great felicity in a so-called Islamic Republic. I tell you sirs, they are dead wrong. That man Khomeini plans to bring the entire structure down in ruins. If the people in Khuzestan get wind that I am out of the country for a month, particularly those QashQai tribes around Bebehan and Isphahan, they will go totally berserk. Neither the army nor the secret police will be able to control them. What I need and need immediately are American and British troops to patrol the streets 24 hours per day. But what I got is a message from POTUS James Earl Carter suggesting, more than that, urging me to set up a constitutional monarchy. What folly?"

"Shah, you are unduly alarmed," McDonough said in his softest, most soothing voice. "Surely that mullah would not put the cat among the pigeons. He has too much to lose."

The Shah looked at him with disdain. He said, "That shows how little you know about fanatics. Sir George, recall the experience of General Charles 'Chinese' Gordon with the fuzzy-wuzzies in the Khartoum." He let out a long mournful sigh and continued, "Oh, I'll go. I can leave tomorrow if that suits you. But things will not get better. Mark my words."

"No need for you to go tomorrow, Shah," McDonough said in a soothing manner. "But soon. Rest up. Advise your staff in Switzerland that you will be coming for treatment. Think in terms of leaving right after the New Year.

The Shah consulted his calendar. He studied it for several minutes and then said, "Very well, gentlemen. I have several chores to complete but I will depart on the 16th of January. He rang a small bell and his secretary appeared with notepad in hand for dictation.

The Shah began:

Dear POTUS Carter:

I have studied your message of recent date and I take your sagacious advice. I am today preparing a *firman, which* will establish a constitutional monarchy for Iran. In it I name the distinguished minister, Mr. Shahpur Baktiar as Chairman of the Temporary

Regency Council. This *firman* will be presented to the Majlis in the next day or two for ratification and I will announce it as an imperial edict before the end of December. Additionally I advise you that I plan to depart Teheran on January 16th for Geneva where I will undergo treatment for my distressing illness. During my absence, which will last for several months, Deputy Shah Richard Milhous Nixon will be in charge of all governmental affairs. The Temporary Regency Council will report to him and you may look to him for protection of American interests in my beloved country.

With fondest regards, respect and admiration I remain

Mohammed Reza Pahlavi Shahanshah of the Imperial Throne of Iran.

Teheran
December 22, 1978

"Well written Shah," McDonough said enthusiastically.

"Yes, I agree," O'Reith said rising and offering his hand.

"Short and to the point," Trevelyen added.

The Shah addressed his hovering, unscrupulous-looking, yellow-toothed secretary. He said, "Haroon, please call the American Embassy. Ask for a copy of the American Constitution. When you have it, rewrite it to conform to our circumstances. Translate it into both Farsi and Arabic. When that is complete, and I wish it done today, draft a *firman* of execution and I will sign it."

The secretary nodded and departed.

McDonough asked, "Will you have a problem with Majlis? Will they ratify it?"

"They are all in hiding," the Shah said. "They are worried that they will be shot by those howling mullahs. It really doesn't matter. I will issue it as an imperial edict. Deputy Shah Nixon can attend to the application of it. It should be easy for him. It is a carbon copy of what he knows about already."

"Just as you say, Shah," McDonough said.

As planned, the Shah departed for Geneva on the 16th of January. Until January 31st, Teheran was tumultuous but manageable. Deputy Shah Nixon ably assisted by the Colonel who was shooting troublemakers by the thousands, thought he was bringing things under control. But then Ayatollah Khomeini descended from the ramp of an Air France 747 on February 1st. That day, the streets were filled to overflowing with hordes of screaming Muslims. Flagellating each other with small chains, the blood ran from their happy wounds. Anarchy reigned. With no small trepidation, Richard M. Nixon looked out the window at the weaving, waving, shouting multitudes. The Golestan Palace was protected by troops still more or less loyal to the Shah but Nixon had a feeling in the pit of his stomach that he could be in trouble. On his glass-topped desk was a stack of the newly issued green and yellow 5 thousand rial notes. One of the oriental-eyed, pigtailed tea boys had brought them in. Hot off the press, in place of the crowned Mohammed Reza Shah, these notes had a picture of a beaming Nixon wearing a red fez with a black tassel. When he authorized the printing of them, he thought it was one of his better ideas. Now he was not so sure. The bills had been placed in circulation that very morning. He didn't know how many were floating around out there where those crazies could get an idea of what he looked like. Suddenly he felt a little giddy. He needed a drink and sent for the gin bottle.

It was Mid-March of 1979 and O'Reith was back in Paris. Conferring daily with Cook in Omsk on the progress of the Poghdar to Vladivostok pipeline, his life was a series of phone calls and telex messages. Although there were many difficult river crossings and mountain tunneling, progress was steady. They could begin filling the line by April 1. Hamilton in San Francisco got a telex each morning advising him of the total welded joints as of the previous midnight. When the Oil Company ceased operating in November of 1978, the Poghdar to Gach Saran pipeline was shut down with the rest of the system. The Casinghead Company declared force majeure on the contract with Standard Oil. Two people, Clive O'Reith, and Bill Hamilton were ready to end that sorry state of affairs. So the April 1 expected date was critical. With 40 days to fill the line, Standard Oil could begin loading a tanker on May 10.

McDonough, commuting back and forth between Rome and Moscow, tidied up the documentation that would make Poghdar a Soviet Socialist Republic. With Mikoyan out of the picture, he relied on Occidental's Frank Ashley. The question of Russian 'honorary' citizenship for Nixon and the Colonel had to be resolved. Under existing law, all Poghdar functionaries had to be Soviet citizens. A bit of a flap arose because neither Flor Jiménez nor Pat Nixon wanted to become Russian citizens, even on an 'honorary' basis. In fact, since Pat Nixon's stroke in 1976, she hardly participated in affairs of state, preferring the seclusion of the Nixon apartment in the Waldorf Astoria. And Flor definitely preferred Madrid to a dusty, wind-swept tent-city on the Afghan plains. Other questions still needed to be resolved. For example, the Soviet Government wanted to put a transit tax on the crude flow. Standard Oil would put up with a lot to get the oil but it had to make economic sense.

Just as he was feeling good about the entire affair, O'Reith was jarred by a late night telephone call from Scotty Trevelyen in London. "Clive, bit of bad news. Richard M. Nixon and the Colonel are both in Evin prison, said to be in irons."

"Jesus Christ!" O'Reith exclaimed. "I had the idea that they were holding it together."

"Khomeini picked a guy by the name of Mehdi Bazargan to head up a provisional government," Trevelyen continued. "He stormed Golestan Palace with a horde of religious troops. They took Nixon and the Colonel prisoners. Bazargan says they will be tried and shot. The mullahs set up a Revolutionary Court. They've already shot 50 or 60 of the Shahs top dogs, generals and ministers and high poobahs. There is no doubt in my mind whatsoever that they mean what they say. Bazargan and Khomeini say they will proclaim Persia to be an Islamic Republic beginning April 1. An Islamic Revolutionary Council will replace the Majlis. Anyone disloyal to the new government will be executed out of hand."

O'Reith was silent for a few moments and then he said, "Well Scotty, we need those two in Poghdar. We must get them out and we have to be quick about it."

"Yes, I agree," Trevelyen responded, his voice rising nervously. "With the chaos in Teheran, we can probably spring them loose but we will have to act before they organize the police. I'll instruct Ahwaz to smuggle a battalion of Gurkhas into Teheran. They can come into town disguised. We still have good informants in both Ahwaz and Teheran. I will put it to Black Rod that we have to have a few officers. Majors or light colonels."

"Is George in the picture on this?" O'Reith asked.

"I have not called him yet."

"Let me do that, Scotty. We can stage out of Baku. George knows how to line that up. We'll meet you and your cadremen there. How do we enter Persia?"

"A disused RAF airstrip near the Howz-Sultan salt lake between Teheran and Gom has a 3,000 feet runway. Won't take a jet. The lake is twenty kilometers long. Should be easy to spot by moonlight. The airstrip was macadamized during the war but I can't say what it's like today. We'll fly over it at low altitude to check for ruts and obstructions."

"Scotty, in addition to the usual prison break-in equipment, what about cutting torches?" O'Reith asked. "We may have to cut our way through the main gate. If we can't get our hands on the keys to the cells, we'll have to cut the locks off. We won't be able to use explosives."

"I have driven past Evin," Trevelyen said. "It is a several story building occupying a square behind a high gray stone wall with watchtowers at each corner. It appears to have a large courtyard. The front gates are steel grill work. Our Gurkha commander in Ahwaz can hijack some Leyland oil well hookup trucks equipped with oxy-acetylene torches. Must be a couple of dozen of them in the Ahwaz motor pool. We once had an employee in there that reneged on an IOU to a merchant in the Bazaar. One of our men took meals in to keep him alive. I may be able to locate him. Possibly get inside for a look-see."

"That's a good idea," O'Reith said. "OK Scotty, when I get George on the line, I'll tell him to oil up his Webley-Fosberry .44. He's in the dumps since he lost two papal elections in a row. He needs a good fight to bring his spirits up."

Trevelyen laughed. "I can't say that I look forward to *that*. But it looks like we may have one on our hands. Might just as well get it over with."

"Scotty, what about bug spray?" O'Reith asked. "If the inside of that prison is anything like the pisser at Abadan Airport, it will be foul."

"That's an easy one. We'll have a case of it on board when we land at Baku. Anything else?"

O'Reith was pensive for a minute and then said, "Scotty, this is from instinct, I don't know exactly why but we may need an air compressor."

"Discharge hose?"

"Maybe five or six. Twenty or thirty feet long. When the Colonel was caught in the tunnel near Caracas, they threw him in a foul underground cell. We might face a similar problem at Evin."

"I'll take care of that, Clive".

"OK. See you in Baku."

As it turned out, the break-in of Evin Prison was relatively uncomplicated. Trevelyen's informant gave him the layout and described what they would find behind the walls. In the middle of the night, O'Reith, wearing distance glasses, in an army 'Goop Suit', lime green golf cap and combat boots, was armed with a .45 Colt automatic in a pistol belt. Under his right arm was a Thompson sub-machine gun. Unfortunately, even with glasses, his night vision was less than it had once been. He doubted if he could hit anything. McDonough was in black clerical garb, felt hat, and the only black Roman collar O'Reith had ever seen. On his feet were British Army regulation hob-nailed brogans. He carried his huge revolver in a webbed belt with the holster covering his family jewels. Under his right arm he had a Sten gun. Attached to his belt was a bag of potato mashers. Trevelyen and his seasoned Commando officers were similarly armed.

As the crow flies, from Baku to landfall at Rasht on the north coast of Persia is 450 kilometers and then to Qasvin, another 125. From there it is 75 kilometers to the disused airstrip near Soltanabad. The two Oil Company C-54 aircraft, flying by dead reckoning at 20,000 feet required two hours to make it. The raiding party arrived at the deserted airstrip around ten o'clock at night. A platoon of Gurkhas in Oil Company pickups was waiting for them with hook-up trucks and trailer mounted air compressors. Trevelyen's Kurdish driver came down from Teheran with the Zim limousine. The caravan drove north, headlights dimmed down. The only hitch was a roadblock set up where a bridge crossed a gully about 20 kilometers south of Teheran. A firefight followed in which several Persian mullahs were killed. None of the Gurkhas were hit. The two trucks blocking the bridge were dynamited and the caravan continued.

When the raiders arrived at Evin Prison, they found it surrounded by a second platoon of Gurkhas. The throats of the external guards were already cut. The interior guards in the cobble-stoned prison yard slept as the locks of the heavy steel gates were torched off. After the six massive hinges on the gates were copiously lubricated, they swung open silently. At the moment the gates opened, the watch tower sentinels, sleeping on their feet, were shot by marksmen. When the dazed, sleepy-eyed yard-guards saw the Gurkha's razor-sharp Kukri knives flashing in the moonlight, they put their hands up. Astonished guards inside the prison, rudely awakened by ferocious Gurkhas, were not interested in testing their knives.

Prison administration occupied the ground floor. Above were three stories of cells. On the second floor, the noses of the raiders were assailed by the commingled odor of stale sweat, urine and feces. The bailiff, eyes on a gleaming Kukri, readily turned over the keys. Trevelyen, three British army officers and a platoon of Gurkhas began a flashlight search of the cells, seeking Nixon and the Colonel. On the second floor, McDonough led a similar search party and O'Reith searched the cells of the top floor. In fifteen minutes all three floors had been searched without finding either man.

The frustrated oilmen and their search parties reunited on the ground floor. A Gurkha sergeant held a knife to the throat of the prison commandant. Lifting an arm, pointing to an expanded metal grate in the floor, the terrified man muttered in French, "les oubliettes". The meter square grate had a keyhole in one corner. Behind it on a peg in the gray wall, a foot-long brass key hung.

Once unlocked, the grate opened easily aided by a counterbalanced chain and pulley assembly. A nauseous, visible miasma met their noses. O'Reith exclaimed, "Jesus! Jesus H. Christ!" He jerked out his handkerchief, covered his nose, and said, "We need the air compressors to ventilate this place."

McDonough muttered "Egad!" and similarly covered his nose.

Trevelyen said, "Blimey!" and strode to the courtyard for a breath of fresh air. Within minutes the two air compressors were hooked up and as ventilation of the oubliettes began, a yellow-green miasma arose from the square hole.

Gurkhas pulled off their jackets and fanned the fumes away until the odor dissipated. O'Reith said, "Well fellows, like it or not, we've got to go down there." He beckoned. The Gurkha sergeant shone his flash down the hole. They began their descent down a steel ladder that disappeared into the gloom of the dungeon.

McDonough said, "Let's take the prison commandant down with us with a rope around his neck."

O'Reith nodded. The fettered commandant was trundled over to the hole. Clumsily, two Gurkhas, knives between teeth, escorted him down the ladder. Then two more Gurkhas with Sten guns went down. Then O'Reith followed by McDonough. Trevelyen stayed above to control the guards.

Once down, the party found themselves in a gallery twenty-five meters long and ten meters across, dimly lit by naked drop lights. Long-winged bats, hissing and drooling, ominously circled the bulbs in elliptical orbits. Squeaking sewer rats scurried along the dank floor. On their right was a row of small cells. The prison commandant pointed to a two-foot long key hanging from the wall. O'Reith saw it and immediately realized its significance. He said to the Gurkha sergeant, "Go up the ladder and ask Brigadier Trevelyen for the bug spray. Bring several cans."

When the soldier returned, from a distance O'Reith scanned the cells with a flashlight. He called out, "Mr. President, Colonel Jiménez, where are you?"

Ventilation had greatly improved the atmosphere in the dank prison cellar.

The two prisoners immediately identified themselves. O'Reith continued in a loud voice, "We're going to fumigate you before we unlock the cells. Hold your breath."

Richard M. Nixon and Carlos Pérez Jiménez drenched in bug spray, wearing the filthy, stinking clothes they had on when they were imprisoned, helped by Gurkhas, shakily climbed up the ladder to stand beside Trevelyen on the prison floor. O'Reith and McDonough emerged behind them. O'Reith said, "Mr. President, Colonel Jiménez, go out into the prison yard and take seats in the bed of a pickup. Wait there. We'll release all of these prisoners to cover our getaway."

Opening all of the cells, the Gurkhas herded over 200 men into the prison yard. When the signal was given, Nixon and the Colonel, both nude and wrapped in army blankets, riding alone in the bed of a pickup departed Evin prison, hopefully forever. They were escorted fore and aft. O'Reith, McDonough and Trevelyen followed the trucks in the big Zim limousine. As the caravan left the courtyard, the horde of released prisoners poured out onto the streets. An alarm began to clang. With Gurkhas firing their rifles in the air, the caravan, horns blaring, headlights flashing, rolled south at great speed down Shahid Raja toward Gom. As they went, the Gurkhas tossed hand grenades out onto the streets. McDonough got rid of his potato mashers one after the other. Shrapnel was flying everywhere. Soon they were through the vast bazaar and on their way to the disused airfield. When they arrived, the three oil field executives, Nixon and the Colonel enplaned for Baku. The Gurkhas continued south with orders to drive to Ahwaz, organize a fuel supply convoy and then proceed across Khuzestan to Poghdar.

Rescuers and rescued were finishing breakfast at the Soviet Experimental Agricultural Station south of Baku on the Caspian Sea. O'Reith said, "You fellows can rest up here for a week or so and pull yourselves together. I highly recommend the vodka and the beer is not too bad either. You'll have a car and a driver. He'll show you the sights. Dinner tonight in a converted Silk Road caravansary famous for its Caucasian cuisine. When you're ready to go back to work, we'll line up a flight from here to Poghdar. You'll have to operate out of a tent city for a month or so. We'll have proper housing set up shortly. If Pat and Flor wish to join you we will provide transportation."

He turned to McDonough and said, "George, I never did understand that halo trick you pull, Did you find that in some ancient archive in the Vatican vaults?"

McDonough smiled and laughed. He answered, "Clive, the Vatican had nothing to do with it, Nobody there that smart. The halo trick came from MI-5, John Masterman. It is still tight. Time may come when it will be needed again. If I explained it, Masterman would throw a shoe. The way he tells it, Morgan Le Fey, sister to King Arthur, gave him the secret. But I can tell you this much. To project a halo, one must be religious and not like these phony churchmen of various stripes that drum up large crowds at so-called 'revivals'. The Trinity pay no attention to those charlatans. One has to be sufficiently religious that the Son will be attentive. Only the Son is active. The Father just hangs around with a bunch of female angels, sitting on clouds, drinking honey and singing hymns. The Holy Ghost has never been seen. Nobody knows what he looks like and he apparently has no portfolio. There is more to it, of course. What I have explained to you will be adequate for now. As a Dame of Honor and Devotion, Genevieve Ste Jacqueline is in on the secret."

O'Reith began, "George I was never a praying man until Helen fell ill at Santiago de compostelo. Not a focused prayer aimed at whoever up there was listening. Someone told me that a prayer to the Holy Ghost was in the nature of a last resort. I thought of that when she became ill again but I could not get up any enthusiasm for an unknown quantity. So what about the Holy Ghost?"

"As a starter, he is a wraith. He lacks substance Can't wear a halo, In holy pictures he appears as a small triangle of light, Like the glow of a firefly."

"So the Holy ghost is a mere cipher."

"Just so, Clive. Just so."

O'Reith smiled. His experience with *Foo Fighters* as well as Amanda Macabra's strange powers, led him to accept what McDonough had just related. He turned his attention to Nixon and the Colonel The look on their faces showed that neither were keen on the prospects of a long-term sojourn in Poghdar S.S.R. Nixon spoke first. "General O'Reith supposing we get the pipeline organized and locate some suitable Soviet technicians and managers, is there a chance of my further employment with the company in the U.S? And not too far in the future either."

Before O'Reith could answer, the Colonel began, "General O'Reith, my feelings are much the same as Mr. Nixon's. My heart is not in Asia. This assignment has been a trial for me. I lost my capable assistants and I grieve for them."

O'Reith asked, "Are you referring to Graffito and those other two cats?"

"Yes indeed. "Major Graffito, Captain Anthrax and Captain Taupe."

"What happened to them?" O'Reith asked, already having a good idea.

"Ah sir! They were, sad to say, liquidated by those same animals who placed me in vile incarceration." He drew a line across his throat with his finger, sputtered, "Zsst! Like that."

"We have been through interesting times," O'Reith muttered.

Colonel Jiménez continued, "I am strictly, for better or for worse, a banana republic statesman. I would like to return to South America; preferably Venezuela but I could make a go of it in Colombia as well. In fact I would like to visit San Cristobal again, the place of my birth. Just once I would like to take the shroud off of my statue in the Plaza Commercial. Gaze up at it. I know the name of the sculptor, a gentleman from Florence. Someday I will call upon his with my regards to express admiration for his fine work."

O'Reith smiled. He said, "Gentlemen, anything is possible. Work diligently in Poghdar until it is properly organized. I promise you suitable employment in climes more to your liking. Colonel Jiménez, as to Colombia, we know that it is a dangerous, turbulent place. Do you think you could bring some order to it?"

"I'd have to recruit some boys in San Cristobal. I'd want my own troops in Cali and Medellin. Bogotá of course."

"How would you get them in?" O'Reith asked.

"From San Cristobal to Tibu over the Green Road. Charter a plane there and fly them across the country. I would like to bring my statue as well."

O'Reith nodded, looked at Nixon, said, "Let's suppose that Jimmy Carter fades. We get a Republican administration beginning in 1980. That's just around the corner. Do you have what it takes to lobby the administration to get us an army for Colombia? Say three Corps?"

"It would depend on who gets elected. With a guy like Ronald Reagan, we could do it. Reagan would bring Al Haig back into the government. Nixon said.

O'Reith looked again at Nixon, said, "Fellow named Mulheny, Mr. President. Last time I saw him he was a lieutenant general. Armored Infantryman. You'd have to lobby him up to four stars. Maybe five. We'd need him to run the army."

"With Haig in the government it would be a snap. But I can do it even if he isn't." Nixon said.

O'Reith looked to McDonough, said, "What do you think George? Can you put something like that together?"

"Take over Colombia?" McDonough asked.

"That's it. The Colonel puts his goon squads into Cali and Medellin. Takes out the drug lords. Another goon squad in Bogotá topples the sitting government. Not much there to topple. The new POTUS puts American troops in to clean up the insurgency. When things settle down, Carolyn puts a seismic crew into the Magdalena Valley. We locate a few structures and bring in rotary tools. We hit something big; we'll build a pipeline through the Andes. Bring the crude oil out through a terminal at Buenaventura. How does that sound?"

"Ambitious," McDonough said.

"You fellows want to go for it?" O'Reith asked.

"Count me in", Nixon said.

"And I", the Colonel said.

"Clive what exactly would my role be?" McDonough asked.

O'Reith's eyes became steely and piercing. He fixed McDonough with them, said, "Supremo, George. Supremo. You'd be the Pope of the Oil Fields. For once you'd sit in the cat bird's seat"

McDonough roared with laughter but quickly became pensive. O'Reith sensed that McDonough had grasped the enormity of his assignment. But McDonough stood tall and they shook hands on it and had a few drinks to seal the bargain. O'Reith and McDonough caught an Aeroflot jet to Rome. Trevelyen went to London. Nixon and the Colonel took another shower, their third of the day.

It was the summer of 1981. O'Reith was with Maxine in their flat in the rue de Surenes. In Asia, the company was running a million bbl/day of Poghdar crude oil out of Vladivostok destined for Osaka, Japan under an evergreen contract with Standard Oil. The price was $34.32/bbl. The pipeline was paid out and the company was earning $15 million/day. O'Reith was 75 years old and Maxine 65. For the last two years, they had played golf almost every day. His game leg was greatly improved and his waistline was as it should be. Sharon Mills flew in from Los Angeles weekly to take care of his face and his hair. Sometimes she gave Maxine a facial. His children called from time to time. Helen Simpson had a live-in boy friend that O'Reith had never met, a film editor for MGM. Helen Simpson was certain he would soon be a director. Alice Ridley had become an aunt to Helen Simpson in a relationship similar to that she had with her late mother. His son Clive Colin, after a decade of cohabitation had married Ellen Mae, the heroine of the last remake of *The Song of Bernadette.* They had remodeled the Summit Avenue bungalow. All was well with them. His older daughter, Rae Regan was twice a grandmother. She was happy. Amanda Macabra came to visit once a year bringing tales of intrigue in Miraflores. The Colonel, living in Madrid, was writing a book called: *On Tropical Statecraft.* Occasionally he or Flor would call to say hello. Once in a while he asked O'Reith for an opinion on a human rights issue. McDonough was in Rome with Cook. Although under an order of expulsion and threatened with excommunication, the Vatican found it could not enforce its will. He was in a fine mood. The affair at Evin Prison had lifted his spirits. He and Cook were planning a trip around the world. He too was planning a book called: *From La Roche Guyon to Lake Albano; a Simple Priest's Story.*

A month later, O'Reith, still in his bathrobe, was at the breakfast table looking at Maxine in her Chinese red, silk robe, sitting across from him. His plate held bacon and eggs. The coffee was steaming from a silver pot sitting beside a stack of toast. On the side were a plate of cherries and a bowl of figs. They were up and showered after a French Dip as sweet as any he could remember. Maxine was smiling at him. The telephone rang. Maxine lifted the receiver. O'Reith said to her, "I am not in. I am definitely not in."

"McDonough, Maxine said, "Silver, you have to talk to him." She listened with pleasant curiosity as he took the telephone.

He asked, "George, what's up?"

"Clive I've just had a chat with Nixon. Reagan's chief of staff said OK for a corps of armored infantry. Four stars for Mulheny to lead it. The Colonel is chomping at the bit. I've a company plane lined up to fly him into San Cristobal. Carolyn is ready to put the seismologists in. Insurgents are quiet in that area. She won't have to wait for the Colonel. We're going to survey a pipeline right-of-way through the Andes. All we need now is your sure touch."

"George," O'Reith said. "Really! Hold on. Let me get a map." He was on his feet to get his atlas when he looked over to see Maxine's face become suddenly downcast. She appeared melancholy. O'Reith paused, looked lovingly across the table, and continued, "George I'm not going anywhere. Remember the deal we made? You're the Supremo."

"Clive!"

O'Reith could sense the anxiety in his voice. He said, "George, you will be just fine".

"Coo Bob!" an astonished McDonough gasped.

O'Reith broke the connection and hung up.

Maxine was in his arms, her breasts out of her robe rubbing his nose, her perfume sweet and her laughter lyrical. He was having a rare second erection. This time it was going to be a peter bender.

The most unlikely place to find a statue of William Howard Taft would be in the garden of McDonough's villa at Lago Albano. But when he and Cook returned from their around-the-world trip that is exactly what they found. Cook, rubber-necking in Manila, came upon a statue in the weed-ridden Imelda Marcos Park. Curious, she wire-brushed the accumulated bird droppings from the plaque to discover that the statue was the long ago American POTUS. The corpulent statue honored his governorship in 1902 of the Philippines. Grime and verdigris had rendered him anonymous. With a sense that the old gentleman had been neglected, she bought the statue from the Minister of Interior Affairs. No one had any interest in retaining his 4 ton portly presence. Without telling McDonough, she put it on a boat to Italy. She telephoned O'Reith, pointing out that it resembled McDonough. He remembered the Florentine sculptor the Colonel mentioned in Baku. Thus William Howard Taft was transformed by blowtorch into Hadrian VI. Taft, his felt hat and mustache removed, his features altered *mutatis mutandis*, and a titanium-plated miter affixed to his head, came to resemble, quite remarkably, Sir George P. Cardinal McDonough.

When McDonough saw it, he started. But neither Cook nor O'Reith ever revealed to him its secret.

NEW YORK BIBLIOGRAPHY

1. Carl Bernstein & Bob Woodward *All the President's Men.* New York: Simon and Shuster. 1974.
2. James Bamberg *British Petroleum and Global Oil,* 1950-1975. (*Volume III of The History of the British Petroleum Company*). Cambridge University Press 2000.
3. Daniel Mark Epstein *Sister Aimee (The* Life *of Aimee Semple McPherson). New* York: Harcourt Brace. 1933.
4. Edward Jay Epstein *Dossier: The Secret History of Armand Hammer.* New York:Random House. 1996.
5. Judith Ewell *The Indictment of a Dictator (TheExtradiction and Trial of Marcos Pérez Jiménez)* College Station, Texas: Texas A&M University Press 1981.
6. J.A.S. Grenville *A History of the World in the Twentieth Century.* Cambridge, Mass: Harvard University Press. 1980.
7. Rudolph Grey *Nightmare of Ecstasy* (*The Life & Art of Edward D. Wood, Jr)* Los Angeles: Feral Press 1992.
8. Walter Isaacson *Kissinger A Biography.* New York:Simon & Shuster. 1992.
9. Ephraim Katz *The Film Encyclopedia.* New York: Putnam Publishing Group. 1979
10. J.B Kelly *Arabia the Gulf and the West* London: George Weidenfeld and Nicholson Limited. 1980
11. J.C. Masterman T*he Double Cross system.* Random House Group Ltd. Yale University Press. 1972.

12. Richard P. McBrien *Lives of the Popes*. San Francisco: Harper 1997.
13. Boris Mollo *The Indian Army* Poole, Dorset: Blandford Press. 1981
14. Samuel Eliot Morison *The Oxford History of the American People*. New York: Oxford University Press. 1965.
15. David Quinlan *Quinlan's Film Stars*. London:B.T. Batsford Limited. 1996.
16. David Quinlan *The Illustrated Directory of Film Character Actors*. London: B.T. Batsford Ltd. 1985.
17. Glyn Roberts T*he Most Powerful Man in the World The Life of Sir Henri Deterding*. New York: Covici Friede. 1938
18. Kermit Roosevelt *Counter Coup*. New York: McGraw Hill. 1979
19. Augustine T. Smythe et al *The Carolina Low Country*. New York: The Macmillan Company.
20. Daniel Yergin The Prize. New York. Simon & Schuster. 1991
21. *The Times Atlas of the World*. Seventh Comprehensive Edition. New York: Random House. 1985.
22. *The World Almanac and Book of Facts(2000)*. Mahwah, NJ: Primedia References Inc. 1999.
23. *Political Dictionary of the Middle East in the 20th Century*. Edited by: Yaacov Shimoni and Evyatar Levine. New York: Quadrangle/The New York Times Book Company. 1974.
24. Annual Reports: The Standard Oil Company, New Jersey (EXXON) 1970-82.
25. The Standard Oil Company of California (CHEVRON) 1970-82. The Texas Company (TEXACO) 1970-82.
26. Gulf Oil Corporation 1970-82
27. Newspaper Articles *The New York Times* 1970-82 Obituaries, Fashion, Political and Economic News.
28. *International Herald Tribune* 1970-82 as above.
29. *The Wall Street Journal* 1970-82 as above.
30. *The Los Angeles Times 1970*-82 As above.
31. *The Miami Herald* 1970-82 as above.
32. *Figaro* 1970-82 as above.
33. *El Gráfico* (Guatemala City) 1970-82 As above.
34. *El Nacional* (Caracas) 1970-82 as above and *Panorama (Maracaibo)*
35. *Oil & Gas Journal* Oil and Gas News.1970-82

Glossary

1. Alcabala Venezuelan police check point.
2. API American Petroleum Institute.
3. bopd Barrels of oil per day.
4. Cedula Venezuelan identification card.
5. CFP *Compagnie Francaise des Petroles.*
6. DHL Worldwide Courier Company.
7. FDR Franklin D. Roosevelt.
8. *Gran Tenue* Full Dress Formal Military Uniform.
9. JAG Judge Adjutant General.
10. Majlis Persian Legislative body
11. Montecristo Top grade of Panama hat.
12. Movieola Film editing device.
13. Oil Company Iranian Oil Exploration and Producing Company (The Consortium).
14. Oxy Occidental Petroleum Company.
15. pdq Pretty Damn Quick.
16. Potato Masher World War I German Hand Grenade.
17. POTUS President of the United States
18. PRI Partido Revolutionario (Mexico)
19. Splasher Aid to navigation. Location Finder. 19.
20. VHF Very High Frequency radio transmitter and receiver.
21. Black Rod Gentleman Usher of the Black Rod. Queen's plenipotentiary, Carries Ebony staff topped with a Golden Lion. When he pounds on the door to Parliament, he must be omitted. He usually brings bad news. Position was created in 1350.